Hadrian's
Lover

Patricia Marie Budd

Clink
Street

Published by Clink Street Publishing 2015

Copyright © 2015

Second edition.

ISBN: PB: 978-1-910782-98-9
EB: 978-1-910782-99-6

Dedications

This book is dedicated to all my LGBT students past, present, and
future. I am here for you. I always have been and always will be.

Joseph, I love you! You will always be my Grecian poet.
Wilf, you inspired me! You are not forgotten!

October 6 – 12, 1998

The world must NEVER FORGET what
happened to Matthew Wayne Shepard!

Reviews

Editor's Choice for September, 2013, *So So Gay*, London, UK

Five Star Review "Beautiful, heart-wrenchingly poignant, and brilliantly conceived" Jake Basford, *So So Gay*, London, UK

"*Hadrian's Lover* inspires internal debate and thought. As a text in a high school classroom it would do wonders and possibly change the world." Drew Rowsome, *My Gay Toronto*

Acknowledgments

Many thanks go to:

Christine Marie Scott, Bartley P. Busse, and James Duncan: my initial editing team! You helped me shape my vision!

Monty Henstridge for providing legal advice for all court scenes.

Brendan Toner for providing military intelligence.

Joanne Skilnick for helping me better understand our country's natural resources, global warming, and the future ecological health of our planet.

Christine Marie Scott, Bartely P. Busse, Kimerica Parr, and Tara Nahamko for their endorsement of my work.

Tyler Tichelaar for his professional editing services acquired through ReaderViews.

WARNING!

This is a novel about sexual awakenings and sexual discrimination. You will be reading some sexually explicit material. Two thirteen year old boys begin sexual experimentation; a fifteen year old boy is caught masturbating; a sixteen year old boy wants his boyfriend to have sex; a seventeen year old boy and girl have sex; and a married male couple have sex on more than one occasion. If this warning offends you put the book back on the shelf, do not buy it, do not read it. The odds are you aren't ready to handle the truth. And yet, ironically enough, you are the reason why this book had to be written!

-pmb-

Prologue: Crystal's Report

A Treatise Validating Hadrian's Sexual
Preference and Method of Procreation
by Crystal Albright
submitted to: Ms. Sterne

Homosexuality is the sexual norm in Hadrian while all forms of heterosexual behavior are illegal. Hadrian's citizens have chosen a homosexual
lifestyle side-by-side with in vitro fertilization, to create a stable human
population within the confines of our borders. It had been determined by
the founding families—and is approved every decade, on our country's day
of birth by our citizens through a referendum—that Hadrian's population
shall never exceed ten million.

Our small country was founded three generations ago. My great-
grandmother, Ester Stiles, was among the first families to buy land in
the Hudson Bay region of Northern Manitoba with the express purpose
of creating a safe and stable home for homosexuals as well as a rigidly
monitored and controlled human population. For this luxurious lifestyle,
we have the five founding families to thank: Stiles, Stuttgart, Birtwistle,
Nasser, and Reznikoff. It was they who, in the early years of Canada's
decline, purchased the land of our good country. It was they who established the cornerstones of Hadrian's constitution: that Hadrian's chosen
lifestyle is homosexual; that Hadrian will be a safe haven for homosexuals
from around the globe; that Hadrian's central focus is the creation and
maintenance of a stable human population; that Hadrian will create an
ecologically sound balance between humanity and nature. The key focuses
of this treatise are the cornerstones reflecting Hadrian's sexual preference
and the stabilization of the human population without which humanity
will most certainly decline as surely as the Roman Empire did.

As late as the twentieth century, it was reasonable, perhaps even
essential, that humans should prefer heterosexuality as the sexual norm.
Heterosexual sex is designed specifically for procreation. Humanity no
longer requires such methods, yet the multitudes outside Hadrian's walls

are still reproducing at an astronomical rate. Outside Hadrian's walls, close to twenty billion people are overpopulating this planet—nearly twenty billion people are starving and suffering from uncountable syndromes as a result. Millions of these people resorting to cannibalism just to survive! (*Salve!*, HNN—Melissa Eagleton Reporting, June 2, 21—). These poor unfortunates are forced to live in close quarters spreading disease at a rampant rate. Humanity has overrun the planet like a virus killing all of nature in its path. What food is available to these people is scarce. What medicines limited. Little space lies beyond our walls for farms to grow food and raise livestock. Hadrian, on the other hand, is self-sustaining. We have farms. We grow our own food. We raise fowl. We maintain freshwater fisheries. We house seawater fishery farms. Our people are fed. Our surplus stock accounts for 14 percent of Hadrian's economic wealth as we export what we do not need to those in dire need. We have, in every sense of the word, created a utopia here in Hadrian.

Sometimes our citizens question why, if we are so adamant against heterosexuality, do we not simply allow these people to immigrate to other countries where their lifestyle is not only acceptable but also preferable? The answer to that question should be obvious. These are our children. We do not simply dismiss them—toss them into a torrent ocean of human disease, debris, and decay. Our love for our offspring does not permit us to act in so selfish and irresponsible a manner. Besides, no one born in Hadrian is a pure heterosexual.

One of Hadrian's greatest advances, truly a leap in medical science, has been its work on the human genome project. In the past fifty years, our genetic scientists believe they have identified those chromosomes within our DNA that indicate a strong disposition toward homosexuality. Although the human animal is by nature a creature that needs to procreate, nature has also established its own checks and balances to overpopulation by ensuring some aspects of human DNA lean toward homosexual behavior. Hadrian's scientists, who have worked to increase that component of our DNA, are believed to have successfully eradicated the pure heterosexual gene from Hadrian's genetic database. Our geneticists scan each and every embryo to determine whether the homosexual gene exists before implanting it into a woman's womb. If no signs of homosexuality are present in the embryo's DNA, it is automatically destroyed. Thus, our geneticists ensure that every citizen born in Hadrian is homosexual (Doctoro, *Hadrian's Human Genome Project*, page 882).

Here in Hadrian, we ascribe to the Kinsey scale. According to Alfred C. Kinsey (*Sexual Behavior in the Human Male*, page 638) human sexual preference can be divided into a scale from zero to six. A zero on this scale is said to be 100 percent heterosexual whereas a six is considered pure homosexual. The gradations between show individuals leaning more or less toward either side. Societies outside Hadrian's walls have always elected to accept the leaning toward heterosexual behavior purely for the means of reproduction. Religion has both fostered and festered the "procreation fact" as the foundation for heterosexuality as the pure and natural sexual norm. Yet this choice has not served humanity well. Our small planet simply cannot sustain the burden of human population placed upon it. Our founding families recognized the futility of heterosexual preference and excessive procreation. Thus, upon foundation of our good country, the first article of justice states the need to enhance and nurture human homosexual tendencies as well as create strict procreation laws.

With modern medical advances, our geneticists boast having reduced the Kinsey scale by two points (Billington, *The Homosexual Gene*, page 32). Although our geneticists are, as yet, unable to distinguish between each of the gradations of Kinsey's behavioral scale, they are confident enough to pronounce that no more zeros or ones exist among any of Hadrian's citizens. Every child born into Hadrian society in the last twelve years is, at the very least, a two on the Kinsey scale. We do not deny that a two still has a stronger leaning toward heterosexual behavior; however, inside every two is a latent homosexual. It is our job as citizens of Hadrian to help these individuals release and embrace their true, and socially acceptable, inner desires. Until the day when our scientists have created the perfect human genome, where all who are born will be sixes, we must forever work with our children, reminding them why our country was founded and the critical need to maintain a stable human population.

For this reason, reeducation camps were formed: Not to harm and abuse our citizens but to remind our youth of our country's founding families' ideals and the necessity of maintaining strict vigilance. Many of today's youth are unaware of our early immigration policy. In the beginning, Hadrian's borders were open to immigrants, inviting homosexuals from around the world to join us. Many people swarmed to our gates, and not all of these people were homosexual. In fact, a large number, at least 15 percent, were people who believed themselves to be a one or two on the

Kinsey scale. Two individuals who joined us, Mark and Julie Reiner, a pure heterosexual couple, agreed to sterilization in order to be part of our preferred community. Neither had wanted children anyway, viewing procreation in an overpopulated world as immoral. They also agreed to permanent separation, each locating to opposite ends of the country. They knew when they immigrated to Hadrian that they were entering a homosexual community, a community dedicated to restraining the human population growth, a country dedicated to putting into place the necessary checks and balances to create a stable human population. These noble people chose to deny their heterosexual tendencies, accepting celibacy in its place, for the sake of Hadrian's future, for the sake of humanity. All of Hadrian's citizens are asked to make such sacrifices, if indeed, one perceives being who we are as a sacrifice at all!

Perhaps the greatest sacrifice made by any Hadrian citizen is that of the surrogate goddess. These women open up their wombs, choosing to be the mothers of our men's children. Without these women, our homosexual men would be bereft of the benefits of rearing many of Hadrian's children. No wonder these women are treated like goddesses in our world. In fact, it is the expressed desire of this author to become a revered surrogate goddess.

It is also important to remind our youth that Hadrian's first citizens swore an oath of fidelity to our founding principles. Although our children are not required to swear this oath until coming of age (twenty-one), it is expected of all Hadrian's citizens to raise their children with a clear understanding of not only the world inside our walls, but of the dangerous world that surrounds us. That dangerous world batters against our walls daily as a reminder. Heterosexual barbarians are constantly threatening to overtake our country. Hadrian's ballistic missile detection and tracking system is state of the art. It is terrifying to learn how many incoming missiles our military has protected us from. A virtual wasteland lies outside our walls where many of our intercept missiles have detonated those threats (Dodger, *The Military Sciences*, page 182). Although conscription of our youth into Hadrian's military between eighteen and twenty-two years of age is undesirable, it is undeniably essential; we must defend Hadrian's way of life at all costs.

The worst attack against our peoples occurred a mere eight years ago when an Evangelical Christian drove across our border, exploding a dirty nuclear device in Augustus City. The loss of Quadrant One's southern grassland region and the devastation to our populace was the final straw that drove our people into exile from the outside world. No more are tourists from other countries allowed to visit our fair and spacious country. Although we retain fair trade with friendly countries through export and import, we no longer believe outsiders can be trusted to cross over our borders (Miller, *The Resurgence of the Law*, page 42).

Hadrian's population must remain xenophobic. We cannot allow the ravages of disease to infect the only stable human population. Annually, hundreds of millions of outsiders die of disease and starvation; yet those numbers never seem to impact the ever-growing population. We, in Hadrian, will never send our children to live out there with them. No, it is much kinder, much safer to our wayward youth to be reclaimed through reeducation. Although some of our youth may believe themselves to be heterosexual, it is incumbent upon us to help them understand what it means to be a two on the Kinsey scale and help them awaken and embrace their latent homosexuality.

Hadrian is the savior of humanity. While the rest of the world procreates itself into excessive human waste and decay, our small population will live on. Hadrian's values ensure the human race will survive.

Salve!

As the clock counts down, Hadrian's citizens await the very moment we can all shout gaily, "Happy New Year and Happy Fiftieth Birthday, Hadrian!" It is hard to believe that we have made it this far! Fifty years of gay freedom! Fifty years of a stable human population—maintaining ten million! Fifty years of showing the rest of the world how man and nature can commune as one. Considering all the trials and tribulations Hadrian has been through since we first established our borders, it is truly amazing we have come this far. The wall surrounding our borders is now one third complete, stretching for hundreds of miles on each side of the southeast and southwest gates.

This is it, folks; in less than seven minutes, when the chimes ring in the New Year, we will all shout out with joy, for Hadrian is the only country left standing between humanity and certain death—for without Hadrian, the human race would invariably become extinct! As we look outside our walls and daily witness man's decay, although we are saddened by their sufferings and daily losses, their decline is a reminder of the value and importance of Hadrian's society. Overpopulation is the planet killer. Overpopulation is man's deadliest enemy. Homosexuality, population stability, communing with the earth (that small portion of which we have saved within the confines of our walls): these are Hadrian's gifts to the future. Our scientists estimate that the dregs of the human race will wipe themselves out in the next fifty to one hundred years. But Hadrian will remain! Hadrian will fight for humanity's survival.

Before the clock strikes that magic hour, let us take a moment to remember Hadrian's soldiers, those brave men and women who patrol our borders and guard our wall from the outside world, and the endless attacks against our civilization by the heterosexual barbarians and religious fanatics. Every year, we mourn the loss of another soldier dying to preserve our rights and freedoms. Every year, a grieving mother or father buries her or his only child. No one goes to the wall with illusions. To serve at the wall is to face certain death on a daily basis. To serve at the wall is to be in a constant state of readiness to repel desperate attacks by illegal immigrants threatening to swarm over our borders, threatening to infect us with any one of their endless plagues. To serve at the wall means to battle with organized armed forces determined to steal our land and destroy what little remains of the earth's habitable land. To serve at the wall means to face the threat of religious terrorists who deem our chosen lifestyle as the devil's menace. Our young men and women conscripted into our forces, who serve four years of their lives between the ages of eighteen and twenty-two, are our protectors and saviors from the outside world. Before the countdown begins, let us hold our traditional vigilance—one minute of silence for those of us who cannot enjoy this night's revels—one minute of silence for those of us who may, at any moment, die while defending our very way of life and the right to celebrate the way we do tonight. One minute of silence and then one minute of bated anticipation to the final countdown. And then together, we will shout for joy our Happiest of New Years, for this year as we celebrate the fiftieth year of our country's birth, we are also celebrating the rebirth of mankind!

Vale!

New Year's Eve

Facing south, with a convex dome encompassing east and west as well as the entire roof, the Hunter home is one of the most impressive dwellings in Antinous. The northern wall contains a glass bay window opening up to the view of a multi-tiered garden sloping down to the Nelson River. Very few buildings have open windows facing north in this manner. All windows are on the convex of every Hadrian building, designed to double as solar panels, obscuring the interior from the outside, but allowing those inside a beautiful tinted view of all that lies beyond. This design has also eliminated the need for window dressings. To have clear glass windows exposed to the outside denotes either wealth in a family home or a government complex.

The Hunters' backyard is a sprawling garden that slopes down by tiers to the river. Right now, it is lightly dusted white from last evening's snowfall. Come spring, Dean will begin the process of manual tilling, mixing in the mulch from last year's compost, and seeding, weeding, and nurturing the garden. Gardening has been Dean's job for the past two decades. More than just time-consuming, it acts as a relaxant, something Edgar, Dean's psychiatrist, had recommended years ago. It also provides the Hunter family with income tax refunds on an annual basis. Every Hadrian citizen who makes the effort to work with, and not against, the earth is granted hefty tax rebates.

As well as showing pride in his garden, Dean is equally proud of the interior of his and Geoffrey's house. There is little one can do with respect to the exterior. All homes in Hadrian look the same with a convex facing west, south, and east for solar panels and one flat wall facing north. There are no front doors, only a back door facing north. Only size and interior luxuries denote wealth. When you enter the Hunter home, the first thing you see is the wide expanse of the living room to your left and the glistening creams and beiges of the kitchen directly in front. To the right is the long hallway that leads to the central washroom, and four bedrooms, one being the master bedroom. Standing in the lobby closest to the hall entrance, Dean Hunter takes in the full view of the living room. Tall and lean, Dean is standing rigid as he stares at the room before him. Dean is anxious. Geoffrey is never any help when it comes to organizing a party. When asked, he will help, but with limited effectiveness. Sweeping a floor in Geoffrey's mind means sweeping around things. It never occurs to him to move a couch or a chair, to get at the dirt underneath. "Nobody is going to look under the chairs, Dean. I swear." He adds, "Sometimes I think you are more gay than I am!"

Dean finds this old joke annoying, but he knows Geoffrey means kindly by it, so he always shakes it off. Staying focused, Dean pipes up, "Tonight's special, Geoffrey." Although not needing to, he reminds him, "This is not just any New Year we're celebrating! It's also Hadrian's fiftieth birthday!"

Geoffrey smiles fondly at his old lover. *No, not old*, he reminds himself. *Dean is only forty years old*. Not that there is a huge gap in their ages; Geoffrey is only forty-eight. No, he refers to Dean as his old lover because they have been together for over twenty-two years now (not including couple's registration). So many changes have occurred in Dean over the years—from the frightened teenager Geoffrey met to the strong confident man standing before him. Smiling, Geoffrey still appreciates that Dean took his last name. Although he knows it wasn't so much a choice on Dean's part as it had been a necessity, at times like today, Geoffrey is able to convince himself that this is how Dean wanted it regardless. And Dean, he muses, is still so handsome. Geoffrey enjoys checking out his lover when Dean is unaware. Knowing Dean is self-conscious, Geoffrey doesn't try to make Dean uncomfortable. Still, when opportunities like this arise, with Dean fixated on a problem and focused, Geoffrey will often stand back and admire his physique. Dean is tall and slim, no middle-age bulge. Unconsciously, Geoffrey gives his own protruding belly a slight shake. Geoffrey is short and stout next to Dean. And, unlike Dean's thick dark brown hair, Geoffrey's mousy brown curls have all but receded to a horseshoe patch around his head. *Hadrian's Lover*, Geoffrey muses. *Dean is still so good looking*. Even the gray streaks that lace his temples are attractive. With his square jaw and thick eyebrows, he is the classic Marlboro man. No one smokes in Hadrian, but the old image hangs in the city's central museum. When they first saw the original advertisement poster, Geoffrey teased Dean, saying,

"All you need now is a cowboy hat." Geoffrey was so taken by the resemblance that he surprised Dean with a week's stay at The Cattle Ranch horseback riding that year. This, of course, was before their sons, Frank and Roger, Geoffrey's genetic sons, were born.

Geoffrey's musings are cut short by a sudden caustic remark, "I hate that wallpaper." That wallpaper is the one point that takes Dean's pride down a notch when it comes to his home's interior! He despises it wholeheartedly. It doesn't happen often, but every so often, Dean will utter a complaint about their living room décor. Although Dean was responsible for most of their home design, Geoffrey was given free rein with the living room. "Everyone is entitled to one room," Geoffrey had insisted. Dean still regrets giving in to that logic. Besides, Geoffrey already had his study!

"Well, you should have said so fifteen years ago when I picked it out," Geoffrey replies. "It's too late now."

"I wanted to say something, but we had agreed you got to decorate the living room." They have been having this old argument for five years now. The use of wallpaper was still allowed fifteen years ago with the mandatory restriction that it not be replaced for a minimum of ten years. Its use became banned two years ago, three years after they could have replaced it! Geoffrey refused then, and he still refuses now, to change the décor. Wood walls maintained by oil or natural stone are the limited means of décor today. The less one adds to the world's pollution, the greater the tax break. Wallpaper and most paint are now illegal.

Seeing defiance begin to glare in Dean's eye, Geoffrey turns authoritative. "We are not adding to global waste by tearing off perfectly good wallpaper. We've kept it in good condition and it stays up as long as it lasts."

Scowling, Dean says, "But we've kept it long past the ten-year minimum. Can't we just get rid of it—it's so dark!" The wallpaper is black with silver, laced patterns.

Shaking his head, Geoffrey has bragged to too many coworkers about having the same wallpaper up for fifteen years, adding how it will last at least another five. With wallpaper now being illegal, owning one of the few homes with the material still on its walls is a status symbol Geoffrey is not willing to give up. "The silver pattern brightens it up."

"Only because the paper is so faded!"

"It's not faded." Geoffrey is determined to defend his choice to the death.

"It's faded."

"It's staying up!"

Sulking, Dean repeats, "I have really grown to hate it."

Unrelenting, Geoffrey replies, "Well, grow to liking it again because we are not changing it again for at least five years!" Wagging a pointed finger toward Dean, he adds, "And only then if it needs replacing," and he cites a government slogan to end the argument, "Earth First!"

"Fine!" Dean huffs. Glancing down, he glares Geoffrey's way. "Hand me the broom, please. I have to sweep up in here."

Grimacing, Geoffrey bites back, *I just finished sweeping up in there*, but he knows better. Nothing is ever clean enough for Dean when company is expected. Rolling his eyes, he retrieves the broom and hands it to Dean.

Before Geoffrey can execute an escape down the hall to their room, Dean turns to scold him. "Geoffrey, I need your help here." Reluctantly, Geoffrey crosses over and helps pull the couch out so Dean can sweep up the dust and excess dirt.

Appreciating the profile of Dean's form as he leans forward to capture more dirt with the broom, Geoffrey wishes the man would let up with all this cleaning. After Dean finishes his task, Geoffrey leans in close, whispering hotly in his ear, "Anything else you need me to do?" Today's observations have reminded Geoffrey how Dean has matured into a very sexy man, *like fine wine*, he muses. "Our guests won't arrive for another two hours." *And*, he whines inwardly, *if you would just let up on all this cleaning, we could relax and enjoy ourselves in the shower.*

Though no prude anymore, Dean has his mind on more practical matters. His eyes continue to scan the room, landing on the coffee table—it is cluttered. The coffee table—cheese tray! Turning, he orders Geoffrey, "Get the soya cheese out and start cutting slices." Remembering the way Geoffrey put the last cheese tray together, he adds sternly, "Arrange it nicely this time. Use a little parsley as garnish, and put a small bowl of sweet pickles in the middle." Suddenly, remembering an important detail, he concludes, "and set out the crackers I baked—arrange them nicely, too!"

"I don't see why you get me to do these things. I can never meet the standards you set."

"If I had time," Dean answers crisply, "I would do it myself. But I don't." Hands sawing the air frantically, he admits, "I need you to help."

Laughing, Geoffrey bows, "Your servant ever."

Exasperated enough to roll his eyes, Dean sighs, "We only have two hours before the first guests arrive." He points dramatically now toward the kitchen.

"I'm going." Geoffrey's hands go up in defense and he flashes his *please don't shoot me* grin. "Soya cheese tray. Crackers. Pickles. At your will!"

After Geoffrey turns the hall corner, Dean shouts out a reminder, "Don't forget the real cheese. I bought some cheddar and some Brie. Mike loves Brie."

Calling from the kitchen, Geoffrey says, "I don't know why you expect him every year. Mike Fulton never comes."

"He promised me he'd come with Todd this year."

"He never comes!" Geoffrey reminds him gently, but sternly.

"I messaged him through his wave link at work. He replied he was coming!" Dean refuses to see Mike Fulton for what he has become, choosing instead to remember the man he was before his husband passed on.

"Fine." Geoffrey is no longer trying to mask his exasperation. "He'll come. I'll put out the Brie!"

"He promised me!" Dean insists. "He promised both Todd and me!"

Although Geoffrey had not meant to be heard, his low growl still makes its way from the kitchen into the living area. "He's a good one for making promises."

As much as Dean would like to defend Mike right now, deep down he knows Geoffrey is right. Mike Fulton is not the same man who married Dean's best friend twenty-one years ago. That man died the same day his lover, Will Middleton, passed on. Dean and Will had been best friends since high school. Everyone, in those days, had expected Dean and Will to partner for life. But events happened, things changed, and then Dean met and married Geoffrey Hunter. Shortly after, Will Middleton met Mike Fulton in his first year at Antinous Uni; by the end of that year, the two men had married. Dean had always thought his friend had rushed things, but he understood why Will had chosen to marry so fast. Mike had proven to be the best of all partners for Will, and an amazing Papa to Todd.

Only in the last few years has the man changed, leaving Dean to worry about Todd. Mike Fulton is a grown man who can work things out for himself, but at fifteen, Todd is still too young and impressionable. He needs a father's guidance to help him through the confusing years. Dean has done his best to offer Todd help, but his access to the young man is limited. "I wish Mike would let Todd live here with us," Dean often laments to Geoffrey, who always answers, "He is not our son." As if to impress his point, he always asks, "Would you let Frank go off to live with the Middletons if I had been the one to pass on instead of him?" Although partners keep their own surnames, it is traditional to refer to the family unit by the genetic parent's last name. Since Todd was Will Middleton's genetic offspring, his last name is that of his father. Since both of the Hunter boys are Geoffrey's genetic offspring, they, too, go by the last name Hunter. Had Dean been able to keep his last name and provide the genetic material for a child of his own, that child would have borne Dean's original last name. Hadrian's reproduction laws, however, have denied Dean the responsibility and privilege of producing an offspring.

Today, Dean responds to Geoffrey's question by placing his hands over his bowed head. "No! I could not—but I'm not like him!"

Geoffrey reenters the living room as Dean puts the final touches on the coffee table. He has rearranged the candle plates and is now holding a few stray magazines in one hand and a dust rag in the other. Dean remonstrates, "Mike Fulton is still the boy's papa and he loves Todd!"

"But he's never around when Todd needs him!" Dean is so exasperated he begins to weep. "And I promised Will that I'd look out for his boy."

"And you do," Geoffrey says. He wants to embrace Dean, but he knows when Dean is like this, any physical contact only causes him to revert back to old habits.

Oddly enough, it is Dean who reaches to Geoffrey for an embrace. "And he is so much like his father it scares me." As Dean's hands are full, he does not wrap his arms around Geoffrey so much as step in to allow his husband's arms to wrap around his back and clasp the sides of his shoulder blades. Dean bends down to rest his head against Geoffrey's shoulder.

"You don't have to worry about Todd," Geoffrey says reassuringly. "He and Frank are tight. And one day, I swear to you, those two will be a unit."

"I hope so." Dean nods his head against his partner's shoulder. "You're right. I worry too much."

"All right." Geoffrey gives Dean one more squeeze before releasing him and issuing a mock stern order. "We better finish getting ready for your party! It is Happy New Year after all!"

"And," Dean adds gaily, "Hadrian's fiftieth birthday!" The two men kiss briefly. Then, through misty eyes, Dean confesses, "I really love you, Geoffrey Hunter. I am grateful every day that I have you in my life."

Moved by Dean's honesty, Geoffrey kisses his lover passionately. As soon as Geoffrey releases him, Dean springs back into action. When Dean has a party to plan, there is no stopping the man!

*****

Salve!

A Year in Review
HNN—Melissa Eagleton Reporting

This past year has been a quiet one for Hadrian with only four outsider attacks against the wall. According to Lieutenant-General Birtwistle, only one attack was from an organized force. The Alberta regiment, the Manitoba brigade (consisting mostly of descendants from what used to be southern Manitoba), continues to demand we return Hadrian's land to them. Lieutenant-General Birtwistle is confident the losses incurred by the enemy were sufficient to deter any future attacks from this military force. "We had to use incendiary rockets against the enemy." Sighing, he closed his eyes I'm sure in an attempt to block out grim memories. "We took out their entire squadron." He then shook his head sadly. "It was the only way. They were clearly organized and had with them scaffolding apparatus. Hadrian's war policy is very clear. No outsider is ever to enter Hadrian!" An understandable policy after June 13, now commonly known as 6-13, and considering the constant bombardment of plagues ravaging many outside countries. The last thing Hadrian needs is for a contaminated outsider to bring a plague inside our walls. Lieutenant-General Birtwistle feels Hadrian no longer need fear the Alberta regular army. As he reminded us in his interview, "Alberta's Prime Minister has assured us, via wave link, it is no longer providing this regiment with additional forces. Remember," Lieutenant-General Birtwistle said, "it has been over eight years since the Alberta army has sent any regiment besides the Manitoba Brigands to attack our borders." The fact that Lieutenant-General Birtwistle refers to this particular regiment as bandits suggests that they are no longer regular army but are themselves becoming another desperate rabble, outsider victims fruitlessly trying to slip through our walls.

Lieutenant-General Birtwistle would also like Hadrian to recognize Private Katrina Jones, who was awarded the Antinous Sword, posthumously, for her brave actions. Prior to the incendiary rockets being used, she stood bravely at the wall repelling the invaders. She died of a gunshot to the head.

Inside our walls, new progress has been made in strengthening the firewalls that keep the outside net from infiltrating our wave link. Unfortunately, some noxious hate literature, written by Leigh F. Butler, brother of Jeremiah F. Butler, the notorious suicide bomber of 6-13, slipped through last month. In his hate statement, he declared the citizens of Hadrian to be devil spawn and blasphemous sinners. Unfortunately, he was able to spam his cruel words to all our high schools via wires, terrifying and confusing many of our youth. Quoting his antiquated Bible (my apologies to those Hadrian citizens who choose to believe in this God), he referred to us as the abominable villains of Sodom and Gomorrah and warned that the dirty nuclear device his brother exploded was really God raining fire upon us and that more such rain is destined to come our way. Leigh F. Butler and his message of hate is a brutal reminder of the need for vigilance at our borders. Estelle Ramones, head of Hadrian's Institute of Computer Science, assures us that the latest version of the firewall will stave off future attacks of hate literature.

On a positive note, agricultural engineer Quintin Laugharne claims to have biologically engineered an even hardier soya bean than the one Will Middleton introduced to our southern grasslands fifteen years ago. Will Middleton's revolutionary work helped usher Hadrian closer to a fully self-sustaining country. Using Middleton's research as his base, Laugharne has now stabilized the bean's genetics so it will grow even in our milder summer seasons. The soya bean, known for centuries as a life-saving plant with its high levels of protein, has saved Hadrian from over-dependency on food imports from the outside world.

Even prior to the addition of the soya bean industry, Hadrian had always been very close to self-sufficient. Because Hadrian's borders include one quarter of the world's largest inland freshwater lakes (believe it or not, Hudson Bay used to have a high concentration of saline that we harvest along its shores) and numerous bountiful rivers, we do not lack access to fresh water like many parts of the outside world. The boreal forest in our northernmost regions, with careful harvesting and a solid forest reclamation plan, provides us with all the pulp and paper we need. Our fishing industry and farms all boast bountiful harvests, and the mining of quartz and ore meet our basic metal needs. As we enter a new year in the life of Hadrian, we can happily claim the future is in our hands. Happy fiftieth birthday, Hadrian!

Vale!

A New Year's Kiss

The Hunter home is immaculate. You could run a finger into its deepest crevice and not pick up any dust. This obsessive cleaning trait of Dean's only rears its ugly head when company is expected. He has also taken great pains to ensure that both party rooms, living room and kitchen, are decorated to match the evening's festivities. All of the Hunters' guests, when greeted at the door, are presented with one of Dean's hand sewn (and starched!) conical hats. Using colorful scraps of hemp linen he produced over a dozen of these hats with tassels for his guests to wear. Every year he sews a new one, always for Geoffrey to wear. The living room is decorated with a rainbow of cheesecloth strung across the ceiling and others dripping down to the floor. Two of the three living room wall screens are turned on with festive imagery slide shows, the third reserved for the *Salve!* New Year count down. Dean also has a series of handmade noisemakers, including miniature drums, castanets, and whistles. Along with all the traditional New Year's paraphernalia, Dean makes sure each guest starts the night with a glass of wine or his choice of liquor. With all the gaiety surrounding him, the multiple coos over his décor, and the layout of the food, one would expect Dean to be thrilled—but he isn't. It is already ten-thirty and still no Mike and Todd. Frustrated at having no way of contacting Todd, Dean just paces in the front hallway, periodically looking toward the door.

"Dean," Geoffrey whispers, placing a hand on his lover's shoulder to settle him. "Our guests are in the living room, not the front hall."

"I'm just—"

"Waiting for Todd; I know. But," with gentle opposition, "if Mike were going to bring him, they'd be here by now."

"I just hate the thought of that poor kid stuck at home alone on New Year's Eve," Dean laments.

"You don't know that, though, do you?" Geoffrey reminds him.

Dean shakes his head angrily. "Oh, but I do! Mike Fulton is either working overtime for more credits, or he's out with a new boyfriend."

"You have no right to judge the man," Geoffrey remonstrates.

"I'm going to take the bubble." Seeing reservation in Geoffrey's eyes, Dean attempts to justify his actions. "I just want to drive over there and see if Todd is home."

"Dean," Geoffrey reminds him, "the bubble won't run right now. It's been too cold. You know that."

"It's only minus five out there."

"It was minus twenty yesterday," Geoffrey reminds him. "The battery is dead."

"It's been out in the sun all day, it should be charged up by now."

Geoffrey grimaces, "Dean—"

Before Geoffrey can finish Dean jumps in with, "I'll take public transit then."

"Dean!" Geoffrey grabs Dean's arm before he can turn toward the closet. "You're not thinking rationally."

"Please, Geoffrey, let me go."

"No, Dean. Your responsibility is to your guests."

Just as Dean nods his reluctant assent, there is a knock at the front door. Dean rushes to answer it. Todd is standing outside. With his shoulders stooped and his body bundled inside an old black jacket, Todd looks stouter and shorter than he really is. In fact, Todd is 5' 5" and quite muscular since he trains year round for his favorite sport, b-ball. He also likes to wrestle and plays v-ball on the offseason to stay in shape. In the summer, he swims in Hudson Bay. His wavy brown hair (hidden underneath a wool toque) is the same color as his eyes, which currently stand out against his thick frosty eyelashes. His hands are stuffed inside his jacket pockets because he lost his gloves a few weeks ago. "Hi, Papa Dean," he stutters through shivers. "Can I come in? I'm freezing!"

"Of course you can." Dean pops his head over Todd's shoulder. "Where's your Papa?" Seeing no sign of Mike Fulton, Dean asks, "Did you walk here?"

"Yes, sir," Todd answers as he steps inside. Dean doesn't even bother to ask why Todd never took public transit—no thumbprint, no credit, no access to public transit. He doesn't remove his coat, though, since he is still cold. Although winters in Hadrian are relatively warm, never falling much below -15° C anymore and this New Year's Eve is considered mild at -5, Todd still had to make the trek across town. Todd and his Papa Mike live in subsidized housing on the northern edge of Antinous, Hadrian's capital city, whereas the Hunters live in a more posh region, along the Nelson riverbank.

Dean shoots Geoffrey an exasperated look before smiling for Todd and asking, "Is Papa Mike working overtime tonight?"

"Nah, he has a big date," Todd says while shrugging off his coat.

The way Dean glares at Geoffrey over this piece of information one would think Geoffrey was to blame for Mike Fulton's absence. Geoffrey chooses to ignore Dean's pointed expression, welcoming Todd with a handshake. "Well, we're glad you were able to join us, Todd." Gesturing, he adds, "Go on into the kitchen and help yourself to some punch. Frank's in there with Roger and a friend." Following Todd with his eyes as he walks away, Dean calls, "Mind you take from the purple bowl. The crystal bowl is for adults only!"

"And tell Frank to quit eating all our food," Dean adds as Todd disappears.

"Yes, sir," Todd chimes back from the kitchen.

* * * * *

Frank, Anthony, and Roger are the only ones in the kitchen. The three boys are clustered together around the table filled with food. Like most teenage boys, Frank's appetite is humongous, so he has spent most of the night standing at the kitchen table eating. Todd laughs, "Papa Dean wants you to quit pigging out!"

Frank smiles as soon as he sees Todd. He instantly steps forward and pulls Todd in for a bear hug. Being so much taller than Todd, standing 6' 3", he actually lifts his friend off his feet, holding him suspended briefly. "Glad you could make it, pal. We were ready to give up on you." Frank is a very attractive youth. His oval face and reddish brown hair, although slightly feminine, do not detract from his obvious strength, for like Todd, Frank is muscular. He too enjoys playing v-ball, b-ball, and wrestling. He is even a long distance runner for track. His eyes are a speckled green, blue, and gray. When Frank smiles, his eyes always seem to light up.

Anthony scowls as soon as Frank greets Todd, instantly turning his back to concentrate on the cheese and crackers. Like all of Frank's boyfriends, Anthony is short, standing only 5' 5½". He has a small wiry frame, almost too skinny. Although he stands by the food table and appears to pick at the cheese, he doesn't eat anything.

"Hey, Todd," Roger calls out happily. Todd is like an older brother to Roger, sometimes even more so than his real brother. Frank is great, but he doesn't listen like Todd. Whenever Roger is upset and neither father is around, Todd is the next person Roger seeks out for help. Frank is a last resort because he seldom ever takes seriously anything Roger has to say. "Want some Brie? Papa Dean put it out for your Papa Mike. Is he here?"

Todd leans in between Anthony and Frank. "Excuse me, skinny," he teases Anthony, who does not respond, refusing even to move out of the way for Todd. Frank grabs Anthony's shirt collar and pulls him to his side. Anthony's smile for Frank barely conceals his contempt for Todd. Todd is not oblivious; he knows Anthony is jealous, which is utterly stupid since he and Frank are just friends. Cutting off a huge chunk of Brie, Todd slathers it on a cracker before offering it to Anthony, "Here," he teases, "let's fatten you up a little so Frank has something he can grab onto." Roger howls in laughter.

Anthony glowers at Todd; then peering up, he complains, "Frank, your friend is being mean to me."

Todd chuckles along with Roger while Frank fights back the desire to join in. "Anthony, he's just playing with you." Sensing that his little boy is about to explode into one of his famous hissy fits, Frank calms Anthony down by kissing him. Although he still refuses to talk to Todd, Anthony is mollified. As they watch this display, Todd winks at Roger while stuffing the cheese and cracker into his mouth.

* * * * *

"Geoffrey! Geoffrey!" Dean cries out frantically. "Do you have the champagne ready? Melissa Eagleton is starting the countdown!" This bottle, *Champagne Philipponnat Clos des Goisses*, their last bottle of real French champagne, has been waiting patiently for over four years for tonight's special celebration. With major cutbacks on imports, it is not likely they will ever have another such bottle to drink. They had ordered one case on their tenth anniversary, drinking a bottle each New Year and anniversary until

6-13 ended any chance that they could order more. Since then, their last remaining bottle has sat in solitary confinement inside its case in the far reaches of their cold storage awaiting Hadrian's Fiftieth New Year's Eve and Birthday celebration. As Melissa Eagleton's voice drones along with the guests (all eyes glued to the Hunters' wall screen), Dean calls out impatiently, "Geoffrey, please!"

Geoffrey enters the room with the champagne bottle in his hand and the cork teased halfway out. Smiling, he gives the bottle a slight shake—just enough to get the bubbles flowing, but not so much that any of the valuable wine will get wasted on the floor. "Cork ready to pop, dear."

Dean sighs audibly, moving swiftly to the coffee table to retrieve the tray with one dozen crystal flutes, one for each of the eleven men present at their little New Year gathering. The extra flute, having been intended for Mike Fulton, will sit empty on the tray. As soon as the count hits one, everyone in the room cheers "Happy New Year!" along with Melissa Eagleton. Every man turns to his partner or neighbor, extending the traditional New Year's kiss. Geoffrey and Dean kiss gingerly, due to the delicate nature of the tray held between them. Once the first round of kissing is complete, mostly moderate pecks since the only two couples present are Dean and Geoffrey and Frank and Anthony, Geoffrey pops open the champagne and pours everyone a drink. Although he gives full portions to the adults, the four teenage boys only garner a half glass each. Frank tosses his flute back, downing the expensive wine in one dramatic gulp. Geoffrey shakes his head. Dean wants to lecture him on such folly, considering how expensive this particular bottle is and how they are never likely to taste such luxury again, but before he or Geoffrey can express their displeasure, Frank turns Todd's way and pulls him in for a kiss. And not just any kiss. Frank spins Todd as if in a dance, dipping his best friend low before diving down for his lips. It is a very romantic gesture, and as angry as Geoffrey and Dean are at Frank for having downed the expensive champagne, they are both pleased to see Frank engaging in a kiss with Todd. Neither man dislikes Anthony, but both men are hoping for a union between Frank and Todd. Smiling at the sight, Geoffrey feels the need to kiss his lover one more time, a little less gingerly now that the tray of flutes no longer hinders him.

After Frank releases Todd, he dips his flute into the punchbowl; then raising his flute high, he offers up another toast to honor Hadrian's birthday! Anthony does not participate in this cheer. Having watched Frank kiss

Todd, the young man boils over in anger and jealousy. Pushing through the small crowd, he stops briefly to glare at Todd. And then, intentionally banging into Todd's shoulder, he pushes past him to storm out of the front room and down the hall to Frank's bedroom. Frank shrugs his shoulders Todd's way before following Anthony out to set things straight.

Todd turns to leave, figuring he's overstayed his welcome, but Papa Dean catches him by the elbow. "Happy New Year, Todd." Dean tussles Todd's hair as he speaks.

Ducking away to avoid Dean messing his hair too much, Todd laughs in reply, "Happy New Year, Papa Dean." Then, with a half-hearted smile, "and Happy Fiftieth Birthday, Hadrian." He lifts his flute in a token toast.

"Fifty years. Pretty amazing, eh?" Dean is smiling, not having felt the tension yet.

"Uh-huh." Todd is barely paying attention to Dean. He is staring in the direction Frank left in pursuit of Anthony.

Noticing the distant look in Todd's eyes, assuming rightly it has something to do with Frank and Anthony, Dean comments, "That was some kiss you and Frank had."

"You mean Frank *had*!" Exasperated, Todd exclaims, "I wish he'd stop doing things like that to me!"

"So tell me what was wrong with the kiss?"

"It was too much—over the top—Frank always goes overboard. I mean, that's the way you kiss your boyfriend. And I'm not Frank's boyfriend."

"Why not, when the two of you get along so well?"

"Because Anthony is Frank's boyfriend."

"Does that bother you?"

"No." Shaking his head, Todd reiterates, "Really, Papa Dean, I'm not jealous of Frank's dating other guys." Somewhat confused by the truth, he confesses, "I don't know why," and confirms with his eyes, "I love Frank. You know I do."

Papa Dean places a hand on Todd's shoulder. "I know."

"It's just, well, I'm not ready to date yet, and Frank obviously is." He shrugs. "I can't be angry at him for that. Besides," he adds judiciously, "I have no time for that sort of thing. I have to concentrate on school and b-ball. Keep my average up and my game sharp so I can get into uni. That way I won't have to be a soldier and can work toward being an agricultural engineer like my dad!" Excited by the prospect, Todd adds, "You know Dad introduced soya bean to

Hadrian. I want to introduce rice. That's the last food substance we still have to import. Can you imagine if we could grow our own?"

Dean smiles, pulling Todd in for a hug. "That's an admirable goal, son. It would make your father proud." Dean hugs Todd a little too hard but the young man doesn't mind. Both men are re-experiencing the grief of loss: for Dean, the loss of a dear friend, and for Todd, the loss of a father. Releasing Todd, Dean takes a moment to brush a lock of hair out of the boy's eye. "There is so much about you that reminds me of your father."

Todd beams. He loved his dad. There are nights he will dream his father is still alive, only to wake up and suffer the crushing reality of his death all over again. The transition of joy to sorrow, though seemingly infinitesimal, is very real. The light in Todd's eyes blurs and tears begin to fill. "Why did he have to die?"

Papa Dean re-submerges Todd in his arms. "I don't know, son. Life is seldom fair. Sometimes all a man can do is make the best of it."

"I want to make Dad proud of me. I want to be just like him."

Todd breathes these words against Dean's aching chest. "You are, Todd, like him in so many ways." *Perhaps too much*, Dean worries. "But you have to be your own man, too. And I know," he says, now pushing Todd back slightly so he can look him in the eye, "whatever you decide to do with your life, your father would be very proud of you!"

"Thanks, Papa Dean."

Dean frowns. His little pep talk has not removed the shadow covering Todd's mood. "All right, out with it."

"Out with what?" Todd asks, shifting his eyes away.

"You are still upset about that kiss, aren't you?"

"Sort of."

Todd is evasive. Papa Dean will not let Todd escape telling him about his anxiety. "Why does the kiss bother you this much? It just looked like the two of you were having some fun."

Todd's eyes darken. "It may have looked like fun to you, but as sure as Hadrian was gay, it didn't look that way to Anthony."

"Ah, Anthony."

"Yeah, Frank's boyfriend. How could Frank kiss me like that in front of him? That's the way you kiss your boyfriend! Not your best friend."

"So, you're worried about Anthony's feelings, then?" Dean is not convinced.

"Yes—no." Todd knows better than to lie to Dean. Papa Dean always has a way of wriggling the truth out of him. "I'm worried about all the hateful rumors he's going to spread when we go back to school."

Papa Dean is concerned. "Does this happen a lot?"

"Every time Frank does something stupid like that in front of one of his boyfriends." Exasperated, Todd says, "Everybody he has ever dated hates me! And they have all called me horrible names behind my back. Last year, Iggy told everyone I was a *strai*."

"A *strai*?" Dean asks, angered. "I hate that word! It's so derogatory. It's no one's fault if he's born straight. He's to be pitied, not mocked."

"And then," Todd barges on to avoid discussing Iggy's accusation, "Frank avoided me for six weeks because Iggy made him choose between him and me. The same thing is going to happen with Anthony; I just know it!"

Although sensitive about the topic, Dean will not let Todd pass over such a volatile accusation. "Whoa, back up, son. Have his boyfriends accused you of being straight?"

"Iggy told everyone I was a *strai*—a cu—cunt—hammer—." Todd closes his eyes, trying not to cry. "And he's not the only one. Just about every boy Frank's ever dated has said that about me." Shaking his head in disbelief, he adds, "They never say it to my face, of course, but Crystal tells me everything."

"Is Frank aware of this?"

Todd shrugs.

"I plan to ask him," Dean says.

Todd opens his eyes, fear evident. "Please, Papa Dean—no." He sighs. "It's going to be strained enough between Frank and me as it is. After he's done talking to Anthony, I'm willing to bet you won't be seeing me around here for a good month—at the very least." Looking down at his feet, Todd concludes, "Anthony is not the type to put up with competition."

Dean turns grim. "That explains all those times you've been absent from our house the past few years." He shakes his head. "That is not to happen anymore." Lifting Todd's chin to look at him, Dean says, "I promised your father I'd keep an eye on you. How can I do that if you're avoiding my house? Promise me you'll come over at least once a week."

"But—," Todd stutters.

"No buts." Papa Dean is stern. "Sunday dinner is the easiest. Promise me Sunday dinner at the very least."

"Papa Dean—Frank's boyfriend will nev—"

"Frank's boyfriends come and go like the wind through foliage. You are a son to me." Refusing any argument, Dean adds, "Frank can tell his boyfriends what he should have been telling them all along." Todd looks up quizzically. "That you are like a brother to him!" Taking a moment to calm down, Dean finds his smile. "So, Sunday supper?"

Todd smiles, relieved he doesn't have to lose touch with Papa Dean. "Thanks, Papa Dean!"

"Try not to let petty, jealous slurs hurt you. Surely you can see the irony?"

Todd expresses his gratitude by giving Dean a grizzly bear hug. "I love you, Papa Dean," he blurts out unexpectedly.

Dean laughs and hugs the boy tighter. "I love you too, son." Kissing the top of Todd's head, he promises, "And I will always be here for you."

* * * * *

Salve!

Illegalizing Outsider Technology
HNN—Melissa Eagleton Reporting

As many of you are aware, Hadrian's government officials have met numerous times to discuss whether or not outsider technology should be made illegal. The debate is proving to be a most volatile one, and our opinion polls show that many of Hadrian's citizens are divided on the issue. For some, it is a matter of cost. Outsider technology comes cheaper than the contact vocal lens. For others, anything brought into Hadrian from the outside world could potentially be contaminated. We must remember that disease is rampant in the outside world, and the possibility that some deadly bacteria, for which there is no cure, can spread through such importation is very real. Yet, as my producer wisely puts it, "We still import rice, sugarcane, fruits, and vegetables that are unable to be grown this far north. Coffee and cocoa," two of his favorite vices, "although nearing impossible to acquire except at exorbitant prices, are also among those items imported into Hadrian." As these are items we consume, it seems, he claims, to be rather ironic—silly in fact—for Hadrian citizens to be over-zealous when it comes to the use of outsider technology. "These, after all," he stated at our pre-production meeting, "we do not eat." I must admit, what he says makes sense, yet it still sends a chill down my spine when I think of Hadrian's citizens making use of outsider technology. When one citizen uses outsider technology to contact another connected by voc to our wave, the ramifications are frightening. Viruses intended to damage our wave network can do substantial damage to Hadrian's businesses, government, and educational institutions. Then there are the numerous instances of spam messages, voicemails, and videos containing hate sent intentionally to destroy our citizens' morale and frighten our children. Too many times have these insidious viruses littered our wave network. The importation of food items does none of these. As inconvenient as it might be for some of our citizens to abandon the less expensive communication devices purchased through outside companies, remember, Hadrian's government offers wall screens and tablets credits below the least expensive outsider tech. Everyone in Hadrian can still be connected to the wave. The potential ban of outsider technology will not see the less fortunate of Hadrian citizens bereft of communication. Government devices may be slower but they are definitely a lot safer for Hadrian.

Vale!

Illicit Communication

The following Sunday, Todd fails to join the Hunters for their family dinner. Dean demands to know why. Frank's answer is evasive, "Todd's sick."

Angered by Frank's dismissive attitude, Dean stretches his hand across the table, demanding, "Give me your cell phone!"

Frank gasps, flabbergasted. "My what?" He has not told anyone that Todd, Crystal, and he own cell phones. No one knows they communicate through an outsider satellite phone service. Although using such a service is not illegal in Hadrian, it is certainly frowned upon.

Geoffrey looks up, dismayed and discontented. "You have outsider technology?" His voice is curt and solemn.

"No!" Frank protests.

"Don't lie!" Dean insists, still holding out his hand, palm upward, waiting for the recalcitrant technology to be handed over to him. "It's how you communicate with Todd, isn't it?"

Geoffrey glares at his son. Frank shivers. Roger pales, suddenly very afraid for his older brother. Neither father has ever raised a hand against his children, but the look in Geoffrey's eyes suggests he is fighting back the desire to cuff Frank right now. Frank, too, notes the rising anger in his genetic father. Continuing the lie will only land him in even more trouble, so Frank capitulates to the truth. "Please, Dad," he begs, "Todd can't afford a voc. No one knows, I swear!"

"Your Papa Dean knows! He found out, didn't he?"

"It's not like it's illegal," Frank mutters weakly.

Growling now, Geoffrey asks, "Are you aware that people are currently debating making use of all outside technology illegal in Hadrian?" Staring intently at his son, he continues, "And if it becomes a crime, that means one of only two punishments: exile or death." Pausing to the let the gravity of the situation sink in, he concludes, "You know we have no prisons in Hadrian."

"I know, sir," Frank mutters into his chin. Frank is now pale with fear. Roger begins to cry.

"And," Geoffrey adds, a little too cruelly, "they are suggesting anyone who would want to use outsider technology must be straight. To be caught with a cell phone could mean a one-way ticket to a reeducation camp. I do not want either of my boys to be thought of as a *strai*."

"Don't use that word, please," says Dean, surprised by his husband's word choice when Geoffrey knows how much he hates this commonly accepted slur.

"But," a horror-stricken Roger cries out, "Frank's not straight!"

Turning to his youngest, Dean attempts to calm him. "Roger, dear, dry your eyes. Frank is not in that kind of trouble."

"But he could be," Geoffrey growls.

Dean begins to regret that he brought up the subject in front of Geoffrey. "It is not necessary to frighten the boys, Geoffrey."

Geoffrey gives Dean a knowing stare. "Yes, I think it is. You of all people should understand that."

Neither boy catches the undertone of Geoffrey's remark, but Dean feels its sting. He closes his eyes briefly before re-summoning his strength. "Well, owning outsider tech is not illegal yet, and we've caught the boy before anyone else has." Waving his open palm as a reminder to Frank, he says, "As soon as he hands over the device, this whole uncomfortable business will be over."

"You heard your Papa, Frank!" Geoffrey orders. "Give him the phone!"

"Give it to him, Frank. Give it to him," Roger begs. Frank obeys.

"Now, Frank," Geoffrey instructs, "you can forget about the rest of your supper. Go to your room and study."

"Yes, sir," Frank says as he stands and turns to leave.

Before Frank can walk past his father, though, Geoffrey grabs hold of his arm. "Promise me right now that you will never use outsider technology again." When Frank's response comes a second too late, Geoffrey tightens his grip and growls, "Promise!"

"Yes, sir," Frank weeps. His only contact with Todd is lost now because Anthony won't even let him look at his friend in school. "I promise."

Geoffrey releases his grip. "All right, go to your room."

* * * * *

Later that night, after Geoffrey retreats into his study to prepare for another week at the office, Dean sneaks up to Frank's room. He brings the remains of Frank's dinner with him. Because Frank is tall, he often gets lightheaded if he doesn't eat properly. Dean often wonders where the boy gets his height since Geoffrey is so short by comparison. *Obviously from his genetic mother*, he reminds himself, and yet, Roger, Frank's genetic sibling, is also short. *Ah well, there really is no explaining the oddities of genetics*, Dean muses. Knocking lightly on the door, Dean waits for Frank's acknowledgment before entering. Frank is sitting at his desk studying (as his father had instructed). Dean crosses the room and places the plate next to the computer slate Frank uses for school. The Hunters are wealthy enough that they were able to purchase Frank his own slate rather than make do with the school's slower version.

Frank smiles when he sees the food. "Thanks, Papa Dean. I'm starving."

"I knew you would be, a big boy like you. You shouldn't go without food." Shaking his head, he adds, "But your father was angry, and he was right to send you to your room."

Pulling Frank's cell phone out of his pocket, he studies the ancient technology a moment. "Come over to the bed and sit down with me." Shaking the phone slightly, he says, "I want to talk over a few things with you." Frank complies and follows his papa to the bed. Dean pulls open the poster curtain and the two sit side-by-side on Frank's king-sized mattress. "Whose idea was it to buy these things?"

"Mine, but Crystal agreed. I mean, without a voc, it's really hard to keep in touch with Todd. And vocs are just too expensive. We couldn't buy him one of those."

"No," Deans concurs. "That's for certain."

Pleading now, Frank says, "We're the three gay caballeros, Papa Dean; we need these to communicate."

Dean smiles briefly, "The three gay caballeros. I like that.' More sternly, now, he asks, "Do you understand why your father got so angry with you over this?"

"Not really," Frank admits. "He went a little crazy if you ask me."

"What you need to understand, Frank, is that Hadrian went a little crazy after 6-13."

"I know 6-13 was bad, but that was eight years ago."

"Yes, it was. Even so, fear of the outside world hasn't abated. To have a dirty nuke explode in your borders, killing so many people, destroying so much of our fertile land—well, surely you understand there is a lot of distrust for anything outsider—especially technology."

"I'm sorry, Papa Dean. I just wanted a way to keep in touch with Todd is all."

"I understand. But we all have to make sacrifices for Hadrian's lifestyle. You know that, right?"

"Yeah—I don't know—I guess."

"One of those sacrifices includes importation of many fruits and vegetables we used to enjoy and delicious items like coffee and chocolate and," adding sternly, "outsider technology."

"But it's not illegal yet."

"But it's frowned upon and you know as well as I do that it'll be illegal soon enough. Now," handing the phone to Frank, he says, "show me how this thing works."

"Huh?" Frank is flabbergasted. After getting into so much trouble, he can't believe his papa wants to use the phone.

"I want to ask Todd why he didn't come tonight." Dean is matter-of-fact in his request. He understands that neither Mike Fulton nor his son, Todd Middleton, have vocs. There is no way of messaging them either since their wall screen broke down a few months ago.

Frank is uneasy about phoning Todd. He has been avoiding him to placate Anthony, and he knows how much he hurt his friend when he texted him not to come over tonight. "But, Papa Dean, Todd's sick."

"Really?" Papa Dean is not fooled. "Call him now!"

"But Dad said—"

"And, I'm telling you to phone him. Now!"

Frank takes the phone out of Dean's hand and begins pressing different keys, "Yes, sir." When the number starts to ring, he hands the phone back to Papa Dean. Listening intently, he can just make out Todd's voice as he answers, "Hey, Frank, what's up?"

"You don't sound sick to me."

"Huh?" Todd is confused. This is not Frank's voice.

"It's Papa Dean."

"Papa Dean." There is a moment of reflection. "How did you—?"

"Frank is not as circumspect as he thinks he is," says Dean.

Frank lowers his head as if he can feel Todd glaring at him through the phone.

"Oh." Todd remains silent, waiting for Dean to pass judgment.

"Don't worry. I'm not going to tell on you." Todd's sigh of relief is audible even to Frank. "These little devices are not illegal—yet. But they are more conspicuous than the vocal contact lens so you boys have to be doubly careful." When Dean stares intently at him, Frank nods in agreement, corresponding with Todd's reply of, "Yes, sir."

"Now, Todd," says Dean, quickly changing the subject, "I have a bone to pick with you."

"Sir?" Todd feigns confusion, but he knows exactly why Dean is upset.

"You promised me Sunday dinner—and," he adds swiftly, "don't pretend you're sick!"

"I'm sorry, Papa Dean, but Frank—"

Dean cuts Todd off instantly with a curt remark directed at his son. "I know—Frank!" Dean is staring so intently at him that Frank begins to sweat. "I understand, but that doesn't mean I am letting you off the hook. You promised me Sunday dinners, and if need be, I will pick you up and take you out to eat. That is until Frank gets his 'love life' settled." Frank responds by staring at his feet. "So," Dean states crisply, "I will be around to pick you up next Sunday; let's say 6 p. m."

"But Papa Mike, he's so proud—he'll say no."

"You let me deal with Papa Mike. Does he know about this phone?"

"Yeah." Then adding in his Papa Mike's defense, Todd adds, "He doesn't like it, but he understands."

"Okay, put him on the phone, then. I'll talk to him now."

"He, uh…" There is an awkward silence.

"He's not home, right?"

"No, sir."

"On a date?" Dean is bitter at this news. It is not that he holds anything against Mike for forming a new relationship; it's just he has been forming new relationships since, well, within weeks after Will died. It seems Mike turns to the arms of strange men to help him forget, and Dean suspects he also turns to whiskey. Sighing at circumstances beyond his control, Dean adds with determination, "I'll get a hold of him at work this week. Papa Mike will agree."

"Thanks, Papa Dean." Todd is relieved. He is lonely right now. When he's not at school or in b-ball, he's stuck at home alone, with nothing but studying or the odd text with Crystal to keep him from dying of boredom.

"Now," Dean is quite stern, "before I give this phone back to Frank, I want both of you boys to promise me to be more careful! No one—and I mean NO ONE, is ever to know the two of you are using these things. Is that understood?"

Although in separate rooms in different ends of the city, both boys answer in unison, "Yes, sir!"

* * * * *

Salve!

Masturbation Rules
HNN—Melissa Eagleton Reporting

Earlier this week, we had quite the heated debate over the topic for tonight's *Salve!* In all honesty, I was at first uncomfortable about discussing such an issue so openly on air. I suggested this topic be best left to the education system to deal with. Hadrian's Sex Education Curriculum is one of the finest worldwide. However, my producer pointed out, quite correctly, that this topic is not something meant only for our children. Parents, too, need some coaching—not in terms of "how to"; most of us can figure that out quite nicely on our own—but rather in terms of how to talk to our children about this issue. So today's topic is masturbation and what to do if you accidentally walk in on your child—doing—ahem—pleasuring him—or herself privately.

Often when a parent accidently walks in on his or her child masturbating, the moment becomes one filled with consternation and embarrassment for both parties. What is really important in this situation is not to allow our initial emotional reaction to take precedence. Allowing discomfiture and disquiet to dictate the now critical discussion, or worse yet, to allow these emotions to avoid the issue all together, is not instrumental in helping your child develop a healthy attitude toward his or her body and the act of masturbation. Clearly this is an act everyone has committed once or twice, perhaps many times over. The old religious myth fanatics used to scare their sons' hands away from their penises. "You'll go blind ' is, as my producer succinctly put it, "hooey." Therefore, the question begging to be asked is: Why do some parents still react badly upon the discovery of their child's masturbatory acts? When we respond unfavorably to such a natural instinct, we are perpetuating the folly that masturbating is sinful Again, to quote my producer, "That very notion is absurd." As the parents of Hadrian's children, we need to remind ourselves that masturbation does not hurt anyone! On the other hand, it is actually beneficial to both body and spirit. Masturbation is a great stress reliever, and the release of sexual tension is something every single human body demands.

In fact, masturbation is a great sexual alternative for our youth. The startling rate at which our teens become sexually active suggests the need for proactive measures. What better pro-active measure than masturbation? It allows your son or daughter to release built-up sexual tension without sexual bonding and forming of intense relationships prior to being emotionally ready. For, as we all know, the body is often ready for sexual release long before the average person is emotionally ready for a serious relationship.

Still, it is important that your child understand how masturbation, colloquially referred to as "petting the kitty" or "lengthening the leather," is a very private act and not one to be shared with others—and no doubt, many a parent has been embarrassed by the accidental discovery of his or her child's private affairs. But it is critical you step past these uncomfortable feelings—wait out enough time to allow the embarrassment to abate, and then discuss the issue with your teen. This is critical. Children of Hadrian should never feel wrong for committing such a natural, useful act. Murad Nasser, Hadrian's top medical practitioner, recommends that we orgasm at least once a day, even if one does not have a sexual partner. Masturbation, he says, is a necessary act, possibly even vital to maintaining good physical and emotional health.

In fact, parents, don't wait for that accidental moment; be pro-active. Sit your son or daughter down today and hold a frank discussion about this matter. Let your child know that it is okay to masturbate—just remember, it is a very private act that should never be expressed in public. As well as ensuring your child understands and accepts masturbation as a natural act, make sure he or she knows masturbation is something best done alone.

Vale!

Images of Crystal

Todd's room is actually a walk-in linen closet. Because his and Todd's bungalow has only one bedroom, Papa Mike removed all the shelves in the closet and restructured the middle shelf as a bed with dresser drawers underneath. The shelf is long enough and wide enough for one single mattress. Screwed into the wall above the head of Todd's bed is a small reading lamp so Todd has some light. The door to Todd's room is the original folding door that came with the linen closet. About two feet are between the closet door and the bed shelf for Todd to move around in. More often than not, he leaves the folding door open to give the illusion of more space, but today, he has the door closed.

Currently, Todd is half-lying, half-sitting up on his bed, with his upper back and neck pressed against the wall. Images of Crystal Albright (his and Frank's other best friend and fellow sport fanatic) moving in slow motion waft through Todd's brain. He envisions her musky cinnamon scent and the way she looks in her tight green dress. The fingers of his one hand are actually caressing the smooth lacquered pages of a very old *Hustler* magazine, circa 2010. Open to the pullout image, the woman Todd pretends is real looks alarmingly like Crystal. Both women are tall, thin yet muscular, have short dark hair, stunning brown eyes, *and* big breasts.

Todd found the magazine in the recesses of Papa Mike's closet. There a small box lay hidden, and curiosity, though deadly to the cat, is fodder to Todd's desire. He doesn't even question what contraband porn is doing hidden inside his papa's closet. He simply found the match to ignite his wakening desires. Without being self-conscious, Todd returns with the magazine to his small bedroom.

Down the hall, Papa Mike is opening the door.

"Hey, Papa Mike, is Todd in?" Frank asks as he enters.

"Yeah. Was he expecting you?"

"No. I'm just hoping we can talk."

"What's wrong? You look distressed."

"I just broke up with Anthony."

"Break-ups," Papa Mike replies conciliatorily, "are the worst at your age."

"Yeah."

"Well, come on in then. He's in his room." Gesturing, Mike adds, "Just head on down."

It only takes a moment for Frank to walk to Todd's room, open his door, and walk in on him in the act. Giddy at the sight, Frank blurts out, "Hadrian's Lover, Todd! Are you jerking off?"

Todd gasps, quickly rolling over to face the wall, his actions immediately abandoned. Suddenly, all his heat is spent, and his sun collapsing pulls Todd's psyche deep inside its black hole. One thought alone resonates: *Thank Hadrian, my pants aren't down.* Fortunately, Todd did not bother removing his pants so he is not revealing an exposed buttock to his companion. Panic stricken, a second thought suddenly emerges: *What if he finds out?* Shaking, Todd tries desperately to hide the magazine clutched in his left hand.

Frank quickly slides the door shut behind him, hoping Todd's Papa Mike didn't hear his outburst. There is just enough room for Frank to stand in front of Todd's shelf. "Oh, man," he whispers. "That is the sexiest thing I have ever seen."

Hoarse, Todd blurts out, "Go away, Frank."

"No way." Frank sits down beside Todd. Tickling his hand up Todd's spine, slithering it over his shoulder, Frank's hand begins to make its way back down Todd's chest. Todd curdles, contorting into the fetal position, ironically bringing Frank's hand closer to its mark.

"Please, Frank, don't."

"Just go with it, baby." That is when Frank feels the magazine clutched in Todd's hand. "Are you using porn?" Giggling. "I love it!" He clasps the magazine and gives it a gentle tug. Todd's grip tightens. "Come on; let me see, too."

"Please." Todd is now in tears. "Go away."

Becoming suspicious, Frank tugs harder at the magazine. "Why?"

"Just let go."

"Give me the magazine."

"No."

"Give it over!" Frank practically yells as he pulls the contraband free of Todd's grip. Standing up, he stares at the magazine in horror. "What the fuck is this?" When Todd fails to answer beyond a whimper, Frank screams, "What the fuck is this?" Rolling the *Hustler* tight in his grip, he begins to beat Todd with it. "*Strai* porn? You're using *strai* porn?" Todd cringes under each blow.

Before Frank can get too carried away, Papa Mike slides open the door. "What in Hadrian's name is going on in here?"

"Todd was whacking off when I walked in." Frank is so incensed his voice makes even the simple act of masturbation a sin.

"Every man, woman, and child masturbates, Frank!" Although embarrassed for Todd being caught in the act, Mike would never chastise him for it.

Frank swirls around to throw the trash rag in Papa Mike's face. "He was using this!"

It takes a moment for Papa Mike to regain his balance and senses. His inspection of the magazine is accompanied with a moment of silence, punctuated by Todd's truncated sobbing. Knowing his are the only sounds being made, Todd tries desperately, even more so unsuccessfully, to control himself. Finally, Papa Mike asks, "Where did you get this, son?" Todd can't answer. His voice is currently being choked by shame. Looking at his son's friend, Mike orders him, "Do not tell *anyone* about this."

"What are you going to do?" Frank demands.

"I will deal with this." Papa Mike is curt, his voice suggesting Frank leave immediately.

"How?" Not even waiting for a response, Frank barges on, "Where would he get something like this?"

"From my closet."

"*Your* closet?" Incredulity doesn't even come close to describing Frank's emotions at this moment.

"Yes, my closet," Mike repeats with no offer of an apology. Looking toward Todd, Papa Mike nods knowingly.

"What the fuck is something like that doing in *your* closet?" Frank is nothing if not persistent.

"I used to sell contraband." Still no apology; just a blunt declaration.

Incensed, Mike states, "How the fuck do you think I got his father through Uni? On a mechanic's pay?"

Flabbergasted, Frank asks, "But this? Who would buy——"

"Yes, Frank, there is a black market in *strai* porn, and the older it is, the more costly. Bound paper magazines like this," he says, shaking his head in regret, "had I remembered I still had it, might have brought in a thousand credits or more. Damn, I wish I had found it first. I could have bought Todd new b-ball shoes and decent clothes for school." *Maybe even some whiskey and cigarettes,* he ruminates. Pointing its remains at Frank, he says, "Now that you've ruined it, I doubt I could score a credit for it."

"That's what you're worried about?" Frank can't believe his ears.

"What? You think Todd's the only kid in Hadrian who has ever masturbated to *strai* porn? Shit, I stroked the snake a few times to this myself." Mike doesn't even pause in his lie. He has spent most of his adult life helping a *strai* very close to him hide. He knows exactly what to say and do. This sort of posturing has become second nature to him, even if it has been a while. "And, why not? Who in Hadrian's name does it hurt? It's a great way to get rid of some of that straight tension." Eyeing Frank circumspectly, he adds, "But you wouldn't know about that, would you?" Mike shakes his head in disgust. "Well, guess what, Frank? Not every one of us is a six on the Kinsey scale. Some of us actually have some battling to do!" Looking back at his son, he adds, "Todd may be a five or a four; hell, he may even be a three or a two. I don't care. Do you?" Gesturing with the magazine toward the front door, Mike shames Frank into looking down at his shoes, but Frank still refuses to take the hint and leave.

Frank wants to say, *Yes, it does matter*, but he knows the answer is no. "No, sir. No, I don't care."

"I'm working with him." Papa Mike is blunt and still motioning with the magazine toward the front door. "That's all you need to know."

"Can you," asks Frank, feebly pointing to the now decimated magazine, "get rid of this?" Searching for the right words, anything to justify his frustration, he states, "It's—it might be too much temptation for him."

"Yes.—And, I will go through my closet to see if I have any more.— And, if I do, I will throw it all out. Happy? Satisfied?" Once again, Mike gestures as if to say, *Will you now get the fuck out?*

"Thank you." Frank begins to cross in front of Papa Mike.

Stopping Frank suddenly, Mike demands, "And you? What do you plan to do? Expose him?"

Todd cringes in fear. Frank looks down on his friend. Feelings of compassion overwhelm him. "No, sir."

"Thank you." Frank turns and goes down the hall.

Waiting until he is sure Frank has left the house, Papa Mike finally sits on the bed beside Todd. *Fuck*, he mutters to himself, *not this again!* "I m sorry, son. I should have told you Frank was here."

"P-Papa, am I straight?"

Breathing deeply before sighing, Mike responds, "I don't know. Most of us have something straight in us." Glancing down at the magazine, he adds, "That's why I was able to make so many credits selling these damn things." *I should get back into it*, he considers. *We're so fucking broke.* It was too dangerous, though, and Mike no longer wants to risk his life in that racket. Turning his mind back to Todd, he rubs a hand over his forehead "But we all have that latent homosexual in us, too."

"Do we?"

"Yes. Most of us—just—" Shaking his head, he suddenly turns his explanation into a command. "Just never act on those straight tendencies."

"Yes, sir—I mean, no, sir—I won't."

"Good boy." Getting up to leave, Mike pauses to look down at his late husband's son. "Just remember," he adds (something used to tell Will) "you don't have to do anything until you're ready." *Will you ever be ready?* He wonders. *Will never was.*

Todd sniffles, "Thanks, Papa."

"You *okay*?" Not bothering to pause, he adds, "'Cause I gotta go. I got a date."

Todd doesn't answer. Papa Mike has already left the room. Still holding himself, Todd notices how his penis has shrunk inside his hand like a turtle.

* * * * *

Salve!

Hadrian's Lover
HNN—Melissa Eagleton Reporting

Hadrian's Lover is scheduled to air this Friday on the wave. Don't miss the pilot episode of this inspiring, historical fiction that traces the lives of Hadrian, Emperor of Rome, and his young Greek lover, Antinous. The producers of this docudrama do not wish to refer to their work as historical fact, preferring the newly coined phrase "factition," even though much of the script is founded on solid research. That Hadrian was ruthless like many Roman Emperors will receive little emphasis at the start of the mini-series. Initial emphasis will be placed on the fact that he was deemed one of the five good Emperors of Rome. Much of the scandal surrounding his love affair with Antinous will also play a significant role. It isn't until after the sudden death of young Antinous, only nineteen years of age, drowning in the River Nile, that the more vicious side of Hadrian will be presented. It is said that after the death of Antinous, Hadrian went mad. In fact, most of the cruelties for which Hadrian is known occurred after he lost Antinous.

That Antinous was the most sexually alluring and beautiful of men caused a great deal of difficulty for the casting director. Abigail Williams searched tirelessly throughout Hadrian for a young actor who would meet this bill as well as be able to perform the role. She finally found her match, but it has been decided not to identify him until the show's airing. Rest assured that Hadrian's best and most beautiful young man has been chosen for this most illustrious role. Indeed, this is the role of a lifetime.

Long time favored actor Royston Birley will be playing Hadrian. Royston, thrilled at having landed such an auspicious role, is said to have spent months completing in-depth research into Hadrian's reign as well as finding everything the wave has to say about Hadrian's love affair with Antinous. "What is great about this role," Royston said in a recent interview, "is the highlighting of Hadrian's arranged marriage to Vibia Sabina, clearly a political maneuver that caused much misery to the noble emperor. The only real joy and love of Hadrian's life was his young Greek lover Antinous."

As we all know, after Hadrian met young Antinous, the boy became his closest confidant. Antinous provided Hadrian with lively conversation as well as the obvious attraction of physical beauty. Theirs is perhaps one of the most heart-wrenching love stories of all times, as Hadrian and Antinous' relationship was severed all too quickly by the sudden drowning of the young man on the River Nile.

The mystery surrounding Antinous' death will be dealt with in-depth. A fictional character, Centurion Detective Giustino Romano, has been created specifically for the storyline. This character, Director Aaron Ganis says, will consider all the various theories about Antinous' death. Was it a ritual killing, a murder, or an act of suicide? Ganis will not reveal what, if any findings, are given in this series, but he assures us, that all conspiracy theories of Hadrian's day, as well as a few invented by our writers, are thoroughly investigated by Centurion Romano.

Vale!

Sweet Sixteen!

Todd's birthday is celebrated at the Hunters'. Mike Fulton is working over-time and contacted Dean earlier through his work wave messaging system to let him know he wouldn't be attending. With frustration brewing, Dean is determined to throw all his energy into preparing the perfect dinner for Todd. *The boy will turn sixteen only once; why can't Mike see that? Sixteen. Next thing you know he'll be seventeen—seventeen—*Dean closes his eyes. A swirl of anxiety rushes through him—*No!* Shaking his head, Dean refuses to allow memories of his youth to ruin the night's jollities. Todd's birthday cake, Dean decides, will be extraordinary. He plans to bake the young man a thick, very heavy, chocolate fudge cake. Cocoa beans are rare, not being grown in Hadrian, so he had to purchase them through the black market; Geoffrey will be upset when he finds out, and Dean anticipates a scolding, but he doesn't care. This is Todd's day and Dean knows how much the boy loves the taste of choco-late, so a chocolate cake is essential for Todd's birthday! *Will*, he remembers fondly, *also loved chocolate. And,* Dean smiles, *he grew his own cocoa beans in Antinous Uni's agricultural hothouses.* Remembering Will causes Dean to compare Mike's behavior with what he feels it should have been, like that of Will. *Will*, he firmly believes, *would have been here!* Dean silently berates Mike Fulton. *Will never would have missed Todd's birthday!*

The doorbell rings. *Someone's here already?* Dean rushes to the front door, ripping off his baker's apron before answering it. Crystal Albright stands before him. *Hadrian's lover, who invited her?* The Hunters rarely have women over, and Dean is always warned in advance so he can make himself scarce. "Hello, Crystal." Dean's voice remains smooth, even though a sharp shock is racing through his body. Crystal is beautiful. Today, she is wearing a low-cut blouse, exposing deep cleavage and tight-fitting jeans. Crystal takes a deep breath, exposing even more cleavage. Another shock wave hits Dean and he jerks slightly. His hands instinctively reach for his temples, which are throbbing.

Concerned, Crystal asks, "Are you all right, Mr. Hunter?" Crystal thinks it is so romantic that Dean chose to change his name to his husband's, so, unlike the other kids, she never calls him Papa Dean, but always refers to him as Mr. Hunter.

"Yes, Crystal," Dean mutters as his head jerks. "Just a slight headache. Go into the living room. Put Todd's present with the rest and I'll get you a drink."

Sensing Dean's distress, and unwittingly making his agony worse, Crystal offers, "Let me help you, Mr. Hunter. That's why I came early." After depositing Todd's gift in the living room, she joins Dean in the kitchen. He keeps his back to her, but her cinnamon scent wafts through the air. Dean starts to rub his forehead. She watches from behind as his back muscles tighten. "What can I do?" Crystal asks. *Give her something. Give her something.* Dean tries desperately to think. He can feel her walk closer. She touches his waist. Instantly, a shock rips through him. He stumbles. Nausea begins to build. "Mr. Hunter, are you sure you're all right?" Dean tries to speak, but the need to vomit is so extreme that he lunges for the sink and begins to throw up. "Oh, dear." Crystal is concerned. "Mr. Hunter, you should go lie down. I'll take care of everything here."

Dean agrees by nodding his head. He instantly leaves the kitchen for the safety of his room. *Who is going to bake Todd's cake now?* He groans, calling back, "Just don't do the cake. Leave the cake. I'll tend to it later."

"Don't you worry about anything, Mr. Hunter. Mama Elena taught me how to bake. I can handle this. Now, where is your recipe?" As her voice fades, Dean groans in disappointment. He had wanted to do all this for Todd, had it all planned out, and then that girl had to show up. *No, it's not her fault,* he tries to remind himself, *stop blaming women.* But he can't stop himself, and even though he is aware of the unjust nature of his thoughts, he continues to berate Crystal Albright for her presence.

* * * * *

After dinner, Todd slips away from the festivities to visit Papa Dean in the master bedroom. Although surprised to see Dean looking quite healthy, Todd believed Crystal when she said he was really ill. He had thrown up in the kitchen sink, she said. Besides, Papa Dean would never abandon him. "Hey, Papa Dean, how are you feeling?"

Dean sits upright on the bed. Blinking his left eye, Dean turns off the news wave he was watching through his vocal contact lens, colloquially referred to as "the voc." The voc was the last of the new technology to enter Hadrian pre-6-13: phone, video, game console, timekeeper, camera, and wave link (with holographic screen and keyboard all in one). Microscopic solar batteries combined with the salt water of the eye help to keep the vocal lens charged. Coupled with a tactic tattoo or ear jewelry installed with microphone and speakers, the individual is constantly connected with Hadrian's information wave. "I'm feeling a lot better, son. I'm so sorry I'm missing your party." Concerned that Crystal might have botched Todd's dinner and the cake, he asks, "Did everything taste all right?"

"O, wow, Papa Dean; that supper was amazing." Todd's smile fans Dean's heart. "Crystal said you had everything ready and that all she had to do was pop the buns in the oven. That beef stew was really something else. What were those big doughy things in it?"

"Those are called dumplings. My papa…" Dean pauses momentarily, feeling the loss of dear family connections before continuing, "used to make them for me all the time."

"They were delicious." Todd sits down beside Papa Dean. Dean reaches forward and rubs the back of Todd's new shirt. It is made of thick hemp, a plant grown in Hadrian, so a common fabric, and dyed dark beige with a green foliage pattern (all dyes made by Dean using plants from his garden). "This shirt is really nice, Papa Dean. Thank you so much. Where did you get it?"

"I bought the fabric and designed the pattern myself. I chose to handsew. I thought that would make it more personal."

"Wow!" Todd looks down at his shirt with new eyes, filled with admiration. "You handsewed this?"

Dean smiles. "Designed the pattern myself." Musing, he adds, "I sewed one for Frank's birthday last month, but he's never worn it. Isn't flashy enough for him, I guess."

"Well, then Frank's just stupid. I think this shirt is amazing!"

The shirt is simple in its construction. The collar is only one-inch wide and is double the thickness of the rest of the shirt. The front panels, where the buttons and buttonholes go, are also double thickness and folded identically to the collar, as are the cuffs. Dean would have liked to create two buttonholes for cuff links, but Geoffrey advised him to go with buttons. "There is no point giving the boy what he can't afford, and you always go overboard for his birthdays," Geoffrey had remonstrated with Dean quite sternly. "How do you think Mike feels when Todd comes home bearing your expensive gifts—things he can never afford to buy the boy?"

"If Mike paid more attention to his son, I'd care," Dean answered back.

To which Geoffrey reminded Dean, "Todd is not your son, and you have to trust that Mike Fulton is taking care of him."

But he's not taking good care of him! Dean wants to yell back at Geoffrey when he suddenly realizes he is not arguing with his husband but sitting in his bedroom talking with Todd. It is amazing how powerful some memories can be, creating their presence so strongly in the moment.

Todd, sensing Papa Dean's distress, reaches forward to wrap his arms around the man's neck. "I love the shirt. Thank you so much, Papa Dean."

Still hugging Todd, Dean asks, "Is your friend still here?"

"Crystal? No. She had to go home."

"I'm sorry she left so early," Dean lies while smiling freely. "You know I am feeling a little better. Would you mind if I rejoined the party? I'd like to taste some of that cake I had hoped to make for you."

"Crystal did a really good job!" Todd doesn't realize how much his words hurt Dean.

Swallowing his disappointment, Dean determines to sound chipper, so he claps his hands together and declares, "Well, then I better taste it to make sure it really is good." Winking, he adds, "It's not like we get chocolate every day."

Todd winces. "Mr. Hunter wasn't too happy when he saw that cake."

Dean laughs. "I didn't think he would be. The chocolate I purchased was contraband. But today is your birthday so he simply has to endure it."

"You shouldn't get yourself into trouble for me, Papa Dean."

Dean gets up and Todd follows him to the door. "I can handle Geoffrey. Let's you and I go join the rest."

As they walk down the hall, Todd proposes, "Hey, Papa Dean, how about when I become a bioengineer like my dad, I genetically alter the cocoa bean so we can grow it up here?"

Dean wraps an arm around Todd's shoulder. "That's a wonderful idea, Todd. Best I've heard in years. Until then, though, let's go enjoy what's left of your illicit birthday cake."

* * * * *

Salve!

Extreme Weather
HNN—Melissa Eagleton Reporting

The legacy our forefathers have left us is never more prevalent than in days like this one. We all know of the changes to the earth's weather systems as a result of global warming. We live in what used to be a thick boreal forest that is now more grassland. We live near what used to be tundra, now mostly boreal forest. Hudson Bay was once the world's largest inland body of salt water—no more. As well as having to live with radical changes to earth's bio-system, we also have to contend with the excesses of extreme weather. Without warning, the weather will change and, suddenly, we find ourselves swamped by torrential rainstorms or tornadoes descending where least expected. Worse yet are the super cell thunderstorms that used to show up only over locations much further south such as Montana in what used to be the United States of America, now a smattering of smaller countries, much like our own old Canada. What we are experiencing right now, over both southern quadrants and all of Antinous, is equivalent to the kinds of storms that used to hit desert regions in the rainy season. Meteorologists suggest that the rains pounding down on us will last for weeks. Tighten your belts, Hadrians, as very little yield is likely to come from this year's crops. Already, city dwellers are complaining of having lost the bulk of their precious topsoil, and farmers are looking out, not onto the fields they have planted (if indeed they have planted any seed at all!), but at lakes! The question that sits in everyone's mind right now is whether, after the rains finally stop and all the drainage has occurred, there will be enough time, and *top soil*, left for planting, growing, and harvest. I do hope you have taken precautions over the years and have extra preserves from last year's growth since it is very likely our grocery stores will suffer a shortage of fresh fruit, grains, and vegetables this year! Remember, we do not bring in the same level of import as we have in the past. When a rough year hits

Hadrian, we must all be prepared to ride out the worst of it. If your stores are low, do not be proud; speak to your neighbors. I am certain many a prudent man or woman has extra rations and will be more than willing to share.

Vale!

Spring Fever

As it nears the end of May, planting season is quickly passing. Numerous rainsqualls attacking Antinous in the past couple of weeks have aborted all of Dean's early attempts to get his garden in order. According to Melissa Eagleton's report on *Salve!*, there is very little chance of the rains letting up any time soon. The loss of this year's garden is too much for Dean, and his sigh is both weary and discordant. The Hunter family garden is his pride and joy. Every year during the spring and summer months, he spends hours each day planting, weeding, trimming, pruning, and ensuring that the finest fruits, berries, and vegetables grow in the sprawling ledges of their backyard. It is a garden to please the eye as well as provide sustenance. The top three tiers are Dean's flower and herb gardens, each with at least two fruit or berry trees: apples, pears, and Saskatoon berries and choke cherries. Cutting through the garden's center is a path that helps Dean navigate up and down the various tiers. As one descends closer to the riverbed, Dean has one tier for sweet corn, another for a wide variety of vegetables including tomatoes, potatoes, beets, peas, carrots, cucumbers, onions, radishes, green and yellow beans, broccoli, lettuce, cabbage, and asparagus. The last tier is split with one side strictly for raspberries while the other half is divided between strawberries and blueberries. Dean is careful to keep the berries covered with cheesecloth so the birds cannot consume his crop. Interspersed throughout are the fallow tiers in which Dean alternates his vegetable and corn gardens. These tiers are kept well weeded so the soil can replenish and be used for compost storage. To keep these areas out of sight for visitors, Dean constructed temporary partitions to surround the unused areas. Geoffrey surprised Dean one year by commissioning an artist to paint images of the flowers and plants Dean most loves to cultivate on each of his partitions. This gift was given the first year after Dean's garden won Hadrian's Home Garden Award. Dean has garnered this award six times over the past ten years; the last three years consecutively.

This year is different, though. Dean isn't thinking about winning any awards, or trying to grow a new crop. Nor has he begun his annual ritual of digging his hands into the earth, spreading manure and compost, lovingly planting seedlings, carefully thinning and weeding. Instead, Dean has been holed up inside the house, watching the rain fall—too much rain. Not enough dry time has passed in between the rain for him to work the dirt, which, rather than being in soft beds, is now in thick muddy pools.

Seated on the cushioned bench inside the bay windows, Dean stares morosely at the rain pounding down on his backyard. Gardening is his lifeboat, a ritual routine that keeps his mind from focusing on harsh memories—memories that recur every spring—always beginning on the Ides of March. "*Et tu, Brute?*" he mutters. Tears roll down his cheeks.

This depression has been creeping up on Dean for over two months. Success at keeping it hidden and at bay was destroyed when the rains came. Prior to the steady downpour, Dean was keeping his mind focused on planning out the garden, getting seedlings ready, and cleaning out his garden shed. But the rainstorms came. And although it rains every spring, and Dean suffers low days as a result, this year the pounding down of the endless stream has swollen the river, flooding the first two tiers, drowning, and eventually washing away his precious berries. The other tiers have also been ruined as the heavy rains washed off all the topsoil he had worked so hard to build up and maintain over the years, reducing much of the garden to the stone and clay that lies beneath. To make matters worse, Geoffrey has been working late nearly every night for close to three months. With too much time on his hands, not seeing other outlets like sewing or house cleaning as options, Dean slowly has sunk deeper and deeper into a funk. So overwhelmed by emotion and memories he no longer tries to restrain in his mind's recesses, Dean doesn't hear the bubble pull up; they are such quiet vehicles. Its sudden appearance in the small parkway next to the backdoor startles Dean into awareness and fear sends the blood racing through his body. Quickly wiping his eyes, Dean dashes into the washroom where he splashes cold water over his face, hoping to hide his tired red eyes from his lover. *What time is it?* Dean wonders. The boys aren't home from school yet. *What's Geoffrey doing here?* In a panic, Dean blinks his right eye, looking at the clock to check the hour. *It's only 2:30*, he groans. Geoffrey is two full hours early. *Why is he home now? Maybe he knows. What to do? Go to the bedroom? Pretend to sleep? No*, Dean realizes, *that would tip Geoffrey off*. Rushing into the kitchen, Dean begins to pull out pots and pans, quickly planning an elaborate meal that should take him a good two hours to prepare. *Maybe Geoffrey will see that I'm busy*, Dean hopes desperately, *and go straight to his office instead of—of—of whatever it is that brought him home so soon*. Terrified of being found out, Dean doesn't even notice which vegetable he pulls out of the fridge. He just slams it down on the cutting board and begins chopping. Without realizing it, he is chopping apart a gourd he recently retrieved from the pantry for decorative purposes.

* * * * *

Salve!

Our Oceans Overflow
HNN—Melissa Eagleton Reporting

Yes, the title for today's *Salve!* is deceiving. Indeed the earth's oceans have grown over the last century. The loss of over half the Arctic and Antarctic polar icecaps has reduced the size of every continent while increasing the oceans exponentially. Albeit a terrifying truth, tonight's *Salve!* is on another type of overflow: the garbage barrage. When our satellite takes images of the earth's oceans, one has to wonder whether there is more water or pollution. The oceans are literally overflowing with debris. Observe as our wall screen reveals horrifying images of garbage islands. So much human waste in the form of plastics: bags, bottles, utensils, you name it. Then there are various metals, from tin cans to car parts! Even human clothing! Everything man-made can be found in the swill that was once a beautiful ocean. There are simply too many refuse items floating out there for me to attempt naming them all. All of this garbage has collected over the centuries until now one can actually stand and walk on these debris mounds. There are literally thousands of these garbage islands. Our cameras even detected a small colony of humans living on one. There is so little livable land left in the outside world that some poor souls have resorted to making these floating rubbish heaps their homes. It is frightening to wonder what they eat and drink on their floating cities of garbage.

Where the oceans' waters still flow free, what was once a beautiful aquamarine has been contaminated yellowish orange, a sulfurous byproduct of oil spills. In other areas, the thick black oil of recent and centuries old spills has turned this once azure bowl into a region of Black Death. Compare these images of Mexico's Gulf Coast, taken in the early twentieth century, to those taken now! The sight is absolutely grisly.

Eutrophication, possibly one of the most deadly of ocean killers, is entirely man-made. Having used the ocean as our waste disposal system for too many centuries, we have added more than just toxic chemicals into our planet's essential waters. We have flooded the oceans with fertilizers, causing exponential growth of algae. These little creatures have flourished to such an extent that they have literally consumed all of the oxygen in their surrounding ocean area, killing off all other marine life in the vicinity. Where there used to be the odd "dead zone" in our world's oceans, now more than half of earth's oceans are lifeless.

Is it any wonder that our marine biologists work endlessly to ensure that the water we consume from our rivers connected to the Hudson Bay is clean? We also patrol our water border endlessly with a new breed of fisherman: the "detritus fisherman." These brave men and women work tirelessly to keep humanity's excess pollution from entering our waters. It is an endless, dirty, and backbreaking job. The worst part is our not knowing what to do with much of what we prevent from coming our way. In most cases, it is simply rerouted back to where it came from, as we have nowhere to put this accretion of decay. Our detritus fishermen do, however, continuously dig through and salvage from this garbage any materials we can use. We have salvaged glass for windows and metals for building. Much of what we can no longer dig deep into our earth to find is simply floating out there, waiting for us to grab and reuse. Being a detritus fisherman is a thankless, heart-wrenching, and backbreaking job. These people are the real heroes of Hadrian.

Perhaps the most sorrowful images of our oceans are the hundreds of thousands of refugee ships floating among all the garbage and decay. These ships' passengers were either forced off their land due to overpopulation or were desperately hoping to be allowed onto the North American continent where pockets of sustainable land still exist outside of Hadrian. Most of these people will die in their crafts on the ocean, either from thirst, starvation, or disease because no one will allow them onto their shores. As painful as it is for us, we too must turn these ships away. Time and again, refugee boats navigate their way into Hudson Bay from both the Atlantic and the Arctic Oceans, hoping to immigrate to Hadrian. I honestly cannot imagine how difficult it must be to turn away crying and emaciated children. But Hadrian's borders must remain closed. There is too much risk of widespread disease, and as all our outside images have shown, where too many men dwell, the earth inevitably suffers. Our population is ten million. We will not allow that to grow either through baby booms or immigration. Population control is the first of the four cornerstones of Hadrian's civilization. It is the very crux, the very pillar upon which our society was founded.

The earth's ocean waters are a grim reminder of why the human population must diminish and then be restrained from ever growing out of control again!

Vale!

Good News!

Geoffrey seldom comes home early from the office. Today, however, is special. Thrilled by the morning's success, he is anxious to find his partner and share the good news with him. The last thing Geoffrey is expecting is to find his husband suffering from another episode. Dean has been stable for over three years now. Their psychiatrist, Edgar, was like a gift from Hadrian. He prescribed Seroxat (an anti-depressant that has helped Dean cope with brooding fears and panic anxiety) as well as Zolam (a benzene for immediate relief when Dean suffers from a panic attack). Their monthly appointments have been worth every chit. The possibility that Dean is crumpled over inside does not even register in Geoffrey's mind, though the steady rain of the past two weeks should have been warning enough. Unfortunately, Geoffrey is often too preoccupied with work to take note of the subtle changes occurring in his home. And, now that the boys are older, they don't complain when Papa Dean is morose and not spending time with them like he used to. So, when Geoffrey arrives home, he is in a state of ignorant bliss: a man of all smiles.

The deal Geoffrey has been working on for the past three months (years actually, but only these past few months have led his hopes and dreams in the right direction) has finally come to pass. Although his father was hurt when Geoffrey told him of the plans to sell Hunter Enterprises to Hadrian National, the need was too great. Since Hunter Enterprises runs the detritus fisheries, much of the financial burden of coping with waste disposal falls on his company's shoulders. For years, his grandfather and father had fought with the government for subsidies to help cover the devastating cost of effective, earth-friendly disposal of all wastes retrieved from Hudson Bay. Seeing as Hunter Enterprises received the benefits of profit from the usable wastes they fished out of the bay, the government insisted the company also carry the financial burden of disposing of all non-usable materials. Anything retrieved from Hudson Bay that is harmful to the planet must be disposed of in such a way that it no longer poses any threat to the earth or Hadrian's citizens. The respect gleaned from being the corporation responsible for eliminating much of the pollution from Hadrian's main water source, as well as providing the country with nearly one fourth of all its usable resources, pales at times next to the astronomical cost of providing safe, clean disposal of many of the toxic wastes left behind by humanity's forefathers. Geoffrey's grandfather and father compensated for this financial loss by offering their employees little support—no medical benefits, no retirement savings packages, and, of course, being such a dirty job, it was also low paying. Geoffrey, however, has a stronger moral streak than his elders. Rightfully, Geoffrey credits Dean for helping him acquire a more philanthropic perspective.

When Geoffrey's father retired and Geoffrey took over the company, he decided to listen to his workers' needs. The end result was an added financial burden on Hunter Enterprises, cutting great swaths out of company profit. Try as they might, the board members could not persuade Geoffrey to change his mind because he saw reason and right behind providing for his detritus fishermen. These men and women handle much of the toxic wastes found in the Bay, and they have done so for far too many years without health benefits. Geoffrey made this decision within weeks of discovering that the majority of his employees, over two-thirds, in fact, were from the reeducated class, those members of Hadrian's society who had been found out as heterosexual before the age of twenty-two (the age one pledges an oath to Hadrian's four cornerstones). These citizens were placed in government run reeducation facilities that guided them back toward Hadrian's chosen lifestyle. The taint of having being registered as straight remains a blight on their lives, as very few opportunities are open to these men and women. As a result, many take jobs as detritus fishermen since few others want such arduous, dirty, and mentally draining jobs and few other employers will hire them. All job applications must be accompanied with full disclosure as to one's education and military service. As no heterosexual is allowed in the military and re-education camps are considered educational institutions, such "full disclosure" would immediately reveal anyone who was once deemed heterosexual. When Dean had learned this fact, he extracted a promise from Geoffrey that he would treat his employees fairly.

Knowing how important it was to Dean, Geoffrey labored endlessly to convince the board to improve working conditions for the detritus fishermen and offer them a benefits package. Very few board members had supported Geoffrey's bid for his employees. That the reeducated are desperate for employment makes them an easy target for exploitation. Geoffrey had argued that their role was too important to ignore as, he rightly pointed out, "Outside of the military, no other man or woman in Hadrian puts his or her life on the line daily the way detritus fishermen do." Although the vote was close, he did secure a slight raise and a basic medical plan for the detritus fishermen. Unfortunately, the cost of doing so was breaking the back of Hunter Enterprises. The board members were upset, stockholders were calling for changes, and Geoffrey had been forced to determine what those changes needed to be.

Today's success brings forth those changes: secured financial resources for the stock investors, the value of their shares doubling with the take-over, and all cost of waste disposal now being handled by the government. Selling Hunter Enterprises to Hadrian National, making it a subsidiary to the government giant, is the finest move Geoffrey has made so far for his business. Granted, Geoffrey is no longer majority owner, but he does retain his post as company head as part of the deal. He is now on a salary that doubles what his wages were when he owned and ran Hunter Enterprises. As well as further improving the detritus fishermen's wages and working conditions, which he knows will make Dean happy, Geoffrey has not only secured but substantially improved his family's lifestyle as well as his children's future. To be rid of the worries and financial burden of waste disposal has made his mind and heart light. Now that Hunter Enterprises is a subsidiary of Hadrian National, Hadrian taxes will be used to pay for all waste disposal and renewal. Hadrian citizens pay the highest taxes in the world, most of which are reserved for cleansing and maintaining Hadrian's little portion of the planet. In fact, the majority of Hadrian's taxes are split three ways: funding the military; funding education (of which reeducation is a subsidiary); and continuous research into effective earth-friendly waste disposal. Tax rebates are offered for those who show extra care with earth-friendly practices, but these pale next to the expense of cleaning up Hudson Bay, the world's second largest inland body of water: a veritable ocean-sized slough filled with waste discarded over centuries by billions and billions of humans.

Today's victory is one Geoffrey longs to share with Dean. When he prances into the front room, he calls out merrily, "Dean, Dean, come out here. I've got something I want to tell you."

"I'm in the kitchen, preparing supper."

Dean's petulant response should trigger a warning in Geoffrey's mind, but it does not. Being far too engrossed in his own joy, Geoffrey does not notice the sullen tone in Dean's voice. "Put that away," Geoffrey chants. "We're going out for supper." When no sound comes in response, Geoffrey calls out, "Come in here, Dean; this is important." Dean slowly walks from the kitchen into the front room, shamming a smile. Joy, success, and pride have a way of blinding a man. Geoffrey does not see the obvious signs of depression in Dean's eyes.

As soon as Geoffrey sees his lover, he rushes to him and lifts him up in his arms. Being shorter than Dean by a good three inches, Geoffrey has to lean back in order to lift Dean off the ground. Dean also has to cooperate by bending at the knees and lifting his feet. After swinging Dean around, Geoffrey lowers him and reaches up for a kiss. Dean complies, but with little fervor. Geoffrey has enough fervor inside to compensate, enough to keep him from noticing Dean's lack of participation. "Your daddy's done it, baby!" he says between bouts of kisses. "I sealed the deal today!"

"What deal?" Dean asks, now leaning against the wall. Geoffrey's swinging and plunging into him have driven his body up against the hideous black velvet wallpaper.

Geoffrey has to kiss Dean again before answering, "Hadrian National now owns Hunter Enterprises!"

Dean tries to smile. "That's…great." Geoffrey kisses him again and then turns Dean to face the wall. Dean's face is now squishing up against black velvet. He knows Geoffrey can't tell. Dean's depression is rooted so deep inside that, like a dandelion that's been dug out, it continues to resurface, sprout its yellow head, and just as quickly, wither white.

"Um…" Geoffrey mutters as he kisses the back of Dean's neck. His hands are running up the front of Dean's shirt, catching the buttons and flipping them open adeptly. His nails scratch down the front of Dean's chest, gripping and pulling at his chest hairs. Making his move for Dean's belt buckle, he steps back slightly so Dean can give him room to undo it. Dean obliges. He knows what Geoffrey wants. Soon enough, Dean's pants and briefs are a bundle of cloth around his ankles and Geoffrey has the front of his pants open. Not able to accomplish much standing tip-toe, Geoffrey makes a request of Dean, "Bend your knees for me, babe." Dean obliges but snaps when Geoffrey thanks him with, "That's my boy."

"I am not a fucking child! I know what to do. You don't have to instruct me like an idiot, you know!"

The resurgence of Dean's spring depression hits Geoffrey like a wrecking ball. He releases his grip on Dean's penis and steps back, flabbergasted by this sudden attack. "Whoa, where did that come from?"

"You!" Dean is still facing the wall, hands positioned, his body waiting, only his mind reacting. "You treat me like a little baby. 'Come to Papa.' 'Who's your daddy?' 'Bend your knees.' 'Good boy!' You'd think I was a fucking dog!" Turning now to face Geoffrey, eyes wet and red with anger, he shouts, "I'm a man, damn you! Not a fucking dog and not a child! For the love of Hadrian, treat me like an adult!"

"That…is…not…fair!" So stunned by the blow of Dean's curse, each word Geoffrey utters stands alone. Backing away to the opposite wall, Geoffrey holds his hands up in a defensive position. Shaking his head, he says, "I don't deserve this!" Taking a moment to inspect his lover, he sees that Dean, now facing him, still has his pants and briefs tangled at his feet. His limp penis exposes itself as an affront to Geoffrey. "For Hadrian's sake, pull up your pants," he sneers. "You look ridiculous."

It is cruel, malicious, yes, even evil to say such a thing to Dean at a moment like this. When trapped inside his anxieties, Dean truly is as vulnerable as a child. Insecure and riddled with depression, desperate to dig himself out of his hole in the sand, every attempt to claw at the edges sinking him deeper, Dean collapses to the floor. First his back thumps against the wall, as if Geoffrey's voice had been a fist slamming into his chest. Tears spring forth anew and his body slowly drips down, his shirt pulling up and away from his torso as he lowers himself, making him even more exposed. Geoffrey, knowing he has done wrong, fears the extent of the damage he has just caused. Rushing to his lover's side, he sweeps Dean up into his arms and apologizes. Geoffrey, too, breaks down as he blubbers his regrets.

"No," Dean whimpers. "I'm sorry. I'm sorry. I'm sorry. I'm sorry." Geoffrey has to put a hand to Dean's mouth to stop this skip recording. When Dean gets completely overwhelmed like this, he simply can't stop saying, "I'm sorry."

Gently holding Dean's mouth closed, Geoffrey tries again. "I didn't mean that, babe. Please forgive me."

Shaking his head free, Dean wails, "It's my fault! I hate myself! I hate my life. I just—I just—sometimes, I just want to die."

Fear tugs at Geoffrey's heart. "Please don't talk like that." He hasn't heard Dean utter these words in years. *What's gone wrong? What's happened?*

Dean continues his self-recriminating rant. "Why do you love me? Why do you stay with me? I'm nothing! I'm pathetic!"

"No, babe. No," Geoffrey tries to reassure him. "That's not true." He rocks him now as he caresses his hair. "You're a good man, Dean. We have a good life." Gently cradling Dean's head in his hands, Geoffrey turns Dean's face upwards to look at him, now pleading with him. "You know that, don't you?"

Dean's voice becomes soft. "You have a good life. The boys have a good life. I have nothing—I'm useless—I'm fucking useless. I hate myself." Frustration builds to a fever as Dean begins pounding his fist on his thigh.

Following Dean's fist with his eyes, Geoffrey now notices the bruising. *Not again!* "Dean, stop!" He demands as he grabs Dean's fist and fights for control. "You promised me you would never do this again."

"I hate myself! I hate what I've become! I had wanted so much—when I think of what I might have done…"

Geoffrey tries desperately to reassure Dean, knowing his words fall on deaf ears. "No, Dean. You're an amazing man, a great cook, a fabulous dad, and the clothes you sew, the garden you keep—" Then it hits him—*the garden*—Dean hasn't been able to work in his garden. "All this rain—that's what brought this out, isn't it, sweetie?" Shaking his head, self-recriminatingly, he adds, "I should have known. I've just been so busy with this deal."

"That's the thing," Dean says. "You've got your deals. You've got your business. You've got your life. But what have I got? Nothing! I've been reduced to—to—this!" With that final cry, Dean regains control of his fist and begins slamming it into his thigh again. Both thighs, Geoffrey notices, are black and blue—mostly yellow and purple, actually.

Enraged, Geoffrey wrestles Dean onto his back, pinning his arms down with his knees. Bellowing so that spit showers Dean's face, he demands, "Stop it!" For a moment, he just kneels there, dominating Dean, growling down at him, pressing his knees into Dean's arms to keep him from harming himself further. Trying to control his anger, knowing rage only exasperates Dean's condition, Geoffrey works to slow his breathing before speaking. "You swore you would never hit yourself again."

"I tried not to—but—I just—I hate myself so much—I couldn't stop myself."

Closing his eyes, thinking briefly, Geoffrey asks, "When was the last time you saw Edgar?" He had been so busy he had stopped attending sessions with Dean.

"Last fall."

Nodding, Geoffrey continues, "And why did you stop going?"

"He said I had improved so much he didn't see the need to keep up with our sessions."

"Right." Opening his eyes, looking into Dean's, Geoffrey asks, "And why didn't you tell me this?"

"Things were going good."

"What about the Seroxat?"

Dean evades the questions. "My arms hurt, Geoffrey. You're cutting off my circulation."

"If I let you go, will you promise not to hit yourself?"

Dean shudders a few breaths before replying, "I'll try."

Geoffrey tightens his grip, "Try isn't good enough."

"I…" Dean trembles, "promise."

Releasing his knees, Geoffrey slips off Dean to sit on the floor beside him. "The Seroxat, Dean—when did you come off the Seroxat?"

"Edgar started tapering me off in the fall. I took my last dose in February."

Geoffrey looks dejected. "Why didn't you tell me?" Ire forming once more, he demands, "Why didn't Edgar tell me?"

Still lying on the floor, Dean covers his face with his hands. "I told him I would."

Geoffrey snorts. "And he believed you?"

"I was doing so good."

"*Well*, Dean! You were doing *well*! And, you were doing *well* because you were on the Seroxat!" *Dear Hadrian, why*, he chastises himself, *did I correct his grammar?* Closing his eyes, Geoffrey pauses for a moment to regulate his breath, attempting to calm himself. Sadness is so overwhelming and fear for the mental and physical health of a lover can cause one to consider acting outside of reason. At this moment, all Geoffrey wants to do is hunt down Edgar and pummel him into dirt. In anticipation, quite involuntarily, his hands form fists. Geoffrey has to force himself to relax them, and almost against his will, shake these thoughts away. Looking back at Dean, Geoffrey notices that his pants and briefs are still tangled around his ankles, his shirt still strewn open, exposing his chest. Geoffrey reaches for the waistband of Dean's briefs. "Let me help you, sweetie," he says soothingly. After helping Dean pull his briefs and pants back into place, Geoffrey watches as Dean buttons them shut. "You left your shirt open," he says. Dean stares at the wall, oblivious. Pondering the situation, Geoffrey wonders whether Dean has any benzies left. "Do you still have some Zolam?" When Dean only whimpers, Geoffrey becomes insistent. "Where is it?"

"It's probably expired."

"Where is it?"

Dean succumbs to the inevitable. "My top dresser drawer—under the socks—back right corner."

"I am going to get it now and you are going to take some." Considering Dean's current state of mind, Geoffrey adds, "Your full dose."

"Please," Dean begs. "I want to do this without drugs."

Geoffrey shakes his head. "It didn't work for you, did it, Dean?" Adamant now, he says, "No. You need Zolam right now. You know you do." As he gets up and walks down the hall to their room, Geoffrey blinks and mutters, "Edgar Fraser." Dean cries softly. Geoffrey's voice fades out as he enters the bedroom, but he will make an appointment with Edgar that evening at seven o'clock. There will be several evening appointments to come since Geoffrey will insist on attending them. From their room, Geoffrey calls out, "The boys will be home soon, Dean. You better come into the bedroom."

Accepting his circumstances, Dean rises slowly to join Geoffrey. "After the Zolam kicks in," he says softly, "we can have sex like you wanted." Geoffrey doesn't hear this since Dean is only muttering to himself.

* * * * *

Salve!

The Eighth Anniversary of 6-13
HNN—Melissa Eagleton Reporting

For seven years now, I have been asked to revisit the pain that was inflicted upon our people that fateful June day in 21___. That June 13th was, ironically enough, a Friday. In the early hours of that ill-fated morning, the fanatical Christian, one Jeremiah F. Butler, believed to hail from Tex (formerly the state of Texas within the United States), drove into our border city of Augustus. At 5:57 that morning, with the summer sun already hanging high above the horizon, he was asked to please step out of his vehicle. Border Patrol Officer Acilia Zangani, who died the instant the bomb exploded, having voc'd in prior to the explosion, was quoted as saying, "Although there is no reason to mistrust this man, something about him feels dangerous." The Border Patrol Office in Antinous, which later said Officer Zangani's instincts were always 100 percent accurate, approved her request to retain him for questioning. When instructed to leave his vehicle, the man must have panicked because, at that instant, the dirty nuclear bomb hidden in his trunk exploded. Five hundred and eighty-eight thousand of Augustus' citizens died that day. Their deaths were followed by another forty-four thousand: those who were at the city's northern edge or working peacefully on the surrounding soya farms. Those closest to the bomb's explosion, but far enough away not to die under its initial impact, suffered slowly from radiation burns, sickness, and the onset of various forms of cancer. Many working out on the farms would not know how their lives would be dramatically changed due to contracting cancers anywhere from six months to even as late as, yes, even today: cancers we know to have been induced by the deadly radiation. As a result of 6-13, Hadrian lost one of its greatest innovators in bioengineering, Will Middleton, the man responsible for genetically altering the soya bean to grow in our northern climate.

Since 6-13, many of Hadrian's citizens have suffered from apocalyptic dreams. This is understandable since Augustus is the third city to have suffered from a nuclear attack. For some time, it appeared that the world had learned and people were unwilling to unleash such devastating brutal power against their fellow man, but it seems that fanatical faith is not prone to learn from past human mistakes. Please, fellow citizens, if you are one of the many who suffer from such horrifying nightmares, seek out one of Hadrian's many competent and compassionate psychiatrists. There is no need to suffer alone.

So there you have it, Hadrian. As well as 6-13 stealing one of our greatest minds, Will Middleton, it has left many of our citizens subjected to psychological trauma. We will never forgive the heterosexual world for condemning us. Never again will an outsider cross our borders.

Vale!

Apocalyptic Nightmare

Mike's recurring nightmare always begins in an idyllic setting, at the Fulton family cottage on an isolated beach north of Antinous on the Churchill River. This is where, every summer for the first thirteen years of their marriage, Will Middleton and Mike Fulton would pack up the bubble and take Todd for vacation. As well as the golden sand that runs for miles along the river's southern shore, there is the scenic beauty of the boreal forest still growing in this region. The dream always opens here. It is always early evening and Todd is always busy building sandcastles, digging moats, and filling them with water. The scene is tranquil, the skyline lilac, interspersed with dark blue. Will Middleton, six inches taller than his partner, rests his arm on Mike Fulton's shoulder. Mike, as always, pulls in tight to Will's side, walking at a slight angle as a result. Will laughs along with Todd, enjoying the sights and sounds of his play. Then he looks down at Mike, smiles, and ruffles the shorter man's hair. Mike soaks in every gesture from his spouse. Will Middleton is not one to express feelings physically, nor verbally, so moments like this are rare. Although the sun is behind Will, his face appears radiant and Mike feels himself at his most in love. Reaching up using his toes, Mike is pleasantly surprised by Will's leaning down to meet his lips for a kiss. Todd's laughter flaps like butterfly wings in Mike's chest, causing his heart to beat rapidly. For a fleeting moment, Mike wonders whether now is the time for them to have their second child, his genetic son or daughter. Just as Mike's lips are about to connect with his lover's, Will Middleton disappears.

Mike is stunned. "Will? Will?" he cries out. And then he sees him; Will Middleton is inside a mirror—*what is he doing inside a mirror?* Mike always wonders—bent over working on a soya farm just outside of Augustus City, the city shimmering in the background. *What is Will doing outside Augustus City?* But his question is never answered. All Mike can do is watch in horror as a thunderous explosion occurs behind Will and a mushroom cloud billows over Augustus City in the background. The ensuing winds, shooting out from the city and racing across the field, form a hand that clutches Will Middleton. Tauntingly it lifts its victim, suspending him by digging one gnarly nail into his neck. Will screams and struggles against the force lifting him, but he can do nothing to escape its grip. Slowly, Will's life force begins to drain away until all that remains is a limp bag of skin. When nothing remains of what was once Will Middleton, the wind whips his husk against the inside of the mirror shattering the glass, its sharp shards slashing Todd, cutting deep into his skin. Screaming, Todd leaps up from his sandcastle and runs wildly into his Papa Mike.

In horror, Mike Fulton stares at the boy clutching him. He pushes Todd off, but the boy climbs back on, crying, begging for his daddy. It is as if Todd is made of glue and is now stuck to him. Mike, using both hands, grabs one of Todd's arms, and with great effort, plucks it off. As soon as Mike releases his grip and reaches for Todd's other arm, the first arm, as if being pulled by magnets or gravity, slams back into him. Every time Mike plucks one of Todd's hands away, the other hand slams back into him, gripping, clutching, sucking onto him like a river leech. Suddenly, a war of gripping and plucking occurs until Mike, unable to bear it any longer, sits up in his bed, screaming at Todd to let go of him—to get off—to leave him alone!

Sweating in horror, Mike leaps out of bed and races to the linen closet—now Todd's small bedroom. The closet door is open as usual, but there is no Todd. Relieved, Mike sinks to his knees. Todd is not here to hear him scream. Too many times, Mike has awoken from this nightmare to discover Todd sleeping. Never will Mike wake him to ask whether Todd can hear him. It is safe, Mike believes, to assume Todd knows nothing of his inner loathing for the boy—Todd lives while his husband died. Todd lives while his responsibility to produce a child has been relinquished due to impoverished means. Todd lives while his sperm is being used to provide barren men and women with children. His children! "At least one child should have been given to me to raise." Having had a loving relationship with his genetic mother, Mike had longed for his own parenting role. Riddled with guilt, Mike cries as he grieves and self-recriminates. "I'm sorry, Todd," he blubbers. But his apology is insincere.

* * * * *

Dating Devon

June is coming to its end, and like every other Friday afternoon that school year, Frank Hunter and Todd Middleton arrange to meet at Todd's locker. It has become a tradition for these two to spend every Friday after school having supper at the Soya Baron (where *"the Soya Burger is King!"*). The Soya Baron is conveniently located across the street from Pride High. Lacking the special thumbprint to connect him to an account, Todd has no purchasing power, so it is always Frank's treat. Being more like brothers than "just friends," it never makes Todd feel awkward to have Frank pay for him. Frank and Todd are best friends, having been best friends since they were in the cradle. Will Middleton, Todd's genetic father, and Dean Hunter had been best friends since their high school years. Papa Dean often reminds Todd and Frank how the boys used to sleep together in the crib. In fact, sleepovers were a common event for these two until the onset of puberty. With sexual awakenings apparent in both boys (thirteen being a critical age), Frank's fathers sat Frank and Todd down to warn them how sharing a bed now would be too awkward. Papa Mike, Frank's fathers assured Todd, would agree. Papa Mike did not participate in this crucial parent/son discussion. Ever since Will Middleton's death, Mike Fulton had taken very little notice of Todd's growing needs. Still, Geoffrey Hunter and Papa Dean assured Todd that Papa Mike and they did not want their sons becoming sexually active at so young an age. Well, they had nothing to worry about with Todd. Although he had yearnings, he wasn't interested in having sex with anyone yet. Frank, on the other hand, unknown to his fathers, began sexually experimenting when he was thirteen. Although Frank wants to be with Todd, he has begrudgingly come to accept that Todd is still listening to their parents. It doesn't help that Papa Dean constantly reminds Todd that Papa Mike and he approve of his choice to wait until he is ready, or at least eighteen.

Today, Frank is late. Todd sighs. He is starving! Leaning against his pink locker, Todd settles in for the long wait. Disappointment begins to swell in Todd's chest. Frank is already fifteen minutes late. It is not unusual for Frank to be late, but he is seldom ever ten minutes past the appointed time: three-thirty (ten minutes after the school bell). If he's later than ten minutes, Todd knows Frank will usually not show. Todd is used to Frank standing him up. It seems like the older they get, the hornier Frank gets, and the more often he ignores Todd to go off with one of his boys. Frank's absence really stings tonight because, once again, Papa Mike is working overtime. The last thing Todd wants is to spend another night at home alone. *Where are you, Frank?* Todd wonders.

"He's on a date." Leaning up against the purple locker next to Todd is Devon Rankin. Devon is slightly taller than Todd, standing 5' 8", but he has less muscle definition. He too plays b-ball, but unlike Todd, Frank, and Crystal (the three stars of Pride's Panthers and known by all as the three gay caballeros), his dedication level only landed him on the junior team in grade ten. The three gay caballeros played on the senior team last year. Even so, Devon is in good physical shape. His smile is radiant and his blonde curly locks dangle over his shoulders. Today, he is wearing his hair tied back in a loose ponytail. He wears silver stud diamond earrings and a thick silver chain to match. Leaning with his back to the locker, Devon's hands are hidden behind his backside. He offers Todd his profile, definitely his most handsome feature.

"Huh?" Todd looks around at Devon, unaware that he had expressed aloud his thoughts concerning Frank's whereabouts. Devon smiles, exposing for Todd perfect teeth. "Uh, we were supposed to meet," Todd mumbles.

"Yeah, well, I saw him leaving about five minutes ago with Davie." He clicks the inside of his cheek as he winks. "Davie's pretty sweet. And they say he'll even tumble on the first date."

Todd smirks. "I guess he's Frank's type then."

"Yeah," Devon concurs, "which explains why the two of you are only friends."

Todd laughs outright at that. "Yeah. I can't imagine myself ever looking, or acting, like the tinsel tarts Frank dates."

"Tinsel tarts," Devon chuckles. "I like that." Studying Todd briefly, Devon is very agreeable at the moment. "Yeah, I don't like guys looking like women either. I mean, what's the point? It feels too, het'ro, if you know what I mean."

Todd assumes a serious expression. "Yeah, yeah, I know what you mean."

"Now you," Devon says, nodding Todd's way. "You dress the way I like a man to dress."

"Really?" Todd is flattered. Devon is actually the first person to compliment his style of clothing. "Everyone else says I look too much like a 'mechanic'." He feigns quotation marks with his fingers.

"Hey," Devon asks, "isn't your father a mechanic?"

"Papa Mike is."

"What does your father do?" Seeing gloom in Todd's eyes, Devon immediately apologizes, "I'm sorry, Todd. I didn't know."

"That's okay," Todd replies. "I don't really talk about it."

"That's okay; I understand." Devon's compassion touches Todd. "Do you mind my asking what he did?"

"Nah, sure. Dad was an agricultural engineer."

"Wow!" Devon exclaims. "That's big!" Suddenly Devon realizes Todd's last name is the same as the famous bioengineer Will Middleton. "Your dad was *Will Middleton?*"

"Yeah," says Todd, proud of his father's accomplishments.

"No wonder you're so good at b-ball. Will Middleton was one of the greatest college b-ball players ever."

"He also helped establish the soya farms in Quadrant One," said Todd. No one had believed Will Middleton when he had said soya would grow in the grasslands of Quadrants One and Two, considering it was not that long ago on the evolutionary scale that the region had been mostly boreal forest. But with the rapid increase in planet temperature, the temperate marshy grasslands quickly moved north, and with the onset of hot summers and moderate winters, the southern tips of Quadrants One and Two proved to be fertile soil for the valuable, lifesaving plant. With less room for raising livestock, the soya plant has become crucial in providing Hadrian's citizens with much needed protein, especially since cattle are nearing extinction. With over twenty billion people crowding the earth, very little room is left for cattle ranches. In fact, the national government only allows one cattle ranch to exist within Hadrian's walls because the methane gases released by the cattle were a major cause of global warming. Living in an environmentally sound and balanced environment is, and will always be, one of Hadrian's central principles. Todd is proud that his father was instrumental in ensuring Hadrian's ability to live in harmony with its small portion of the earth. "Yeah," Todd continues, "Dad used to travel there a lot…" Pausing, Todd squeezes shut his eyes, trying desperately to hold back the hot tears fighting to stream out. "He travelled to the southern tip—soya farms—he was there when—"

"Oh, shit!" Devon is truly sorry. "6-13!"

"Yeah, well,—" Todd loses focus and begins to sob. He misses his father so much his whole body aches in agony. Will Middleton's death had spun both husband and son into such a state of despair that their parent–child relationship has never recovered.

"Hey, hey." Devon reaches his arms around Todd and pulls him in for a hug. He rocks Todd gently in his arms, allowing him time to cry while he whispers soothing hushing sounds. There are no words for a moment like this, and Devon doesn't even try to find them.

"I'm sorry," Todd utters through gasps. "It's been eight years; you'd think—"

Devon won't even let him finish. "No, I wouldn't be able to get over it." Still rocking Todd gently, he says, "You cry as long as you want. As long as you need!" Todd accepts Devon's offer and releases a flood of pent up grief. He has only been able to share this level of emotion with Frank and Crystal. Having another person feel empathy is relieving.

After Todd is spent, Devon asks whether he'd like to have dinner with him. "At your place?" Todd asks.

Pleased that Todd is responding on a positive level, Devon replies, "I was thinking maybe we could go to a Japanese restaurant. How about *Rezu*?" *Rezu* is Japanese slang for lesbian. The restaurant owners have chosen to embrace the slang term and make it their own.

Todd shudders. "Oh, man, I can't—I mean—" Todd is not sure how to tell Devon he doesn't even have a thumbprint, let alone credits.

Devon smiles. "I'm asking for the date, so it's my treat." After waiting a moment without reply, he asks, "So, what do you think?"

A date? Todd wonders what this might mean. *He won't pressure me, I don't think.* Remembering Devon's description of Davie (tumbles on the first date), Todd feels reassured that Devon isn't likely to expect anything. "Okay," Todd replies, still sounding uneasy, "if it's not too expensive—I mean, I've heard *Rezu* is pricey—I don't want you blowing all your credits on me."

"Nothing's too pricey for my first date with you." Laughing, Devon says, "I can't believe you said yes. Man, I've been wanting to ask you out all year."

Todd blinks, "Really? Me?" He shakes his head in wonder. "I'm nothing special. I'm certainly not good looking or—"

Devon puts a finger to Todd's lips. "You are a prize, my friend. Half the guys at Pride want to date you, but we're all too scared to ask."

"Why?" Todd is truly dumbfounded.

"Mostly out of fear of Frank," Devon answers. Suddenly realizing Todd really doesn't understand why anyone is afraid of him, he adds, "But, also because you're the best damn b-ball player on campus. You got Rookie of the Year at Quadrants. I think everyone's intimidated by that."

Intimidated by me? Todd finds that concept hard to believe. It is amazing how humble a man can be when he is afraid of what other people might think.

"Come on," Devon says, squeezing Todd's shoulder muscle, in antici-pation. "I got my mothers' bubble. We'll drive to *Rezu*." Devon's mothers own a 'double bubble,' a slightly larger vehicle designed to sit four. Only registered couples with one or two children are eligible to purchase one. All other residents of Hadrian are confined to owning a single bubble. Once partners register as a legally bound couple (the equivalent of marriage), they are required to sell off one bubble, reducing the number of vehicles driven throughout Hadrian, thus limiting congestion and the number of road accidents. It also helps ensure less energy waste. When a registered couple is preparing for the arrival of a newborn, they are free to trade in their bubble for the family-sized double bubble.

As the two boys approach the small vehicle, Devon laughs, remembering when he and his mothers went in five years ago to trade their old double bubble in for a newer, more reliable version. The salesman had a bowl of an odd-looking gum on his desk. He said it was called double bubble! "Did you know that the name double bubble once was a type of chewing gum?" Devon asks Todd. "From way back when." Just to add emphasis to how long ago this really was, Devon not only extends the vowel in 'way' but also gestures with open palms a very long extension. Todd shakes his head. "Yeah, the guy who sold us this bubble told us all about it. It's a small pink rectangle with an indent in the middle. It comes wrapped inside a joke comic. When I first tasted it, I thought it was really great—super sweet, but the flavor only lasted a few minutes. The man said they used the original recipe to make it. I mean it was really good, but for such a short period. I ended up spitting it out." Todd's look of surprise that anyone would so blatantly litter encourages Devon to add, "Don't worry; I learned my lesson. Mama Rena caught me and gave me such a tongue lashing when we got home." Laughing, he adds, "Mama Rena believes a spanking every now and again never hurt anybody, so she actually paddled my backside that day." Reassuring his new friend, he adds, "I've never done anything like that again."

Todd nods his approval. "You're lucky only your mama caught you!"

"Tell me about it," Devon agrees. Both boys shudder at the thought. No one litters in Hadrian. The fines if caught are astronomical, and if you amass a record of three offenses, the government will exile you from Hadrian!

Devon opens the bubble for Todd by tapping on the roof, causing the transparent door to slide down. Todd steps up and then down into the small vehicle. It looks so small that it seems impossible for anyone to fit into it, but it is surprisingly roomy inside. Even a man of 6' 5" can sit inside a bubble and not feel cramped. After settling into the driver's side, Devon turns Todd's way. "I can't wait till we get to *Rezu*." Smiling, he adds, "I don't know about you, man, but I'm starving!" As if on cue Todd's stomach growls, causing Devon to laugh. "Good, you're hungry too! I know just what to order us when we get there!" Todd can't help but laugh along with Devon, his playful mood infectious.

* * * * *

Salve!

Rezu—Still Hadrian's Top Restaurant
HNN—Melissa Eagleton Reporting

When was the last time you took your lover out for a quiet romantic meal? Where better than Hadrian's oldest restaurant, *Rezu*? One of Antinous' most popular restaurants and listed as Hadrian's top dining establishment in the bestselling restaurant guide: *Hadrian's Finest Victuals*, published last year through Sappho Press. *Rezu* is nestled nicely in the corner of Backstreet Bay where it offers its customers a scenic view of the Nelson River that complements its tantalizing cuisine. Opened the year of Hadrian's founding, *Rezu* has always held its mission to be to provide Hadrian's citizens with an authentic taste of traditional Japanese cookery. Kyoko Yokomoto was among the first immigrants to join Hadrian's family. With her, she brought everything she knew about preparing traditional Japanese food, having apprenticed under her father at his restaurant in what was then still Vancouver, British Columbia, Canada. Her daughter, Etsuko Yokomoto, inherited *Rezu*, and today Etsuko's daughter, Chiyo, and grandson, Jun, run the business. *Rezu* still upholds the quality that founded this fine eating establishment. You are guaranteed one of the finest meals in all of Hadrian when you visit *Rezu*. Bring your lover and reserve a private room. There is no better way to spend the perfect romantic evening than dining at *Rezu*.

Vale!

Rezu

Devon offers his thumb to the host, teasing him with little wiggles back and forth. The man adeptly retrieves his pad, allowing Devon to press his thumbprint on the face of it. Subsequent to his print, Devon follows up with a few taps, transferring credits from his account to the host's. Devon's generous tip opens up for him one of *Rezu*'s private rooms. Before sliding open the thin rice paper doors, delicately decorated with cranes in flight above a low bamboo marsh, Todd and Devon respectfully remove their shoes. The tatami mats, they are told, are very old and almost impossible to replace since Hadrian has limited imports from the outside world. The devastation to Quadrant One caused by 6-13 radically diminished world trade, having created for Hadrian a barometer of fear that seems permanently stuck in the red zone, resulting in Hadrian's choice to become xenophobic. There will be no new tatami shipped to *Rezu* for quite some time.

Upon entering the room, Todd is impressed by its sparse but beautiful decor. Along one wall is a low stand with a flower vase and small statue. "This," Devon explains, "is what my moms calls the tea room." Smiling sweetly, he adds, "She says you are supposed to admire the beauty of the flower arrangement and art work." In this case, the art consists of a small statue of a crane taking flight, and a print of *Courtesan* by Hokusai. "It's supposed to put you in some kind of mood," he says slyly.

"Wow, that's beautiful," Todd responds, transfixed by the beauty of the courtesan.

Devon lies on his side, his head closest to where Todd is seated. When they first entered the room, Devon motioned for Todd to sit on the right side of the long, low dining table, but Todd judiciously chose to sit at the head where there was only room for one body. Lying sideways is Devon's attempt to get in close to his new partner.

Although the drinking age in Hadrian is twenty-one, Devon is able to schmooze the young waiter with a few circular motions of his thumb. The Rankin family often patronizes *Rezu* and is known for its exorbitant tips. Soon the two boys are drinking *biru* (Japanese for "beer" Devon translates for Todd) and warm *saki*. "Rice wine," Devon explains. "Very strong rice wine," he adds with a chuckle when Todd sputters out his first sip of the strong bitter alcohol. "Trust me," Devon winks. "Keep drinking. It's strong enough that it'll start tasting good soon enough." The two boys laugh, and Todd, taking Devon's advice, continues to sip and scrunch up his face in disgust. Soon their meal arrives. Devon, knowing the menu well, orders them a variety of sushi with tempura. Todd balks at the idea of eating raw fish, but he has no problem gobbling down the deep-fried and lightly battered vegetables and tiger shrimp. And even though he has never eaten tofu on its own like this, he is amazed by how good the white block covered lightly with dried fish flakes tastes when dipped in a combination of soya sauce and rice wine vinegar.

"By all that's gay and glorious," he declares, "but this is good food!"

Devon consumes the majority of the sushi, the most expensive portion of the meal. He is a little disappointed that Todd won't even try any of the raw fish placed delicately over the sweet rice. He ends up overstuffing himself because he had ordered enough for a whole murder of crows. Devon really wants to impress Todd and win him over as his boyfriend.

Attempting to use the chopsticks, having only learned that night, Todd fumbles to pick up another piece of tempura, the light batter coating an orange slice of something truly delicious. "Umm," Todd says as he barely manages to pop the item into his mouth. Talking with his mouth full, Todd spits out small bits of the food in the explosion of words. "What's this stuff called?"

"That's yam." Devon is enjoying the sight of Todd luxuriating over the food he is consuming. When Todd trickles some of the soya sauce rice wine mixture down his chin, Devon leans forward, and with his index finger, he wipes the stray dribble and ensures it (along with his finger) makes its way inside Todd's mouth. There is a moment of silence, in which Devon feels a flame and Todd feels awkward. "Nice stubble," Devon says admiringly. "Most guys I know can't even shave yet, let alone hope to grow stubble."

Embarrassed that he is not presentable, Todd self-consciously rubs his cheek. "Ah, Papa Mike forgot our razor at a friend's house." Devon chuckles. Lowering his eyes, feeling shame, Todd admits, "Papa Mike said he'd, ah, bring it home, but he forgot again. So, I, ah, couldn't shave this morning."

"That's okay." Lightly licking his lips, Devon giggles, "I've never kissed a guy with stubble before."

Todd slowly sets the chopsticks down. *I'm going to have to do this*, he figures. *Devon's used up a lot of credit here tonight.* He swallows hard, sips a little sake, and then closing his eyes, turns his head and waits for Devon's lips to touch his own. Todd had only meant for a quick little peck, but Devon's lips cover his, his teeth gripping Todd's lower lip. And then Devon's tongue slips inside Todd's mouth. Todd panics and pulls away. Devon is not worried. "Wow." He smiles. "That was nice." Todd blushes, unable to speak, muted by embarrassment and anxiety. Devon peers up at Todd. Noting the dark flush, he asks, "Am I the first boy you ever kissed?" Todd shakes his head. "Of course not," Devon reasons, "Frank, right?" Todd nods. "Of course, Frank. But you're not his type, so that's why the two of you never went anywhere."

"We…we're…we…are…friends," Todd stutters.

Devon runs a hand up Todd's leg. Todd's hand flutters against Devon's and lowers it to the floor. Devon pushes his side up and rests firmly on his elbow. "Are you still a virgin?" Devon knows the answer as Todd's face turns dark purple. "Wow, a virgin," Devon mutters in awe. He is now lying on his back, hands cupping his head. "Hey, man, that's cool." Lying back on his side, Devon once again faces Todd. "We all start this world off as virgins." Truly admiring Todd now, hoping he will be Todd's first, Devon asks, "Have you thought about when you want to do it?"

"Ah…" Todd can't look up. He has never been good talking about sex. His father died when he was only eight so Will Middleton had never had a chance to discuss awakening sexuality with his son. Papa Mike, unfortunately, turned aloof after Will Middleton passed on, lacking both desire and energy to raise Will's son properly. He did, at least, give Todd some good advice once, shortly after Todd had turned thirteen. "Papa Mike says I shouldn't…um…" Todd swallows uncomfortably, "do anything, until… well, just, until things feel right. He says I should w—" Certain this next line is going to make him sound foolish in Devon's eyes, he cuts himself off.

"Hey," Devon says kindly, "you don't have to be embarrassed. I'm not going to make you try and do anything tonight."

"Thanks," Todd sighs, relief heavy in his exhale.

"So, what else did Papa Mike say?"

"He...um...thinks I should...um, well...maybe wait until I get married. That's what he and my dad did."

"Really?" Devon is amazed. Although Hadrian has a very strong notion of family—only registered couples, committed to monogamy, confirmed in marriage a minimum of ten years, can apply for a third child—there are no religious laws dictating a couple wait until marriage before having sex. "Why?" he asks, truly dismayed. "I mean, sorry," he says in response to Todd's look of alarm. "It's just, that's a little unconventional. Most people don't worry about that sort of thing. I mean, if it feels right, why not share what you've got with the other person?"

"I guess that's what Papa Mike means." Todd is so embarrassed now that he is studying his knees, wishing the rest of him could be ducked under the table, too. "He just thinks I need to wait until it feels right."

"Yeah," Devon says. "That makes perfect sense." Since that expression gives him hope, Devon reaches his hand around Todd's head, pulling him down onto the tatami mat flooring for another kiss. Not wanting to scare Todd off, though, he just lies there with him, kissing until Todd pulls free and asks Devon to take him home. "Sure," he says.

Devon wraps his arm around Todd's waist and they exit their private room. Meeting up with their waiter near the front entrance, Devon thumbs the man's pad, tapping in a hefty tip of extra credits. As they leave *Rezu*, Devon leads Todd back to his mother's bubble. Playing the gentleman, Devon moves to open Todd's door for him. Before opening the door, though, Devon summons up his courage, "I'd like to see you again. Can we go out again tomorrow?"

Devon's heart drops as Todd shakes his head. "I, ah..." Todd swallows. "Tomorrow I promised Papa Mike I'd help him fix the bubble. I...I won't be able to...both day and night...busy."

Devon wraps his arms joyfully around Todd, hugging him close. "How about Sunday afternoon? Are you helping Papa Mike then, too?"

Todd gives in and puts his arms around Devon. "No."

"We could go to The Cattle Ranch Restaurant that opened up last month."

"The Cattle Ranch Restaurant?" Todd turns pale, gasping. "I heard a beef burger alone costs fifty credits!" A credit in Hadrian is akin to what the old country of Canada used to consider a dollar bill. Anything less than a credit is called a chit; one hundred chits equals one credit.

Devon laughs, finding Todd's level of nativity appealing. "Not quite that bad. A beef burger is only thirty credits."

Only? Todd shakes his head. Thirty credits are enough to buy groceries for a week: soya beans, soya milk, soya bread, soya cheese, a few greens, and one serving each of fish or chicken (a leg or a thigh—not the breast). The concept of tossing that many credits away for one little slab of meat is beyond comprehension for someone barely scraping by like Todd and his Papa Mike. *Rich people*, he muses cynically.

"Yeah," Devon continues, oblivious to Todd's musing. "It is, if you ask for all the extras like a bun, lettuce, tomato, onions, sauce that sort of thing. A beef burger can easily run up to fifty credits if you're a fussy eater." Grinning, he adds, "Like me."

"No, Devon," Todd states firmly.

Although disappointed since a meal at the burger establishment always leaves one's partner feeling obliged to put out, Devon can tell Todd is serious. "Okay," he reconsiders. "How about the zoo? That won't cost too many credits. A few credits each to get in, a little more on top for junk munch, which…" he adds in his own stern manner, "we can't live without." Todd chuckles; everyone loves junk munch and it is relatively cheap. Papa Mike brings some home every second or third week, so it can't be that expensive. Smiling sincerely, sensing Todd's leaning, Devon asks, "You can afford that, can't you?"

Todd's mood darkens as he shakes his head. "I…" *How do I tell someone this?* "I…don't have a thumbprint—or a credit account." Todd lowers his head in shame.

Devon blinks. "Why? Won't your Papa give you one?" An individual without a thumbprint implant has no purchasing power, which is why nearly everyone in Hadrian over the age of twelve has a thumbprint.

"We just don't have the credits—" Todd trails off, feeling deeply his shame.

"Hey," Devon says soothingly, "let me pay for the zoo. Come on," he cajoles Todd. "It's nothing expensive like The Cattle Ranch Restaurant or *Rezu*. Again, it's me asking for the date: my date, my credits. What do you say?"

The zoo. Todd begins to smile against his will. Todd hasn't been to the zoo since before his father died.

Devon, noting the slight transition, tickles Todd into a more playful mood. "Come on," he encourages. "It'll be fun."

Todd nods his head slightly. "It does sounds like fun!"

"Are we on then?" Devon asks as he leans in for a kiss. When he finally releases Todd's lips, Devon waits for him to say yes. "It's a date, then." After planting another kiss on Todd, Devon laughs gaily as his new beau blushes. "Hadrian's lover, you are so cute," he declares.

"Cute?" Todd sputters.

"Not cute like one of Frank's boys' cute." Shaking his head slightly and laughing, Devon adds, "What did you call them?"

Both boys answer, "Tinsel tarts."

After a further chuckle, Devon says, "It's just refreshing to be with some-one for whom all this is new." He kisses Todd again and then asks, a little tentatively but with hope, "Can we tell everyone at school it's official; that we're a unit?"

Todd shrugs, "I…I guess so. Just…just…" Trying not to sound too pathetic, Todd says, "Just don't push for—you know."

"I won't," Devon promises and then hoots out his joy. "One more kiss, one more kiss—just one kiss and then I'll take you home. I promise."

Todd complies.

* * * * *

Before getting out of the bubble, Todd turns to face Devon. Thinking Todd is going to initiate a kiss, Devon leans forward. Not quite knowing what to do, Todd kisses his cheek. Devon giggles and turns Todd's head to face him, kissing him fully on the lips. "We've come this far," he smiles. "I won't push forward, but I'm definitely not going backwards," he says coyly. "Did you want to say something?" he asks to help relieve Todd's tension, which, oddly enough, Devon finds very erotic.

"I…ah…forgot," Todd mutters.

Devon laughs. "Well, if you remember, voc me. My I.D.'s devran—" he pauses, taking a moment to kiss Todd before continuing, "—hgvoc."

Too embarrassed, Todd is unwilling to reveal to Devon he doesn't even have a vocal contact lens. The latest in high tech communication is too expensive for Papa Mike. If Todd were to get a part-time job, he could probably buy one, but Papa Mike has asked him to concentrate on school and b-ball. "A b-ball scholarship is the only way you are going to get into uni, Todd," Papa Mike had said, shaking his head sadly. "We just don't have the credits." No thumbprint means no access to spending money; no vocal contact lens means limited access to the wave, especially since Papa Mike won't even pay to fix their wall screen. "It saves credits," he reasoned. "This way we don't have to pay government rates for the wave link."

"But we could get the reduced rate, Papa Mike," Todd had pleaded. But Mike Fulton is too proud to apply for services made available to low income families, so they don't even get the wave coming through their wall screen anymore. *Thank Hadrian for school!* All educational institutions provide free access to the wave, but only through school slates, and the wave only works when at school. So Todd has to live with old school technology and the generosity of his friends. This past New Year's Eve, Frank and Crystal had given him an old cell phone with unlimited calling (a three-year contract obtained illicitly through an outsider phone company!) in celebration of Hadrian's fiftieth birthday.

"Thanks," Todd says, smiling sheepishly for Devon. Tapping his temple, Todd pretends to have memorized Devon's voc I.D., suggesting it is something he can actually use. Then, after "one last kiss," Devon opens the bubble door. Todd jumps out, and as quick as a rabbit chased by coyotes, he runs inside his house.

* * * * *

Salve!

All but Extinct
HNN—Melissa Eagleton Reporting

Looking for a way to spend your Sunday afternoon? Why not take in Hadrian's Zoo? Hadrian boasts the last remaining zoo planet-wide. Pre 6-13, it was a hot spot for tourists around the world. With fewer visitors due to closed borders, Hadrian's Zoo is suffering from financial distress. Rest assured, Hadrian's National Government will not allow this worldwide treasure to lapse into disrepair, or risk the deaths of any of its animal occupants, many of which are the only living relics of their species. Lucy the elephant, for example, is the last of her kind. Thanks to the preservation of sperm and eggs dating back to the mid-twenty-first century, our zoologists have been able to impregnate Lucy, as they had her mother and her grandmother before. The zoo has always been one of Hadrian's most affordable locations, costing a mere three credits for adults, two credits for students and senior citizens, while children under twelve get in for free. If numbers do not improve, though, zoo officials say they may have to increase admission credits to as much as fifteen credits for adult admission, ten credits for students and seniors, and they are even considering a charge of five credits for children between the ages of two and twelve. These high prices, zoo officials claim, may be necessary for them to maintain the various hothouses they have for growing exotic foods as feed. Then there is the difficult and very expensive chore of regulating the temperatures of their animals' living quarters. Pearl, for example, being from the now extinct species of polar bear, requires a much colder environment than Lucy, the elephant. Remember, Hadrian is preserving our planet's vast array of animal species in the world's last remaining zoo. Your patronage will help ensure the future of our planet's wildlife. One day, after the hordes of heterosexual barbarians finally die off, the future citizens of Hadrian will reclaim the planet. We will be the earth's surrogate parents to its future wildlife population. So, don't delay; spend your Sunday afternoon at Hadrian's zoo!

Vale!

Hadrian's Zoo

Time spent at the zoo is such an incredible experience that Todd begins to think he might actually come to like Devon that way, *maybe*. Their walk through the various animal exhibits is both awe inspiring and a sobering one; both boys remain silent, staring at what is said to be the last of its species. Such signs are posted everywhere. "Have we seen an exhibit without one?" Todd asks solemnly.

"I don't remember one," Devon replies. Not wanting their date to be so gloomy, Devon decides to liven things up. "I'm hungry," he chimes.

"You're always hungry," Todd reminds him.

"I'm a growing boy, with a hollow leg, as my moms like to say." They laugh as Devon leads them to the closest junk munch stand.

Devon insists Todd let him buy them soya dogs, causing Todd to protest. "You're spending too much on me, Devon. I mean—you know I don't have credits or a thumbprint." It never seems to matter to Todd that he's told Devon this fifty times already. Something inside keeps urging him to repeat himself. Perhaps Todd is hoping Devon will finally understand why he feels so uncomfortable. "All our credits go to paying off Papa Mike's debts." Actually they mostly go to buying whiskey, hallucinogens, contraband cigarettes, and taking out various young men, but Todd doesn't wish to share this information with Devon. "He can't spare a single chit, let alone get me a thumbprint."

"Come on, Todd," Devon says reassuringly. "None of that matters to me. I don't care if you don't have any credits. But," trying not to sound judgmental, "why don't you get a job? Your employer would have to arrange for the thumbprint, and then it would be free. Once you got that, you could set up your account with your first download."

"Papa Mike wants me to concentrate on school and b-ball. They're my only hope for uni." Sighing, he adds, "And I want to go to uni. I want to be a bioengineer like my father." Sensing he is not getting through to Devon (*why can't rich people understand?*), Todd gets straight to the point. "The fact is, Devon, it makes me feel awkward watching you throw away all those credits."

Devon laughs. "I'm having fun. Besides, I like spending credits on you."

Todd sighs. "It just doesn't feel right. It's like…" He pauses to consider his words carefully. "It feels like I'm using you."

I wish you would, Devon thinks in response, but he merely says, "Well, you're not. I want to spend credits on you. I want to do things for you." Devon is sincere. "I want to do stuff with you. I don't care if it costs a few credits. Why not? I've got it."

Frustrated, Todd sighs deeper. "It's just, well, maybe we could do something less expensive. I mean, something that doesn't require credits."

Devon shakes his head, flabbergasted, unable to conceive of anything that wouldn't cost a fortune in credits to have a good time. "Like what?"

"I don't know. Go for a walk in the park or—I like working out. Maybe we could get together and train for b-ball."

"The school year's almost over," Devon replies, a little bemused. "That makes no sense."

"You know you're pretty good," Todd encourages him.

"Right," Devon mutters. "That's why they kept me on juniors this year."

"No, really," Todd says. "With a little training, I bet you could make first string on seniors next fall. I mean, why not? We got all summer."

Devon smiles, *All summer—he's thinking long-term dating now!* "Are you serious?" Devon is beaming. Hooking up with Todd Middleton is proving to be the highlight of his year! "I would absolutely love that!" He hugs his new boyfriend, smothering him in kisses. Embarrassed, Todd pushes Devon off. "Hey, come on," Devon says, dismayed. "What's wrong?"

"We're…" Todd's eyes shift side-to-side. "There's people…" His head tilts to the right, indicating two women walking arm-in-arm toward the aviary.

"I keep forgetting how private you are." Although slightly annoyed, Devon is still thrilled at Todd's offer to help him train for b-ball. "No more kissing in public, I promise."

"Thanks," Todd replies shyly.

"Time for dessert," Devon announces merrily.

Todd shakes his head. "We just agreed not to use up any more credit."

"No," Devon counters. "We just agreed that some of our dates could be credit free, like training." Willing to compromise, he suggests, "How about this? When you pick the date, we'll do it your way. When I pick the date, I get to spend as many credits as I please. Come on," he says encouragingly. "Let's shake." He offers his hand. "I'd say, kiss on it, but…" he pauses, looking upward and tilting his head, "we're in public." Todd nods in agreement and they shake. For the rest of the afternoon, Devon fills Todd up with every form of sweet treat and junk munch he can convince his new boyfriend to eat, including a red candy apple and a caramel one!

* * * * *

Salve!

Hot Summer Nights
HNN—Melissa Eagleton Reporting

It's another hot Hadrian summer day! Can you believe this used to be one of the colder regions in the old country of Canada? Believe it or not, Hudson Bay once had an ice-free period of only four months, dating back, of course, to the late seventeenth century! One would have expected, though, with the radical decrease in salinity in Hudson Bay's waters, that there would have been a decrease in the ice-free time on the ocean-sized inland lake. Fresh water freezes much faster than salt water. Unfortunately for much of old Canada's northern wildlife, such is not the case with Hudson Bay. The constant rise in global temperatures has made our summers hot and our winters warm, far too mild for the bay to freeze over for any substantial length of time. During the mid-twentieth century, the mean temperature for Hadrian this time was year was 10° C. Today we enjoy a mid-June mean of 30° C. Also, winter often used to arrive in late August, early September. Now, old man winter (who has aged to the brink of death) seldom worries us until mid-to late December. Yes, global warming has changed our planet's ecosystem considerably. Hadrian, which was once mostly boreal forest, is now one of the most fertile of grasslands regions around the globe. It is our mild winters and hot sultry summer nights that made Hadrian one of the world's top tourist spots prior to 6-13! The loss of the foreign tourism industry has been a blow financially, but I am sure I speak for everyone in Hadrian that it is no loss, but rather a relief, no longer to have to cater to those hypocritical heterosexual barbarians.

Vale!

Summer Craze

It is a crazy and frustrating summer for Devon. The closer he feels he is getting to Todd, the further Todd seems to be pulling away from him. One night, their last weekend before school starts up, as they are sitting on the bed in Devon's room, watching one of Devon's voc vids through the wall screen, Devon begins to come on to Todd. This time, he is pushing for more than just a few kisses. He wants them to undress so they can see each other's bodies. "We don't have to do anything serious," he reasons, "just touch each other." Todd's heart starts to pound inside his chest. He can barely breathe, let alone try to answer. Devon takes his silence for consent and he begins to reach his hand inside Todd's pants.

Todd leaps off the bed like someone had just lit him on fire. "Stop! Stop it!" he shrieks.

"What's going on in there?" Alisha Rankin calls from the living room.

"Nothing! We're okay, Mom," Devon responds. Standing up, he turns on Todd. "What's wrong with you?" he whispers. "Do you want my moms coming in here?" Annoyed, he gestures for Todd to sit back down on the bed.

Todd refuses, squeezing his eyes tight. "Just, please, don't touch me there. I'm not ready yet."

"Why not?" Devon is perplexed. "It will feel good if you let me." Shaking his head in wonder, he adds, "I could make you cum." When he gets no response but a further lowering of Todd's head, Devon demands, "Look at me, Todd."

"I…" Todd can't seem to open his eyes.

"Okay," Devon sighs. "I won't touch you. But baby…" He kisses Todd lightly. "I'm aching here. I want to feel you touch me." Devon takes Todd's hand in his and, though Todd shakes he allows Devon to manipulate him, as if he were a puppet. Soon Todd's hand, held in place by Devon's. is gripping Devon's penis through the rough folds of his jeans. Devon groans and kisses Todd. Squeezing Todd's hand, Devon gasps, "Oh, baby, put your hand inside my pants." Although Todd struggles some, Devon. having unzipped his jeans, moves Todd's hand up through to his cotton briefs. Slipping Todd's hand through the front opening, he helps Todd grasp his penis. Devon groans in ecstasy.

Unable to cope, Todd pulls his hand free. "I can't do this," he pleads.

"For Hadrian's sake, Todd." Devon is angry. "I have been waiting all summer for this." Exasperated, he has to slow down his breathing to avoid yelling. "I can't take this anymore. I want you and I know you want me."

"No!" Todd shrieks. "No, I don't." Todd is terrified. Feeling Devon like that has repulsed him. He notices the hurt look in Devon's eyes. "I...I... I'm just not ready. I don't want sex right now. I just want to date...to hang out—not sex—not yet."

"When?" Devon is becoming quite demanding.

Todd is in tears. "I don't know."

"No." Devon shakes his head angrily while zipping up his pants. "No, you don't, do you?"

"I'm sorry, Devon," Todd pleads. "I just. I can't."

"There is no can't about it!" Devon spits. "You won't!"

"It's not like that," Todd tries explaining.

Devon turns his back. "Get out." Todd is stunned. He didn't expect this. Even with his back turned, Todd can feel the anger glaring out Devon's eyes. "I said get out!" Turning and pointing toward the door, Devon yells, "I'm through with you." Stunned, Todd turns, makes his way out of Devon's room. Blindly he makes his way to the back door and heads home. He has to walk the five miles since Devon is so angry he doesn't offer Todd a ride.

* * * * *

Salve!

Back to School
HNN—Melissa Eagleton Reporting

Well, it's that time of year again, children, teenagers, and parents! School has started! As of the wee hours, with the sun still rising early in the sky, Hadrian's youth were seen walking back toward school. It is always an exciting time of the year when friends who lost touch over the summer months are able to reunite inside the halls of academia! There is no doubt in my mind that Hadrian's education system is by far the finest in the world. Our children come first in Hadrian, and preparing them to meet the challenges they will face upon commencement in the adult world is our teachers' top priority. At Antinous' own Pride High, for example, students study courses in our planet's ecological history, the impact of climate change, and the ways we in Hadrian are working toward a positive reversal, or at the very least, a partial resurrection, such as we have obtained in Hadrian, of the earth's natural resources. Some students look forward to classes in population control while others will approach life from a much lighter perspective. Pride High is renowned for its glorious fashion and cosmetics programs. Whatever your son or daughter chooses to take in preparation for his or her future career, you can be certain that schools like Pride High will be working toward the betterment of your child's education! As Principal Gavin is often heard to say, "Pride High! Where all our children walk with heads held high!"

Vale!

Back to School

Todd is not looking forward to going back to school. Breaking up with Devon was so sudden and unexpected that Todd is left profoundly confused and isolated. Devon refuses to answer any of his wave messages, and Papa Mike never seems to be around these days, leaving Todd with no one to talk to. Compounding the matter is that Frank and Crystal are miffed at him. He never called either of them over summer vacation, being too busy dating, and now when he calls Frank, all he gets is "Can't talk, Todd; I'm busy." Whenever he tries calling Crystal, all he gets is a generic recording telling him "Crystal Albright is currently unavailable." *She must have turned off her phone*, Todd reasons. Now it's Sunday night, and tomorrow is the first day of school. Todd knows his classes. His first class is math with Ms. Sterne (which causes him to grimace), followed by Hadrian history with Mr. Reiner (which brings on a smile). Frank and Crystal are taking those classes, too. Last spring during fall registration (and pre-Devon), the three friends had tried to get into as many of the same classes as possible, but they weren't so successful with the afternoon. After lunch, Todd has physical education while Crystal is studying world religion and Frank is taking fashion studies. For their last class of the day, Todd is enrolled in agricultural sciences, Frank in cosmetology, and Crystal has a spare. *At least I'll be with my friends in the morning, or will I?* Todd wonders. Worried, Todd realizes he should have made an effort to spend time with his friends over the summer, but Devon had sucked up all of his time.

His break-up with Devon hits Todd hard. He really thought they were forming a strong friendship, granted a friendship in which Todd felt obliged to kiss, but they were sharing some really deep thoughts. They talked about the concept of a god or gods, and why some of Hadrian's citizens still believed in these deities regardless of the obvious hate literature toward homosexuals in many of their holy texts. They also argued over whether Hadrian citizens had subconsciously made gods of Hadrian and Antinous, and both expressed confusion over why some citizens slipped outside the wall, simply to vanish. Why anyone would want to live in the outside world was unfathomable. And they always shared a good laugh over the boys' and girls' washrooms remaining segregated. "That is so *strai*," Devon would always say. "I know; how stupid," Todd would respond, and then they both would utter, "Like, that makes any sense!" That this expression was simultaneous every time the boys had this conversation always made them laugh. But, most of all, they had shared a love of b-ball. Todd had really brought Devon a long way with the game. Without doubt, Devon is now first string material. *B-ball's going to be toughest of all*, Todd realizes. *But I'll make it work, somehow. It's good for the team*, he reckons, *and I will recommend Devon to Coach Miller.* As always, when it comes to b-ball, Todd lines up the team and its various positions in his mind. *Frank is center*, he decides. *He's tall, fast, and is almost unbeatable with his jump ball. Crystal is point guard, I'm shooting guard, Millicent will take small forward, and Devon will be perfect as power forward.* The thought *Devon will be perfect* cloaks Todd like a dark cloud shadowing over the moon. Todd is so confused about his feelings for Devon; at times, he simply can't contain his emotions.

Everything with Devon happened so fast and ended just as quickly. Todd still hasn't gotten over the staggering blow. What Todd fails to understand is that Devon, too, is smarting. While Todd was building a friendship, Devon was falling in love. When Devon had asked Todd out, he wasn't looking for a friend, he was looking for a lover; and although he tried hard to understand that Todd needed to go slow, when he saw in Todd's eyes that they would never make love, he lashed out, angrily tossing Todd aside. Devon is now a walking wound, and thoughts of Todd, the very sight of him, are like salt water for him.

Day one of school is brutal. Todd and Devon are in the first three classes together. Devon inevitably arrives early and is already sitting in Ms. Sterne's math class when Todd walks in. As soon as he sees Todd, Devon starts singing an old tune dating back to the late twentieth century: "Day Tripper" by some group called the Bugs or the Beetles. But Devon knows the group, he knows the song; his mothers are music historians. Actually, both women are librarians. Music history is their passion, and though they call themselves music historians, no one in Hadrian gets paid for acquiring such knowledge. At any rate, Devon is able to take full advantage of their quirk and taunt Todd with it. At first, Todd has no idea what Devon is saying with that song, but eventually, the words take on meaning. Devon is calling Todd a tease through these antiquated lyrics. Someone who leads a man on, only to refuse to follow through on promises made. *But I never made any promises,* Todd insists. *Or did I?* Every kiss, he realizes now, was a subtle intonation. With that sudden self-awareness, Todd begins the process of self-recrimination. Once the seed of self-recrimination has been planted, all it needs is a good dose of self-loathing to keep it well watered.

By the end of school's first week, Devon has a new boyfriend, Roger Hunter, Frank's little brother. Roger, now in grade nine, is thrilled to be Devon's new beau since it means he is dating one of the big boys. When Todd sees them walking arm-in-arm or kissing goodbye in the hallway, he feels a pang of hurt. He knows Devon brings Roger to their classroom door to kiss him goodbye, to rub into Todd's face that it took him no time at all to find a replacement.

Finally, Frank caves and asks Todd to hang out again. He has been watching his friend from a distance and can see how dejected Todd has become. Although jealous that Todd spent his summer dating Devon and not him, Frank can't bear to witness Todd always walking with his shoulders down, never a smile on his face, eating alone—Hadrian only knows where—*no,* Franks reminds himself, *I know where he is.* When Todd feels the need to hide, there is only one place in the school he can go—behind the back stairwell leading up to the girls' locker room. Crystal designated this "the safe space" when she discovered the security camera broken last year. The three gay caballeros refuse to share this safely guarded secret with anyone else.

Frank decides it's time to go looking for Todd. He has started skipping out of class, something hitherto unheard of. Todd's Papa Mike stresses the importance of good grades and b-ball since he cannot afford to pay for Todd's higher education. Frank knows Todd wouldn't skip class unless something was really wrong in his life. Todd may have hurt him, but Todd is still his best friend and he will always love him. "Hey, buddy," he calls out before showing himself. "You hiding back there?"

"Frank?" Todd's heart rises slightly at the sound of his friend's voice. "You talking to me again?"

"Yeah," Frank sighs as he swings in underneath the stairs to join Todd. "I guess it's time to get over my hissy fit."

"I'm sorry I ditched you this summer." Todd is sincere. He realizes now how much he misses his friends. Two weeks alone can be brutal when you are used to constant attachments with others—especially when home life is even emptier than the school halls. "I don't know what happened, really. It was like the summer with Devon turned into a whirlwind. He picked me up, spun me around like a twig, and then shot me out at the end of it."

"I guess you really liked Devon, eh?" Frank asks, trying hard to hide his disappointment.

"I thought we were..." Todd is truly befuddled. "I don't know—connecting on some level." Looking over to Frank, slightly misty-eyed, he adds, "Like you and me used to be."

"Yeah," Frank sighs. "I know." Considering his behavior last June, Frank admits, "It's kind of my fault, too. I did stand you up that one Friday."

"Yeah," Todd agrees, "the day Devon asked me out."

Nodding, Frank says, "I was busy dating Davie, and you were looking for a surrogate friend." After musing for a moment, he says, "And I'll bet any amount of credit that Devon was just looking for a boyfriend. He's certainly found one in Roger." Wincing, knowing he just touched on a sore topic, Frank adds, "Sorry, Todd."

"That's all right." Although they sting, Todd realizes Frank's words were not meant to hurt. "He had to move on. I guess I ought to as well. It's just hard when—"

"When you're all alone?"

"Yeah," Todd says, looking over to his friend. "I had no idea how important you and Crystal were to me until you two decided I was no longer worth the effort."

"Well, I got over it." Slapping Todd's thigh as reassurance, Frank adds, "I'm sure Crystal will too."

Todd's sigh of relief is audible. "Thanks for taking me back."

"We're friends, the best of friends, man," Frank confirms. "And that is never going to change. Come on," he invites, slapping Todd playfully. "Let's go find Crystal. It's time to get the three gay caballeros back together again!"

* * * * *

Salve!

A Veritable Vortex in Time
HNN—Melissa Eagleton Reporting

It is an undeniable truth that autumn in Hadrian is one of the loveliest times of the year. By mid-September, the leaves will begin their glorious changing of color. By October, they will dance in the air on their branches in a beautifully golden array. Such beauty will flicker on the limbs of the various trees in our northern boreal forest for a good month, so now is the time to take advantage of this incredible beauty. And where better to enjoy such sights than at The Cattle Ranch, stretching along the northern bank of the Churchill River? The five hundred acres owned by Jake Matonabee and Jeremy Stoker also extend north in a blended mixture of pastureland and boreal forest. Needless to say, the trail rides across their land offer some of Hadrian's most beautiful views, especially now that fall is approaching.

As well as producing beef and mutton for our consumption, leather for coats and boots, and wool for our winter clothing, The Cattle Ranch is renowned for its horseback riding. It offers a variety of vacation packages as well as day rides. A stay at The Cattle Ranch is all inclusive: your room, three meals a day, and all the horseback riding you can handle—they offer three trail rides a day! One of the best parts of visiting The Cattle Ranch is that you are introduced to your horse the morning after your arrival. You will ride this horse your entire stay at The Cattle Ranch, and the proprietors encourage you to bond with your horse by helping with its grooming. They will teach you how to brush your horse down before and after your day's ride. You can job shadow the wrangler if you want, and depending on how long your stay is and how much upper body strength you possess, you may even be taught how to saddle the horse yourself. Don't worry, though; no one has to clean up horse manure. The hired hands take care of that job.

Seriously, though, the best part about The Cattle Ranch is its historical value. It has chosen to operate (as do all farming institutions, be they family or corporate) as did those ranches of old, modeling their style on the mid to late nineteenth century. Horse, mule, oxen, and human power are the rule. It makes sense when you think about it. No large trucks or tractors are allowed in Hadrian due to the excessive use of fossil fuel required to operate such machinery. With a complete ban on all fossil fuels in Hadrian, one is restricted to operating all devices on electric, hydro, wind, or geothermal energy. According to Jake Matonabee, the decision to work as of old came about forty-eight years ago when the farming community met and determined that historical farming was the best possible approach. "It is," as Matonabee says, "a positive environmentally sound approach to working the land and raising cattle. With livestock comes animal waste, which we then recycle into fertilizer." When asked about using biomass energy to run larger equipment, Matonabee was adamant in his rejection. "It still releases carbon dioxide into the atmosphere." Even though the carbon dioxide released by biomass balances out with the carbon dioxide absorbed in its growth, The Cattle Ranch and Farmers Association rejected its use since it removed from them all possibility of tax rebates. Hadrian's government is very generous when it comes to rebates given to any individual or company, with proven methods of reclamation and meeting high environmental standards. More importantly, according to Matonabee, ancient methods of farming and ranching require the community to work collectively during planting, crop growth (weeding and insect control), the birthing of and rounding up of livestock, and, most especially, harvest. As we well know, the use of fossil fuels, all chemical pesticides, and herbicides are illegal in Hadrian, which has led to the choice of a much simpler lifestyle in rural areas. As a result, when one visits The Cattle Ranch, one walks through a veritable vortex in time, stepping out of the twenty-second century into the year 1878.

Vale!

Second Anniversary

Although back on the Seroxat, Dean still suffers from low days, remaining uncomfortable in his skin. Too much of his time is spent in morbid contemplation. Struggling to find value and worth in his life, Dean tries to focus his mind on days that were good—all those times when he truly did feel in love with Geoffrey and believed he wanted to be with him. Today, his thoughts are centered on the first time he lay down with Geoffrey. This was a time of bonding, an awakening and strengthening of their love. Dean, desperately needing to feel this way again, indulges in the memory of their second anniversary. Knowing, on this day, Seroxat isn't enough, Dean takes two milligrams of Zolam, allowing its altering powers to stupefy him. His mind, feeling free now, contemplates his and Geoffrey's second anniversary.

* * * * *

Twenty years ago, as it is today, The Cattle Ranch was nestled in the rolling hills and forests of Quadrant Three. As well as pasturing their livestock (horses, cattle), Jake Matonabee and Jeremy Stoker, owners and proprietors, cut numerous riding trails across their land for paid ranch guests. Yet, not all of this land was reserved for cattle and horseback riding. Jeremy's little sister, Sissy Hildebrand, ran the sheep herd in the northern, more remote section. Sissy, being straight, had chosen a life of isolation to avoid being found out. Jeremy, then and now, knows well his sister's sexual preference, and not only does he accept her, but he has worked hard over the years to help her keep her secret effectively concealed. Even so, he often encourages her to find a woman with whom she can live—someone to register with for security reasons—but she is always ardently opposed.

Her one concession is to hire only women for hands. Taking her brother's advice, she has never hired any men. "Avoid temptation, Sissy," Jeremy always cautions her. "That way no one can expose and expel you." Today, Sissy is forty-six. When Dean and Geoffrey visited the ranch, she was but twenty-six years old. Even then, she was far too old for reeducation camp. Her fate would be worse than death if her secret were known.

Always irate at the implication behind Jeremy's repetitive lecture, Sissy's retort is like a broken record: "I don't think of sex every time I look at a man. It doesn't work that way, you know!"

"I know, Sissy," Jeremy always replies in consolation. "I didn't mean that—it's just, well, even the wrong glance a man's way can lead to suspicion." Twenty years ago, the conversation was even more perverse. "Even Jake," Jeremy one day sprang on her, "has questioned your sexuality more than once."

"What did you say?" Terror welled in Sissy's breast.

"I told him he was being stupid—that you just don't have much opportunity to meet women. So he asked if that's why you only hired women—in hopes of meeting someone and I said yes."

After a long sigh of relief, Sissy said, "Thank you."

These conversations between Sissy and Jeremy about her sexual orientation always end with Sissy bursting into ire. "I hate having to feel this way. It's not fair!"

"It is what it is, Sissy."

"That doesn't make it right," she always grumbles.

"I know."

"Nor is it any answer."

"I know that, too, Sissy, but," he inevitably adds with a sigh, "it's all I've got to offer."

Such conversations only occur when they meet in person—and when they are alone. Fortunately, Jake stopped expressing his concern fifteen years ago. That was only after Sissy actually hired a man as a sheepherder and Jeremy was no longer required to travel north all the time to help her.

* * * * *

For their second anniversary, Geoffrey brought Dean to The Cattle Ranch. After having seen a picture of the original Marlboro Man in the Antinous

City Center Museum and being impressed by its resemblance to his partner, Geoffrey searched the wave for information on The Cattle Ranch. It was just as he had hoped it would be—Geoffrey was pleased to discover it offered vacation packages. For two thousand five hundred credits per person, the all-inclusive package included three square meals a day, a horse to ride and care for every day during the five night, four day stay (with as many as three trail rides a day), walking trails, camping options, even job shadowing for those who were interested in learning the everyday workings of an historical ranch.

At twenty, Dean was tall, lean, muscular, and coltish. He had been broken, though, roughly at the hands of his guardian at the Northeast Reeducation Camp. Only Geoffrey's supportive, gentle ways kept him from committing suicide. Although having been married for two years, the two men had yet to consummate their registration. Geoffrey had won Dean's respect and love, the two men having formed a strong friendship, yet Dean still shied away from sexual contact. Holding hands, wrapping arms about each other's waists, hugging, and even occasional experimentation with kissing occurred. But thus far, kissing, if held onto too long by Geoffrey, had only ever ended with Dean pulling away. Bringing Dean to The Cattle Ranch for their second year Registration Celebration was not an attempt on Geoffrey's part to seduce Dean. He had come to accept, long ago, that winning Dean would take time—even that it might never happen. Mike Fulton and he often confided in one another about their frustrations, both having partnered with a straight, and many times, it seemed as if neither would ever win the sexual love of his partner. Mike would succumb to despair more often than Geoffrey, and the two men spent many an evening or Sunday afternoon venting out their frustrations. They had even considered partnering with each other on the side, but that idea never did come to fruition since, for both Geoffrey and Mike, it was as much about bonding with the man one loves as it was about sexual fulfillment. "True sexual fulfillment," Geoffrey reasoned one night during these conversations with Mike, "comes from making love with the man you love. It's not just about ejaculating and feeling good physically. It's about feeling good with and for someone you love."

"But what if Will never comes around?" Mike was despondent. Then, after looking hard at Geoffrey, he expressed concern for his friend. "What if Dean won't?"

"I don't know," was Geoffrey's reply. "This is brutally hard. I masturbate a lot. I wish—I hope—I just don't know." Then he looked Mike's way. "The fact is, we both knew what we were marrying ourselves into. Will was open and frank with you. Dean, I met at reeducation. I know he only pretended to be cured," after snorting, "with my help. I know for a fact he only took my last name to avoid—"

"Avoid what?"

"Nothing."

Mike let the question drop. Once Geoffrey decided to clam up there was no hope of getting any more out of him. He just waited patiently for the man to continue.

"Although I'd like to think he married me out of love," Geoffrey added despairingly, "our marriage was just an opportunity to him to escape reeducation."

"Then why did you marry him?" Mike asked gravely.

"The same reason you married Will. I fell in love. He's my other half. All I can do is hope one day he'll be ready to share himself with me."

So, twenty years ago, when Dean came into their cabin room and sat down on the bed next to where he lay, Geoffrey was taken completely by surprise to hear Dean say he thought he was ready. It was late, well past the midnight hour. Geoffrey had left Dean sitting by the mock fire (a geothermal heater designed to look like a small campfire) with Jeremy Stoker telling stories about horses, cattle ranching, and singing old country songs for their amusement.

Sitting up, still half-asleep, at first Geoffrey thought he might be dreaming. "Really?" He asked bewildered. "Are you sure?"

"Yes." Although his reply was in the affirmative, Dean was shaking, his voice so low Geoffrey could barely hear him. Not looking at Geoffrey but sitting hunchbacked on the edge of the bed, holding his hands atop his legs, rubbing the palms together nervously, Dean was avoiding eye contact.

After pulling himself closer to Dean, Geoffrey gently held his chin in his hand, turning Dean to face him. Dean's eyes were closed. Geoffrey noticed the tears. "We don't have to if you don't want to, my love," he said soothingly. His body was aching, desire for Dean overwhelming him.

Dean nodded his head, "I…" He shook his head, "I—do…" He nodded once more. "…want to. We…" He opened his eyes, looking directly into Geoffrey's, seeing in them an honest expression of love. Before him sat a man who would do anything for him. As he burst into tears, Dean blurted out, "I love you, Geoffrey, but I'm afraid."

Cupping Dean's face in his hands, Geoffrey reassured him, "I love you too, and I would never do anything to hurt you."

"Then…" Dean swallowed. Turning his face, he kissed the palm of Geoffrey's hand, "make love to me."

As the two men kissed, Geoffrey discovered everything he believed about intimacy to be real and true.

* * * * *

Less than an hour before Dean gave himself over to Geoffrey for the first time, he had been opening his soul to Jeremy Stoker. Jeremy was the kind of man who seemed to invite confidence. His quiet, self-assured ways suggested understanding—and a willingness to accept. Someone willing simply to listen and nod can have a powerful influence. Without even realizing it, Dean had told this man about what had happened to him in high school; what it had been like to be straight and live in a pretend gay relationship.

Having shook his head in wonderment, Jeremy mused, "Two years— and you two ain't never—"

Dean lowered his head and shook it. "He won't ever make me—he promised." Taking a moment to breathe in and out with short staccato, he added, "He's a man of his word."

"Does he—" Jeremy paused, wondering how to put this. "Does he get it somewhere else?"

"No—sometimes I wish he would, but—"

"But yer glad he don't."

Dean shuddered with shame at the realization.

"By all that's gay and glorious," Jeremy muttered, "that man must love you." Worried he might have touched on a sore spot, he asked gently, "And you, Dean, how do you feel about him?"

"I love him," Dean blurted out. No thought had gone into his answer— only expressed emotion. He took a moment to take in what he had just said. "I do love Geoffrey; he's a wonderful man," Dean pleaded. "It's just that I'm not that way, and it's hard having to crawl into bed with him every night, knowing he wants me to do things I can't seem to bring myself to do."

"I can imagine," Jeremy replied, nodding again for Dean to go on.

"I just—I just don't know what to do. I can't keep faking it—I can't keep on hurting him like this, but…" Dean shuddered at the thought. "I can never go back to that place."

"What was it like?" Jeremy asked with sincere interest.

"It was…it was…" Even with all of Jeremy's ease and willingness to listen, with every ounce of the man inviting confidence, Dean could not bring himself to speak of what had happened to him during his time at the Northeast Reeducation Camp.

"It's all right, son," Jeremy said soothingly. "I don't need to know." That Dean was straight was something Jeremy had figured out even before the two men had arrived at The Cattle Ranch. Changing the subject, but only just slightly, Jeremy commented, "Your partner must be a very wealthy man."

This comment seemed so odd so soon after Dean had just exposed himself as het'ro that he couldn't help but bluster, "I don't understand?"

"Notice how you and he are the only two guests here." He paused to allow the young man a moment of reflection. "This is peak season. This time of year, early fall being so lovely, all our cabins are usually full. We can service up to six couples—men and women—don't matter. Business is business. Though, we do tend to attract more men, being men ourselves." Having given Dean a knowing look, he added, "Don't see any women here about, do you?"

Dean pondered the implication. "He bought out the whole place?"

Jeremy smiled. "Rented out." Dean blushed. That was what he had meant to say. "He even asked if we had any women hands."

Dean sat up straight. "Do you?" His eyes opened wide to reveal both hope and fear.

Jeremy nodded. "Some. Cowfolk come in both sexes you know."

Dean flushed an even deeper red. "I…ah…"

Jeremy pointedly ignored Dean's obvious embarrassment. "I told him as much and he asked whether we'd mind keepin' 'em outta sight while the two of you were here. He paid extra for the favor, so I sent the ladies up to the north pastures to help my little sister, Sissy. She tends to our sheep up there." After having eyed Dean briefly, Jeremy rested his eyes on the faux fire. "Now. The way me and Jake figures it, if a man don't want no women around, he's either reeducated or has a real hate on for women. Either way, it likely adds up to his being straight." He chuckled slightly. "There ain't nothing straight 'bout your man…" He paused momentarily to wave his hands, "which leaves only you. Now yer twenty, why ain't you at the wall? He's a mite older, clearly been educated. Well, it doesn't take too much to put two and two together. You was straight when you was younger, and as you jes' told me now, you still is."

"You…you…" Real fear flashed in Dean's eyes. "You aren't gonna expose me, are you? Have 'em send me back there?"

"No, son, I ain't gonna do that to you. 'Sides," he stated judiciously, "my understanding of the law says it is illegal to act on being straight and you ain't been doin' no straight acts far as I can tell."

"No, sir," Dean expostulated vehemently. "No, sir, I haven't."

"Ever done?" Although his curiosity was pushing the bounds of propriety, Jeremy simply couldn't help but ask.

"N-no, sir—just the kissing stuff I told you about."

"Well, that's good, I suppose. But…" Here Jeremy paused, rubbed his chin, then sighed deeply. "Even if you did and I knowed 'bout it, I don't reckon I'd turn you in." Dean was stunned. Sitting before him, for the very first time in his entire life, was a man who wasn't judging him for being who he was. Dean felt so overwhelmed and touched that he was unable to speak. Having sensed the need to change the topic, Jeremy offered up a song. "How 'bout a little good ol' fashioned country fer ya?"

Dean smiled. "I'd like that."

Jeremy turned to his right where his guitar case leaned against one of the vacant stump seats. After opening it and retrieving the instrument, he took a moment to tune the strings. "Let's see now," he said while retuning the G string; his ear was close to the string as he listened intently until he was sure the sound was just right. "How about a little more Tim Hus?"

"Who's he?" Dean was clearly intrigued.

"Tim Hus, he was from Alberta country back when Alberta was still a part of old Canada. I sung y'all one a his songs yesternight. the one 'bout a bull rider."

"A bull rider?" Dean was intrigued, his eyes widening at the wonder. He remembered the song he just hadn't put the picture together in his mind. Blushing Dean adds, "I, ah, thought a brauma bull was a wild horse."

Jeremy laughs. "You remembered that line, did ya?" Then shaking his head between chuckles, he adds, "No. It's the bull they say no one can ride." Unable to let a good joke pass he adds, "It also means the man with the big penis." Dean joins in on the jocularity. Then nodding his head thoughtfully, Jeremy adds, "Anyway, cowboys—note girls ain't added here—don't think there were any women folk done this—men would saddle up the biggest, most ornery bulls they could get a hold of an' try an' ride 'em. Compete to see who could stay on its back the longest. Well, them bulls would buck mighty hard. I guess it was considered a real act of manhood to be able to ride on the back of one of them like that."

"Were any of them ever killed?" The idea of risking his life to prove his strength above others was intoxicating to Dean.

"Oh, yeah. I reckon lots were. It would be mighty dangerous. Our old bull is one mean bastard. I sure wouldn't want to git on the back of him—but these good ol' boys did and made good money doing it, too. Anyhoo, this here song I'm gonna sing ya's called 'Silver in the Buckle' and its 'bout a broncin' horse rider." Jeremy chose this song specifically for the one verse in which the Montana man meets a girl "across the line that stole his heart away." Under normal circumstances, Jeremy would adjust the verse, even though most folk, he knows, don't really listen to the lyrics. But not tonight—tonight Jeremy sings the song exactly the way Tim Hus wrote it. If he had judged the lad correctly, Dean would make out the intent of the lyrics. And when he was singing that verse, he would watch the youth closely to see whether or not he was game. Sissy was mighty lonely and Jeremy knew she needed a man in her life. He couldn't keep up this charade; Jake was far too suspicious, and as much as he loved Sissy, his true love was Jake. The fear of losing him had been building up lately.

Jeremy was correct. Dean picked up on the lines, gasping as soon as he heard them—taking off his hat, Dean used it to cover his lap. Without even finishing the song, Jeremy chimed out, "Sissy? Sissy, little girl, is that you?"

Jeremy had turned the voc mic off so Dean couldn't hear the woman's response. "Jeremy? For Hadrian's sake, don't you know what time it is?"

"It's late, sweetie pie. What you callin' fer?"

"ME? Why you dirty ol' swamp rat—" Jeremy blinked, turning on his eye cam to show her Dean. "Ohhh." Intelligence dawned. Although he was obviously much younger than Sissy, she couldn't help but find herself drawn to his masculine beauty. "Can he—hear me? Can he—see me?"

"Naw, little girl," Jeremy teased. "You know I don't got time to come running up there to help you herd in a bunch of sheep. Why didn't you fence up them pastures like I told you to?" He then confused the young man by giving Dean a wink. "Why didn't you jes' call me in the morning?" Feigning chagrin, he added, "Now, little sis, you know I'm too busy. We got guests to entertain this week." Having trouble containing himself, Jeremy laughed outright.

"So, what's your game, Jeremy? Is he for me?"

"Maybe." Grunting as if punched lightly, he added, "It might be possible." His smile spread wide. "Of course you can meet them—well, one of them, one guest went to bed early. Here—" When Jeremy blinked on the holocam, the grainy image of a blonde, curly haired young woman in her mid-twenties appeared. She was sitting up in bed with the covers dropped down to her waist.

"Hello." She spoke shyly, having never met a man other than her brother with straight tendencies. And since Jeremy is bi-sexual, she has to share him with Jake, who, she reasons, would likely kill her if he knew. The very idea of a fully straight man only interested in women excited her. Jeremy moved his head, bringing Sissy's image closer to Dean. "I'm Sissy. I herd sheep for my brother up north."

Dean looked up, smiling clumsily. "My name's Dean Stu—Hunter." Blushing crimson, Dean squeezed his eyes shut and dropped his head.

Sissy giggled awkwardly, "Stuhunter. That sure is an odd name. What's your cultural heritage?"

"No, uh…" Dean stuttered. "I…it's just Hunter."

"Okay, just Hunter." Dean was so embarrassed by her teasing that he could not bring himself to look up. Beginning to feel sorry for him, Sissy added, "It's nice to meet you, Dean." Since Jeremy had placed her holo image close enough, Sissy reached up with her hand to touch Dean's cheek. The cool thing about holo imaging through the contact voc is that the salt-based electric current charging it can be felt as a slight shock, which had given a whole new meaning to the concept of phone sex! Unfortunately, when Sissy's holo fingers lightly feathered Dean's face, he was stunned. His mind reeled back to reeducation and a bolt of lightning crackled in his brain, searing all of its energy out of his extremities. The suddenness of this impact caused the young man to have a seizure. Sissy quickly pulled her hand back, watching on in horror. When the attack finally abated, nausea set in. Turning his back on Jeremy, Dean vomited into the bushes behind his seat. When he finished, Dean got up, and without looking back, stumbled toward his and Geoffrey's cabin, pausing briefly at the water trough just outside their door to wash his face and rinse out his mouth. Turning to look at her brother, Sissy inquired, "Jeremy, what just happened?"

"He's a re-ed…" Then shaking his head, he suggested, "They must've done something."

"For the love of Hadrian," she gasped. "What?"

"I don't know, Sissy."

"Poor boy," Sissy lamented.

Jeremy sighed. "I only hope he can adapt." His eyes had followed Dean walking in the direction of his and Geoffrey's cabin.

Sissy was miffed, "Like m—"

Jeremy never let her finish. His eyes had hardened, "*Likely*, yes, likely, I agree. It's very *likely*." After a pause and having softened some toward his sister, he said, "But what might have happened to him—it frightens me more than you can possibly know."

Trembling at the implication, she inquired, "How so?"

"He could be—" Jeremy stopped himself in time. He knew he must avoid saying anything that might implicate Sissy. He had taken a foolish risk doing introductions over the voc—anyone on the government wave could have overheard.

For a brief moment, brother and sister stared into one another's eyes. Sissy was the first to break the silence. "I really do need help—with—the sheep, Jeremy."

"I sent you three women," he replied dryly.

Closing her eyes, Sissy tried desperately to squeeze back the tears. "Please come," she begged. "I really need you—your help."

"All right, baby girl," he answered soothingly. "I'll saddle up first thing and get there by nightfall." Although Jeremy and Sissy are brother and sister through their fathers' marriage they are not genetically related. Even so, if anyone ever learned of their affair most people would find it disturbing.

Suddenly, Sissy blurted out, "I love you!"

Jeremy's eyes grew stern again, and he responded quickly with, "I love you too, *little sis*."

* * * * *

Salve!

Today's Sexually Active Youth
HNN—Melissa Eagleton Reporting

Too many of today's teenagers are sexually active. This is a concern for numerous of Hadrian's parents. Many are seeking professional advice for ways to discourage our youth from beginning early experimentation. The fact is, early sexual experimentation has been a problem for parents of teenagers since the beginning of time. The accusation of outsiders that our teenagers are promiscuous due to our sexual orientation is balderdash. The teenage years are ones of sexual awakening. Teenagers' hormones begin to pop and dash around like the ball from the old pinball machines in the arcade museum. That is not to say I condone early sexual behavior in our youth. I only say this to let parents know they haven't done anything wrong if they suddenly discover their young adult is no longer a virgin.

Many young people find themselves hurt and confused by their first sexual experiences. What our children need to learn, through open and honest communication with their parents, is that touching, allowing another to touch you, is a very intimate experience. One becomes quickly attached to the person to whom she or he makes love. The greatest danger our youth face is the wretched psychological hurt that comes with a break-up. The pain of breaking up is compounded deeply if one has been intimate with another. Encouraging our youth to restrain from acting upon their sexual impulses at an early age is crucial. Early experimentation may shatter a child's self-esteem, creating an emotional turbulence that can deter an individual from creating a stable emotional bond with a future partner.

No doubt, parents, you are wondering what it is you can do to help stave off your child's sexual yearnings for a year or two. To begin, you need to be open and forthright with your sons and daughters. Be prepared to answer any questions they might ask regardless of how uncomfortable it may make you feel. And, yes, it is essential that you consider their questions about heterosexual behaviors. Remember, many of our citizens know what it feels like to be attracted to the opposite sex. Even though our geneticists have done a wonderful job isolating the gene for homosexuality, the fact still remains that some of our children are born with heterosexual tendencies. Let's remember the Kinsey scale: anyone between a three and five is easily swayed to accepting homosexuality as the sexual norm. Youth who are a two, on the other hand, feel the heterosexual drive a lot more strongly than their latent homosexual tendencies. If you suspect your child might be a two on the Kinsey scale, you can help him or her release the inner homosexual. Encourage your children to reach deep inside and discover what they like most about their own sex. Nurture these inclinations and help your child turn them into honest desires. For a child who is a two, it really is just a matter of finding the right man or right woman.

Now, for parents whose children are easily attracted to the same sex, you need to talk to your children about how to move slowly, as they may not take the time necessary to formulate solid relationships. Many of our youth find they get involved too quickly in a sexual relationship and are ultimately hurt. Parents, speak candidly with your child. Let him or her know what it was like for you as a young adult. Discuss how you controlled your sexual urges; or be honest, let him or her know about the hurt you felt when you gave of yourself too soon. It never serves a parent to mimic a virgin countenance. A false face forces even the finest into floundering. We are not saints; we are human beings, and we are all prone to flaws. Let us leave that "holier than thou" nonsense to the religious fanatics outside our walls, shall we? Rather, Hadrian's parents need to help their children understand how emotional the sharing of one's body is and encourage their children to restrain from entering into such a commitment at too young an age, and the best way to accomplish this is by sharing our own experiences openly. But perhaps the two most important pieces of advice I can offer you are these: be honest and never judge your child.

Vale!

Study Date

Frank's room is huge. Todd laughed the first time he saw the bathroom attached. "By all that's gay and glorious, man, your bathroom is four times the size of my bedroom!" Frank's bed is a four-poster queen-size; Todd's is a single. As soon as he enters Frank's room, Todd always rips open the poster's curtains and tosses himself onto Frank's bed. "Man, I wish I could have a bed this size. And the mattress." He always says this as he luxuriates in the feel of a mattress that actually bends and forms to his body, immediately placing him in the perfect rest position and realigning his spine at the same time. "Hadrian's lover," Todd groans in delight, "it just cracked my back for me."

Frank laughs heartily. He enjoys watching Todd squirm in delight on his bed. "You can sleep over any time," is Frank's chirp reply, always knowing, but never fully prepared, for Todd's inevitable response.

"Forget it, Frank. I'm not one of your tinsel tarts."

"I think you'd look cute in makeup." Frank never quits.

"You're not slathering that shit on my face ever again." Todd sits up and studies his image in Frank's mirror. The silver center is a beautiful oval surrounded by a highly decorative cherry oak frame. "It made me look stupid; the stuff smells. And, worst of all," he adds emphatically. "It gave me acne." Now looking at his friend, he exclaims, "I hate acne!" Frank sits next to Todd, placing his hand on his knee. Todd swats it away. "Hands off, buddy!"

Frank shrugs off the rejection. Todd may play hard to get, but they are still best friends, and that relationship always gives him hope. "And how old were we then? Ten? Twelve?"

"Thirteen," Todd replies crisply. Todd has grim memories of that day. Frank and he got carried away dressing themselves in as festive a manner as possible. After painting each other's faces, Frank exclaimed how beautiful Todd was, and suddenly, they were kissing, making out quite heavily. The experience became awkward for Todd when Frank began dry humping against him. Todd didn't know what to do, and the incident hadn't stopped until Frank had groaned during ejaculation. Todd had leapt up from the floor at that point, crying, "I'm not ready, Frank! I'm not ready. This is too soon."

As Todd ran out of the room, Frank had chased him. "Todd, come back! I'm sorry."

Todd wouldn't listen. He had just hopped on his bike and raced home. He never even bothered to change. When he ran inside, he saw Papa Mike sitting on the couch with a new "friend." "Well, well," the man said smiling, "look at your little fella." Todd stood rooted to the floor, unable to move. He was so stunned that when the man stood up and walked toward him, Todd stumbled back against the wall. The older man, trapping him there, leaned in so close Todd could smell the whiskey on his breath. It wasn't until the man hooked his finger through the silver loop of Teika's dog collar and gave it a slight tug that Todd remembered Frank had put it on him. All the clothes Todd had chosen to wear were pinks and purples, and Teika's dog collar, being dark purple, matched perfectly. Frank had taken it off the old German Shepherd and strapped it on Todd. They had both laughed hilariously when Todd had pretended to be Teika. Frank started petting him, saying things like "Good girl!" Todd had pretended to wag his tail and leap up to lick Frank's face the way he had seen Teika do. That was when things between Frank and him got crazy.

"I like the dog collar." The older man's seductive whisper ripped Todd out of his memory. "Do you want to do it doggy style? Is that what you're wanting to do?" Todd winced. That was how Frank had dry humped him. The man continued his seductions. "You are one beautiful little boy. Do you know that?" he asked Todd in an enticing manner. Todd just stood there, glued to the wall, and quaking. "You are going to have all the men chasing after you when you get older."

Timid and terrified, Todd called out, "Please make him stop, Papa Mike. Please."

"Leroy, leave the kid alone." Papa Mike didn't even sound annoyed. But Leroy listened. He blew Todd a little kiss first, then returned to the couch to sit beside his lover. "But, Todd," Papa Mike began to chastise, "go to the mirror and look at the way you are dressed." Todd did as instructed. "With those clothes," he said, shaking his head, "that dog collar and all that makeup—well, face facts, son; you are just asking for sex."

"Your Papa's right, little man," Leroy concurs. "Makeup was designed to help make a person more attractive. It's a tool. You wear it because you want to enhance your appearance. And if you want to enhance your exterior form, it's because you want somebody to take notice of you. Just like I did." He topped off his lecture with a wink.

Todd shivered. He didn't mean to. He thought Frank and he were just fooling around, but then it got crazy and they had done stuff, stuff Todd felt was wrong—*No*, he thought, *not wrong, just not right*. He looked at himself questioningly in the mirror. *Why*, he wondered, *if it's not wrong, didn't it feel right?*

"So, Todd," Papa Mike asked, "are you ready for sex?"

"No, Papa." Todd knew he wasn't ready; he wondered whether he'd ever be ready after what he and Frank had done. "No, Papa, I'm not."

"Then go wash your face, change your clothes, and for Hadrian's sake, take off that damn dog collar!"

"Well," Todd recalls the other man laughing and saying, "at least you know the boy is gay."

"Shut up, Leroy." After sighing, Mike had added, "You can dress for attraction when you are ready to attract."

Still staring at himself in the mirror, Todd mouths the words, "Yes, Papa," both in the past and in the present.

Frank looks at Todd oddly, wondering what is going on inside his friend's mind. "Thirteen," Frank waves the age off dismissively. "We didn't know what we were doing." Walking over to his dressing table, he opens up a cosmetic case. "I've been learning all kinds of ways to use makeup creatively in Cos class. Makeup doesn't have to make anyone look tawdry. You don't have to slather it on, wear blush, or anything. Just use a little base to keep from looking too pale." As if to further his case, Frank adds, "No tinsel, no trash."

"Yet," Todd reminds him, "all the boys you date wear it to look kitschy."

"Kitschy," Frank laughs. "Good word! That's going to be my nickname for you."

"Don't you dare—" Todd begins to protest.

"Okay, Kitschy," Franks says, winking Todd's way. Frank is constantly threatening to give Todd a pet name.

Todd's face reddens. "I swear by Hadrian's lover, Frank. I'll kick the shit out of you if you ever call me that again."

"All right, gee whiz, learn to take a joke." Frank shrugs off his annoyance by turning to the mirror and begins to brush the light beige powder over his face. Taking his time, sensing the mood of the room, Frank decides to chat lightly until Todd calms down. Unfortunately, he does not choose a very good topic. "Really, Todd, it's like you're living back in the Dark Ages, embracing old world concepts where men weren't allowed to dress freely. No makeup, no skirts, no flashy clothes."

"You don't wear skirts," Todd interjects.

"The point, Todd, is I could if I wanted to." He turns to face Todd, brush in one hand, powder case in the other. "And nobody would abuse me for it!" Frank insists, "So could you!" Before Todd can object, Frank barges on, lecturing, "There was a time, before Hadrian, when men's fashion was limited. We weren't allowed to choose the way we dressed." Looking with emphasis toward his cosmetics, he adds, "Or the way we looked." Turning back to face the mirror, Frank finishes his touch up. When done, he swivels to face Todd, presenting his newly formed image: "See," he smiles proudly. "You can't even tell I'm wearing any. It just covers up the blemishes."

"You don't have any blemishes," Todd interjects.

"That's because I cover them up." Adding more powder to his brush, Frank moves in closer to Todd. "Here, let me put some on you."

Annoyed, Todd pushes Frank's hand away. "I said no."

"Oh, come on, Todd. Everyone wears makeup!"

"That doesn't mean I have to."

Spinning on his heels, returning the cosmetics case to his dressing table, Frank exclaims, "You are so stubborn!"

"You said men have a choice in Hadrian. So, why can't I choose the way *I* look?"

"Of course you can," Frank says a little too harshly. "Did you know," he adds in his own defense, "that when makeup was first used by the Egyptians, it was worn by men as well as women!" Todd shakes his head. "I learned that in Cos, too!" Huffing a little to release his anger, he states, "Well, here in Hadrian, like in ancient Egypt, men are free to wear makeup if they want to!"

"It's just," Todd counters, "some guys use way too much goop and it looks awful."

Frank takes this comment to mean his personal use of makeup is vulgar. "Just because a guy wears a little base doesn't make him cheap or gaudy."

"I didn't mean you…" Todd stumbles, trying to avoid hurting his friend's feelings. "It's just that's the way the boys you date look—garish, flashy, showy. I mean—you never date anyone who just looks normal." *And they all wear that stupid fucking collar!* "It's like you want every guy you're with to look like a tart or something." His frustration growing, Todd expresses his real fear, "And I know if you're trying to put that crap on me, it's because you want me to look that way, too!" To avoid further discussion, Todd stands and crosses over to the bedroom door. "What's taking Crystal so long?" Todd reaches into his jean pocket to retrieve his cell phone and begins to text.

"What are you doing?" Frank is clearly annoyed. Todd hit home when he suggested Frank wanted him to look pert and cute like his "boys." It's almost as if Frank is trying to relive their time together when they were thirteen. Todd seemed so anxious to kiss him, so anxious to pet and play then, but he suddenly changed. Frank still doesn't know what he did wrong, and they can never talk about that day. It has become taboo—almost as if it never happened. Sighing, Frank realizes a truth about himself; everyone he dates has that same boyish look; they all remind Frank of Todd on that day, and they all end up wearing Teika's dog collar.

Todd has his back to Frank so he doesn't see his friend's facial expression. He simply answers Frank's question. "Texting Crystal to see what's taking her so long."

"Put that away," Frank growls. Todd obeys his friend, hearing something dark and ominous in Frank's voice. "She'll get here when she gets here!" Allowing all of his annoyance to spill out, he adds, "Crystal, our little chaperone."

Todd turns around. "That's not fair, Frank! She's smart. Besides, we both need to pass this test." He adds as a reminder, "Everyone needs Hadrian history to graduate."

"I know." Frank lets go of his aggravation. "I just would have preferred you and me alone."

"You're the one who got the three of us together to form a study group last year!"

"I know." Somewhat frustrated, Frank replies, "I had no idea you two would hit it off."

"We're just friends, Frank," Todd insists. "Like you and me."

"No," Frank reminds him, "not like you and me."

It is Todd's turn to get irritated. "I am not a tinsel tart! I am not trash! And I will not join your little harem of boys!"

Frank is offended. "I never said you were any of those things." Frank sits on the bed and pats the spot next to him. Todd refuses to take the bait. "You would be the only one!" As if to defend his behavior, he adds, "I only date all those guys because I'm waiting for you!"

Slightly mollified, Todd sits back on the bed, searching for a way to word this delicately. "Frank, I don't want a boyfriend." Seeing the look of shock in Frank's eyes, Todd begins to backtrack. "I mean, not so soon after—it just hurts too much." Sighing, hoping this will placate Frank, he says, "I'm just happy being able to hang out with you again."

"And what's wrong with dating?" Frank sees hope in everything Todd says.

Squeezing his eyes shut, Todd replies, "Nobody just dates." Then complaining, he says, "A date means getting laid and…" Feeling foolish, blushing a little, Todd stares at his feet as they shuffle uncomfortably. "I'm not ready for sex." He harrumphs, "That's why Devon dumped me."

Frank laughs gaily as he wraps his arms around Todd's shoulder. He and Devon didn't do it! He can still be the one Todd falls in love with! The first and only one Todd shares himself with! *Just like Dad and Papa Dean*, he tells himself. Todd wants to shove Frank off, but he knows that will hurt his friend too much so he lets Frank hug him instead. "I respect you, Todd. I wouldn't make you do anything until I knew you were ready."

"That's what Devon said," Todd mutters gloomily.

"I'm not Devon." Then whispering in Todd's ear, he adds, "Dating would be no different than the way things are now, except for kissing and," a little naughtily, "maybe a little petting." Frank leans in for a kiss.

Todd quickly turns away. "Kissing leads to petting and petting always leads to sex!" Glaring back at Frank, he concludes, "And if it doesn't, he dumps you!"

Frank gently brushes away one of the tears Todd is desperately trying to hold back. Frank reaches out to Todd and holds his friend tight in his arms. "He really hurt you, didn't he?" *Hadrian exile you, Devon*, Frank curses.

Although he would like to struggle against Frank's hug, Todd merely closes his eyes and tries to explain. "Frank, I—" Unable to finish, he tenses into Frank's embrace.

Encouraging him, Frank says, "You can tell me anything, Todd."

No, I can't! Todd starts to cry. *Why can't I feel anything if I'm at least a two? Isn't it just a matter of finding the right man? Isn't Frank the right man? I love him. I don't love anyone better! Why don't I feel anything then?* Summoning up the courage, he asks, "Everybody's at least a two, right, Frank?"

Frank smiles reassuringly at his friend, "That's right, babe. Everybody in Hadrian is at least a two." To prove his point, he asks Todd, "You look in the mirror, right?"

"Of course I do. Everybody does."

"Everybody, good. Remember last year?" Todd shakes his head, unsure of Frank's allusion. "When we took the history of homosexual themes in cinema?"

Todd smirks, "Yeah, great class. All we did was watch short flicks and movies!"

Frank becomes annoyed. "It was more than that; we learned some important things too, you know."

"Yeah, yeah, I know, but," he smirks, "it was slack!"

Truly annoyed now, Frank states, "Beside the point. Remember the short film we watched by the twentieth century director David Blythe—oh, Hadrian, what was its name?"

"Don't ask me. All I remember about that class was not having to do any work. I spent most of it sleeping. It was sweet."

Frank is almost irate. "Todd, please, I'm trying to remember—*Circadian Rhythms!*" Frank is pleased with his excellent memory. "In it, he said, and I quote, 'All mirrors are homosexual.'"

Todd screws up his face in disgust at this logic. "What?"

Frank walks over to the mirror to illustrate. "See, I'm looking at myself, and what I see is a man. As I admire my own image, I am admiring someone of the same sex."

"By that reasoning," Todd utters sarcastically, "everyone who masturbates is gay."

Frank spins to face Todd, pleased by the logic, "Yes! That's right! And Todd," he says, remembering back to the day he walked in on his friend, "you can't be—you know—that way—having masturbated."

Todd blushes as the memory surges through him. When Frank walked in on him, he had been masturbating to thoughts of Crystal—while looking at heterosexual porn. Shame floods his body. Franks, sensing his friend's unease, sits down beside him and wraps an arm around Todd's shoulder. "Besides," he adds, giving Todd a gentle shake, "everyone born in Hadrian has homosexual tendencies. It just takes some people a little longer to find themselves than others; that's all."

Todd nods his head (a little too quickly) in agreement. "I'm just not ready—right, Frank?" As his breath quivers, he tries to sound confident. "I'm just not ready yet." *If Devon taught me anything about myself*, he thinks, *it was that!*

Frank begins kissing the top of Todd's head. "I can wait, babe. I can wait."

Although Frank's action is innocent, Todd panics. Pushing Frank away, Todd stands, a bit too aggressively, before crossing to the other side of the room. Positioning himself next to Frank's desk with his back to his friend, Todd picks up his school slate and begins tapping the screen, searching for the doc they need to study from for tomorrow's test. After finding what they need, he holds the slate against his chest, a feeble armor against Frank's lust. Finally summoning up the courage, he rejects Frank's offer. "No, you can't." Turning back to face Frank, he states, "You can't wait." He pauses, losing some of the conviction in his voice. "At least, not for as long as it could take me." Silencing Frank with a wave of his hand, he adds, "I know you, Frank. You're horny. You'll start dating all those pretty boys and I'll look like a fucking idiot." Just as Frank is about to deny the charge, Todd interjects, "Really, Frank? Admit it. What if it takes two or three years before I'm ready?" His eyebrows cock. "My father wasn't ready until he was twenty-four years old!" What Todd doesn't mention was that his father was "piss drunk" at the time; something his Papa Mike often slurs in drunken lament when he doesn't realize Todd can hear him. With barely a pause for this thought Todd continues, "Are you really going to stay celibate that long?"

That is the clincher. Frank cannot deny the fact that two years—with the possibility of eight years—without sex is way too long. He would never stay faithful to Todd, not for that long of a stretch, and Todd, as he has come to learn over the years, is the most steadfast of friends. "That's why I love you, you know."

Todd tries to laugh; pretending to be coy is not something he is good at. "Why?"

"Because you're faithful, loyal. You're the best friend I've ever had, will ever have." Standing up, Frank crosses over to join Todd as his desk. "Papa Dean says you're one in a million!"

"That's nice of him." Todd likes Frank's Papa Dean. He is down to earth, although Todd can't quite figure out why he feels an affinity toward the man. Ever since his father died, Todd has felt like Papa Dean adopted him. He's proven to be an even better father than Papa Mike. Todd flops down on the floor, the school slate now face up in his lap.

Frank pulls out his desk chair and sits down. Swiveling around so he can look down at his friend, Frank ends with, "Okay, so you're not ready." Pointing his index finger at Todd, he warns, "I'm going to continue dating."

"I never said you shouldn't." Todd is not looking at Frank, tapping and sliding his finger across the slate, ostensibly in search of the page they need to study.

"But one day," Frank continues, "you will be ready, Todd Middleton." Todd laughs and shakes his head. Frank's dogged determination is what makes him such an excellent b-ball player. The man just never knows when to quit. "And when that time comes, just know this." Frank bends down and lifts Todd's face up by the chin. "I will be standing in the wings ready to sweep you up into my arms."

"Okay, Frank." Todd sees no point in continuing to resist since he's won a stalemate, "but until then, please remember, we're just friends."

* * * * *

Salve!

Hadrian's Wall Still Holding
HNN—Melissa Eagleton Reporting

Another wave of heterosexual barbarians attempted to force their way through a portion of Hadrian's Wall and cross our border last night. This time, the attack was waged against the Mid-West Gate Battalion. According to Captain Collins, 12th Platoon commanding officer, "This was no regular army. Had it been, they never would have concentrated all their men on so heavily a fortified zone." Having anticipated an intelligent military attack, dressing regulars like thralls, Captain Collins had immediately contacted the bases located fifteen miles south of the Mid-West Gate, those camps stationed near the electric wire fencing, warning them to be on alert for what he believed would be the real attack. However, no such attack came. It truly is a wonder that the hordes did not attempt an attack in one of these locations, which are, as Captain Collins assures us, the preferred location for armies or organized gangs to attempt breaking into Hadrian's borders. Even so, rest assured, folks, that these border fences are not left undefended. We have watchtowers placed every fifty feet with trained snipers to keep the heterosexual barbarians at bay. At the Mid-West Gate, heavy fighting was reported by Captain Collins. After taking small arms fire, and coming under insurgent rocket attacks, the 12th Platoon used superior tactics and its upgraded M4A2 assault rifles to push back the enemy and seize the objective. The rifles' extremely high rate of fire and 30 round 5.56mm magazines provided the necessary force multiplier to inflict maximum casualties with minimal losses. In fact, Captain Collins believes that last night's attack was more of a suicide run than a battle. Considering the desperate living conditions of many outsiders, this does not seem so unlikely. "All the bodies of the heterosexual dead," Captain Collins is quoted as saying, "were emaciated," adding, "had they been successful at climbing the wall or breaking through the front gate, not one of them would have stood a chance in hand-to-hand combat against the men and women of Hadrian." His eyes were filled with sorrow as he spoke, and shaking his head, he told me, "Even our oldest citizens would have stood a better chance. It was worse than an old fashioned turkey shoot!" A turkey shoot for those voc, or wave, viewers who are unfamiliar with the term, means having all the advantage. Apparently a turkey hunter would scatter the flock and then sit back and wait while all the birds reconvened in the same spot. He would then just sit back and shoot them at his leisure. I can assure you, folks, that under no circumstances did Captain Collins mean to suggest his soldiers and he shot the barbarian hordes at their "leisure." Rather, for the soldiers of the Mid-West Gate Battalion, this turkey shoot was far too painfully easy. Many of our young soldiers have requested psychological aid, as their training did not include assisted suicide. Captain Collins has made a recommendation to his commanding officer that the military begin looking into the possibility of training our soldiers for what he believes will be more future acts of euthanasia. Once again, we are reminded of our good fortune, extending gratitude for the wisdom of the founding families in creating the only safe haven remaining for humanity on planet earth. Is it any wonder we have no crime in Hadrian? Is it any wonder we have no jails? Who, in his right mind, would commit a crime knowing that the only punishment available is banishment with the option of assisted suicide? It is truly amazing how many of our convicted criminals request black henbane when sentenced with exile.

For those viewers unaware, black henbane is a highly poisonous plant because it contains several alkaloids. It grows wild throughout most of Hadrian. To ensure its availability to those who would choose euthanasia, the plant is grown in a hothouse here in Antinous. Even our most hardened criminals do not want to live in the outside world, so daunting, so terrifying is the prospect. If put to the test, I daresay I too would choose death over exile. Really, when you think of the alternative—life outside our walls—wouldn't you choose death?

Vale!

Enter the Vixen

"Frank," Papa Dean calls from the front room. "Your friend Crystal is here."

"Finally," Todd mutters. He really does need Crystal as a chaperone.

"She says you guys have to study." There is some trepidation in Papa Dean's voice, a note Todd picks up on, but to which Frank appears oblivious.

"Thanks, Papa," Frank hollers back. "Send her in."

Todd shakes his head. "Why can't you just open the door and talk like normal people, instead of yelling?"

Frank, very good at being coy, replies, "I'd have to walk all the way over there and I prefer being close to you."

The door bursts open and Crystal enters. She is tall—5' 11½"—but it has always irked her that she never hit six feet. She has never forgiven her mothers or the doctor for making her take heterosexual birth control in order to stunt her growth. "Gigantism," her doctor had warned, "is a serious concern. An enlarged heart would mean a shorter lifespan." This warning was enough to convince her mothers, so Crystal was required to stunt her growth.

With her short, dark brown hair swept up and over to the right side, accenting her oblong face, cute little nose, and jade green eyes, Crystal is truly beautiful. Like Todd, she refuses to wear makeup. Everyone, boys and girls, wears makeup these days. No one seems to care that a girl won't, though. More girls than guys can get away with the natural look, even if their numbers are far and few between. At least Crystal isn't the only girl at Pride who refuses to wear the goop. And a girl without makeup isn't instantly tagged as straight. By comparison, Todd has set himself up for razzing because he is the only boy at Pride who won't wear any facial enhancements. Even, still, Todd begrudgingly admits most people don't wear makeup to look like sluts—*only Frank's boys!* What Todd will never admit to himself, though, is that his perspective on this is more than slightly skewed.

"Hey, guys," Crystal chimes as she walks across the room. When she reaches the middle, she gives a model spin so they can better appreciate her figure. "So," she asks, beaming in their direction, "how do I look?"

"Wow! Girlie girl, you look amazing!" Frank stands up to admire her image more thoroughly. "Do you always dress like this for a study date with boys?"

Crystal giggles. "Silly, I have a date with Lolita after." Spinning slowly to show off her beauty, she says, "I'm wearing this for her!"

"Do your moms know you're dressed like that?" Frank utters his amazement.

"Don't be insane," Crystal replies. "They don't even know I own this dress."

Crystal is stunning in her light green dress, snug to the body. Thin straps reveal snowy white shoulders, a low cut bodice exposes a deep cleavage, and her hips are accented by the rippling of material sewn into elastic. The skirt is a mini and hugs her buttocks neatly. Frank leans in to inspect her backside. "Aren't you wearing any underwear?"

The question is rhetorical, but Crystal answers anyway. "Of course not," she giggles. "Can't risk showing any lines." Still twirling in constant show of her beauty, Crystal smiles. "What do you think, Todd? Do I look okay?"

Todd's eyes are wide, his mouth hangs open and he is staring. He stutters, "You, uh—gee, Crystal." Swallowing hard, he manages to say, "You look great."

"What do you think, Frank?" Crystal swirls again. "Will Lolita like me in it?"

Frank is more than pleased with Crystal's question. "She is going to like you so much, girlie, you won't last sixty seconds in that dress." Crystal's giggle suggests that that is the plan. "Let me dab some makeup on you," Frank adds. "And I can cut that time in half."

Turning coquettishly to Todd, Crystal winks, "What do you think, Todd? Should I let Frank doll me up?"

Frank notices Todd staring Crystal's way—gawking actually. Jealousy rages as he slams back down on his chair. It creaks but doesn't break. "Fuck it!" he spits out. "You look fine the way you are." Todd blushes and turns away.

Crystal, ever the expert deflector, turns a teasing eye on Frank. "Oh, oh." Feigning a little pout, she says, "Crystal came at a bad time, didn't she?" Poking Frank, attempting to jostle him into good humor, she adds, "Were you trying to make it with the boy again?"

Frank, although not feeling very spirited, forces a laugh. To make it look like he's giving in to Crystal's jocularity, he spins gaily in his chair, retorting, "Can't blame a guy for trying."

Todd turns, hoping to change the conversation. "Shouldn't we start…" Red splotches now cover the whole of Todd's face. "I mean…" Embarrassment causes him to stumble over his words.

Misinterpreting Todd's bashful demeanor, Frank smiles Crystal's way.

Giving Frank a knowing wink to deepen further his misconception, Crystal feigns concern as she bends forward to shake Todd's shoulder, exposing her deep cleavage in the process. "Awe, Todd, are we embarrassing you?"

Todd bends his head down quickly; even the back of his neck is red. He mutters, "Can we study? Please?"

"First, you two kiss and make up." Then taunting Todd, she adds, "Otherwise, I might think you're a *strai* and attracted to me." Looking up stunned, Todd is clearly hurt by the accusation. "Oh, I'm just teasing." Crystal's voice is not as reassuring as it should be. "I know you're not straight. But seriously," pouting again, looking to Frank to take the initiative, "I won't feel right until you boys kiss and make up."

Frank stands, taking full advantage of Crystal's suggestion. Walking over to Todd, Frank motions for him to stand. Then, after placing both hands behind Todd's head, and with his back to Crystal, he carefully mouths the words, "Make this look good." Using his eyes, Frank gestures Crystal's way. "She's a gossip." As he looks into Todd's eyes, he waits for him to initiate the kiss. When their lips finally meet, Frank holds them together for over a minute. Crystal squeals in delight and claps during the whole ordeal. As Frank returns to his chair, Todd shakes before awkwardly sitting down on the floor.

"Wow, Frank," Crystal remarks. "That must have been some kiss. You got the boy all a tremble." She, too, sits on the floor in front of Todd. "You know," she still goads Todd, "I love watching boys kiss."

Frank smiles. "Well, that's all you get to watch us do!" Although he is speaking to Crystal, his eyes are locked on Todd. That kiss has his whole body on fire. Reaching across his desk, he slides his personal slate over, using it discreetly to cover his groin.

Todd musters up the courage to speak, "Can we…" Even now, addressing these two is difficult. His hands, still gripping the school slate, shake it slightly for emphasis as he finishes, "study now?"

"Study?" Crystal claps her hands together, her eyes open wide in excitement and she gives her head a little shake. "Okay! Tomorrow's test!" As always, Crystal is highly exuberant, (kids love associating with her due to her excessive energy bursts and constant upbeat mood). "Hadrian's legal system. Tomorrow's test will be on Procreation Laws, the impact of 6-13 on Hadrian's foreign policy and conscription laws—"

Frank rolls his eyes in disgust. He is sorely displeased with the fact that all Hadrian's youth must now serve four years in the military. Prior to 6-13, youth were only conscripted for two years.

Crystal ceases listing and begins to chastise him. "And what is your problem?"

"I wish we didn't have to have conscription," Frank mutters. Although he doesn't like the idea of having to serve in the army, he, like every other Hadrian citizen, is required by law to do so.

"Exceptions are made for scholarship winners," Todd reminds him.

"A very good reason to study," Frank declares, posturing himself now for hard work.

"I disagree," Crystal argues. "Conscription is essential." Quite stern now, she adds, "Even if I win a scholarship, I plan to ask the uni to hold on to it until after I serve." Both boys stare uncomprehendingly. "We are all responsible for helping to defend our country. Four years of service ensures more experienced men and women defending our walls, something we need considering that the world out there is getting more and more insane." Shaking her head sadly, "Surely you remember 6-13?"

Todd certainly remembers, Frank thinks, as he watches his friend for any sign of emotional disturbance. Fortunately, there is none.

"Besides," Crystal remonstrates, "you can't depend on a scholarship." Shaking her head disapprovingly, she says, "Sorry, Frank, but your marks are just not high enough. Todd may get a sports scholarship, but you are going to the wall." Hadrian's wall, although envisioned to surround the entire country (and one day it will!) only spans one hundred miles across those lands where the heterosexual barbarians have been known to concentrate the bulk of their attacks. There are, however, watchtowers and electric fences spanning the rest of Hadrian's borders. "Unless," Crystal smiles wickedly, "you expose yourself."

"What?" Frank stands, face flushed with anger. Todd stands to calm him. "She's just kidding, Frank." Looking down at Crystal, miffed that she would upset Frank to such a degree, Todd says, "Tell him you're just kidding."

Crystal can barely get the words out from laughing so hard, but she does manage to execute an apology of sorts. "Don't worry, Frank," she finally utters after her stomach and diaphragm calm down. "No one in their right mind would ever believe you're straight. Which again means, you're going to the wall." This brings on another fit of laughter.

Todd, knowing Frank's temper, pulls the man in for a hug. "If you go to the wall, I go to the wall," he whispers. "We go together." This mollifies Frank, and he returns Todd's light hug with his own grizzly bear. The physical contact, Todd rightly surmises, is just what Frank needs to get his mind off wanting to punch Crystal.

After kissing the top of Todd's head, Frank whispers his appreciation. "Thanks."

As the two boys resume sitting, Crystal, oblivious to her guffaw, smiles Todd's way, whispering to him her dream. "I'm thinking of making the military my career."

Suddenly, Frank is forgotten as the two have a brief tête-à-tête. "I thought you wanted to be a surrogate goddess?" Todd asks earnestly. "You'd look beautiful pregnant," he blurts out.

Frank scowls as Crystal smiles and says, "Thank you." To Frank's further annoyance, she blows Todd a kiss. "I can do both. The military has great maternity leave benefits, and a surrogate goddess never has to get pregnant more than once every two years."

"It seems to me a surrogate goddess would be ten months of wasted time and money for the military," Frank utters discouragingly.

Impervious, Crystal insists, "It's amazing how many compensations are made for a surrogate." Then, smiling at Todd for encouragement, she adds, "I really could do both!"

"Cool," Todd replies, finding everything Crystal has to say fascinating right now.

Frank shakes his head in disgust. "Typical Crystal, always wanting to be in the limelight!"

"You shall not dissuade me, Frank Hunter." More determined now than ever, she states, "I shall be a surrogate goddess *and* make the military my career!" Now, looking back at the school slate in Todd's lap, she smiles. "Let's get back to our study list, shall we. Where was I? Oh, yes, listing off study topics. Procreation Laws, the impact of 6-13 on Hadrian's foreign policy, and…" glaring at Frank, "conscription laws, the resurgence of the anti-heterosexual campaign, and reeducation camps!" Once again turning to face Todd, Crystal opens wide her eyes. She accents the expression by sticking her tongue out of her mouth and rubbing her hands together while giggling. "Let's start with Procreation Laws, shall we?" Trying now to recapture a teasing mood, Crystal slaps Frank's thigh, "So, tell me, after you two boys wed, are you planning on having your babies right away or waiting?"

Before Frank can even answer, Todd's head is shaking. "We're not registered!"

"I know that," Crystal laughs. "I said *when*."

Frank steps in before Todd can reject him thoroughly. "Yes! We do plan to register!" The look he gives Todd brooks no objection, so Todd simply looks down at the slate in his lap and waits, wishing fervently for the other two to finish kidding around. Frank, however, has more to say on this issue. He wants to make sure everyone in the room is clear on his intent. "We'll wait a couple of years, I think, but have them both within the first ten years. That's what my dads did—and I want them close in age—like Roger and me. What about you? Right away or later?"

"Never!" Crystal says this a bit too emphatically.

"What?" Todd looks up, his face exposing disappointment.

Crystal shrugs slightly and then looks to Frank, almost as if he would be more likely to understand. "When I register…" Mischievously, she adds, "*if* I register, I certainly don't want to add a child into the mix."

"But you have to," Todd admonishes. "And your partner will have to."

Crystal pointedly ignores Todd. "A child just complicates everything."

Frank looks concerned. "You and Mama Elena at it again?"

Crystal, dropping all jocularity, becomes instantly somber. Her eyes roll up into her sockets. "And then she and Mom go at it. Mom always takes my side and that pisses Mama Elena off. 'Just because you passed her through your loins doesn't mean she's always right.'" Crystal shakes her head and joins the boys in laughter at her mimicry of Mama Elena's shrill accusations. Crystal laughs, "Mama Elena's right, though. Mom lets me get away with everything." Taking on a stern expression for this imitation, Crystal shrills, "You've spoilt the girl rotten." After they have all had a good chortle, she adds, "And I am spoilt—rotten. I could never have a kid, especially if she turned out like me." Frank and Todd guffaw in agreement.

"But," pulling them back to his original argument, Todd insists, "You still have to have a baby. Everybody has to—it's the one child law."

Crystal's green eyes sparkle. "There are ways around that. Your Papa Mike figured a way around it, didn't he?"

"But Papa Mike wants to have his child."

"Then why doesn't he?" Crystal asks.

Todd cringes. When drunk, Papa Mike will often throw this issue in Todd's face. "Do you see me with my own child? No! And why not, might you ask? Because of you, I've no fucking money! Because of you, I've no fucking child of my own! You are so fucking needy. New running shoes—new clothes—more food!" Todd no longer points out the fact that it was Papa Mike who drank through all his father's savings after 6-13.

Frank, cognizant to the sudden pallor of Todd's face, shakes his head in dismay. Crystal always manages to ask the wrong questions. Frank leaps in to save him from having to explain. "His Papa applied to pass his responsibility on to others. They use his semen for men with low sperm count." Watching Todd's head droop, Frank cringes at now being the one to make Todd wince.

Papa Mike's voice roars in Todd's brain. "I've probably got a thousand kids out there I'll never meet!"

Crystal's voice breaks through Todd's memory, "Why?"

"For the love of Antinous, Crystal! They're poor, all right! His Papa can't afford another kid." Fearing for Todd's emotional balance, Frank insists, "Drop it already."

"Sorry, Todd."

"It's all right, Crystal." Todd smiles meekly. "I don't mind not having a kid brother or sister. Frank and Roger make up for that."

Crystal's smile widens. "You always look at everything in such a positive light, Todd. I so admire you."

Todd beams, all discomfort washed away by Crystal's compliment. Frank seethes with jealousy. *Crystal caused Todd pain, I defended him, and one silly compliment on her part and he's all's good.* Wanting to lash out at Crystal, Frank throws the argument back in her face. "You don't have poverty as an excuse, not with your Mama! How do you plan to avoid raising your own child?"

Crystal replies slyly by tapping Todd's school slate, suggesting the answer lies inside today's study session. Although still confused and curious as to her meaning, Todd uses Crystal's gesture to suggest the three of them actually begin preparing themselves for tomorrow's test. "Do you guys want me to quiz you?"

Crystal and Frank both roll their eyes. "Goodness gracious me, Todd!" Crystal shoots her next remark Frank's way. "Is he always so serious?"

"Yup!"

"Okay. Let's begin, but give me the slate. I'll drill you two. I already know this shit by heart. Mama Elena's been making me study every night this week." Rolling her eyes upward to the ceiling, opening her hands into fat jazz fingers, Crystal adds, "She is such an extremist!" After snatching the slate away from Todd, Crystal begins, "Let's start with an easy one. When was the one child law instigated?"

Frank answers instantly, "The same year as our founding."

"Good." Crystal is now settled into a studious pose, sitting on her knees, causing her skirt to rise even higher up her thighs. Todd struggles not to stare at the soft brown fuzz she has exposed for him.

Frank notices Todd fixated on Crystal's legs—no, not her legs—the space between them. "Hey, peach fuzz." His annoyance evident, he kicks Crystal's thigh. "Save it for Lolita."

Crystal giggles; blushing, she looks to Todd as if he is a conspirator. "Oops!" Grabbing at the skirt between her inner thighs, she gives it a slight tug, covering what she had previously exposed. Mischievously giving Todd a wink, she says, "It's a good thing I'm with guys!" Then, as if nothing untoward just happened, Crystal continues their study session. "Todd, you answer this next one." Todd closes his eyes, a study method he has perfected over the years to help him visualize the answer. He believes his brain works like a computer, and he simply waits for it to show him the answer. Sometimes it works; most of the time, it doesn't. "Why..." Crystal's voice sends shivers down Todd's spine, "since our sexual preference is the perfect form of birth control, did our founding families believe it necessary to instigate such a radical law?"

Todd's eyes stay closed. The answer has appeared for him. "In order to ensure a stable population that neither declines or increases, it was determined that each man and woman be responsible for bringing in another life to replace his or her own. This way, we could maintain a stable population of ten million and…and—"

Crystal, never noted for her patience, doesn't give Todd any thinking time. "And?"

"And," Frank continues for him, "we have the outside world as our example of what happens when there is no government control over human procreation."

"I know that," says Todd, opening his eyes and looking Frank's way. "Just let me finish, will you?"

"Okay. Finish." Frank isn't offended. Crystal notes how fondly he looks down on his friend.

Todd's eyes squeeze tight. "What Frank said and…um…" He lifts his hands up, turns them into fists, and begins pumping (Frank and Crystal try very hard not to laugh at him). "To ensure the future of humanity…" Here, Todd claps his hands together, opens his eyes, and points directly at Crystal, "As well as to keep mankind from ever again overwhelming the earth with its presence." Satisfied with his answer, Todd releases a contented sigh.

"Very good, Toddie." Crystal pats him on the back.

Annoyed, Todd responds, "My name is Todd!"

"Sor-ry!" She extends each syllable to dramatically ridiculous proportions. Then looking to Frank, she says, "Doesn't like pet names, eh? Whatever are you going to call him?"

"Actually, I call him 'Ki—'"

Before Frank can call him "Kitschy," Todd butts in. He is clearly infuriated, "He calls me what he always calls me—by my name!"

Frank laughs a little uneasily. "Just don't call him 'Toddie.'"

In order to lighten the discomfort she's created, Crystal pipes up, "You guys hear what happened to Millicent at school?"

"No." Franks leans forward in his chair, hoping the gossip is malicious enough for Crystal to have to whisper. Todd too leans forward, his face precariously close to her breasts. His heart quickens.

Crystal, sensing the collective desire for dirt, embellishes the story with facial expressions, elongated vowels, and crisp consonants. "She got caught cheating using her vocal contact lens."

"No!" Both Todd and Frank utter in dismay.

"Yeah. Lolita voc'd me today. Millicent is in major hot water. Her mothers grounded her, and she has a week's worth of detention at school!"

"Yikes!" Frank exclaims.

"That's gotta hurt," Todd adds sympathetically.

"That's not the worst of it. Apparently, the school is banning the use of vocs during school hours."

Shaking his head, Frank scoffs, "That is so *strai!*"

"I know," Crystal agrees.

"There is no way they can do that," Frank adds. "You can't even see the thing, let alone determine if someone's using it."

"People move their mouths a lot," Todd responds. Not having a vocal contact, he has noticed how stupid everyone looks, talking or whispering to the air. "It looks like you're talking to yourself."

"So?" both Crystal and Frank say, offended.

Crystal carries on with the harangue. "You can always claim to be reading to yourself."

"Yeah," Frank agrees. "Some people read better when they mouth the words."

"But that's not how they're going to stop us," Crystal says.

"How are they going to catch you guys?" Todd asks. This situation doesn't affect him since he can't afford the vocal contact lens, but as his friends are clearly upset, he feigns interest.

"I guess they've got some kind of blocker and can stop voc signals."

Todd smiles and shows off his cell phone. "The three of us can still text."

"That's right!" Frank exclaims happily. He and Frank slap hands and grip fingers. Then Frank and Crystal do the same. Crystal raises her hand for Todd, who pretends not to notice by picking some lint off his sock. He really wants to slap hands with Crystal, but he is petrified of making physical contact with her.

Looking up, trying to appear jovial, Todd exclaims, "Thank Hadrian for old school!"

"Yeah, but," Crystal adds, a little miffed by Todd's rejection, "old school tech can never replace a voc." With vocal contact lenses, one can contact a friend anytime by simply blinking an eye and saying his name. By searching for the right icon and blinking it open, a visor scans out from the eyes to form a nearly invisible screen, allowing for virtual face-to-face contact.

One can watch vids, movies, and concerts, play games—a person can do just about anything using the voc. For the more flamboyant, microphones and speakers come in nicely camouflaged jewelry, often worn as an earring. For the artistically bent, there are options like tactile tattoos or, for the more modest individuals, a small implant that can be easily installed behind one earlobe.

Franks muses over the situation a little and declares, "The ban won't last long anyway."

"Why not?" Crystal looks on inquisitively.

"All the teachers have contacts now, even Mr. Gavin!" Mr. Gavin is Pride High's principal. "It won't be long before they'll want access again."

"So true," Crystal agrees. "Nobody wants to be unhooked from their voc."

"At most," Frank figures, "this ban will last two or three days."

"Can we get back to studying?" Todd asks, weary of a discussion that has nothing to do with him.

"Okay." Crystal recaps what they've covered. "Hadrian maintains ten million. We've reviewed the rationale for the one child law, and now, Frank, it's your turn. How many children can a registered couple apply for?"

"Easy. Two."

"Nope." Looking Todd's way, Crystal asks, "Do you know?"

Clearly confused, Todd defends Frank's answer. "How could it be anything but two?"

"Come on, you guys," Crystal is clearly disgusted. "That was a trick question. You know Mr. Reiner loves trick questions." They both look stunned, neither knowing the answer. Crystal sighs, answering for them. "A registered couple can apply for as many children as they want." Smiling now, enjoying the boys' confusion, Crystal explains, "The majority of couples only get approved for two babies, BUT it is possible even today, mostly due to 6-13, that some couples get approved for a third child. It's like slots on a roulette wheel. The majority say two children, two or three slots say three children, *and* one slot even says four." She accents the number by wiggling four fingers.

Frank is intrigued; he would love to have a lot of children. "You mean to say there are registered couples out there with *four* children?" The size of the family seems incomprehensible.

"Yes," Crystal replies triumphantly. "Since 6-13—"

"You said that already," Todd remonstrates. He is trying not to feel any remorse, but so much emphasis on this one date is beginning to bother him.

Frank gives Crystal a daunting stare and mouths the words, "His father."

"I'm so sorry, Todd." Leaning forward, she places a hand on his knee. "But," she adds gently, "this will be on the test."

Todd closes his eyes briefly to summon up his inner strength, "I know. You're right. We have to study it. I'll be okay." Looking now to Frank, the one he knows is truly worried, he states, "I will...I am...I'll be...I'm fine."

Crystal, sensing the need to move past this part of their review as quickly as possible, pushes on. "So, since...that date...the government put together a lottery for which only registered couples can apply. And they get *hundreds of thousands* of applications!" Crystal is quite exclamatory. "Every year since...five hundred registered couples' names are drawn and awarded the privilege of having a third child. These couples are given extra tax credit for raising a third, and in the odd case, a fourth child. The need to rebuild our population, to maintain a population of ten million as established in our constitution, requires a little levity with the one child law. And, remember, this opportunity is only for registered couples." Giving both boys a stern look, she adds, "I guarantee you this will be on the test. It was part of our required reading." When Todd and Frank flush with shame, Crystal rightly surmises that neither boy bothered to download the text assigned them by their teacher. Sounding more like a parent now than a friend, Crystal lectures the two young men, "You had better take the time to read through that material tonight." Switching smoothly, too smoothly, from lecture mode to teasing, Crystal's green eyes begin to gleam. She has been looking forward to this next topic of study. "So, which of you boys can tell me how a woman might avoid having to raise a child of her own?"

"Easy," Frank chimes. His eyebrows rise and he smirks Crystal's way, pleased at being able to return taunt for taunt. "Expose yourself." Enjoying the moment, he adds, "One of the first things they do to a *strai* at re-ed is sterilization." Any youth exposed as straight either has her tubes tied or, for a young man, a vasectomy. The DNA of an exposed individual is deemed tainted and not worthy of future Hadrian citizens. Clapping his hands triumphantly, Frank rubs them together before shooting an index finger into Crystal's face. "You'd never have to have a baby then!"

"True!" More than irked, Crystal's answer is clipped. "If my question were in reference to the re-ed class, you'd be right, but it wasn't, so you're wrong!" Barging on now to keep Frank from interjecting, she explains, "I'm talking about normal lesbians." Smiling with superiority, she states, "There is a way for a lesbian to avoid raising her own child if she so chooses."

A little irked at Crystal's superior attitude, Frank becomes demanding. "Quit beating around the bush, then. How do you plan to avoid raising a child?"

"The surrogate goddess is free to exempt herself from raising her own child."

"Why?" Todd asks, confused.

"Since a surrogate is asked to give up all but one infant at birth, and psychological studies found it too hard on a woman's psyche to keep one child and give up the rest, a surrogate goddess has the option of not keeping any of the babies she births. Apparently," she explains, "once you've raised a child you have given birth to, it becomes exceedingly difficult for a woman to give up the other children she births for men."

"Makes sense," Todd says.

Although miffed at having to agree with Crystal's reasoning, Frank adds, "That's why most surrogates quit after they birth their own child."

"Meaning she has to be an elder parent! But enough of this," Wanting to avoid having it out again with Frank, Crystal decides it is time to move on. "Next topic." Looking to Todd, her strongest ally in the room, she asks, "What does it mean for a country to be entrapped?"

Leaning back, Todd cradles one knee inside his hands before remarking, "You know, I heard on *Salve!* that nearly two-thirds of the world's remaining countries are entrapped. Eagleton says it won't be long before Hadrian is the only country left that is able to sustain itself."

"That's good, Todd; it shows you understand the concept, but you haven't defined what it means." Looking up, she says, "Frank, you define it."

Frank looks at Todd, trying to remember what he said, lifting the meaning out of context. "It must mean trapped somehow." Looking at Crystal, he says, "Trapped inside their borders, maybe?" Stopping her before she can give him the answer, he adds, "Wait, no. Todd said something about Hadrian being self-sustaining." Looking into Todd's eyes, the answer comes to him. "Maybe a country that is entrapped can't sustain its own people. Too many people and not enough natural resources to keep everyone alive."

"Good, Frank!" Crystal slaps his hand and they grip fingers. They are actually friendly again in this moment.

Looking back into Todd's eyes, Frank asks, "Did you say two-thirds of the world's countries are entrapped?"

"According to Mama Elena, they all are." Crystal once again leaps in with the correct answer. "If what Mama Elena says is right, Hadrian is the only self-sustaining country left on the planet."

"Are you serious?" Todd is shocked.

Crystal adds to the tension. "What's left of Canada can't hold its own, far less the rest of the world. Most countries have collapsed; the world economy is completely shattered." Breathing a sigh of relief, she adds, "Thank all that is gay and glorious we finally cut ourselves off from the rest of the world!" The events of 6-13 created so much fear in Hadrian's citizens that the government cut off all but the most important trade. Although Hadrian continues to export much needed fresh water and grain to the outside world, importation has been radically reduced.

"I know," Todd adds, "There is so little usable land left; most of the soil out there is depleted as a result of overuse and erosion."

"That's exactly what Mama Elena said, Todd." Then turning to Frank with conviction, Crystal says, "You see, Frank, that is why our wall has to be defended, at all cost. If Mama Elena is right and Hadrian is the only sustainable country left, the threat from the outside world is only going to get worse." This sobering thought causes the three to sit in silence, considering what their tour of duty on the wall will be like two short years from now if scholarships are not forthcoming. Even Crystal (who plans to make the military her career) knows their lives will be in danger as long as they remain in the service. Once again, Crystal diverts their attention. "But we digress. Tomorrow's test will be on Hadrian's Procreation Laws and—"

"Wait," Todd cuts her off. "Aren't we missing something?"

"What?" Frank asks. "I thought we covered everything."

"No," Crystal agrees, "Todd's right. We forgot about historical implications—lessons learned from the mistakes of the past. We better go back to the one child law. Thanks for reminding us. So, why was the one child law, first instigated by China in the twentieth century, so unsuccessful?"

Frank doesn't even give Todd a chance to reply. "That's easy. The Chinese were heterosexual. The only guaranteed form of birth control for a heterosexual is abstinence. And nobody," Frank says, looking Todd's way, "likes to abstain from sex." Tapping Todd's knee with his toe, he adds jokingly, "Well, almost nobody."

Todd is annoyed. "Heterosexuality is not why the one child law never worked in China." Conceding slightly, he adds, "It may have been part of the problem, but there was a lot more to it."

"Like what?" Franks asks.

"Cultural stereotypes, boys being more valued than girls," Todd answers. "Families would just keep having babies until they finally gave birth to a little boy!"

Crystal shakes her head in disgust, "Thank Hadrian we don't have that!" Crystal is maddened that her sex has always had to suffer discrimination.

"Homosexuality has certainly made equality between the sexes easier to attain," Frank adds. He and Crystal slap hands and grip fingers.

Suddenly, Todd feels very alone. "You guys make it sound like heterosexual men are to blame for all the world's evils."

"Maybe they are," Frank suggests. "After all," he adds, "the world out there is run by heterosexuals."

"Mostly run by heterosexual men," Crystal adds pointedly.

"By the late twentieth century, homosexual men were beginning to make their mark in politics," Todd counters. "And," he adds to placate Crystal, "there were women leaders, too."

Crystal rolls her eyes. "I can count them all, too, on one hand," she sighs. "That Gandhi woman," tapping her index finger, "Margaret British woman," her middle finger, "some Muslim lady," her third finger.

"Our old country, Canada, had a woman prime minister," Todd reminds her.

"Yeah, right Todd." Crystal is clearly caustic. "And she lasted how long?"

Smirking, Frank adds, "Who even remembers her name?"

"Whereas five out of Hadrian's eight presidents have been women!" Crystal pronounces proudly. Then, feeling sorry for Todd, she leans forward, placing her hand on his. "It might seem like we are blaming everything on the heterosexual male, but seriously Todd, our laws have to be harsh when it comes to heterosexual sex."

"It just seems wrong," Todd mutters. "It feels like we're prejudiced or something."

"We're not prejudiced," says Frank, on the defensive. "We're just realistic. Look at the mess heterosexuals have made of our world."

"But that has nothing to do with sex," Todd replies.

"No," Frank agrees. "But it has to do with who is running everything."

Todd shakes his head. "Is this going to be on the test?" He desperately wants to change the subject.

"No," Crystal answers. "But it does lead us into our next topic: Hadrian's heterosexual law."

"Why is het'ro sex illegal, Todd?" Frank asks pointedly.

Todd talks to the floor. "It is meant for procreation. No one form of birth control invented by man has ever proved a hundred percent effective." Sighing, he admits, "That's all I can remember."

Frank finishes for him. "Heterosexual men are proven to be more violent in nature. A heterosexual male is more likely to commit rape, and it is suggested that heterosexual males are pedophiles."

"I don't believe any of that!" Todd retorts. "That's all subjective. There's no real evidence."

"Frank, Todd's right," says Crystal. "The real reason we abandoned heterosexual sex was to stem the tide of the world's population. We can only guarantee a stable population by combining a homosexual lifestyle and IVF."

"True enough," Frank adds. "But no one can deny the footage taken outside the wall. All those rapes, children beaten. And then, what those murdering bastards did to our female soldiers at the wall."

"What?" Todd shakes his head in ignorance.

Frank sighs. "It happened nearly twenty-five years ago." He shudders. "Dad showed me the vid stream."

Crystal quivers, "Mama Elena showed it to me."

"Why don't they show it to us in school?" Todd asks earnestly.

"Too bloody." "Too brutal." Frank and Crystal's voices overlap.

Crystal finishes, "They left that to the news and parental discretion."

"So, what happened?" Todd asks.

Frank begins. "The heterosexual barbarians broke through the wall. They killed all the male soldiers instantly, but they took their time with the women." Frank pauses for effect. "They raped them first." Another pause ensues, a moment of silence out of respect for the dead. ' One female soldier survived, and only because reinforcements arrived to drive the hordes back into the wastelands. But she had already gone mad. She never did recover."

Trembling at the memory, Crystal adds, "Oh, Todd, it was horrible."

"And it was all done by heterosexual males." Looking down at his friend, Frank states, "They were brutal, Todd; I've never seen anything like it, and I hope I never have to ever again!" Staring intently at Todd, he says, "Heterosexuality has to be banned." Frank is almost a little too emphatic. "Or we will end up just like them." Although he is merely pointing to his wall, Crystal and Todd understand what he really means: "just like those heterosexual bastards outside Hadrian's Wall."

Sensing Todd's discomfort, Crystal leans forward and pats his knee. Todd reacts as if Crystal were a wasp that just stung him. "Don't fucking pity me!" He spits out vehemently, "I'm not one of them!" Leaping to his feet, he points to Frank. "You saw me and Frank kiss."

Crystal is stunned by the violence of his reaction. Frank smiles, slides his personal slate back onto his desk, opens his lap, and pats his right leg. Todd takes the bait and sits down on Frank's lap. Frank immediately closes his legs, hemming Todd in. Desperately needing to prove himself gay, Todd leans in and kisses Frank with fervor. Devouring Todd's lips, Frank uses enough suction to tease Todd's tongue into his mouth. Todd gives in willingly. Frank's heart beats rapidly and his hands begin to roam.

Crystal stands. "All right, enough!" The boys, not listening, continue to kiss feverishly. Frank starts sucking on Todd's neck, hoping to leave a dark red welt as evidence. Feeling out of place, Crystal remarks, "Study session is clearly over; you two will just have to remember the rest of the stuff on your own." Even though she knows she is rambling, Crystal can't seem to stop talking. "I may like watching boys kiss, but this is ridiculous." Turning to face the door, then spinning back again to look at Todd, she says, "I'm not going to stick around to watch this." She crosses quickly to the door. "I'm out of here, guys." Before opening the door, she takes a quick glance back. Neither boy is paying her any mind. "I'm leaving," but still no reply. "Fine." She opens the door. "Bye." It slams shut behind her.

The sound of the door slamming registers in Frank's mind. As much as he is enjoying Todd's fervent attack, a part of him is worried. The way Todd reacted earlier—his forceful claim, "I'm not ready," coupled with the memory of how horribly their last attempt at sex ended, causes Frank to exhibit some restraint. "Todd," he pants out heavily. "You keep this up—" He stops to draw in more of Todd's mouth and flavor. "I won't be able to stop—so." Already Frank is regretting what he is about to say, but his friendship for Todd is stronger even than his sexual urge. "Unless you're really ready," he warns, "you better go." To Frank's infinite displeasure, Todd stands and leaves the room.

* * * * *

Salve!

Fashion Sense
HNN—Melissa Eagleton Reporting

Dressing drag has always been the domain of our men. And why not? Before the days of Hadrian, it was one way to fight back against the mundane fashion men were confined to. This tradition grew out of each man's need to express his inner desires freely in a world determined to clamp down on male expression. Although men are no longer limited in their apparel, the tradition of the drag queen lives on. And why not? Everyone loves a good drag show! Of course, the drag queen still dons the outfit once viewed as the heterosexual female look designed specifically to attract the male sex. No doubt, in a world where a man seducing another man was deemed horrific, this brash and bold expression was both ironic and rebellious! And, of course, Hadrian's favorite, most brash and bold, drag queen is Pepper Tibbits. Pepper, famous for her—sorry, his, feminine beauty and soprano voice, will be performing tonight at Antinous' Bedroom. Pepper's ability to transform from man to woman is truly awe-inspiring and her voice—sorry, he looks so much like a woman—*his* voice is indeed the finest in all of Hadrian.

My little pronoun blip presents a problem faced by some women in Hadrian. Though no one disputes men their right to dress drag, when the transformation is as complete as, say Pepper Tibbits, well then, if such a man is not on stage, how is the average woman to know she is really a he? Honestly, boys, we must be able to differentiate; otherwise, your little game of subterfuge is unfair. There have been complaints about this issue made to Hadrian's Sexual Preference Agency because more than one young woman has been accused of being heterosexual by attempting to seduce a young man dressed in drag. Andrea Hodgson is but one such victim. In her report, she had fallen in love with a woman named Darya, whom she claimed looked 100 percent female. There was absolutely no way you could tell Darya was male. Darya often flirted with Andrea, so the poor woman thought she stood a chance with Darya. When Andrea made her move, though, Darya's delicate soprano voice suddenly dropped down to a baritone, and Darren accused Andrea of being straight. He immediately exposed her to authorities, and had it not been for the excellent skills of defense Lawyer Faial Raboud, Andrea Hodgson, being over twenty-one years of age, would have been exiled. As we all know, the reeducation camps are designed to aid our wayward youth. Once conscious assent has been given to Hadrian's lifestyle, anyone discovered acting upon hetero-sexual tendencies is forced to leave our country and never return! Such was to have been the fate of Andrea Hodgson. Seriously, boys! How can this be fair? Dress in drag and enjoy your tradition, voice your rebellion against the heinous heterosexuals, but please, do not use drag as a weapon against your fellow citizens. Be sure to let the women around you know you are men, and if some poor soul mistakenly assumes you to be female, due to your exceptional talent at presenting your feminine mystique, please kindly inform her of your real sex, and only expose her if she persists in her seductions after your disclosure!

On a brighter note, now that the leaves are starting to change color, it is time to consider new fall fashions. Burnt orange, yellows, and greens are all the rage right now. But not everyone can wear these colors with ease. Fear not; bright colors stay in style year round in Hadrian. Pink and purple are always a hit no matter what time of year. Just remember: never wear white after the long weekend of September. While white works in the summertime, it fails to impress in the fall. That doesn't mean you have to go brown, but it certainly means white should go back inside the closet. Hadrian, let's dress for success, not like a mess.

Vale!

T'Neal

The next morning, Todd walks into his first class to witness Crystal and T'Neal arguing. Aghast he watches them from the other side of the room as if across a vast expanse dividing him from all of humanity. Their voices are loud enough to be heard by everyone, even the kids in the hall. T'Neal looks so short standing next to Crystal—barely 5' 4". Towering over him like she is, Crystal looks like an Amazon ready to impale him. T'Neal is not daunted. Lithe and beautiful, T'Neal has never been insecure. His dark black hair is long and shiny. Although he wears more makeup than the average teenager, his use of cosmetics is tasteful, accenting the slightly oriental lift to his eyes, his sharp cheekbones, and full lush lips. When made up like this, T'Neal goes from being merely good looking to being absolutely gorgeous. Pointing to his neck, he screams, "Are you calling me a liar and a thief?" T'Neal is proud of his new piece of jewelry. Donning the bright purple leather dog collar lets everyone knows he is Frank's boyfriend. A boy has reached the highest pinnacle of teenage hierarchy if he's dating Frank Hunter. T'Neal is now on top, and no one is going to push him down!

"It certainly looks like it to me." Crystal slams each word into T'Neal's chest with her finger.

"And I'm telling you," he spits up, "that Frank gave his collar to me! That I'm his boyfriend! And not some fucking cunt hammer!"

"Todd is not a *strai*!" Crystal yells back. "I saw him and Frank kissing yesterday."

"I was with Frank yesterday!"

"Frank was with me and Todd yesterday afternoon, you lying little piece of shit!"

"I don't care who Frank was with yesterday afternoon. Or what he was doing with the *two of you!* He was *with me* last night!"

Millicent, one of the girls standing behind Crystal, sees Todd leaning against the doorjamb and gasps, "Oh, Crystal, there he is."

Todd shakes his head questioningly. T'Neal spins on his heels to declare, "You are not Frank's boyfriend, *strai*. I am!"

Todd turns white at the accusation. Nobody has ever called him a *strai* to his face before. It doesn't seem to matter that the insult comes coupled with the suggestion that Frank and he are dating.

T'Neal is pleased by the reaction he has coerced out of Todd. Pointing proudly to his neck as evidence, he continues to harangue him. 'He gave me his collar last night." Running his middle finger through the silver ring (ostensibly designed for a dog leash), T'Neal wiggles his shiny purple nails (freshly polished that morning to match his new neckwear) Todd's way. "Did he ever give you his collar? NO!" Todd needs all of his will power not to throw up. Whirling back to face Crystal, T'Neal unhooks his finger and begins stabbing his own chest. "Me! Frank gave it to me." Then pointing toward Todd without even bothering to look his way, he exclaims, "Not him!"

Todd is stunned. "What the fuck?"

As Frank enters the room, he ruffles Todd's hair. He takes no notice of Todd's expression; all his attention is on Todd's turtleneck. Taking a quick peek underneath, he spies the red splotch he left on Todd's neck yesterday afternoon. He chuckles before saying, "Hi." Todd pulls back from him. Frank is again oblivious to Todd's mood as his eyes are now firmly locked on T'Neal. "Hey, baby," he says gaily in greeting, "who's your daddy?"

T'Neal takes a moment to rejoice in front of Crystal before twirling Frank's way, "You are, Frank."

Frank opens his arms. "Then come to Daddy." They kiss and embrace. Crystal blurts out, "Frank, you pig!"

Frank looks up over T'Neal's shoulder. "What the fuck's your problem?"

T'Neal, still snuggled up against Frank's chest, answers, "The stupid cunt says you're dating Todd. She called me a liar and thief for wearing your collar." Frank releases T'Neal, looks slowly and steadily at Crystal, then turns to look at Todd, who is pale and leaning against the doorjamb. Turning back to Crystal, Frank's anger flares. "What the fuck did you say?"

"Don't put this on me, you bastard. Yesterday, you and Todd were making out hot and heavy, and suddenly, T'Neal has your collar. I had to leave your room because the two of you were going at it so hard. It was embarrassing, and then this morning, I see this little prick in that." She points dramatically at the collar around T'Neal's neck. Millicent and the other girls mutter their disapproval of Frank's conduct.

T'Neal chooses to defend Frank. "Well, Todd couldn't have been very good at making out 'hot and heavy' if Frank dumped him so quickly for me. I can't imagine a cunt hammer being able to perform in the way a real man like Frank is used to." Shooting a smug glance Todd's way, he rubs salt in the wound. "That's right, *het'ro*. He picked me, not you."

All Todd can say is "Fuck me" as he stumbles out of the room.

Annoyed, Frank yells at his new boyfriend. "Shut up, T'Neal."

"But Frank—" Poor T'Neal is bewildered. "What did I do wrong?"

"You gloat," Frank says furiously.

T'Neal is offended. "Well, you never told me you and Todd were dating."

"We aren't." Frank pushes T'Neal aside and begins to head toward the door.

Terrified, T'Neal grabs his arm. "Frank, are we still a unit?"

Frank turns around; his anger dissipates at the sight of T'Neal's horrified countenance. Apologetically, he says, "Look, T'Neal; none of this is your fault." He leans in and gives T'Neal a quick kiss. "We're still a unit." Looking past his new boyfriend to Crystal, he adds, "That bitch is spreading rumors is all."

"Rumors are fake," Crystal shoots back. "What I saw yesterday is true!"

Frank glares and points at the woman. "You have no fucking idea what you saw, or what you just did to Todd." He is so angry his face is purple and his fists clench.

At this moment, Ms. Sterne enters the classroom. Ms. Sterne is a no nonsense teacher. She wears a suit jacket, tie, and skirt every day. Her silver hair is cropped short, military style, reminding her students she once made the army her career. She wears no makeup and constantly suffers from dark rings under her eyes. "What is all the swearing and screaming about?" She takes a moment to study Frank's posture. "Frank, you better calm down." When Frank shows signs of releasing tension and his face fades from purple to splotched pink, Ms. Sterne begins to lecture him. "Frank, you know I don't approve of swearing in this classroom."

The presence of his math teacher lets some of the wind out of Frank's sail. "Sorry, Ms. Sterne," Frank mumbles. "It's just that Crystal—" He chooses not to continue.

"Crystal what?" Ms. Sterne asks coldly. Crystal is the woman's niece and clearly Ms. Sterne's favorite. Frank also knows how much the woman detests Todd.

"Nothing," he mutters as he storms out of the room.

"Frank," Ms. Sterne calls out after him, "get back in here! Class is about to start."

"Would you like me to go fetch him?" T'Neal asks half-expectantly.

"No, T'Neal, you sit down. One student missing from class is enough for today. Everyone, sit down." Blinking up her attendance sheet, Ms. Sterne notices one other student missing. "Where is Todd Middleton?" Looking over her glasses and down her nose, she stares at Todd's empty desk. Shaking her head, she mutters loud enough for the class to hear, "I just saw him downstairs. He's not fooling anybody." She blinks Todd Middleton and Frank Hunter absent.

* * * * *

Salve!

Spotlight: The High School Counselor
HNN—Melissa Eagleton Reporting

Today, I wish to offer our wayward youth some advice. Teens, is your biggest fear that you might be heterosexual? Well, don't worry. At the very most, you are a two on the Kinsey scale. That means you just need a little nurturing and more time to find the latent homosexual inside of you. The right man or woman is out there waiting for you. Do not despair. Do not give up hope. Remember, you are not alone. Inside every high school is a loving counselor who is willing to listen to your fears, concerns, and sexual confusion. These men and women have been trained by the finest in education counseling and psychiatry. They know what you are going through, and they can help guide you toward finding your inner homosexual. I know your instincts are to turn to your friends for advice, but they are not always the best ones to guide you. When struggling with sexual confusion, it is essential you turn to trained professionals. Hundreds of teens just like you are questioning who they are, and like you, they too need professional advice. Do not be afraid of your high school counselor; this person is there to help you.

To encourage further both teens and parents to avail themselves of their useful high school counselors, let me tell you about an interview I had with Pan Zhang, Pride High's counselor. According to Pan, he meets with five or six students each year to discuss their heterosexual concerns. Many of these students, he says, come to him in tears and begging for help. The cry he says he most often hears is, "Help me not be straight. I don't want to be a *strai*." It is a heartbreaking plea for aid and one Pan feels requires immediate attention. These youth become Pan's top priority as he takes them under his wing and offers guidance. Parents and a professional psychologist are brought in immediately to help the youth conquer these abhorrent desires. Since these are youth who have never acted on their heterosexual desires, none are sent to reeducation camps except as a last resort. As we all know, the re-education camp is designed to help our active heterosexual youth find his or her latent inner homosexual. Youth who have heterosexual leanings but do not take action are much easier to reclaim through private in home and school measures. Nine times out of ten, Pan says, wayward youth who come forward before acting on their heterosexual impulses can be reclaimed before reeducation camp becomes essential.

Please remember, no high school counselor has ever exposed a youth based solely on a confession of fear. Counselors are there to talk and listen and understand. Rest assured, your high school counselor will guide you in the right direction; help you discover your latent homosexual tendencies. Don't delay. Visit your high school counselor today!

Vale!

Hiding

Frank finds Todd exactly where he expected—behind the back stairwell leading up to the girl's locker room. Ever since Crystal discovered the security camera in this hallway to be broken, it has become Todd's safe place. As he is hidden under the stairs at the very far end, the first indication Frank gets of Todd's presence is a continual banging of bone against brick, punctuated with the repetitive phrasing, "Fuck me."

"Hey, buddy," Frank says as he turns the corner of the stairwell. Bending to fit underneath, he sits down next to Todd.

Todd is no longer hitting his head against the wall. It is now lodged deep between his knees.

"Leave me alone, Frank," Todd mutters.

"Can't do that, buddy," Franks says softly. "Not while you're in this state."

Todd looks up, glaring hate shooting out of red puffy eyes. "You put me here!"

Frank sighs, closes his eyes, and rests his head against the cold brick. "That's not fair, Todd."

"Isn't it?" Todd lashes out all his anger and embarrassment onto Frank.

"I know you don't mean that." Frank hasn't moved. His eyes remain shut, trying to hide the bleeding inside.

"Well, I do!" Todd shouts. Standing now, he walks to the front of the stairwell and sits on the lower steps, using both his back and the stairway to protect him from Frank. He shouts out to the wall in front of him, "Every-thing, Every—Fucking—Thing *is* Your Fault."

Desperately fighting back tears, Frank pleads, "Todd, I came here to help you."

"Help me?" Todd looks up incredulously. Standing, he crosses back behind the stairwell, staring at Frank. "You can't help me! Everything I said would happen is happening. They all think I'm a fucking idiot. That you dumped me—"

Frank shakes his head. "I'm sorry Crystal said that."

"She didn't!" Todd yells in her defense. "Your little boyfriend did!" Ripping at the hair on his head, Todd begins to wail, "How long, Frank? How long after I left you?"

"Todd." Frank finally opens his eyes. They are red and swollen, caused by a combination of anger and hurt. "We're *NOT* dating!"

"I know that!" Todd yells. "But Crystal thought we were, and then you go and hook up with—with—that fucking little tramp! That fucking little tinsel tart."

"Are you jealous?" Frank blurts without thinking.

"I'm not jealous. It's your timing. It's your fucking timing that hurts." Todd slams his back against the sidewall and drops to the floor. His knees knock against Frank's since the two boys are now sitting at right angles. Todd quickly pulls his legs away.

Frank grits his teeth at the gesture. "Todd, I had no idea Crystal was going to say anything. Besides," he adds, almost a little too cruelly, "I wasn't the one who kissed you." Leaning his head back against the wall, he says, "After you left me—what the fuck did you expect?" He looks up at Todd, allowing his tears to flow freely now. "Seriously, Todd, what did you think I was going to do? I really thought we were going somewhere." The pounding of bone against brick recommences, this time much louder, much harder. "Todd, stop that!" When Todd continues his act of self-abuse, Frank grabs him by the head and orders, "Stop that!"

Todd is now mumbling through tears, "He called me a *strai*, Frank. A het'ro! A fucking cunt hammer! To my face!" His hand caresses his forehead. "Oh, Hadrian," he weeps into the palms of his hands. "Help me."

"Todd. Todd," Frank says lovingly. Wishing he could hold Todd, Frank settles for rubbing his hand on his friend's shoulder. "T'Neal was jealous. Nobody believes a jealous man's accusations. His calling you a *strai* is stupid," Frank reasons. "Think about it—he thought you and me were a unit. That's not straight."

Todd's weeping is relentless. "Oh, Hadrian, I'm so sorry, Frank." Todd's voice is barely audible. "It's my fault. It's all my fault." Closing his eyes, desperately needing to confess. "Frank,—" his voice catches. "I think I'm—"

"NO, YOU'RE NOT!" Frank is standing now, towering over Todd. "Don't ever fucking say that!" He pauses to calm himself down. He looks away. For some reason, he can't seem to look at Todd. "I know you're not. Not after yesterday. I felt you. You were hard, man. You were hard when we were going at it."

Todd wants to tell him it was Crystal who did that to him, but he is too afraid. All he can muster is, "Thanks, Frank."

Frank, now squatting down in front of Todd, takes his hands in his. "You're just not ready." He shrugs his shoulders, "So what? Who cares? Just because you don't want sex right now doesn't mean—doesn't mean you're straight—it just means—you're not ready."

But I do want to, Todd laments internally. *Just not with you.*

"What we did yesterday," Frank smiles feebly, "we just did to shut Crystal up." His anger for the girl resurfaces. "She had no right to say those things about you." He spits out his vehemence, "Fucking bitch!"

"She's not a bitch," says Todd, a little too defensively. "I mean, it's not her fault either. It's me." Starting to cry again, he asks, "Oh, Hadrian, Frank. What's going to happen to me?"

"Nothing, Todd. Nothing. I'm here for you. I'm going to help you. I'll do anything. Anything to help you through this."

"Anything?" Todd asks, wiping his nose against his sleeve. "Do you swear—"

Frank answers before Todd can even finish, "I swear."

"Swear on the soul of Hadrian's lover?"

"Yeah," Frank laughs, placing a hand over his heart, "I swear on the soul of Hadrian's lover!"

Suddenly, without thought, Todd blurts out, "I love you, Frank." Recognizing what he just said causes Todd to start crying again. Frank pulls him in for a full embrace, holding Todd between his arms and legs: both boys end up in the fetal position.

"I love you, too, Todd," Frank says as he cradles Todd.

"If it's ever going to be anyone, Frank," Todd blubbers, "it will be you."

"I know. I know. And I'm ready for you. I'm waiting. You and me, Todd," Frank mutters softly. "You and me. But only when you're ready."

"You promise?" Todd is shaking.

"I give you my word." Smiling, envisioning their future, Frank says, "After we graduate. After we register if that's what you'd prefer."

Todd nods. Still shaking, he quivers, "Yeah, after we register." He gives Frank a slight nudge to release him. "I'm okay now. Really." He forces a feeble smile as he wipes his eyes and nose on his sleeve. The two boys separate and once again lean their backs against the cold brick walls.

Even though Todd claims everything is copacetic, Frank still feels the need to lighten the mood. He laughs, reminiscing, "Hey, you remember when you puked down Ms. Singer's shirt?" The mood becomes jocular as both boys collapse into each other in raucous laughter.

"Oh man, she was pissed," Todd sputters out between guffaws. He is forcing out the jocularity, though, since the Ms. Singer experience was the first stirring of Todd's confusion.

"Actually," Frank counters, "she took it amazingly well. You only heard her initial reaction. She saw how sick you were."

This event happened in their grade eight class. Todd hadn't been ill. He had simply awoken that day with a headache caused by too much crying through the night. It always happened near the anniversary of 6-13—the apocalyptic nightmares in which Todd watches his father explode in front of him. After rising, he had asked his Papa Mike for an aspirin and Mike, being hung over, grabbed the wrong bottle. Partying excessively of late (also brought on by the anniversary of his lover's death), Mike had accidently given Todd one of his hallucinogens. By the time Todd got to school, the effects of the drug had started to kick in. Todd was sick and nauseous. His head was swimming; he was even drooling. During math class, Ms. Singer had stood by Todd's desk, helping the student sitting across from Todd. She was bent over, showing the girl how to figure out that day's formula. Ms. Singer was a first year teacher, young, slim, busty, and beautiful. Always delicately dressed in various shades of pink or purple. All the girls were a'titter whenever she was in the room. Her body curves were accented at their best in this position, and her behind was very close to Todd's face. He became transfixed, following her spine from the small of her back down to her buttocks. Reaching up with his hand, he clutched her right buttock. Ms. Singer turned in horror, to stare down at Todd. "Mmm," he whispered, "nice bum." Fortunately for Todd, only Ms. Singer had heard him. More fortunately, she is a very empathetic young woman, seeing before her a very sick young man.

"Oh, you poor dear," ignoring the raucous laughter of the room, Ms. Singer bent down to feel Todd's forehead. Her breasts were now directly in front of his face.

"Boobs," he murmured. Lifting his head to get a better look had caused Todd's stomach to swirl. This, combined with the scent of Ms. Singer's perfume, begot puke. His vomit shot up against the woman's chest. After her initial scream of horror, she placed her hand to her mouth and uttered a soft cry. She looked over to Frank, who was sitting in the desk on the other side of the aisle and asked him if he could carry Todd down to the nurse's office.

Todd had very little memory of those events, but two images remain seared in his brain: Ms. Singer's bum and the beautiful valley between her breasts. He relives, embellishes, upon those images in his fantasies every time he masturbates. He usually emerges from these moments feeling soiled and dirty, as if his mind and body have betrayed him, but he can never seem to stop himself from thinking about her—until lately. For the past year, it has been Crystal, with her burgeoning body, who has replaced Ms. Singer in Todd's imaginings.

"Crystal," Todd mutters.

"What about her?" Frank asks, trying to cover his annoyance. Things are finally feeling good between Todd and him again, so mention of Crystal is likely to resurface the strain.

"You've got to make things right between you," Todd reasons.

"Why?" Frank wants absolutely nothing to do with that girl right now.

"Tryouts for b-ball are in two weeks," Todd reminds him. "If you and Crystal are going to be co-captains, you guys have to work things out."

"They only give co-caps to seniors," Frank replies.

"Not this year," Todd responds. "Coach and I agree you and Crystal are our best."

"You're our best," Frank sputters. It has never dawned on him that he would ever be chosen as a co-cap over Todd.

Todd silences Frank before he can protest further. "Uh, uh, I'm not co-cap material. The coach and I talked about it, and she's right. You garner a lot more respect, so the job lands on your shoulders."

Frank smiles, pleased to have both Todd and the coach's confidence.

Sensing his co-cap role has yet to dawn fully on Frank, Todd warns him, "That means you need to work with Crystal, not against her."

"I can keep the sport and my personal feelings separate," Frank insists.

Todd isn't so sure. "Maybe Crystal can't." Attempting diplomacy, he adds, "Couldn't you put your pride aside and talk things out with her?"

"Only if she's willing to apologize!" Frank isn't feeling very conciliatory. Crystal nearly destroyed his relationship with Todd today.

"How about I talk to her? We're planning on doing some initial training before tryouts." Thinking of ways to make this work, he adds, "Umm, how about you join us after school? We're meeting at three in the small gym. Coach is letting us use it. You could come ten minutes late—give me time to set things right and get her to apologize." Sensing Frank's mistrust, Todd reassures him, "She will; I know she will!"

Frank sighs, pinching the crown of his nose with his fingers. "All right, but only if she apologizes."

"For the team, Frank," Todd reminds him.

"Yes," he replies, "for the team." They slap hands and grip fingers. Before they let go, the bell rings. Frank maintains his grip on Todd's hand and the two boys stand. "We better not miss Mr. Reiner's class. We've got that test to write, remember?"

"Yeah," Todd sighs. He never did any more studying after he left Frank's yesterday. "Let's go."

Together, holding hands, the two boys make their way down the hall toward Mr. Reiner's class. This gentle act does not give Todd any sense of discomfort. It is perfectly natural for two friends, whether of the same or opposite sex, to walk hand-in-hand in Hadrian. If two individuals wish to denote an intimate connection, they will choose to walk with their arms wrapped around each other. Had Frank tried to put his arm around his friend's shoulder or waist, Todd would have balked and walked away from him.

* * * * *

Salve!

Remembering Will Middleton
HNN—Melissa Eagleton Reporting

Yes, folks, it's that time of year again! Hadrian's high schools and colleges are gearing up for b-ball season! Tryouts begin next week when high school and college coaches will be on the lookout for the best possible players for their teams. And speaking of the best of all possible players, who over the age of thirty doesn't remember Will Middleton? Who could forget his graceful presence on the b-ball court during both his high school and college years? While attending Antinous' Pride High, Will Middleton led the Panthers to win at the Quadrants three years in a row and the Nationals two years in a row! Until this past year, when his son joined the team, the Panthers had not been back to the Nationals since Will Middleton graduated. Tall, lithe, muscular, and highly skilled, Will Middleton could dribble, pass, shoot, and always score! High school b-ball was only the beginning for this man. His seven years on Antinous' Centurions were award years, too, leading that team to its only ever seven-year winning streak! I remember his coaches thanking Hadrian profusely for his staying on for both a Master's and Ph.D. in agricultural engineering. Having won both a sports and academic scholarship Will Middleton was eligible to play b-ball his entire uni career. To keep the game fair, no one over twenty-five is allowed on the b-ball court.

Unfortunately, we lost Will Middleton as a result of 6-13. That was a sad day for Hadrian with its poisonous claws digging deep into the hearts of all, killing hundreds of thousands on the day of impact; Will Middleton was one such victim. Although we will never see the likes of Will Middleton again, he did leave Hadrian his legacy, Todd Middleton. Sixteen-year-old Todd Middleton is currently attending Pride High and is, according to Coach Miller, the main reason the Panthers brought home their first Quadrant victory in over ten years. Coach Miller openly admits that Todd

Middleton is the unifying force behind her team. Although Todd is a lot shorter than his father, only 5' 5", whereas Will was 6' 2", Coach Miller says what Todd lacks in height, he makes up for in skill, speed, and spirit. Like his father, Todd Middleton lives and breathes the game.

Todd Middleton is like his father in other respects, too. As was Will Middleton, this boy is humble to the core. When asked whether he plans to win Quadrants for his team again this year, his answer was simple, "No one player wins the game. The Panthers won last year and the Panthers will this year too because our team works together like the gears of a finely tuned machine. I'm only one player—look at Frank Hunter. He's a monster on the court. And I defy anyone to try to get the ball from Crystal Albright once she's got control of it." Well, there you have it, folks. Todd Middleton, like his father before him, is a true team player!

Vale!

B-ball

Crystal is already dressed and ready for pre-practice. She had worn her T-shirt and shorts under her school clothes, so as soon as the last bell rang, all she had to do was run to the small gym and get started. When Todd arrives, she is doing push-ups: flat palm up into a clap. As Todd watches her, he admires her lean muscular physique. Her shorts are snug fitting and her buttocks, clenched tight, show the side indent. Following the line of her leg down to her ankle, he can make out thigh and calf muscle definition. Like her forearms, Crystal's monotone voice, as she drones out the numbers, begins to quiver the closer she gets to her optimum number: fifty. "Wahoo!" Todd cheers as her nose touches the hardwood for that last number. "Way to go, girl. You did it!"

Crystal lies down on her side, smiling triumphantly up at him. *Hadrian's lover, she is beautiful*, Todd's thought flashes impulsively before he has a chance to contain it. He blushes. "Hey, you," Crystal chimes. "Told you I could do it!" She pats the floor in front of her belly.

Todd accepts the invitation and sits cross-legged in front of her. "I told you, you could."

"Frank never believed I could, but you…" She pinches the front of his turtleneck slightly, pulling it forward. Todd suspects she's trying to see whether Frank left his mark, so he tucks his chin to his chest. "But you," she repeats as she lets go of the soft cloth, "you've always believed in me."

"Yeah, Frank," he mutters under his breath.

"Huh?" Crystal leans her head under Todd's and looks up into his eyes. "You want to talk?"

"Yeah." Todd leans back, getting her out of his personal space, and draws his knees up to his chest (feeble protection!). "Yeah," he repeats, his eyes shifting right and left, "we need to talk."

"About Frank?"

"Yeah, Crystal, about Frank."

"He's a dick," Crystal spits out vehemently.

"That's not fair, Crystal. You don't—"

Crystal leans back, unbelieving. "Are you actually defending him? For the love of Hadrian, Todd, he cheated on you!"

Todd looks down to his feet. "He didn't cheat on me."

Crystal sits up and slaps Todd hard on the head, causing him to cry out. "Ow! Damn you, Crystal; that hurt."

"Don't be a driveling fool!" she says, leaning back now. "For Hadrian's sake, Todd, he used you, dumped you, and moved on! How can you possibly not see that?"

Standing just outside the door, Frank sneers. He knew Todd could never convince that girl to apologize. *She is too set, too determined,* he reasons, *to believe I'm wrong!* Leaning back against the old brick wall, Frank closes his eyes, and clenching his fists, fights back the urge to charge into the gym and have it out with her.

Todd looks up, trying to smile, trying not to cry. Crystal feels so much sympathy that her hand goes instinctively to his cheek. He closes his eyes and rests his face against her palm. "It's all right, Todd. I know how you feel. When Millicent dumped me last year, I thought my heart had shattered into a million pieces."

This little piece of intelligence does not help to ease Todd. It angers him enough to embolden him. Looking up, he declares, "Frank did not cheat on me because we are not dating! What we did yesterday—" Todd chokes on his words, giving Crystal the wrong impression. He stops himself because he really doesn't want to talk about what he and Frank did. Sighing, he knows he has to talk about it, though—especially now. The look in Crystal's eyes reflects her realization that he and Frank are more than just friends. "Look," he says sternly. "Frank and I are not dating! We never were dating! When I left him yesterday, I told him it didn't mean anything! In fact," he adds, "we talked about other guys and he confessed to me that he wanted to ask out T'Neal. Said he wasn't sure if T'Neal liked him or not. So," Todd improvises frantically, "I told him not to be crazy. T'Neal was obviously madly in love with him, and all Frank had to do was voc him and they'd be dating like they'd been that way forever." Finally, Todd stops to take a breath.

Frank opens his eyes and smiles. *Nice lie, Todd!* Frank is impressed. He wonders whether he should enter the gym now, but he stops when he hears Crystal react.

"Really, Todd? Really? I don't believe what you and Frank were doing meant absolutely nothing to you."

"Well, it didn't," he insists.

Todd's words sting Frank. He takes a deep breath and readies himself to enter.

"I don't understand guys." Crystal is half-irate, half-befuddled. "That you can actually do stuff like that and then act like you just don't care."

"It's not that big a deal, actually," Todd tries feebly to impress.

Frank snorts, lightly enough not to be heard inside the gym.

"Guys are weird," Crystal says.

"Maybe girls are just too sensitive?"

"Well, I'd rather be too sensitive than kiss and forget the way you two do!"

Feeling some success, Todd asks tentatively, "Would you apologize to Frank, please? I mean, none of this was his fault after all."

Crystal leans back, discontent, battling with indecision in her eyes. "Is that what you want?" Unbelieving, she reiterates, "Really want?"

Todd's sigh of relief is audible even for Frank. "Yes, that's what I want."

"Fine!" Crystal agrees, though somewhat begrudgingly. "I'll apologize."

Frank is impressed. Todd actually managed to bring the girl around.

"Thank you so much, Crystal." In his exuberance, Todd leans forward and kisses her. Quickly sitting back, he apologizes.

"Don't be silly; we're friends." Clearly pleased, Crystal leans forward and returns Todd's kiss. It is soft and sweet and stirring. When she releases him, she leans back. "We're best friends." The rest she whispers. "I always kiss my best friends." A second, more lingering kiss ensues.

When Crystal finally releases his lips, Todd blushes and then turns to look toward the door. Frank, he is certain, is out there. "Okay, Frank. Come in."

Crystal leaps up, stung. "He's been standing out there the whole time?"

Frank walks into the gym. His smile is a little too smug. "Do you have something to say to me, Crystal?"

Scowling, Crystal stands; then she looks down on Todd. "You tricked me!"

Nervous now, Todd feverishly improvises. "I didn't trick you, Crystal. Everything I said is true. I just…I just knew you wouldn't listen if I didn't talk to you first." When all Crystal does is harrumph, Todd presses, "Please, Crystal. You two have to work together, be co-caps. And it wasn't Frank's fault. He didn't dump me like you thought. We were just being a couple of guys acting stupid—I led him on, teased him up, and then left. He calls T'Neal—so what." Talking now to his shoes, he adds, "I don't give a shit; why should you?"

Crystal bends down, squatting in front of Todd. "I saw how you looked this morning." Appraising him now with her eyes, she says, "How you look now. You're upset. You can't deny that."

"Yes, I'm upset!" Todd shouts. "That little fucker called me a *strai*! And, you!" He pounds a finger on her sternum. "You fucking called me one Sunday!"

Crystal blanches. "Todd, I didn't."

Frank leaps in. "Not directly, but you kept insinuating it. That's why he jumped on my lap and started to kiss me. Your suggestion was so fucking blatant even I could see through it. I would have told you to fuck off but for Todd jumping on me like he did." Even though he is still addressing Crystal, Frank smiles down at his friend, "A lot more pleasant than yelling at you."

"Oh, Todd, is that what you thought?" Crystal asks. "That I thought *that* about you?" Todd nods, still staring at his shoes. "I am so sorry." Bending down, she embraces Todd. Crying, she begs for forgiveness.

"Please apologize to Frank," is all Todd can muster.

Crystal looks up. "I'm sorry I misinterpreted you, Frank." After Frank's nod of approval, Crystal turns all of her attention back on Todd. "I'm so sorry you guys thought I was saying that about you. I really am sorry, Todd. Can you ever forgive me?"

"Yeah," he says, looking up finally, wiping his eyes. "We're cool." He extends a hand to Frank, who yanks him up to standing. "All right, you guys," Todd says, clapping his hands together. Trying to put everything behind him, he adds, "Frank and I need to change."

As soon as the two boys return from the boy's locker room, Todd takes control. "Let's get to work."

"What do we do first, Coach?" Frank's attempt at jocularity is feeble, but Todd and Crystal laugh anyway.

"Weaves," Todd pronounces. "Coach, put out a med-ball and a b-ball for us to use. But we should run stairs first."

Both Frank and Crystal groan. "Come on, Todd!" Frank protests.

"Seriously, Todd, stairs? You know Coach only gives us those when she's pissed off." Crystal and Frank form a quick alliance.

"I swear she only does it to make us puke," Frank adds.

"Quit acting like a couple of little babies." Todd is in control. "It's conditioning. Strengthens the thighs on the way up and the calves on the way down. So, quit bitching, kiddies, and let's move." When it comes to b-ball, Todd is cocky and confident. His father taught him the game, and they used to spend hours at the local gym playing one-on-one with Papa Mike on the sidelines, taking turns cheering on one and then the other. Will Middleton played high school and college ball. If Hadrian had had a professional league, Will Middleton would have been an all star. He taught his son everything he knew about the game before his death.

After running stairs, Todd has the three of them weave in and out, up and down the court with the med-ball, making the switch to tossing the b-ball a breeze. When he insists they run lines, Crystal and Frank protest again. "For the love of Hadrian, Todd," Frank growls, "that is so *strai!*"

"Sexual preference has nothing to do with running lines, Frank."

Frank shakes his head in both anger and dismay. "You know I meant stupid."

"Let's go, kiddies," Todd remarks as he heads toward the far end of the gym.

"No Fucking Way!" Crystal's objection is a little over the top, but she takes it even further. "We did stairs—why the hell should we do lines, too?"

"What a couple of whiny little babies," Todd balks. "Line training is different than stairs. With lines, you have to work up instant speed, stop on a dime, and switch directions. It's something you have to be ready to do at any second in the game. Line work is critical! Go sit on the sidelines like a couple of little toddlers, but I'm doing lines." There is no way Frank or Crystal have any intention of letting Todd show them up so they run through the line workout with him. Just to piss them off (a little sadistic punishment perhaps), Todd runs the gym lines three times non-stop. Running weaves is next. First, Todd has them toss the medicine ball back and forth before switching over to the much lighter b-ball. Finally, after thoroughly exhausting his teammates, Todd asks through heavy breaths, "How about a little two-on-one?"

Even two-on-one, Crystal and Frank have to work hard to beat Todd Middleton. He takes after his genetic father in nearly every aspect but height. His genetic mother, whomever she might be, must have come from short stock. That he is only 5' 5" is a hindrance on the b-ball court, but what Todd loses in height, he makes up for with heart and skill! His dribbling technique is flawless and lightning quick! Maneuvering speed is another one of his talents, slipping in between and around the other team like a jackrabbit running from wolves. And his throwing arm is by far the strongest Coach Miller has ever seen! He knows every play in the book by heart and has a keen sense of what other players are going to do by the way they move.

After beating Todd 4-2, Crystal and Frank foolishly gloat. And although it means cleaning the gym before heading out, a condition made by Coach Miller if they are to use the gym on their own time, Todd makes sure to remind his two friends, "Two of you!" Then pointing to his chest with both fingers, "One of me." Topping it off with a smug shrug, he continues, "Just saying! And," he tosses in an extra little jab, "you're both twice my height at that!" They all know he exaggerates now, but the height comment is always enough for Frank and Crystal to look shamefaced and help him clean up the gym (something he never does for them when he wins).

As soon as Todd is out of earshot, Frank confesses his dismay to Crystal. "Why Coach Miller doesn't make him co-cap is beyond me."

Crystal shakes her head in wonder. "Makes no sense to me."

Normally, Frank is offended when someone suggests he is not as good as someone else, but there is no denying that Todd is the real b-ball player at their school. Their team is good; they even won Quadrants last year. But Todd isn't just good; Todd is a player, just like his dad. Coach Miller knows this too. She isn't stupid. She just has good instinct when it comes to teenage dynamics. Frank Hunter is top dog. The kids respond to his word like he was a Hadrian god—almost as if he were Hadrian himself. Todd, though admired for his b-ball skills and always beloved during the season, would never be able to command the same level of respect from his teammates. Coach Miller compensates for this situation by making Todd her unofficial assistant coach. She always discusses tactics with him every game: which way the ball is going and what play would work best. Todd is also first string and on the floor every single game. But at times, the coach keeps him on the bench with her so they can strategize. Todd's father taught him well, and Coach Miller wants to squeeze every bit of information out of Todd while she can. More often than not, these bench times occur when the team is winning. If they ever start to fall behind, though, Todd is always quick to say, "You better put me back in, Coach." Coach Miller never objects. With Todd Middleton on her team, she is confident they will not only win Quadrants again this year, but that they might even take Nationals.

* * * * *

Salve!

The Cattle Ranch Restaurant—Controversial Catering
HNN—Melissa Eagleton Reporting

How many of you, Antinous' citizens, have visited The Cattle Ranch Restaurant? Be honest, now! You may say otherwise, claiming to revile the owners for serving the dreaded red meat—cattle having been a major contributor to global warming due to methane gases as well as the destruction of over two-thirds of the world's rain forests to provide grazing land for these creatures. And then there is all the alarm and apprehension regarding health concerns, red meat being seen as a silent killer. Because trans-fats are consumed when one eats red meat, the danger always exists of increasing bad cholesterol. Stop anyone on the street to ask whether he or she would eat cow meat and the rate of denial is extreme. Now, you may ask, why am I so cynical, suggesting the majority of you are liars when it comes to eating beef—simply drive by The Cattle Ranch Restaurant and see for yourself. Don't be surprised to find a line-up that stretches down the block! Patrons are almost always guaranteed a minimum of an hour wait before getting a table. Although The Cattle Ranch Restaurant has only been open for six months, it has fast become the busiest, most popular eating establishment in all of Antinous. I find this fact amazing considering the extravagant cost. Beef is rare (pun intended), with only one cattle ranch in all of Hadrian. One can expect to spend a minimum of sixty credits for a hamburger deluxe. Salisbury steak with mashed potatoes and gravy (vegetables not included) sells for fifty-five credits, and Hadrian help you if you order veal cutlets, tenderloin, or steak! A fine dining experience for two can easily cost you two hundred credits before coffee and dessert! And yet, The Cattle Ranch Restaurant's popularity continues to grow stronger every day. Face it, Antinous; we like beef!

The décor is reminiscent of the Old West. The owners of both The Cattle Ranch and its namesake restaurant are eager to show how environmentally sound their approach to raising cattle is. In fact, for the sake of our environment, The Cattle Ranch's owners, Jake Matonabee and Jeremy Stoker, use very little modern technology on their ranch. They own no bubble or farm equipment requiring energy to operate. Everything accomplished on this ranch is achieved using manpower and horsepower. As well, recycling is their number one prerogative. Horse and cattle manure is used to keep the soil rich and fertile for growing their family gardens as well as the grass, hay, and oats consumed by their stock.

One cannot help but admire the extent to which these two men go to ensure beef is an environmentally sound part of Hadrian's diet. Clearly, red meat is not for everyday eating, but for that one special night. When you want to impress your date, The Cattle Ranch Restaurant is definitely the place. Go on; it'll help you both feel a little naughty!

Vale!

Family Dinner

Geoffrey and Frank are seated at the kitchen table while Dean organizes the last of their meal. He has prepared tofu chili, green salad, and garlic toast. He places the steaming pot of chili on the table for everyone to help himself. He has prepared each person's salad separately and now places the leafy greens with dried blueberries, almond slices (very hard to find these days being as most nuts are imported), and green onion drizzled over with a Saskatoon berry dressing in front of each man's place. One chair remains empty, though, since Roger is late. After retrieving the garlic toast from the oven and placing it inside a small basket, Dean takes his place beside Geoffrey. "Shall we start without Roger?" he asks Geoffrey.

"We might as well." Geoffrey's sigh is disgruntled. "If we wait any longer, our meal will get cold."

Dean looks across the table to Frank. "Do you know where Roger is?"

Frank merely shakes his head. He has already started digging into the chili, stuffing his mouth with it and some of the garlic toast. After he has swallowed down his first mouthful, he expresses his satisfaction with the meal. "This is really good, Papa Dean."

Geoffrey smiles. "Nice and spicy," he says as he pats Dean's knee.

Dean is pleased. He had never intended to spend his life as a stay-at-home spouse. There was a time when he actually dreamed of becoming a paramedic, nurse, or even a doctor—something in the medical profession. He had even considered becoming a chiropractor at one point, but those dreams ended when he was seventeen. Dean never went to uni, and he was married shortly after his eighteenth birthday. Once he came to terms with the way his life had turned out, though, he had chosen to throw himself into the role wholeheartedly. Teaching the boys hygiene, talking with them, listening, offering advice, helping them with their homework, making sure they ate well, all of these were an enjoyable part of his life. That and having them compliment him on the quality of his cooking gave Dean a sense of pride. With the glowing compliments being showered his way, Dean should have been at his ease, but Roger's empty place bothers him. Blinking as he whispers, "Roger," he waits for his voc to connect to Roger's voc link over the wave. Connection is made. "Roger—Yes, it's me—Where are you?—Really?—Turn your voc cam on—Blink and turn on your camera!—NOW!—Thought so. Say hello to Devon for me. Look around.—I want to see where you are; that's why!—Look around!" Glancing Geoffrey's way, Dean says, "They're at The Cattle Ranch Restaurant." Geoffrey's sigh is almost a growl. "Tell him to bring you home.—Now.—You should have asked us first.—Now, Roger.—I don't care if your food just arrived. You come home now!—I don't care how much it costs. You come home now!" Frank, laughing over his chili, gets a sharp slap from his father. Dean continues relentlessly, "You tell Devon he is to bring you home now or you won't be dating him ever again!" Dean grimaces. Although Roger's voice cannot be heard, what he is saying right now can easily be inferred as very hurtful. "Say whatever you want, but if you are not home in the next ten minutes, I will drive there myself and drag you home.—Good. See you soon." Blinking his eyes, Dean severs his connection with Roger. Turning to Geoffrey, he says, "He'll be home soon."

"The Cattle Ranch Restaurant," Frank says approvingly. "Devon really knows how to woo a guy!"

Dean is not in the mood for any humor. "That's enough out of you. Roger is too young to be dating. He's in way over his head with that boy, Geoffrey. I'm worried about Roger out with the likes of him."

"The likes of him?" Frank is amused.

"Yes," Dean retorts, "the likes of him." Angry he has to explain, "A player," and shaking his head, worried, he clarifies, "That boy is sexually active, and I don't want the likes of him…" Exasperated, Dean closes his eyes and breathes heavily, before concluding, "with our Roger."

"Well," Frank laughs, "you managed to save him from the evil clutches of Devon Rankin for one more night."

Geoffrey intercedes by holding Dean's hand while shushing his son. "That's enough, Frank." In an attempt to soothe his lover, Geoffrey adds, "We'll have a chat with Roger as soon as he gets home." Dean nods, though still disgruntled.

Frank figures the timing is right to share his good news. Papa Dean will definitely revel in what he has to say. "Guess what happened in school today?" Dean is not listening. His eyes are focused on the kitchen entrance as he awaits their prodigal's return. Geoffrey shows enough interest so Frank carries on. "Todd said he loved me today."

Geoffrey laughs. "That's not news, son. We've always known that. Surely you've known all along, too!"

"Well, yeah," Frank agrees, "but the way he said it, well, this time it had meaning." Dean's focus has shifted and his eyes are now locked on Frank with intense interest. Frank smiles. He knew this news would make his Papa Dean happy. "Yeah, he said it's going to be him and me someday. After we graduate, we're going to register. We didn't decide when or anything, just that it's what we both want."

Dean clasps a hand to his mouth and closes his eyes while a few tears shed. Geoffrey reaches over; he runs his hand down Dean's shoulder to his elbow and back up again to hold onto his lover's hand. The two men clasp hands, and Dean, with his free hand, reaches over the table to clasp Frank's.

"Well, this is good news, son," says Geoffrey, approving Frank's choice.

"Oh, Frank," Dean says, "I am so happy."

"Thanks, Dad. Thanks, Papa Dean." Sharing this news with his fathers, feeling the depth of their joy in his future happiness fills Frank with a sense of accomplishment and purpose.

"I always knew Todd was the better choice for you," Geoffrey adds approvingly. "I never did like all the different boys you kept bringing over here. It was obvious you were just biding your time with them."

"Well," Dean says, now standing to clear his bowl from the table, "I, for one, am not going to miss that parade of young men."

Frank is confused. "What do you mean?"

Geoffrey explains, "He just means it will be nice to see you settled with Todd instead of jumping from boyfriend to boyfriend like you've been doing for the past three years."

"But," Frank is a little disconcerted, "Todd and I aren't dating or anything. We've just agreed to commit—"

Dean turns on Frank. "How can you commit to something as important as registration and not be dating? That's marriage, Frank!" Dazed and amazed, Dean just stands there and stares at his son.

"Dean asked you a question, Frank." Geoffrey insists on resolution.

When Frank fails to respond, Dean spins on his heels and throws his porcelain bowl into the sink, shattering it. Shaking in anger, Dean braces against the counter's edge.

"Dean," says Geoffrey, standing and crossing over to his lover. "Calm yourself." Eyeing the broken porcelain in the sink, he becomes critical, "that qualifies as waste." Then he orders, "Clean that up." Dean complies, still shaking with anger. Geoffrey, turning back to Frank, insists, "Explain yourself, son."

"Well—" befuddled, Frank searches his mind for an answer. He has never seen Papa Dean so angry, and it has him baffled. "We tried kissing today, but Todd said he wasn't ready yet so—"

Dean swirls around, "SEX!" Frank's mouth drops open. Geoffrey closes his eyes and shakes his head. "That's it, isn't it?" Dean expostulates. "He's not ready for sex, so you're not going to date him." Dean is snarling now. "Is that all you think defines a relationship between men—SEX? Has it ever occurred to you that maybe, just maybe, two people can spend time together just talking, simply enjoy each other's company, maybe cook a good meal together, shop, or read, or even just watch a vid on the wall screen? Is everything about SEX for you? A man is not just a cock and balls!"

Frank smirks. "'Cock and balls'—good one, Papa Dean."

"What?" Dean, no longer simmering, is boiling over. "Do you think I'm fucking around here? This is no joke!"

Frank is stunned. Never once has he heard either father swear, let alone direct such language at him. Geoffrey, too, is incensed. "ENOUGH!" Gripping Dean's arm, he begins to remonstrate. "Never use that kind of language against our boys!" Dean rips his arm away and turns his back on the scene. Although moved by Dean's words and knowing the truth behind them, Geoffrey is compelled to put an end to this tirade against Frank. Dean's words are by far too descriptive and harsh. "I mean it, Dean. The boy may be wrong," says Geoffrey, throwing Frank a warning glance to let him know he has not been exonerated. "I know you're upset, but that is unacceptable."

Exasperated beyond reason, Dean raises his hands in the air. "I'm sorry I swore, but…" Unable to finish, Dean clasps his hands into fists and releases them without reducing any of the tension. "Fine! You deal with him. I have to get out of here before I break something else." Spinning around, refusing to look at either man, Dean exits the kitchen and storms down the hall to their bedroom.

Geoffrey returns to his chair. "I understand why your Papa is angry, Frank." Sighing, he begins, "I'd like to try to understand—" then squeezes his eyes shut and raises and tightens two open hands, "you."

"Dad," Frank pleads, "Todd doesn't want to date. He says dating means kissing, and kissing means petting, and petting means sex, and he's not ready yet."

Tension begins to release, and although Geoffrey is not entirely satisfied, he can at least understand Todd's perspective. "And you're not willing to date him without all those things?"

"I—" Frank doesn't want to admit his father and Papa Dean are right. "That's not it. Todd really doesn't want to date yet. It's his decision, Dad." Desperate to feel exonerated in his parents' eyes, Frank concludes, "I can't make him date me, can I?"

Geoffrey shakes his head. "No, Frank. I don't suppose you can." *Will Dean understand?* Geoffrey wonders.

Almost as if he can read his father's mind, Frank blurts out, "Papa Dean hates me now, doesn't he?"

"No, son," Geoffrey reassures him. "He's just…upset. And I guess…" he says, not wanting to berate his boy, "I guess he has some right to be."

"Why?" Frank is upset and bewildered.

"Look, Frank." Geoffrey leans forward, elbows on the table, hands clasped, looking over his knuckles at his son. "Papa Dean has more right than I do to lecture you on this subject."

"But, Dad," Frank objects, "he doesn't know what Todd wants." Frustrated, Frank adds, "Todd doesn't know what Todd wants—except that when he's ready, it'll be him and me. And that's enough for me right now. If I push Todd any harder, I'll lose him."

"I understand, son," Geoffrey says, trying to respond judiciously. "But I think Papa Dean understands Todd a lot better than either you or me."

"How? I've known Todd my whole life. We've been best friends since before either of us can remember." Frank is annoyed. He truly believes he is the only one who knows and understands the real Todd Middleton.

"I was your Papa Dean's first and only lover."

"I know," says Frank, getting annoyed. "And I know Todd's still a virgin."

One of the things Frank loves most about Todd is his chaste treasure, waiting to be granted to and enjoyed by only one lover. *I will be that man*, he reassures himself, *but only when Todd's ready!*

"Knowing is one thing, Frank. Understanding what that means to a man is an altogether different matter." Rethinking his strategy, Geoffrey explains, "For some of us, sex comes easy. We're luckier than most, I'd say. But for others, like Todd and Papa Dean, it really does take being in the right moment, in the right place, and with the right person. The building of trust required to bring him to that time and place with you is not so easily acquired as you think." Geoffrey begins rubbing the crown of his nose, unsure whether he is getting through to Frank. "I was a lot like you when I was younger. I dated..." *No*, he reasons, *now is not the time to equivocate.* "I slept with a lot of different men." Waving his hand to silence Frank, sharing an expression that clearly indicates this is no time for pretense, Geoffrey continues, "But that all changed when I met your Papa Dean. You see, I fell in love with him. He was young, frightened, alone, reaching out for help—perhaps, I think, like Todd was reaching out to you, today. Anyway, I was a lot older than you are now. I was twenty-six and you're only sixteen. I guess time and a clearer view of the world gave me a better perspective."

"What do you mean?" Frank asks, truly wanting to understand. He really believes he and Todd are a lot like his dad and Papa Dean.

Geoffrey chooses his words carefully. "Your Papa Dean was only seventeen when I met him, and like Todd, he wasn't ready, but we had this connection."

"Yeah, yeah!" Frank agrees. "That's exactly like Todd and me."

"Perhaps," says Geoffrey, hoping for not *exactly*. "But your Papa Dean came to trust me over time. He knew that for me, he was the only one; that all those other men were behind me. You see, I never lied to Dean. I told him about my past flings."

Frank is getting excited. "Yeah, like Todd knows all about my boyfriends."

"Not quite, son. You see I was ready to give up that life in exchange for a true commitment, a real relationship with Dean. And Dean knew he could trust me." Looking gravely into his son's eyes, he asks, "Is Todd able to say the same about you?"

Frank drops his head in dejection. "No, sir." Looking up, miffed and mystified, he demands, "What is it you and Papa Dean want me to do?"

"I can't answer that, son. Only you can decide what is right for you at this time."

"No, Dad, you have to tell me!"

"As much as you want me to solve this problem for you, I can't. Your life is your own riddle, and only you can puzzle this one out."

"That's no help at all."

"I'm sorry, son. You're only sixteen, I know, and this is quite a heavy burden you have placed on yourself, but you do know the difference between right and wrong. Only you know the depth of your own personal commitment to Todd. Only you know how much you are ready to give of yourself at this time in life." Shaking his head in wonder, he adds, "I doubt I could have given everything to just one man at your age, but then, I'm not you, and you're not me."

"So, you're not going to tell me what to do?"

"No, son. I can't choose your life for you."

Frank is both disappointed and relieved. Without thinking, Frank comes to his decision. "I have a date tonight with T'Neal."

"Do you plan on keeping it?" Geoffrey asks, trying hard to keep judgment out of his voice.

"Yes." After a brief pause, he asks, "May I borrow the bubble?"

Geoffrey looks down at his bowl and picks at the last of the tofu chili. "Do you remember the command code?"

"Yes."

"You going to finish eating?" Frank hasn't touched any of his meal since Dean's outburst.

"No, sir, I'm not hungry."

"All right then," Geoffrey nods. "You can go."

* * * * *

After Frank departs, Geoffrey leaves the table cluttered with the dinner mess and retreats to the master bedroom. As Geoffrey suspected, Dean is sitting on the edge of their bed, slouched over with his head between his hands. Geoffrey's first thought, involuntary but natural, is *I sure married a handsome man.* Dean is tall, thin with a classically sculptured face. His brown curly hair is only now beginning to show the early stages of gray, and unlike for most men, is not thinning away. Before sitting next to Dean,

Geoffrey takes a moment to control his sexual urges. Once in control, he begins lightly to rub Dean's back. "Hey."

"So, what's the verdict?" Dean does not look up, but directs the rhetorical question into his hands.

Instead of responding, Geoffrey wraps his arms around Dean and pulls him in for a hug. "Come here." Dean shudders, trying to hold back tears. "It's all right," Geoffrey replies. "Go ahead and cry. I know this is bringing back a lot of harsh memories."

After a long bout of tears, Dean changes the subject. "Our boys are all that I have."

Geoffrey smiles. "What about me?" he whispers soothingly. "You have me, too."

"That's not what I mean," Dean mutters. "I didn't mean to suggest otherwise; it's just, everything I had ever wanted out of life I couldn't have."

Geoffrey closes his eyes. He knows what Dean is talking about. He often wonders how well he could have coped had he not been allowed to pursue a career in business.

"Our boys are everything to me—my whole life—I love taking care of them—and it is fulfilling, but—I feel so useless sometimes—like I'm losing grip."

"That's because they're growing into men and we can't hold onto them forever," Geoffrey reasons.

"I know. I know. But Roger is still so young. He's only fourteen! That boy only wants one thing from him. And then Frank with Todd—oh, Geoffrey, I'm so worried about Todd. He's too much like his father."

Geoffrey squeezes tighter to help reduce Dean's shaking. "We're watching over him. And after what he said to Frank today, I'm sure he'll be *okay*."

"But not if Frank keeps running around like he does."

"We can't control Frank's choices," says Geoffrey. Dean shudders. "All we can do is give him the best advice possible." Kissing Dean softly on the top of his head, Geoffrey adds, "But yelling at him, suggesting he's… unsavory, swearing like that. You know that doesn't help."

"I'm sorry. I'm sorry I got out of hand down there. I shouldn't have let him get me so angry."

"It isn't Frank that upsets you so much is it?"

"I'm just so worried—I thought, when he said he and Todd were committed, that everything was going to be okay, that Todd was…safe."

"Todd is safe. We'll continue to watch over him. I promise." Geoffrey resumes rocking Dean in his embrace. Soon their lips connect. Knowing what sets his love aflame, Geoffrey reaches up and grasps the thick brown curls at the back of Dean's head—not too rough, but enough to cause a slight twinge of pain. Pulling Dean's head back so his neck arches up, Geoffrey begins to nibble on his Adam's apple. Soon they are lying on the bed. Geoffrey manages to undo Dean's shirt and unbutton his denims, forcing the zipper by pushing his hand into Dean's briefs. Geoffrey hardens as he teases Dean's cock into a similar state. The moan he elicits from Dean is truncated by the sound of the outside door opening. Leaping up instantly, Dean heads for the bedroom door. He offers no apologies for abandoning his lover at such a moment. He merely comments, "Roger's home," as he zips up his jeans, buttons up (and tucks in) his shirt, and exits the room.

Geoffrey groans, but he can't help smiling at Dean's commitment to their boys. Once again, he thinks of how lucky he is to have found a man like Dean Stuttgart to help raise their children and share the rest of his life with. Taking a moment to breathe in the scent of Dean's hair lingering on his fingertips, Geoffrey wonders whether he should head on over to his study and put in a few hours of work. Smiling, he likes the idea that flashes into his head. Undress and wait patiently until Dean comes back to their bed.

* * * * *

Frank and T'Neal are hitting it off hot and heavy. They had met at T'Neal's as both his mothers were working and they would have the place to themselves. T'Neal's room, though much smaller than Frank's, also houses a king-sized bed. T'Neal is lying on his back, showing off his incredible stretch. Being lead cheerleader, T'Neal can not only do the splits front and sideways, but he can, in a standing position, lift his leg up into a point, his knee snug against his ear. Currently T'Neal's exhibition is designed to tease Frank. Although Frank makes every effort to oblige his young lover, he eventually drops to the bed to sulk.

"Ah, honey," T'Neal coos. "It happens to all of us. It's okay. Really." Then squishing up his nose and shaking his face like a little bunny rabbit, he adds mischievously, "We could try a again." When Frank gives no sign of complying, T'Neal rolls onto his side and begins caressing Frank's chest hairs. Feeling incompetent, T'Neal begins to apologize.

"It's not your fault," Frank blurts out, a little too harshly. Unable to say more, all Frank can do is shudder, sigh, and cry.

"I swear, Frank," T'Neal promises. Frank's tears urge tenderness in the young man. "No one at school will ever know." At this moment, Frank doesn't even care. All he really wants is Todd to hold. For the first time in his life, Frank feels like he is being unfaithful. The very act of being with T'Neal is hurtful. He isn't just making love anymore. He is having an affair. Although he doesn't break up with T'Neal, he goes home saddened by this new awareness.

* * * * *

Salve!

Panthers Bring Home the Nationals
HNN—Melissa Eagleton Reporting

It was an exciting afternoon for the Pride Panthers today when they won in the last few seconds of the Championship B-Ball tournament's final game. The Pride Panthers are proud to announce that they will be bringing home the National Cup! Co-caps Frank Hunter and Crystal Albright led their team to this monumental victory with the help of Todd Middleton, son of the late Will Middleton, another Pride Panther National Cup winning phenomenon. It seems the Middleton family is destined to be superstars of the b-ball court. Like his father, Todd Middleton landed the winning basket for his team.

All through the game, the Panthers had trailed the Virginia Wolves by only one point. It wasn't until the last second when Todd Middleton stole the ball from the Wolves co-cap Anita Brown that the tide turned in the Panthers' favor. Weaving in and out of the Wolves team, Todd Middleton passed the ball to Frank Hunter off the right of the court, creating an opening that allowed Todd to hit directly for the basket. Frank Hunter, knowing his teammates' strategy, passed the ball back to Middleton, who successfully loped the ball into the basket just prior to the buzzer going off. The game ended with a 35-34 score in favor of the Panthers. Needless to say, Todd Middleton's team was ecstatic. Co-cap Crystal Albright was the first to plant a kiss on Todd Middleton's lips. Who can blame her with all the excitement of the win? Hers was immediately followed by a kiss from the other co-cap, Frank Hunter. Following the example of their intrepid leaders, all of Todd Middleton's teammates commenced kissing him. When they went through the long line-up of shaking hands with the other team, the Virginia Wolves also acknowledged Todd Middleton's success by each player also giving the young man a kiss. Most of the girls went for his cheek, but none of the guys had any qualms about kissing him on the lips. I don't think anyone has ever been kissed as much as Todd Middleton was this afternoon. When asked about all the kissing, Todd Middleton's only response was to blush a deep crimson. He did, however, speak freely about his hopes for the future. "I'm hoping to get into Antinous Uni. That's where my father went." And like his father, Todd Middleton wants to study bioengineering. "My dad genetically altered the soya bean so we could grow it up here. I want to do the same with rice! If we can grow rice up here," Todd Middleton explains, "then Hadrian will truly be self-sufficient!" Now that is the Hadrian spirit! We need more young men and women like Todd Middleton.

Vale!

Antinous Wants You!

Coach Miller is the only teacher at Pride with whom Todd feels comfort-
able enough to have a heart-to-heart talk. They often speak about b-ball.
Then, the first school day after the Pride Panthers brought home the
National Cup, she seeks him out during lunch in the cafeteria. "Todd," she
chimes. Looking up from his bag lunch, Todd smiles. The coach always
makes him smile. "Would you mind meeting with me after school? I'd like
to ask you a few questions."

"Sure, Coach." Todd's smile widens. He likes that Coach Miller asks
his advice about the game. It makes him feel important, worthwhile. "We
gonna talk about next season?" She raises her eyebrows and smiles. "You'll
see." Punching him playfully in the arm, she adds, "After school, then."

Todd laughs, more than pleased. "Okay, Coach." Frank elbows him,
impressed, and the other boys at the table give nods of approval. B-ball
gives Todd a sense of self-worth and importance he seldom feels in other
aspects of his life.

When Todd enters the gym after school, he spots Coach Miller sitting
on the player's bench, going over plays in her book. Todd crosses over and
sits down next to her. Her welcoming smile is infectious, and soon the two
are laughing without either having said a word yet. Finally, Todd breaks up
the chuckle. "What's up?"

"You are," she replies merrily.

"Huh?" Todd is pleasantly flummoxed.

"I've been waiting all day to tell you." Excitement sparkles in her eyes.

Todd is being lifted into the clouds by her thrill. "What?"

"I got a call last night!"

"Yeah," he giggles. Suspicion tickles.

"From Antinous Uni."

"Antinous Uni?" Too stunned to comprehend, Todd questions, "Already?"

"Already," Coach Miller confirms.

"But, I'm only in grade eleven," a befuddled Todd sputters out.

"They're offering you a full sports scholarship, Todd," Coach Miller reassures him. "Residency, tuition, books, food—everything but spending credit!"

Todd is so excited he leaps up from the bench, shouting, "Wahoo!" Jumping up, he punches the air. Coach Miller, infected by youthful exuberance, bounces up to join him in his victory dance. She picks the boy up in her arms and swings him around in circles as if he were two. When she releases him, they both howl like dogs at the moon. Frank, who has been waiting outside the gym door for Todd (he always thumbs in Todd's fare for transit, so Todd only has to walk to school), pops his head in. "What in Hadrian's name is going on in here?"

As soon as he sees Frank, Todd rushes over to his friend. "Me! Me, Frank! Antinous Uni wants me!" The two boys bend at the knees, both chests thrown back, necks stretching beyond ligament capacity as they howl out joyously. When they finally right themselves, Todd barges on excitedly, "That's my father's old campus!"

"Ha, Ha!" Frank, like Coach Miller before him, lifts Todd high into the air and swings him around in circles. Being stronger and taller than Coach Miller, Frank flies Todd even higher. "Of course they want you!" he bellows in delight. "Who wouldn't want you?"

After Frank finally releases him and a moment passes for his head to stop spinning, Todd asks, "Can I come to your place? I need to talk to Papa Dean. Antinous Uni wants me to graduate this year."

"By all that's gay and glorious," Frank declares, "Todd, that's amazing!"

"I don't know; I don't know," says Todd, so happy he is tripping over his words, speaking so fast he can't seem to say anything. "I don't know if I should. I need to talk to Papa Dean first. I have to ask his advice."

Before Frank can respond in the affirmative, Coach Miller becomes inquisitive. "Papa Dean? Why one of Frank's fathers? Why not your own?" With news like this, Coach Miller would assume the boy would want to rush home and tell his own parents first—*parent*, she reminds herself. Todd's genetic father died eight years ago.

"Ah…" Todd hadn't even considered asking Papa Mike. It wasn't that he didn't love his second father. *I do*, he reminds himself. "It's just that Papa Mike has to work and…ah…" A glimmer of gloom threatens to encroach on Todd's good fortune. "It's not like he can't advise me…" As with every mention of Todd's circumstances, Frank wishes he could get Todd away from Papa Mike, but Todd ardently refuses to abandon the man. "Well, since Dad died, well, Papa Mike, he has to work a lot of overtime—I mean, um…" Todd trails off. It never seems like he can defend Papa Mike in the eyes of others. So few people in Hadrian understand what paucity is really like. It's one thing to see the poverty-stricken hordes outside Hadrian's walls, all evidence of which is photographed from above. It's another thing actually to have to live without. Todd counts himself lucky, though. They may not have all the luxuries like voc implants or fancy clothes, but Papa Mike keeps him fed and clothed, and he has a roof over his head. Over half the world's population lives in squalor facing Nature's elements with no bed, no bread, and no clothes.

At times like this, when it is evident the other person simply cannot comprehend his situation, Todd turns to Frank. Knowing how hard this is for his friend, Frank finishes for Todd. "They just don't have any money, and his Papa Mike works twenty-four seven. Todd can go for weeks without ever seeing his second father. But that's okay because Todd stays with us whenever his Papa Mike has to work excessive overtime. Todd and his Papa Mike know they can depend on us. He's never left out in the cold or anything."

"Oh," Coach Miller says. She raises her palms slightly and gives them a little shake to silence Frank's rambling. She can sense Todd's unease and doesn't want what should otherwise be the happiest moment in this young man's life to be filled with shame and embarrassment. "Well," she says, adeptly changing the subject back to Todd's future success and clapping her hands with forced joviality, "it's good you have Papa Dean to talk with, then." Clasping Todd's shoulders, she adds, "Go ask Papa Dean what he thinks, then, and let me know your decision first thing in the morning."

"Absolutely," Frank concurs exuberantly, determined to recapture their previous moment of glee. "You're coming over to our place, Todd. I'll voc Papa Dean and let him know we're coming. Dad's out of town and Roger's on a date, but the three of us, we're going to have us a celebration dinner!" Then shaking Todd, he adds, "And I don't care what you say! It's going to be The Cattle Ranch Restaurant!" The most expensive place in the city, but Todd does not balk. This news is too good, and he is simply swirling with merriment. As soon as Todd nods his assent, the two boys join hands and race out of the gym, leaving Coach Miller giggling happily.

* * * * *

Papa Dean is thrilled by Todd's news, but his advice is not what Todd or Frank expected. "I think it's wonderful that Antinous Uni wants you to graduate early, Todd. That really speaks highly of you, but are you ready?" Todd is unable to answer because the waiter has just brought out a large tray with three juicy steaks, baked potatoes, and an array of seasoned vegetables. Both Todd and Frank ogle their meals. "All right, boys, it's a steak—not a potential boyfriend."

"This is one potential boyfriend I'd be more than willing to date," Todd pipes up as he begins slicing through the slightly seared meat.

"Me, too," says Frank, also beginning to dig in instantly.

"Okay, Todd," Dean reminds him, "chew your food before swallowing."

"Sorry, sir. It's just so good." A line of steak juice dribbles down his chin. Frank laughs.

Papa Dean leans forward and hands Todd a napkin. "Wipe your chin."

"Yes, sir," Todd laughs.

"You haven't answered my question." After the initial reaction over their meal is done, Dean insists on settling Todd's future.

"Well," Todd begins.

"Finish what's in your mouth first," Dean insists.

"Sorry, sir," Todd says while swallowing. "I'm not sure. My marks are pretty good."

"How good?" Dean inquires.

"I've got a seventy-six average."

"That's not bad, Todd, but," he cautions the youth, "that's not great, either." Considering his words over another mouthful of steak, Dean continues, "Most students who excel a grade have marks in the high nineties." Not wanting to be hurtful, yet remain pragmatic, Dean suggests, "Consider waiting one more year, Todd. If Antinous Uni wants you badly enough to offer up a scholarship a year early, it will wait until you actually graduate."

"But I could go in September. Why wait one more year if I don't have to?"

Frank nods. He thinks Todd should go early. "Why should he pass up such an amazing opportunity?"

Dean passes over his son's comment. "Well, let's think about this. You just turned seventeen a few months ago. You will be younger than everyone on campus. And then, you are going to find uni a lot harder than high school, Todd."

"You didn't go to college," Frank barges in, "so how would you know?"

Frank has no idea how hurtful his comment is. Although Dean had every intention of attending uni, he knew, even having finished high school with a ninety-five average, no uni in Hadrian would accept him. Dean pauses, looks away for a moment, settles his emotions, and starts over. "I saw how much work your father had to put into his final year at Antinous Uni, Frank. And your father, Todd, my best friend, said he had never worked harder in his life than when he was studying agricultural engineering. If you really want to bring in innovations like your father did…" Smiling, he remembers the boy's dream on Hadrian's fiftieth birthday. "Didn't you say you wanted to engineer a new strain of rice, one compatible to Hadrian's climate?"

"Yes, sir." Todd is thrilled that Papa Dean remembers. "That's my dream. And," smiling, remembering his birthday cake, "cocoa beans, too! Then you can bake all the chocolate cake in the world!"

"And you boys can eat it," Dean adds, pleased. "But," he persists, "dreams require hard work. Nothing worthwhile in this life will ever come easy. If you go to uni too soon, before you are really ready, you may find yourself flunking out and the road to your dream caving in underneath you."

Todd, looking down at his plate, studies his steak seriously, as if it held in its red sinews the answer to this daunting question. "Gee, Papa Dean. I never thought about it like that."

"No way!" Frank blurts out. "That is so *strai!*"

"Frank, I told you not to use that expression."

Frank ignores his papa and barges on, "Todd, please don't tell me you are actually considering turning Antinous Uni down?"

"I don't know." Todd is still inspecting his beef. Looking up, he searches deeply into Papa Dean's eyes. This is a man Todd trusts, loves almost as much as he loved his father. *I think I love you even more than Papa Mike.* Smiling, Todd gives the table his answer. "Papa Dean is right. If I can trust anyone's advice, it's yours, Papa Dean. If you think I should wait another year, then that's exactly what I'm going to do."

Frank scowls, but Papa Dean is all smiles. "You've made a wise decision, son."

Frank spits out his dissatisfaction. "If I knew you were going to advise him like this, I would have taken him out for supper all by myself."

"Well, look at the bright side, son," says Dean, patting his boy on the back. "You get to keep Todd around for another year, and then, if you win the academic scholarship, the two of you can start uni together."

That pleasant reality is enough to bring Frank back to rights with Todd's decision so the three men can continue to enjoy their very expensive, very delicious steak dinner.

* * * * *

Salve!

Springtime and Exposure
HNN—Melissa Eagleton Reporting

Parents, I cannot stress enough just how important it is for you to keep a vigilant eye upon your child—especially now that springtime has arrived. I am not sure why it is, but springtime always brings with it sexual awakenings and heightened sexual activity. The lengthening days, stretching the sunlight well into night, seem to have an influence on our passions. As conscious adults, we can control these fevers and channel them appropriately. Our youth, however, need our guidance. If we fail them in their time of need, their hormones will lead them astray. The human sexual need begins to simmer in the springtime and often comes to a boil during the hot summer months. During the fall and winter, attendance at our reeducation camps is minimal. Seldom do we see more than two or three wards during this time of the year, many of these inmates having been exposed during the spring and summer months and simply needing more time to mature, understand, and come to accept Hadrian's ways. Yet, come spring, numbers registered at reeducation camps begin to double, triple, and by summer sometimes have quadrupled. Clearly, we are becoming lapse in our diligence toward guiding and observing the ways of our youth. Teenagers, in particular, are our most vulnerable as they journey on the road of sexual experimentation. Be warned, parents; many of our teenagers are playing with fire as they begin to experiment with heterosexual behaviors. Many teenagers choose to experiment with the opposite sex purely out of the youthful need to rebel; however, others are honestly confused and need our help to understand their contradictory desires. Hadrian's first cornerstone of existence is the key to our country's stability as a homosexual nation dedicated to preserving the balance between humanity and nature. When our children experiment foolishly with heterosexual behaviors, they risk establishing lifelong habits that have historically proven themselves counterproductive to humanity. We all know our planet cannot sustain today's world population. Only Hadrian stands triumphant as a self-sustaining country with natural parks and reserves as well as home to the world's only remaining zoo. Everything we do is to help protect earth's ecological diversity. Over 50 percent of the land within our walls belongs to Mother Earth, and we must fight with every ounce of will to keep the majority of humanity from destroying what little remains of her natural ground. Our chosen values have helped us maintain a stable population. This balance would change if we were to allow our youth to restore heterosexuality as the central means of procreation. Having witnessed how heterosexuals have ruined the world, we must not allow the same to happen here in Hadrian. Parents, please remember, you are on the front lines. It is imperative you help your teenager understand Hadrian's values, not merely for us, but for the future of the human race and the planet earth. You are not just raising your own children; you are raising Hadrian's children. You are raising the future of humanity. And, it is up to you to educate your child, for without your guidance, our children will go astray.

Vale!

Exposure

It starts with the dreaded dance supervision: Ms. Sterne's nightmare. Four times a year, the students of Pride gather in the gymnasium to gyrate and sweat over one another while teachers stand back and watch, keeping an ever vigilant eye open for drug and alcohol use. This special Saturday is an extra duty added to teachers' already hectic schedules: a fifth dance added to the annual school year quota. No one but Ms. Sterne is complaining, though, since this dance is in celebration of Pride High's National B-ball Championship victory! Ms. Sterne, having taught at Pride High long enough, knows only too well the dance supervision drill. and having experienced it at its worst, she uses her seniority to avoid gym, hallway, and bathroom duties. Instead, her job is to sit in Mr. Gavin's office and watch the video surveillance. This duty is considered too dull for other educators, many of whom, unlike Ms. Sterne, actually enjoy hunting down drunk and stoned teenagers. In the early years of her teaching career, Ms. Sterne used to chase down teenagers sodden with alcohol with similar avidity until the day she had to sit with one girl as she puked out vodka and a raspberry-flavored drink into a garbage can. The wretched smell still lingers in Ms. Sterne's memory, and she has sworn never again to suffer the decrepitude of youth. So, for the past fifteen years, Ms. Sterne has volunteered for the long night watch inside the principal's office, entertaining herself with classical music while she watches all security videos. If she spies students attempting to consume illegal substances or making out, she vocs Mr. Gavin, and he or some other unfortunate educator has to deal with the teenage delinquent.

Because tonight's dance is a victory celebration, the anticipated offenses are numerous. Ms. Sterne has already caught a few reprobates while blinking her way through the systems channels. It is purely by happenstance that she discovers maintenance has finally fixed the broken camera behind the stairwell leading up to the girl's locker room. She had put in a work order to have that particular camera fixed over three years ago. As is the case with most school bureaucracy, that particular work order got lost. "Somebody must have found it in a pile of red tape, not too long ago," she mumbles as she switches over to that channel. What Ms. Sterne sees on the security wall screen both shocks and horrifies her. Her niece Crystal is making out with a boy—Todd Middleton. This is no ordinary make-out session either; this is full-out intercourse. Her eyes are riveted to the screen both unable, and desperately wanting, to look away. After her mind has gone through a dizzying array of hateful emotions, she finally feels a slight sense of relief as she remembers Crystal's mothers have been forcing the young woman to take heterosexual birth control to counteract gigantism. "We can thank Hadrian for that much," she grumbles quietly. Suddenly fearing she might not be alone, she unreasonably jumps up to look out the door into the main office. Issuing a staccato sigh of relief, she returns to her chair and locks the door from the inside, so no one will be able to walk in on her unawares.

With some semblance of order to her thoughts, Ms. Sterne ponders the ramifications of Crystal's actions. Contacting Mr. Gavin is out of the question. Crystal Albright is not just any young woman; her mama just happens to be Ms. Sterne's sister, Vice President Elena Styles! Crystal will have to be protected for Elena's sake. But that boy—that boy will pay for what he is doing with Crystal! Unfortunately, dealing with Todd Middleton will have to wait until Monday!

* * * * *

Todd Middleton is late for class, again. He always has trouble getting up in the mornings. He spends too many late hours texting with Frank or Crystal. Having to walk to school makes matters worse since it is a good fifteen-minute hike. As Todd runs, he thanks Hadrian for his recent conditioning due to the recently ended b-ball season. *I should have gone to sleep earlier*, he chastises himself. But even after this bout of self-recrimination, Todd can't help but smile. As his feet crunch through last year's deadfall exposed after the last melt, waiting only for the spring rains to batter it into earth, Todd chuckles. Last night's texts were especially fun since neither

Crystal nor he wanted to let go of the other, texting into the wee hours in an attempt to hold onto the memory of their touch—reminding each other what they had done Saturday night, telling the other what each had especially liked, then both agreeing judiciously to delete all remnants of their text talk before signing off.

As with every other late morning arrival, Todd enters his first class dressed slovenly and with his hair disheveled. Because Papa Mike's work day begins early, before Todd even has to get up, no one is at home to make sure Todd gets up on time, washes, and looks appropriate. Todd, more often than not, is left to his own devices. When late like this, Todd usually just grabs whatever he can find on the floor, not even looking to see whether it's clean, has been ironed, has the appropriate flare, or even matches. Papa Mike is a mechanic (a necessary field but looked down upon due to the straight connotations associated with that line of work, so it is one of the least paid professions). Consequently, he seldom buys Todd new clothes. Most of the clothes Todd wears are hand-me-downs from Mike's closet, which, unfortunately, reflect a more rugged-looking man. When Todd goes to school, he gets teased all the time. These days, though, Todd doesn't care. Nor does he take any of the ribbing seriously anymore, convinced everyone accepts him as gay due to his prized position on the basketball team and his longstanding friendship with Frank Hunter. He is far too popular now that he helped the Panthers bring home the Nationals! That and the offer of a full scholarship to Antinous Uni improved his status considerably among the student body. But Todd is not like the other boys, and although it remains unspoken, there are those, like Ms. Sterne, who have always suspected and now know for sure.

"Late again, Mr. Middleton." Eyeing the young man austerely as he sits in his desk, Ms. Sterne shakes her head disapprovingly, her silver hair flashing like lightning. Looking down on Todd, over her reading glasses, she inquires, "What foolish behavior kept you from getting a good night's sleep?"

Todd smiles sheepishly. "Just on the voc again."

Millicent snickers, "You can't afford a voc!"

"Shut up!" Frank, ever ready to defend Todd, offers up "I gave him one for Hadrian's fiftieth birthday last New Year's Eve." Actually, Frank and Crystal gave Todd a cell phone. T'Neal scowls as soon as he hears Frank confessing to buying Todd such an expensive and elaborate present. Frank growls back in retort, "He's like a brother to me, T'Neal. Get over it!"

"And what's wrong with your parents, Todd?" Millicent asks.

"Millicent, you are so ignorant!" Frank declares. Looking Crystal's way, he wonders why she doesn't say anything in Todd's defense.

Millicent ignores Frank's outburst. "Why won't they buy you one? Are they too cheap?" The class joins Millicent in laughter. Todd leans back in his chair, refusing to hide, pride burning greater than embarrassment.

Ms. Sterne does nothing to stem the tide of mockery. Her eyes squeeze into slits. "Just voc'ing?" There is suspicion in her glare. She eyes him from head to toe, inspecting every inch of his apparel. "Did you take time to look at yourself in the mirror this morning?"

"Ah," Todd shifts his eyes away from her daunting stare, "no, ma'am. I was running late and—"

Tossing up her hands in disgust, she finishes for him. "And you just threw on whatever first came to your face? That's it, right?"

"Ah, yeah." Todd shifts in his seat. Ms. Sterne's interrogation has him sitting on hot coals.

Crossing over to her desk, she retrieves a hand mirror. Flashing it at the young man, she demands, "Look at yourself." Todd obeys. One does not contradict a teacher like Ms. Sterne. "Now what do you see?"

"Ah, messy hair."

"That's right." Waving to the student body, she asks Todd, "Do you see anyone else in this room with messy hair?" Todd is required to swivel in his seat and look at all the other students. Most of them, Frank excluded, are smirking at him. No one laughs outright, though, as Ms. Sterne is clearly livid. Crystal, he notices, is not laughing. She has her head lowered, hiding her face from everyone. *She's not participating in this*, he thinks reassuringly. A little smile blooms on his face. Ms. Sterne notes the subtle intensity of his look and who inspires it. She doesn't bother to wait for a reply. Angered by this slight act of communication on Todd's part, she slams her mirror onto his desk, cracking the glass in the process. Startled, Todd leaps up and turns around in his seat. Ms. Sterne is shaking her head, hands on her hips, condemning him with her eyes.

"I—I—I'm sorry. I—I won't be late tomorrow, I promise. It's just—" He quickly runs his fingers through his hair, getting them caught in the tangle.

"It's not just being late!" Ripping Todd's hand away from his head, taking with it clumps of hair, she barges on. "It's not just your messy hair! It's not just the clothes you wear that reek of *strai*!"

Frank can stand no more. "Ms. Sterne, that's not fair. Todd's not straight. He's gay like the rest of us. It's just—he's just—" He gives Todd an apologetic look, "his Papa Mike—well, he's raising Todd by himself—his partner, Todd's dad, died eight years ago." Todd closes his eyes. He misses his father fiercely.

Ms. Sterne throws Frank a warning glance. "I know his father died. I know his Papa Mike is poor. But Todd is what? Sixteen? Seventeen? He could still go to The Charity Bin and get himself clothes that look less straight!" A few students snicker at this.

"But he's not straight, Ms. Sterne. I know him."

"Do you, Frank?" She glances quickly at Crystal and then sharply at Todd. Todd, fixated on his teacher's eyes, registers this look and cringes. Ms. Sterne, although still addressing Frank, smiles cynically at Todd. "Do you really?" Turning abruptly, Ms. Sterne returns to the front of the class, erases the day's lesson, and begins afresh. "I think this is a good time to review why we formed our good country Hadrian and exercised sexual reformation. Why today, more than ever, we discourage all forms of heterosexual behavior." Turning back to face the class, her eyes shoot down like lightning bolts on Crystal. "Crystal, dear, remind the class why Hadrian chose to enforce a homosexual lifestyle, eradicating heterosexuality."

Crystal's shoulders start to heave. It is evident she is sobbing. Todd instinctively raises his hand to answer for her, the urge to protect her is strong. "Put your hand down, Todd. I specifically asked Crystal." Todd instantly obeys.

After a sniffle, Crystal recites, "Human population has grown to such excess that the earth is overcrowded. There are close to twenty billion people in the world, on a planet that can barely sustain ten billion. The majority of humans living outside Hadrian's wall are starving, dying of disease, scratching out a desperate living."

"That's right." Ms. Sterne shows a little pity toward the girl and continues for her. "These poor unfortunates are still propagating at an exponential rate whereas we in Hadrian do not suffer that problem. Having eliminated heterosexuality from our genetic code our population remains stable, and there are no unwanted pregnancies in Hadrian." Turning to another student, she requests, "April, explain how we have managed to eradicate all unwanted pregnancies in Hadrian?"

"All pregnancies are the result of in vitro fertilization and all insemination is recorded in the Centralized Hospital Records."

Now staring intently at Crystal, Ms. Sterne asks, "What happens to a woman who finds herself pregnant outside the official process? Eduardo?"

"She is immediately tagged as a heterosexual. If under the age of twenty-one, she will receive reeducation. If over the age of consent, she will be exiled."

"Good." Ms. Sterne is pleased at the rote recitation. "But," she continues, "before all that, what happens?" Looking around the room, she selects another boy. "Devon?"

"State officials interrogate her to determine who the father is. The unwanted fetus is aborted and the *strai* gets sent to reeducation." Before speaking again, Devon Rankin raises his hand.

"Yes, Devon?"

"Ms. Sterne," Devon asks cruelly, "can the het'ro woman choose death over exile? If she's over twenty-one, I mean."

"Yes, Devon, she can," Ms. Sterne answers curtly. Turning now to another boy, she requests, "Jared, explain how our lifestyle serves Hadrian."

"Hadrian, unlike the rest of the planet, has a stable human population. Our country never exceeds ten million."

"Excellent!" she replies, nodding approvingly before turning to enquire of another student. "Millicent, how else does Hadrian benefit?"

Millicent responds eagerly, "We have housing for all our citizens, everyone has a job, no one starves, and, unlike the rest of the planet, we have farms where we raise livestock and grow all our own food."

For the first time since Todd entered the room, Ms. Sterne smiles. "Very good, Millicent. Frank, continue."

"What more is there to say?" There is hint of anger in his tone. He knows where this lesson is going and he doesn't like it. *Todd is gay!* he reminds himself. *Why is Ms. Sterne doing this?*

"Plenty, Frank." Ms. Sterne glares at him. Usually a boy or girl showing rebellion during these lessons is instantly tagged as straight, but Ms. Sterne knows, everyone knows, that Frank Hunter is in love with Todd Middleton. *The sooner we get Todd reeducated, the better for you Frank*, she thinks solemnly before answering for him. "Hadrian also has the last five remaining wildlife parks on the planet." Turning again to Devon Rankin, assured of getting the right response from him, she says, "Devon, name them."

"The Wapusk, Caribou, Numaykoos, Amisk, and Sand Lakes."

"Very good," Ms. Sterne congratulates the young man. "And all five preserves help retain but a sampling of the indigenous wildlife."

"We actually have indigenous wildlife," Millicent boasts freely.

"That's right," Ms. Sterne adds. "And no other country can boast that!" Reconsidering, she adds, "Except perhaps for the desert regions." Continuing, she states, "We would never be able to maintain that much free land if our population continued to explode like the rest of the world." Turning back to Crystal, she says, "But, let's return to the topic of Hadrian's sexual preference. We scorn heterosexuality because of the world population explosion. Even so…" She stops and tries to sound pragmatic. "No, let me ask this as a question. Crystal?" The poor girl heaves a sob. She knows why she is being singled out. "Will a woman get pregnant every time she has intercourse with a male?" Although rhetorical, Ms. Sterne expects Crystal to answer her question anyway.

"No, ma'am."

"No, she won't." Unsympathetic, she demands, "Look up when you speak." When Crystal complies, she exposes red, swollen eyes.

Witnessing Crystal's distress causes Todd to drop his head on his desk. *What have I done?*

"Then, tell me, why have we made heterosexual behavior illegal?"

Todd groans, and for a brief moment, he rebels. Lifting his head defiantly, he demands, "Why do we have to take this, again? Everyone knows this. We've been repeating this shit since grade one!"

The class gasps. Ms. Sterne smiles grimly. This is the very sort of outburst she was hoping for from the boy. It is all the justification she needs for exposure. Actually, she has all the evidence necessary for exposure, but she is determined to land all responsibility on Todd's head. As for Crystal, an agreement was made with the girl's mothers to complete reeducation, privately, at home, not in a government camp. "The very fact that you think this is 'shit,' Todd, is the very reason we repeat this lesson year after year." Looking now to the students of her class, Ms. Sterne lectures, "As you are in the most vulnerable years, the time of sexual awakening and experimentation, it is imperative that we revisit our laws and the rationale behind them. Inevitably, it is during the teenage years that exposure occurs." Feigning sadness in her expression, Ms. Sterne now reveals the true intent of this lesson: "Today, students, I must expose among you a male heterosexual." All eyes, following hers, shift wonderingly to Todd.

"You can't mean Todd," one boy pipes up. Devon, on the other hand, feels a sense of relief. He nods his head, no longer feeling inadequate. Looking Todd's way, his facial expression, though suggestive of pity, with his downturned, pierced lips, says, *So that's why you wouldn't let me.*

Frank is so flabbergasted that he can't even speak at first. How did this ever come out in the open? Finding his voice, he practically shouts with exasperation, "Being a two is no crime!"

"No, of course not." Ms. Sterne replies, not too kindly. "But acting on those impulses is criminal."

As this statement begins to register in the students' minds, one boy pipes up, expressing similar confusion, "But he's on the b-ball team," while a second exclaims, "He's our best player!"

Ms. Sterne, having anticipated the majority's claims, reminds the students of sports history. "As we know, homosexuals were considered among the finest of athletes during the time of the first Olympics, but recent history shows otherwise. As many of you may not know, just prior to the sexual reformation, the sports industry used to be heavily dominated by heterosexuals. Many homosexual players were afraid to reveal their preferences due to the degree of prejudice against them. So," she says emphatically, "it is really not so strange that we should find a *strai* on a sports team."

Frank turns to his friend. "Todd, say something!" Desperation and urgency are evident not only in his voice but in his wide open eyes. "Defend yourself." Begging, he cries, "Please!"

"He can't," Ms. Sterne says sharply. Staring down on Todd, who has assumed the position of hiding his head under his arms, she states, "He committed the act Saturday night." The class gasps, even Crystal. "The act itself is on tape, captured by one of the school cameras." Todd groans. He had thought the camera in the back stairwell was broken. *It looks broken.* He feels like crying. Not only has he condemned himself, but he has also exposed the woman he loves. "And that act," Ms. Sterne adds harshly, "was forced upon Crystal!" A chorus of girls gasp and three young women leap out of their desks, rushing to comfort Crystal. A few of the boys utter, "Gross!"

Todd's head shoots up. "What?" He can't believe what he is hearing. He didn't force anything. *Crystal kissed me! She gave me the note!* He can't bring himself to state these thoughts, though.

After a brief moment, attempting to glare Todd back to hiding his face and failing in the attempt, Ms. Sterne turns on Crystal. In a voice like broken glass, she demands, "Right, Crystal?"

Todd's head swivels. He knows he is looking at Crystal, but she is a blur, her image distorted by his tears.

Crystal looks in Todd's direction, her head shaking in contradiction as she sobs out, "Yes, ma'am."

"Tell the class what he did to you."

Todd is stunned. He can't see, only hear, as Crystal's voice echoes over and over, the damning accusation. Suddenly he bursts out, "If there's a video—" but Crystal's wail silences him. Wiping his eyes, he gives Crystal a closer inspection. She has a black eye. Someone has thrashed her good. *To make it look more like rape, no doubt*, he reasons. *All the blame must rest on me.* Todd hides his face in his hands.

Now yelling, almost hysterical, Ms. Sterne declares, "I know it was forced; just look at her bruises. But Crystal refuses to accuse you. She says reeducation camp would be better." Turning away in disgust and then swinging back around on her heels, she shouts in Todd's ear, "As far as I'm concerned, reeducation is too good for the likes of you!" Now hateful, her voice dripping venom, she says, "You deserve the death sentence." The class gasps in horror. Todd turns a ghostly white! "That's right, children," Ms. Sterne states emphatically, now wanting solely to intimidate and terrify the lad, "When a straight man rapes a woman in Hadrian, that act is punishable by death!" Staring hard at the pale youth shirking from her glare, Ms. Sterne punches hard. "Regardless of age!" Once again, Ms. Sterne reduces Todd to tears. Sensing that the boy is crumpled and beaten, she demands, "Do you admit to having—" She pauses briefly, choosing her words carefully, "to being an active heterosexual?" Todd shakes. "Do. You. Admit. To. Being. An. Active. Heterosexual?"

Shivering, Todd answers, "Yes."

Straightening, Ms. Sterne towers triumphantly over the crumpled youth. "And now," in a voice dripping with satisfaction, she says, "you can go down to the office where your Papa Mike is waiting to retrieve you." Todd looks up, gasping and pale. Ever since Todd's father died, Papa Mike has barely acknowledged his existence. Todd has no idea how the man will react. Although she doesn't say it, you can see in Ms. Sterne's eyes that she hopes the man will beat Todd senseless.

* * * * *

Papa Mike does not beat Todd. He doesn't even look at him. They drive in silence. They do not go home. Instead, Papa Mike drops Todd off at Riverside Park. Numerous thoughts race through Mike Fulton's brain. *Thank Hadrian, he doesn't bear my name or genes.* He wants to call Todd a fool for getting caught. Tell him he's a shame to his father's good name. But he doesn't. The only words he utters the entire time are when he stops the bubble and motions for Todd to get out: "Never come near me again." The harsh whisper lashes Todd's heart.

Frightened and abandoned, not knowing what else to do, Todd texts Frank and asks whether he can spend the night at his house.

Frank texts back, "Yes. I'll come get you."

* * * * *

Salve!

Another Brutal Attack
HNN—Melissa Eagleton Reporting

Another brutal attack, this time against the Mid-West Wall, has been reported. This morning, barely an hour prior to the change of guards, over one hundred outsiders drove at top speed in armored cars and tanks with the clear intention of ramming through Hadrian's walls. The hour of the attack was clearly meant to be strategic, our soldiers being exhausted after a full night guarding the wall. Although tired, our brave men and women were not lax in their response time. They moved swiftly in our people's defense. The alarm was rung as soon as the first vehicle was seen racing toward our border. Bazookas—or as our soldiers like to refer to them, stovepipes—were immediately used to counter the onslaught of tanks. That many of the front-line vehicles were suicide assaults with explosive devices meant to bring down the wall was evidenced when the first explosion occurred. "The explosion that occurred when our first missile detonated was greater than that particular device was capable of." It was at that moment that Major Janice Cardinal knew drastic measures needed to be taken. "There were far too many tanks heading toward our border," the major was reported as saying, "for the one-man portable recoil rocket launchers to have the necessary impact. And those racing toward our wall were clearly heavily loaded with explosives." With no time to consider options, the major immediately determined that the only way to counter this attack was to bring out incendiary weapons. Major Cardinal, notorious for her military discipline, insists all planes be manned and ready whenever an alert is given. All pilots and bomber crews were at the ready seconds after the attack began. Thus, Major Cardinal was in position to launch an immediate counterattack and white phosphorous bombs were dropped on the attacking hordes, wiping out their entire contingent. Although it is not customary to use incendiary weapons during a battle,

Lieutenant-General Birtwistle commented that these weapons are only utilized when all other attempts at aborting an enemy attack have failed. This particular attack against the wall was so sudden, and the barrage so imminent, that precious little time was available for debate. In the case of this morning's attack, however, Lieutenant-General Birtwistle is confident that the major in charge made the right decision. "The enemy was racing toward us at such high speeds there was little time to deliberate. Had Major Cardinal not issued the order when she had, the wall surely would have been breached." Major Cardinal justified her action, by saying, "The catastrophic explosions that occurred every time one of our missiles struck an oncoming vehicle was evidence enough. If even one of those tanks had hit our wall, it would have come crumbling down. I could not allow that to happen!" We can all thank Hadrian for Major Janice Cardinal's fast thinking and instantaneous leap into action.

This latest attack is yet again a reminder of what we have achieved in Hadrian and how much we have to lose if the hordes outside our walls ever break through. Every Hadrian citizen is employed, clothed, fed, and sheltered. Without the burden of overpopulation, we are able to ensure a healthy lifestyle for all our citizens. Anyone who cannot afford luxuries like voc implants can still have a government installed wall screen with access to the central wave at minimal cost. No one is disconnected, and no one goes without in Hadrian.

And yet, our greatest achievements are still being threatened by the desperate and jealous hordes outside our wall. As much as we may pity their misfortunes, we cannot allow any man, woman, or child to cross our borders. The purity of humanity is in our hands. The cleansing of the planet is a responsibility we have chosen. To allow members of the outside races to fester inside our walls would be to destroy everything Hadrian has so far accomplished. We will never allow that to happen. As a result of our refusal to allow the plague-ridden, overpopulated masses to enter our borders, we are constantly battling back starvation-crazed hordes, slamming against our walls like tempest tossed waves.

Hadrian's military is sending out the call to all of Hadrian's citizens between the ages of twenty-two and forty to reenlist and help reinforce our strength against the heterosexual hordes constantly ramming our walls. The future of Hadrian as a self-sustaining country committed to protecting the planet and the human species is critical! We must triple our military strength and reinforce and continue building our border wall. Hadrian's wall needs to be deeper, taller, and to span our entire country's edge. Seriously consider rejoining our forces to help Hadrian's military continue successfully to thrust back those who are determined to steal and destroy all that we have accomplished.

Vale!

Taming the Strai

As Frank prepares to go fetch Todd, he realizes it is fortuitous for him that his fathers are going out. Monday night is their date night. Geoffrey proposed this standing date when Dean and he were first wed. He believed, quite rightly, that in order to develop and maintain a close loving relationship with Dean, they needed to commit to spending time together on a romantic level. Thus, for over twenty years, the two men have dedicated their Monday nights to their mutual amusement.

Usually looking forward to their private night out, on this particular Monday, Dean is far too disgruntled to enjoy the upcoming dinner and a movie. Frank's voc call this morning about Todd was worrisome. Dean had called Geoffrey on the instant and insisted he come home from work. Dean had rightly judged Todd's circumstances to be an emergency.

Once Frank had gotten home from school and Geoffrey had arrived, the three men had gathered in the kitchen to discuss the situation. Frank had many questions about what might happen to Todd, which led to Dean and Geoffrey revealing Dean's family history, sparing nothing, to Frank. Shocked, Frank learned that he is, by his genetic father's marriage, a member of a founding family. Papa Dean was a Stuttgart. *Was* being the operative word. What should have been an illustrious status is, in their circumstances, a more than frowned upon association. To reveal Papa Dean's founding family genes would cause the Hunters to be shunned by all good society. In fact, sometime after Dean's exposure, his father had put into words the machinations of a story depicting the tragic death of his son in a devastating accident. According to the police report, Dean Stuttgart had been driving his father's bubble when he hit a moose. Everyone knows the bubble vehicle is fragile compared with the older car models that once pumped toxic carbon dioxide into the air, contributing to global warming.

It was deemed an acceptable risk to drive the smaller, lighter electric vehicle, even though crashes were far more lethal. It actually encouraged safe driving. As the story goes, Dean Stuttgart chose to take a Sunday drive into the forest just north of Antinous city. There he rammed a moose, dying on impact. There was to be no challenging this story and Dean never tried. The death of his only son opened the door for Dean's father to apply for another child. Dean has a genetic little sister he has never met—whose name he has never even known.

Just as Dean and Geoffrey finished telling Frank this information, Frank's voc had received the call from Todd that Mike had abandoned him at Riverside Park. Dean had wanted to be the one to collect the boy, but both Frank and Geoffrey insisted Frank go. Since Frank was the one Todd had called, Frank was the one to go get him. Geoffrey and Dean argued heatedly over this, but Frank and Geoffrey eventually won.

Frank, able to sense his Papa Dean's dissatisfaction, reiterated his position, "What Todd needs right now is a friend." Unable to sway Papa Dean, he tried again, "I need to talk to him alone if I'm going to make him realize he and I need to start dating right now."

"You don't even really have to date, Frank," Dean tried hard to explain. "People just need to believe the two of you are a unit." Worried that Todd is too unstable right now for a lover's bond, Dean strongly encourages Frank only to offer up a pretend relationship. "Just act it, like Will and I used to."

Yeah, Frank muses, now getting ready to leave, *and that really helped you, didn't it?*

"Let him know," Dean persists. "Let him know you are there for him, will wait for him, won't abandon him. Make sure he understands we won't ever abandon him." When he turns his bleary eyes to Geoffrey, he is startled at the sight of the man standing stock still, seemingly so impenetrable, resistant to all pity. Dean pleads uselessly, "Geoffrey, please, what the boy needs right now is adult guidance."

Geoffrey is not a cruel man so it pains him to see Dean in such agony, but he also knows that Dean is in no condition to help Todd. He has a lot of calming down to do because his own demons have resurfaced. Dean is Geoffrey's top priority. "Too many haunting memories have surfaced. I need to help you settle those first." Geoffrey truly believes it is in Todd's best interest to let Frank fetch him. "Frank is correct, Dean. If the boys are to pretend to be lovers—"

"They don't even have to pretend to be lovers," Dean cuts him off. "They just have to act like they are dating."

"No, Dean," Geoffrey counters, shaking his head sadly.

"Yes, we do Papa Dean," Frank insists. "You know we do."

Reasserting Frank's position, Geoffrey states, "Todd confessed to being sexually active. If Frank is going to convince others he has tamed him, people are going to have to believe they had sex." Sighing, wishing there were another way around this, he adds, "To do that, the two boys will need to be alone." Before Dean can protest, Geoffrey silences him. "Dean, enough." Geoffrey's tone is stern. He is in command mode and there is no reversing him. "The boys need privacy in order to talk this through. We are going to give them that necessary time alone." Gripping Dean's arm, he states, "Both boys are mature enough, close enough to being men that they can deal with this, and will deal with this, a lot more effectively alone. You and I will only muddle matters." Sighing, he adds, "Besides, you are in no condition right now to offer anyone moral support." Then conceding slightly, he concludes, "We won't stay out long. We'll just go for dinner and be home by seven."

"Make it eight," Frank says. He knows what he needs to do, and he wants more time than their being home by seven will allow.

"All right," Dean reluctantly agrees. "But only dinner and," staring defiantly at Frank, he states, "we'll be back by seven."

"Absolutely," Geoffrey nods, but as soon as Dean's back is turned, he reassures Frank by mouthing, "eight."

Frank is relieved when the two men finally leave. Todd and he need privacy all right. Frank knows he and Todd need to do more than pretend.

* * * * *

As Frank emerges from his bedroom, he forms a wry, telling grin on his face. Devon and Roger are in the living room, as expected, necking on the couch. Roger had promised to invite his boyfriend over so Frank could prove unequivocally that Todd was no longer a *strai*. Frank knows they need a witness beyond himself. There is simply too much evidence against his best friend. And since they are best friends, everyone expects Frank to lie. He stood up for Todd in class today, before Ms. Sterne exposed him, Crystal denounced him, and Todd foolishly admitted to being straight!

Todd straight! It was inconceivable, but there you have it! *Really, Frank?* he berates himself. *Inconceivable? When you've known all along?* Frank shudders; everything he's ever been taught about straight males is heinous: pedophiles, rapists, chauvinists, and all stupid, smelly, messy, dirty pigs! None of that describes Todd. *Okay*, he admits, *he isn't the neatest individual.* The fact is Todd's clothes are seldom tidy. *But he's poor,* Frank insists. *We can excuse him that*—but not anymore. Not after his admission in class. *Even so,* Frank reasons, *Todd is no rapist! There is no way he raped Crystal! No way!* But not even Frank can deny Todd's declaration, and that confession is all the damning evidence anyone needs. Ms. Sterne has even suggested Todd deserves the death penalty. The memory of her implied threat causes Frank to wince. *Again,* he asks, *why do they have to be so cruel about exposure?* But he knows why. It really is the only way to warn *strais*. *Straight men, especially,* he reasons, *are difficult to tame.* Feeling a surge of pride, yet still rueful, he thinks, *Todd may have been a strai, but not anymore. I've made sure of that!*

As soon as Frank walks into the living room, Devon begins admiring Frank's physique. Frank has purposely left off his shirt, and he only begins zipping up his jeans after he enters the living room. Everything about him from tousled hair, to his bruised and sweaty chest, to being half-dressed has to suggest sex. Everyone must know—no *believe*—that what just happened really *did* happen. Todd is a confessed *strai*, but Frank means for everyone to understand that he is just confused! Still, this is not going to be easy. Todd is definitely not what everyone perceives to be Frank's type. Frank only dates the more effeminate boys—boys he can easily manipulate— boys who like to pamper him and treat him like a god. That is definitely not Todd. Todd, like Frank, has the bearing of the alpha male—especially on the b-ball court. Unfortunately, Todd never dated anyone but Devon. And Devon certainly didn't help matters when he announced that Todd's exposure explains everything. He added even more damaging evidence when he said Todd never once initiated and was always the first to pull back from a kiss. *That's Todd's biggest problem,* Frank surmises. Everyone expects him to be the aggressor, but he has never once approached any boy on campus. Everyone now believes that if Devon hadn't approached Todd, he never would have dated anyone. Some even say he used Devon to throw people off the scent of his being a *strai*. Even that Todd is the official star of the b-ball team holds no sway in his favor anymore, not after what Ms. Sterne said about sports and heterosexuals in class. Oddly enough, Frank muses over Todd's position on the team. *He should have been co-cap, not me*, but Frank surmises that his being the taller and stronger got him the position. There is no doubt about it; Frank is definitely stronger than Todd, height and extra weight being his advantage. *Thank Hadrian for that*, Frank muses as he studies the raw skin of his knuckles. Licking off the blood, he remembers how hard Todd fought. It was not what Frank wanted, but Todd had to be subdued. *It had to happen*, he reminds himself again, though it feels more like a reprimand than justification.

Roger smiles. He knew if anyone could tame a *strai*, it was Frank. "So you guys did it?" he asks half-expectant, half-hopeful. Roger likes Todd, seeing him as a part of their family. The last thing he wants is to see Todd sent away for reeducation. Frank grins slyly. He is wearing his "I just got laid look." Devon is not falling for it, though. Todd's exposure today redeems for him what he had seen as his own personal failure. Besides, Todd Middleton had kissed a girl, had straight sex with that girl—Ms. Sterne even implied rape. *No*, he says silently, *Todd is straight, and as far as I'm concerned, there is no taming that kind of man. Besides*, he reaffirms, *if I couldn't get him to do it, no one can!* Turning to Roger, he laughs, "You don't really believe they did it, do you?" Scorn ripples across his face. Looking back at Frank, he says, "You can't possibly expect people to fall for this? No one is ever going to believe Middleton went down for you. He's a *strai*—a fucking little cunt hammer. And, if what Ms. Sterne suggests is true—a rapist!"

"Todd never raped anyone!"

Ignoring Frank's outburst, spitting out derision, Devon exclaims, "They ought to lock the cunt hammer away!" Amused by his own consideration, he adds, "Frankly, Frank, I don't know why they don't just castrate the bastard."

Roger, caving to Devon's perspective, begins to worry. "Did it really happen?" His eyes squint as his shoulders shrug upwards in quandary.

Frank grimaces; he had expected as much, which is why he had insisted on making it really happen, and not just be a pretend act like Todd had begged him. Even so, he couldn't help feeling betrayed. *Roger could at least back me*, he thinks grimly. Crossing over to the couch, he sits next to Devon. The two men stare down until Devon looks away. Then Frank calls out, "Todd!" When there is no response, he looks toward the hallway leading to his bedroom. "Todd," he says more urgently, a hint of anger in his voice, "get out here." Devon and Roger stare expectantly at the hallway.

A smothered cry emerges from Frank's room. "Now, baby," Frank states emphatically. "Your daddy's calling, so come!" Another moan is emitted prior to the subtle sound of a door handle turning, followed by the slight creak of a door beginning to open. Frank offers up his grin to Devon and Roger. "Did you put on the clothes I bought you?" A stifled cry replies. "Come on, baby; I want to see you dressed nice." The door closes with barely a sound. Devon and Roger look at each other curiously. "I've given him a new look," Frank replies matter-of-factly.

Actually, the impromptu shopping spree was in reaction to Ms. Sterne's initial attack on Todd's appearance. The whole time Frank was picking out clothes and throwing them Todd's way, Todd kept throwing them back swearing, "There is no way I am ever going to wear these things!"

Frank whirled on him, insisting, "We have to convince people you really are gay!" Frank won that war, too. "You are going to look like one of my boys and that's that!" There was no more discussion to be had. Frank bought the clothes, and then, as soon as they got home, dragged Todd into his bedroom.

Once again, Devon and Roger stare intently at the hallway, listening to the muffled sounds of shuffling from inside Frank's bedroom. Soon enough, the sounds of a moving door handle followed by the opening of the door can be heard—a little less faint than last time. *Good, he's starting to accept,* Frank muses. The shadow of a body walking tight against the wall appears. It is as if Todd is trying to push himself deep inside the wood in a desperate attempt to escape. Slowly, Todd comes out. He can't enter the living room, though, and stays glued to the corner where the hall and the living room meet. The black velvet wallpaper, though elegant in design, feels repulsive against his skin. Frank has him wearing a tight short-sleeve hot pink T-shirt accenting Todd's muscular torso. Frank wanted this effect. It would make Devon drool, and anyone who could make Devon hard was someone of whom he would approve. Todd's sudden transformation into a meek demeanor is very erotic.

"Wow," Devon mutters appreciatively. "You can really make out his package in those jeans." Todd's hands instinctively drop down to hide himself. Frank also insisted Todd wear a pair of skin-tight jeans with stovepipe pant legs, unnecessarily held up with a hot pink belt to match the T-shirt. To ensure his dominance, the only way people would believe Todd tamed, Frank had also demanded Todd wear Teika's dog collar made of thick purple leather with a huge ring for a leash. All of Frank's boyfriends have worn this collar, even at school. It is like being given his ring or sweater, and it lets everyone else know he, Frank Hunter, is the sole proprietor of this boy.

Frank leans back casually, opens his lap slightly, and pats his left knee. "Ignore him, Todd. Come to Daddy," he invites seductively, patting his knee a second time. Every word, every action, every physical image must literally reek of sex if he is going to save his best friend. "Come on, Todd," Frank urges. It is hard for Todd to move, but he manages to release his grip on the wall. Walking is uncomfortable as the tight jeans chafe against him.

"Parade for us," Devon taunts. "Get him to spin, Frank." Devon is enjoying the show. Todd can't even look up to beg Frank not to make him spin around. He just stops and shakes in the center of the room.

"Shut up," Frank orders Devon. "Don't worry, baby," he coos softly. "Just come to Daddy." Todd slowly begins his death march. "There's Daddy's boy." With Todd standing in front of him, still sheltering himself with his hands, Frank gently turns him around and then roughly pulls him down on his lap. Todd winces. *They have to know he's in pain*, Frank reminds himself. *"I must be cruel only to be kind," as Shakespeare aptly put it.* Frank hates treating Todd so roughly, but word has to get out that Todd has been tamed—that he is no longer straight—that Frank has made him one of them. Tears bloom in Todd's eyes—tears he has been fighting back since he managed to stop the flow after what Frank did to him. Frank gently wipes the tears from Todd's face, caressing the bruises and his cut, now swelling, lower lip. "Who's your daddy?" Frank asks in a teasing manner. Frank is now caressing Todd's legs, squeezing them periodically, and allowing his fingers slowly to climb higher. One of Todd's hands flaps like a bird with a broken wing in an attempt to arrest Frank's movements. Frank grips Todd's hand tightly in his, hard enough to indent Todd's fingernails into his palm. Lowering his voice so only Todd can hear, Frank whispers, "Answer me."

Todd mumbles, "You."

Frank's whisper becomes threatening, "Louder!"

Obeying, Todd replies, "You, Frank!" a little too loudly, enough to cause raucous laughter from Devon and Roger.

Even Frank joins in with a chuckle as he pats Todd's head. "Good boy." Frank kisses Todd as a reward.

Sneering, Devon remains skeptical. "Listen, Frank; play this up all you want, but nobody's going to believe you planked this cunt-hammer."

After glaring Devon's way, Frank turns to look at him. Todd knows exactly what Frank is thinking: *You have to kiss me.* Leaning in to initiate Todd is startled when Frank stops him. "Ah, ah, ah, you didn't ask "

A shudder precedes Todd's request. "Frank, kiss me."

Slipping one finger into the collar ring, Frank tugs slightly, reminding Todd of his new place in the pecking order. "Say, Frank, may I kiss you, please." Todd quakes. Unrelenting, Frank warns, "I won't do it if you don't beg," pulling a little harder on the collar ring.

"Frank," says Todd. Although it is a low whisper, Frank knows Devon can still hear, "may I please kiss you."

Looking straight at Devon, Frank replies, "Of course you may, baby." Turning back to look at Todd, Frank waits for him to initiate. When their lips unite Devon and Roger slap hands and clasp fingers.

"By all that's gay and glorious," Devon chimes, "I think you've really done it."

Roger, congratulates his brother, "Good work, Frank!"

"Now get the fuck out of here," Frank orders before he kisses the top of Todd's head. "My boy and I want a little alone time."

Devon and Roger leave quickly, but not before Devon can call out one last derogatory remark. "One minute a cunt hammer, and in the very next, Frank's buggering board." Chuckling, he adds as he exits, "Impressive."

"Devon, you can be so crude sometimes," Roger says as he pulls his mate through the front door.

Frank waits a few moments after the front door closes behind the two young men. Expecting Todd to dart away any moment, he wraps his legs and arms tightly around his friend. He wants so badly to cry, to beg forgiveness, but he knows he can't. If he is to tame Todd successfully, he can't back down. Not now. Not ever. Papa Dean taught him that. Frank explains, "We had to do it, Todd; you know that, don't you?" His muscles begin to shake from holding Todd so tight. "You know that, right?"

Todd gives Frank the answer he knows he wants to hear. "Yes, Frank." Frank's relief is audible in his sigh. No longer fearing Todd might try to escape, Frank loosens his grip. He does not release Todd, though, as the need to hold him close is too great. Although Frank tries to hold them back, tears begin to stream down his face. Todd doesn't even notice; his eyes are glued shut by shame and exhaustion. "This isn't how I imagined us." Frank releases one arm to wipe the tears from his face. "I always knew it'd be you and me one day—but I was willing to wait, till you were ready. I didn't want to—" He couldn't say it. "I wanted you to want me, too."

"Why, Frank?" Todd's voice is a shattered whisper. "Why did it have to happen?" It was a contemplative moment, solemn and sore with rage.

"Papa Dean was a *strai*," Frank says, looking down at Todd. "Did you know that?" He harrumphs. "My father tamed him—at a reeducation camp. Dad took a summer job there. That's where he and Papa Dean met. Said he wanted to do something to help the nation—said he actually believed taming *strai*s was essential for national security." Frank shakes his head at the wonder of it. "Said he had actually fallen for that claptrap." Resting his head in his free hand, Frank continues, "When I voc'd home, Papa Dean insisted I come straight home. When I got here, Dad was with him; he left work early because this was so important. The two of them sat me down and told me what reeducation camp is like—what had happened to Papa Dean—what will happen to you. They said we needed to make people believe we are a unit—a sexually active unit. That this was something we had to do." Frank swallows his guilt. His fathers had only said to make people believe they are a unit; they never actually said to "do it." *But we had to*, Frank reminds himself. Needing justification, he adds, *This was the only way anyone would believe us*. Openly sobbing now, he begs, "Believe me, Todd; it was better this way."

At this moment, Dean and Geoffrey return home. Because the entry hall opens into the living room, the first thing Dean sees is Todd sitting on Frank's lap, wrapped in his arms, both boys sobbing. Instinct takes over and he rushes to them. "Frank, Todd, what happened?" Quickly taking in the bruises on both boys' faces, he demands, "Hadrian's lover, what happened?" Looking his husband's way, he exclaims, "Geoffrey, they've been beaten!"

Geoffrey moves into the room to stand behind Dean. Frank instantly begins to babble some story about *strai* bashing. Dean cringes as he listens to a gruesome tale about a gang of boys from school jumping Todd at Riverside Park and Frank leaping in to save him. Dean, kneeling in front of the boys, opens his arms to envelop Todd as he slides off Frank's lap. Papa Dean cradles and rocks the boy like an infant. Geoffrey takes great care to observe the scene before him. Frank is shirtless. Todd is dressed like T'Neal—no, like the way Mike Fulton said he had been dressed that Sunday over three years ago when the boys had first experimented with sex. "Dean," Geoffrey places a hand on his partner's shoulder, "you take care of Todd. I'll look after Frank." Frank, Geoffrey also notes, is avoiding eye contact. "Frank," says Geoffrey, his voice mimicking soft and soothing, but Frank can hear the edge of displeasure. The instant their eyes meet, Frank is conscious of his father's awareness. His father, Frank rightly surmises, is not as easily overwhelmed by the current circumstances—empathetic, yes; fooled, no. Having borne witness to Dean's suffering, seeing now Todd crumpled and broken, he wonders at the depth of emotions Dean and Todd are forced to endure. "Frank," he repeats, "come with me." As Geoffrey's eyes brook no opposition, Frank rises and slowly follows his father down the hall and into his bedroom.

After taking in the damage done—the bed curtains ripped off—one of the curtain cords tied to the front right poster—Geoffrey turns and confronts his son. "Tell me what really happened!"

* * * * *

Salve!

Spotlight: Gideon Weller!
HNN—Melissa Eagleton Reporting

"Tonight's episode is unique in that the guest I am interviewing is actually present with us on stage. It is with great pleasure that I introduce to my viewers the warden of the Northeast Reeducation Camp, Mr. Gideon Weller. Mr. Weller, thank you so much for taking time out of your rigorous schedule to speak with us tonight."

"Well, Ms. Eagleton—"

"Please, call me Melissa."

"All right, Melissa. It is an honor for both myself and for the Northeast Camp that you have offered me this interview."

"First off, our viewers would like to know what it is you do at the reeducation camp."

"My job is quite hefty. I oversee all stages of each ward's transition back into Hadrian society. When they first come to us, many are unruly, undisciplined, angry, and hurtful youth. It is the job of all who work at the reeducation camp from the warden all the way down to the janitorial staff to help encourage these boys to embrace Hadrian's lifestyle."

"That must be a very daunting task if they come to you as unruly as you suggest."

"Indeed it is, and indeed they do. Remember, these are boys who believe they are heterosexual. Many are a two on the Kinsey scale, so we have to help them battle against and then vanquish the stronger heterosexual drive. It is essential we cleanse them of their heterosexual tendencies before we can help them find their inner latent homosexuality."

"And how is that done?"

"We have a very tight schedule by which the boys must abide. From the minute they wake to the very minute they return to their beds, they are kept active in sports, classes, private counseling sessions, and other activities deemed necessary for their reeducation."

"How long is their day?"

"Our boys rise at six a.m. and bed down at nine p.m."

"Nine is a little early, don't you think?"

"Not after the rigorous day we put them through. By nine o'clock, many of our boys are so tired they collapse as soon as they sink into their mattresses."

"How long is your day?"

"My day begins at five a.m. I need to wake a good hour before the boys in order to ensure everything is in readiness for the day's activities. I, and all our staff, then join the wards for breakfast and exercise. As soon as the boys begin class, I head over to my office and continue working through all the paperwork that comes along with each ward, and not just the wards currently in my possession. No, no, no. At the Northeast Camp, we keep track of all our wards after they leave us. We like to know about their successes in life. Husbands report back to us on an annual basis. I enjoy reading those reports most of all. Often, I will share these reports with our new wards so they know the hope and happiness that await them in the future."

"That sounds wonderful. How uplifting. How inspiring that must be for these young men."

"For some, yes, depending on what stage of their reformation they are at. It is always delightful, though, when the wards are nearing graduation. These young men truly appreciate news of their predecessors' fates."

"So, is that the end of your day, then?"

"Oh, no, no, no, not by any stretch. The morning is barely over for me by this point. I always dine with the boys, as I mentioned—breakfast, lunch, and supper. Everyone in the camp comes together for meals. I like the boys at Northeast Camp to feel like we are a family. As you may know, many of our youth have been disowned by their real families so we embrace them as our own."

"That is the best way to win our children over, I think."

"So, after lunch, I will go around the camp and participate in various events. All wards have private sessions with their guardians, and sometimes, the charge, or the ward, needs a third ear to listen and help out with difficulties or concerns."

"My word, you are a truly amazing man."

"Thank you, Ms. Eag…Melissa. As I was saying, my days are as full as the boys' days are. I will sometimes join them in viewing films about the outside world or help them learn to reject what they perceive as feminine seduction."

"So far everything suggests an easy time for these young men."

"Oh, no, no, no. Don't be fooled. Reeducation for the straight male is never an easy process. Disciplinary measures are often necessary. Remember, heterosexual males are violent by nature, and one is often caught in a situation where offense is the best defense."

"Of course. Do you suppose it is the same at the young women's reeducation camp?"

"I have no idea what our female counterparts have to deal with. What I do know is that heterosexual males are among the most volatile and dangerous people in Hadrian. I have never forgotten the brutal attack on the wall over twenty years ago."

"Oh, yes. That was horrendous."

"The woman who survived—"

"You knew her?"

"She was my genetic mother. A kinder, more beautiful woman never existed. Those brutal, bloody barbarians, what they did to her—the scars that would never heal. Those bastards—those rapists—those murdering sons of—"

"Of course, of course, what those men did was horrible."

"They are the epitome of heterosexuality, and they are why we must never allow any of our young men to accept or act upon such unruly physical emotions."

"No, of course, you are right. I think what our viewers need to know is that the Northeast Camp has one of the highest success rates at retraining and transitioning our wayward young men back into Hadrian society."

"Yes. I am committed to bringing our boys back to the only truly loving and kind sexual lifestyle. No boy leaves my camp with any inkling of heterosexual tendencies. Until I am one hundred percent certain a ward can live in harmony with Hadrian's chosen lifestyle, he will not leave the confines of my camp. As long as there is any indication of heterosexual tendencies, I consider him to be a threat to Hadrian's citizens and our national security."

"Please explain for our viewers how heterosexuals might affect national security."

"Heterosexuals need to commune with heterosexuals, so these boys will do anything in their power to aid the hordes outside our wall to enter into Hadrian. We all know the story of how it was one of our very own soldiers, who had admitted to being straight, who aided the horde that attacked our wall, murdered our men, raped our women, and killed the soul and sanity of my mother. Every heterosexual is a danger to our society. They will try to make contact with the outside world and bring them in to destroy our guarded and cherished lifestyle."

"No more need be said, Mr. Weller. You are clearly a passionate and dedicated man. Your devotion to the reeducation of our young men and the protection of our cherished society is admirable. And, although viewers, there was never any hard evidence against the accused soldier who also died in the attack, we can surely understand Mr. Gideon Weller's point of view. Mr. Weller, thank you again for sharing your valuable time on *Salve!* You, sir, are our spotlight of hope!"

Vale!

The Principal's Office

Fank! Todd's text is urgent, his typing frantic. He doesn't even take the time to read what he's written. *ppal clled. papa deana dn me. offce. meetig help.* Frank understands everything. Raising his hand, he asks Mr. Reiner whether he can go to the bathroom. Permission is given and Frank races down the stairs, up the hallway, and into the office. He practically slams into Coach Miller, who is leaning rather dejectedly against the doorjamb.

"Coach?" Frank's eyes plead with the woman.

She shakes her head, grimly pronouncing, "It's bad, Frank." Tears begin to spill. "Why?" she asks, seemingly of Frank but really of no one. When she gets no response (not that she had expected one), she continues, "It's so wrong." Her hand caresses her forehead. "Who gives a damn if he's straight!" She has to put a hand over her mouth to stifle her outburst of tears. Chewing now on the knuckle of her thumb, Coach Miller shakes her head in dismay.

The secretary is not impressed. "Being straight is illegal!" he declares.

"Why?" Coach Miller turns and demands of the younger man.

"Population control!" He rolls his eyes as if talking to a dummy. "Everyone knows that."

"So give him a vasectomy! SNIP!" Her gesture, so sharply pointed in Mr. Whalen's direction, suggests she would like to snip him. "Problem solved."

Stupid woman! He sniffs in contempt as his eyes roll upward. "They'll do that to him too, I believe. It's standard procedure upon entering reeducation."

"No!" Frank whispers in despair.

Mr. Whalen, paying the young man no heed, taunts the teacher. "You just don't want to lose your star player!" Sniffing, he adds sanctimoniously, "You should be thinking of your students' needs, not those of the game."

Coach Miller desperately wants to shout back *FUCK YOU!* But because they are standing in the main office with a student present, she has to content herself with a sullen glare.

Mr. Whalen decides he has put up with this woman long enough. "Don't you have work to do?"

Coach Miller wants to scream out, *You're not my boss!* She seethes instead, knowing better. The school secretary may be lower on the employee hierarchy, but when it comes to political clout in the office, this man wields all the power. Turning, Coach Miller attempts to walk away with dignity, but her stride clearly indicates defeat.

Frank instantly runs to the secretary's desk. "Mr. Whalen, please, I need to see the principal."

"Incoming," Mr. Whalen chimes. Waving his hand impatiently at the youth, he blinks to answer the call. Taking his time with the call, Mr. Whalen records all information in infinite detail before blinking off. Finally, he looks Frank's way. "Yes? May I help you?" There is a slight edge of annoyance in his voice.

"I need to speak with the principal. Where is he?"

Grimacing, Mr. Whalen points to the chairs against the sidewall. "Sit down, Frank." Being co-cap of the National Championship team, Frank is known by everyone at Pride.

"I don't want to sit down. I want to talk to the principal."

"Well, Mr. Gavin is busy." Pointing with eyes to the man's office door, Mr. Whalen says, "He's in a meeting."

"I know," Frank replies. "I need to get in there."

Annoyed, Mr. Whalen replies, "It's an important meeting. He's not to be disturbed." Gesturing to the chairs, he says, "Sit down and wait."

"I'm not waiting." Frank rushes to the door but is stalled by a locked handle.

Exasperated, Mr. Whalen calls from his desk, "Sit down, Frank."

"No! I want in." Frank starts to knock, his knuckles rapping harder against the wood as his request is blatantly being ignored.

Finally, the door opens and Mr. Gavin pushes his head past Frank. "Whalen, I said no interruptions." Mr. Whalen, raising eyes and eyebrows, complementing the look with chagrin, flicks open palms, then nods toward Frank's back.

Frank, meanwhile, pushes past the principal into the office to kneel next to Todd's chair. Terror strikes deep into his heart at the sight of the strange man sitting beside his friend. Although in his fifties, there are no lines of age etching this man's face. Nor is there any suggestion of cosmetic surgery. His hair, however, has been dyed black, so black the look is unnatural against the pale white of his skin. His legs are crossed and his hands are folded one atop the other over his knee. His back is so straight he looks more like a mannequin than a human being. Papa Dean stands behind Todd's chair, his hands on the boy's shoulders. Todd is bent over crying. "Papa Dean," Frank asks dismayed, "what's going on here?"

The strange man silences Papa Dean with one darting look. Then, cocking an eyebrow, slightly amused by this new turn of events, he asks, "And who might you be?" His voice is soft, soothing, and sickeningly sweet.

"Who the fuck are you?" Frank demands.

"Such language! Really, Mr. Gavin," the man addresses the principal, who has followed Frank into the office, "the way your students speak to their elders."

"Frank," Mr. Gavin is clearly upset, "I must ask you to leave." He holds the door open and motions Frank toward the door.

Gripping Todd's hand in his, Frank declares, "I'm not leaving my boyfriend."

The stranger snorts. "Your boyfriend, you say?"

Smiling grimly, Mr. Gavin asks, "Since when?"

"Since yesterday. See this," he says emphatically, pointing to Todd's neck, "this is my collar. Only my boyfriend wears it."

"Yes," Mr. Gavin is curt, "and only yesterday T'Neal was wearing it."

"We broke up." Frank is equally brusque.

"That was sudden," Mr. Gavin replies pointedly.

The strange man is clearly amused by all this. "Well, isn't this delightful." Swiveling in his chair, he addresses the principal. "Mr. Gavin, introduce me to Todd's—boyfriend." The pause serves to amplify his sarcasm.

Releasing a long sigh, begrudgingly accepting Frank's presence, Mr. Gavin closes his office door. Before resuming his seat, he begins, "Mr. Weller, Frank Hunter—apparently Todd's boyfriend." He, too, expresses doubt with acerbic slurring. After sitting down, he swivels in his chair and resumes working at his computer, determined to shut out everything that has to happen here. *This is not my business*, he reminds himself. And just last week, he had taken Todd's hand in his, before the entire school body, congratulating him on making the winning basket and receiving the well-earned most valuable player award at the Nationals. *This is a government affair*, he adds in a feeble attempt to justify his act of betrayal.

"Amazing!" Mr. Weller claps his hands with mock glee. "One day a confessed heterosexual—an active one to boot—and the next day he is one hundred percent gay." Getting up out of his chair, he extends a hand Frank's way. "Let me shake your hand, Frank Hunter; your accomplishment in taming this boy is truly amazing." Looking with delight Dean's way, he continues, "You have even outdone your father!" Looking back at Frank, he adds, "Why, in less than twenty-four hours, you have accomplished what takes reeducation camp no less than six months and sometimes up to four years to achieve."

Frank stands, irate; he pushes Weller's hand away. "I didn't say he was fully tame, but I am taming him. He's agreed to let me tame him."

Papa Dean pipes up. "If the girl can receive reeducation at home, why can't the boy?"

"Oh, Dean, Dean, Dean." Leaning over Todd's slumped shoulders, Weller taps Papa Dean's chest. "You of all people should know the answer to that." Turning to face Frank, he continues, "Yes, young man, your Papa Dean is a confessed *strai*—sorry, bad language—heterosexual—a 'zero' on the Kinsey scale in his own words." Weller pauses to feign ignorance. "What exactly did you say, again, Dean?" And, then as if the answer suddenly strikes him like a bolt out of the blue, he exclaims, "Oh, yes! 'You'll never tame me! Never!'" The word "never" is extended like a growl. Mr. Weller's fingers flick out into fat jazz hands, his eyes widen, accenting his sardonic demeanor. "Yes, Dean, I remember." There is jealous animosity in his eyes. Dean Stuttgart had been his ward—yet he had failed in all his attempts to tame the man. It riles him that a summer temp, Geoffrey Hunter, in less than two months, won the boy away from him. Dean Stuttgart, a founding family descendant, would have been a coup indeed. Weller had personally promised the trading baron he would tame his son, even had dreams of marrying into that prestigious family. *I could have kept your father from disowning you*, he thinks grimly. Bitter in his discontent, he studies Todd. *I am not going to lose this boy to any Hunter!* Now, patting Todd's head, he watches dispassionately as the boy shivers and pulls away from his touch. Defiant eyes blurred by tears dart up. Weller's head tilts questioningly. "Is the boy here a zero on the Kinsey scale, too? Whom only the great Hunters can tame?" Todd drops his head in shame. "No," says Weller, shaking his head. "Dean wasn't a zero, and you're not one either. There are no zeros born in Hadrian anymore." Then, adding as an after-thought, "Or ones for that matter. We have genetically removed them from Hadrian's human genome."

"That's impossible," Dean expostulates.

"Really?" Mr. Weller's eyebrows cock at that. He grins contemptuously. "Then explain you. If there weren't a little two in you somewhere, how did the mighty Hunter tame you?"

Frank looks up dismayed, "Papa Dean, what is he talking about?" It's not that Frank doesn't understand the concept; it is simply that fear has him befuddled.

"The Kinsey scale, boy," Mr. Weller answers in place of Dean. Turning on Mr. Gavin, he asks, "Don't you teach your students anything in this school?" Mr. Gavin pointedly ignores the man's insults. Mr. Weller, equally dismissive toward the principal, turns back to explain the elementals to Frank. "A zero on the Kinsey scale is said to be a pure heterosexual with no homosexual tendencies at all. A one only has the slightest inkling of what a homosexual is, much like the fives who have some inkling of what it means to be heterosexual. Some people say fives make the best tamers." Looking directly at Dean, he states, "I say that's nonsense. And then," with a twinkling in his eye, he adds, "there are the sixes," pointing proudly to himself. (Dean shakes his head knowingly at that!) "Well, we are the ideal state of human being. The rest of you poor bastards are somewhere in between. Twos, like your Papa Dean here, are the most difficult to contend with. Many believe they are zeros, but we know better. There are no zeros in Hadrian, and only reeducation can reveal that." Weller's grin actually widens. "Isn't that right, Dean?" Looking down at Todd's slumped shoul-ders, he says, "I suspect your little boy here is a two as well!" Lifting the boy's chin, Mr. Weller forces him to look up again. Inspecting his bruises, he turns to Frank. "It looks like your method of taming includes iron fists."

Slightly confused, Dean glances Frank's way. Frank claimed their bruis-ing came as a result of *strai* bashing. A group of boys had jumped Todd in Riverside Park, and Frank had leaped in to defend him. Frank shakes his head, easing Papa Dean's distress.

Smiling sardonically, Weller says, "Don't worry, Todd; we won't beat you like Frank, here." Dean winces, knowing that promise for a lie!

Todd yanks his face away, his knuckles turning white from gripping the arms of his chair. Ready to scream, only Papa Dean's soothing words ease him. "Shh, Todd, it's okay."

"Yes, Dean, it is okay." Mr. Weller concurs. "Or, at least it will be after reeducation."

Todd's face drops into his hands, his wail expelled through clenched teeth, "Frank, you promised!" Looking up at his friend, through tears and desperation, he says, choking on his words, "You said if we—You said I wouldn't have to go!"

Franks kneels instantly by Todd's side. Both hands are clutching Todd's. "You don't!" Looking up, eyes pleading, he asks, "Does he, Papa Dean?"

Before Dean can answer, Mr. Weller leaps in, "Oh, Dean, Dean. Dean." Each repetition of the name accompanies a jarring shake of his head. Mr. Weller's smile is vicious. "Did you make promises you can't keep?"

Dean attempts to stare the man down, but Mr. Weller is too secure in his position to worry. Although he looks away in defeat, Dean persists with his position. "No, Frank," Dean insists. "He won't have to go." Once again, boring his eyes into Weller's, he states, "If the girl doesn't have to go, Todd won't have to."

Mr. Weller shakes his head sadly, with mocking, heartrending distress, "The girl, Crystal Albright, is not a confessed heterosexual." With a circular swirl of the hand, he points to Todd. "Your boy here is."

Dean is steaming, "She initiated everything!"

"Not according to the girl—" Weller pauses to glance Todd's way before adding, "or the boy."

"Why don't you look at the video and see what really happened?" Frank demands. "Todd told me. She came on to him."

Mr. Weller shrugs condescendingly, "I would, but the video has been destroyed."

Dean, Frank, and Todd all cry out, "What?"

"Now, Todd," Mr. Weller says tersely. "You confessed. What need is there to hurt the girl further? None. So, at her mothers' request, the video was destroyed."

Todd leaps out of his chair. "That's not fair!"

Mr. Weller is no longer willing to play games. He shoves Todd roughly back into his chair as he yells, "Sit down!" Todd winces. He is still raw from yesterday. "Your confession has been made. You agreed to the girl's account. We had, we *have*, no need of video evidence." With biting insistence, he adds, "It is too late to change your story now! You are going to reeducation camp."

"No!" Dean demands.

"You have no say in this, Stuttgart!" This is the first time Todd has ever heard Papa Dean's birth name. He's a Stuttgart. Maybe there is hope. The Stuttgart family is a founding family. Surely Papa Dean has some pull. As if sensing what Todd is thinking, Mr. Weller chuckles, shaking his head contemptuously. "Don't get your hopes up, boy; not even a Stuttgart can circumvent the sexual reformation laws."

He was going to add, *especially one whose father has disowned him*, but a bitter, discontented Dean interjects, "But clearly the girl's mothers can."

Now, as if addressing children, Mr. Weller speaks slowly, over-emphasizing each word. "The girl committed no crime. The boy did." In a more menacing tone, he addresses Todd, "You can thank Hadrian and his lover that Ms. Albright and Vice President Stiles aren't charging you with rape!" *Vice President Stiles!* The thought looms in everyone's mind. Todd always knew Crystal's parents were rich, but she never spoke of her mama's founding family status. Mr. Weller gleams at the prospect. He may not be able to marry into her family, but he can most certainly ingratiate himself. Twisting the knife in the jugular, he adds, "Otherwise, you'd be swinging from a rope!" Todd pales.

"You don't have to do this," Dean pleads. "We are working with him at home."

"Home?" Mr. Weller shakes his head, "No, no, no. Todd has no home. Not anymore." Reaching behind him, on the principal's desk, he retrieves a document.

For a brief moment, Mr. Gavin is acknowledged, or rather, the high back of his chair, as he sits frozen, concentrating on his computer screen. He has nothing more to say or do with this issue. The *strai* belongs to the government, and it is in his best interest simply to give them the boy.

Shaking the document Dean's way, Mr. Weller proclaims, "His legal guardian, Michael Fulton, has signed the form. The boy is now my legal ward!"

Dean gasps, mouthing the words, "Not you!"

Weller smiles as he mouths back his response, "Me."

Todd, oblivious to their silent communication, mutters, "Papa Mike." As his chest caves, his shoulders heave with sobs. He feels even more betrayed than when he had been abandoned by the man the day before.

Squatting now, Frank traps his head under his hands and between his knees. He sobs with heart-wrenching abandon as Papa Dean begs, "Don't—don't—don't—"

Mr. Weller ignores him. "Stand up, Todd. We have to go."

"NO!" Todd shrieks. He darts up from his chair and races for the door. Before he can grab the handle, though, Mr. Weller has retrieved a smart tranquilizer dart from his coat pocket. It's a simple blowgun, and the dart, now sticking out of Todd's shoulder, knocks him out instantly.

Being the closer of the two men, Dean reaches Todd's body first. Although he knows this battle to be lost, he feigns denial, allowing him an opportunity to fumble around the boy's shirt pocket, retrieving Todd's cell phone.

* * * * *

Salve!

Inside a Reeducation Camp
HNN—Melissa Eagleton Reporting

"I always enjoy these episodes where I am able to leave the studio and visit a location live. After our successful interview with Northeast Reeducation Camp's warden, Mr. Gideon Weller, we have been invited to his reeducation camp to meet with some of the wards and their guardians.

"This camp is beautifully situated on the shore of Hudson Bay. With thick forest to the north, farmlands to the west and south, and the lake to the east, the boys sent here are kept physically active all year round. In the spring, plowing and planting the fields occurs. During the summer months, the boys enjoy fishing, hiking, biking, swimming, canoeing, even singing around the campfire. Come fall, the boys actively participate in the harvest. All the vegetables and grain consumed at the Northeast Camp are grown right here.

"Over here is the nucleus of the entire complex. As you can see, the boys' cabins encircle the central compound. It is in this main building that the hub of activity occurs. In this one building, all wards and guardians meet to celebrate victories and or discuss difficulties each individual ward may be facing.

"Let's go inside, shall we? As we go down these stairs and turn right, we enter into the kitchen galley where all the food is prepared, and let me tell you, viewers, it smells really good in here. This next room is the central cafeteria where even Mr. Weller sits down to eat his meals, seven days a week I've been told. Mr. Gideon Weller has married himself to reeducation. He lives, eats, and works here. His entire life is dedicated to the welfare of our young men.

"This next room, as we move down the hall, is the central meeting area. Here, I'm told, is where the young men hold dances and parties where they learn to have good clean healthy gay fun! Here in this room, we are going to meet Little Stephie Chatters and his ward Mattie Molloy.

"Hello, Stephie."

"Hello, Ms. Eagleton. This is so wonderful. Thank you so much for coming here. May I say hi to my fathers?"

"Of course you can."

"Hi, Daddy. Hi, Papa Steve."

"Now, Stephie, is it true, were you really a ward here once yourself?"

"Oh, yes. I came when I was twelve. But I'm no longer straight, in any way! I am one hundred percent gay, and I am so happy now. I was so miserable when I thought I was straight. I was always depressed and even thought about killing myself. When I first got here, I begged Papa Gideon—Mr. Weller lets me call him Papa Gideon—to help me be gay. I knew being straight was awful—Papa Gideon calls it abhorrent—but I had no idea how to fix things. This camp saved my life. And now I'm able to help out other wards like Mattie here."

"So, you must be Mattie. Tell me, what's it like having a ward like little Stephie? He must be a huge inspiration for you, knowing he too once suffered like you do."

"Yes, ma'am."

"Mattie's shy, Ms. Eagleton. He's only been here a couple of months, but he's come such a long way. When he first got here, he was very angry. He always swore, and he wouldn't listen to anything anyone had to say. But now he is so demure. I am so proud of him. I just know that he will be cured before the year is up."

"Well, Mattie, that is such good news. I'm sure you will be so happy when you get released."

"Yes, ma'am."

"Stephie, Mattie, thank you so much for sharing your stories with us. What a great inspiration it is to see success and how a victor is able to turn around and use his experience to help another young man flourish. It truly is awe inspiring and rewarding. So there you have it, folks, the success of the Northeast Camp firsthand!"

Vale!

Interview with Salve!

Geoffrey and Dean are snuggled up tight on the couch, watching a comedy on the wall screen. Dean has been so despondent after Todd's exposure and transfer to the Northeast Reeducation Camp. Geoffrey is hoping a little humor will help cheer him up. It is not working. Halfway through the vid, Geoffrey gets an incoming call; blinking, he pauses the film. A second blink and then, "Hello?—Hey, Aaron, how are you?" Dean smiles slightly; Aaron Hillier stood up for Geoffrey at their wedding. What Dean doesn't know is that Aaron had also been a volunteer that summer at the Northeast Reeducation Camp when Dean was being held there. In fact, he ended up studying reeducation psychiatry and now works full-time under Gideon Weller. Geoffrey pulls away from Dean. Dean sees nothing odd in this act, thinking Geoffrey simply needs to focus on his conversation. "Yes, yes, it has been too long…So, how's Mateo?" Mateo is Aaron's partner. He, too, unknown to Dean, works in reeducation psychiatry. "Nice. Good to hear. So what's up? Why the call? Really? Dean and me?"

Dean looks over. "Dean and me what?" Although curious, Dean's voice holds no excitement.

Geoffrey, hushing Dean, looks straight at the wall as if at Aaron. "Why?" A dark film covers Geoffrey's eyes. "Are you serious? He can't do that?"

"What? What? Do what?" Dean asks nervously.

"What?" Geoffrey voice is a mixture of horror and ire.

Dean reaches over and grabs Geoffrey's shoulder, turning the man to face him. "What is it? Is it Todd? Tell me!"

Geoffrey tries to calm his voice. "We've been asked to do an interview for *Salve!*"

This is dumbfounding. Why would an offer to be on TV cause such consternation? Dean shakes his head in dismay. Shivering, he inquires,

"Why?"

"Aaron," says Geoffrey, focusing once more on the wall, "Dean and I need to talk. I'll give you our answer tomorrow." Now it is Geoffrey's turn to shake his head in dismay. "When?—Fine. I'll call back in one hour." Blinking once, he disconnects. After he blinks a second time, the image on the wall screen disappears. Leaning back into the couch, he closes his eyes and purses his lips. Dean's stare burns deep into his consciousness. "We've been asked to participate in an upcoming *Salve!* episode titled 'Happily Married After Reeducation.'"

Shrinking away, Dean groans, "No!" His head shakes spasmodically. "No!"

Geoffrey smiles sadly at his terror-stricken lover. "I—" He doesn't want to do the interview any more than Dean does, but he knows better. *How to explain?* Opening his eyes, he can see by the look on Dean's face no level of understanding is attainable right now in his fragile mind. Even so, the truth must be revealed. "We don't have much choice."

Dean's scrotum turns to ice. "Why not?"

There is no easy way to say this so Geoffrey doesn't even try. "Weller filed a report against you."

Dean screams, "They can't send me back there! They can't! We're married! We're married!" Geoffrey moves closer to his lover, but Dean rejects any physical contact. Leaping off the couch, he begins pacing the living room like a caged tiger.

"Apparently, you said something today, something Weller says indicates you might still be straight."

Dean's voice becomes shrill. "What? What? What did I say? I didn't say anything. I just tried to help Todd. I was just trying to help Todd."

"In his report, Weller said you claim there are still ones and zeros inside Hadrian. And," he adds hesitantly, "that it is impossible to tame them."

Dean's body jerks as if hit with an electric shock. Doe-eyed, anticipating the bullet, Dean turns to Geoffrey. "I never said that!" Words become disjointed as Dean's breath turns sporadic. "I swear I never said that!" No longer pacing, standing now on the other side of the room, Dean wraps his arms around his shoulders, rocking his upper body.

Crossing over, Geoffrey places his hands on Dean's (still clasped tight around his shoulders). "He says…" He turns Dean to face him. "He said you declared yourself a zero when you were inside the camp…" closing his eyes to avoid showing Dean the dread he feels, Geoffrey adds, "And that today's statement suggests that might be true." Dean shrieks. Geoffrey pulls him in tight. As much as it pains him, Geoffrey needs to finish telling Dean everything that was said about him. "Weller has recommended you be re-assessed by his reeducation psych team." Dean starts to scream wildly, shaking inside Geoffrey's grip. "That's how Aaron found out. He works in assessment under Weller." Trying not to grimace, Geoffrey continues, "He said Weller wants you back inside the camp so they can determine whether or not…" He closes his eyes, fear beginning to shake his resolve. "Whether or not you should be exiled."

Suddenly, Dean is seventeen again—desperate and willing to do anything to avoid further punishment. He drops to his knees and begins undoing Geoffrey's pants. It is Pavlov's dog all over again. Blowing Weller was the only sure way of avoiding punishment.

"No! NO! Dean, stop it!" Geoffrey kneels down so he and Dean can be on the same level. "I promised you then and I'm keeping that promise now. It will never be like that between us! This is your fear acting, not love." Dean collapses into his lover's arms. Both men shed tears. Recovering his voice, Geoffrey tries to offer up some hope. "Aaron believes if we go on *Salve!* and talk about our lives, it will exonerate you." Dean nods. He is broken, beaten the way he was back in the camp. He really is willing to do anything right now. "We'll just answer a few questions. Tell Hadrian we're in love—only say what's true." The ceaseless nodding of Dean's head against his chest discombobulates Geoffrey. "I won't let them take you back there. I won't let them exile you. I swear to you, on the soul of Hadrian's lover, I will fight them like a grizzly protecting her cub." Geoffrey slides into a seated position on the floor, and Dean falls helplessly into his lap. Holding Dean tightly, Geoffrey tries desperately to reassure him with gentle strokes and soft cooing noises.

* * * * *

Melissa Eagleton is even more beautiful in person than she is on the camera. They say the camera adds a good ten pounds, and Melissa would not lose weight to look normal so when one first encounters the real life woman, the first reaction is always how much slimmer she appears. She is also a lot shorter than most would expect. One seldom sees Melissa standing when she gives one of her broadcasts. Her dimples seem just a little deeper and her smile a little wider too. No one is quite sure why, but instead of doing the woman's beauty justice, the camera actually diminishes her. Perhaps it is because she refuses to wear extreme amounts of makeup. She does comply with the need for makeup for the camera, but she never lets the cosmetics team do more than make her look healthy and normal. Off camera, the light makeup proves to be very stylish. Her blue eyes twinkle in such a way that the interviewee is immediately put at ease. Well, almost every interviewee. Nothing, not even Melissa's sweet demeanor and perky smile, can help ease Dean's tension. In fact, her feminine beauty has the exact opposite effect. For Dean, being in close proximity to such an attractive woman sets off a series of residual electric shocks that shake his body in a series of disjointed jerks—akin to Pavlov's dog—destroying any potential attraction or emotion he might have felt for her. Having been attached to electrodes, with high voltage shocks tearing throughout his nervous system every time his body responded erotically to a beautiful woman, has proven to be a lifelong lasting and very effective deterrent. Although Dean remains attracted to women, his body has been successfully conditioned, and his brain sets off the memory of the shock so strongly that he feels the very currents as if they were still ripping through him. This, now natural reaction, is why Dean avoids women as much as humanly possible. Regrettably, the shock waves he now feels remind Dean not only of past horrors, but they also bring to mind what Todd is going through this very moment inside that camp.

"So, gentlemen…" Melissa's voice is melodious. "Come sit down next to me." Geoffrey, understanding Dean's dilemma, takes the chair closest to Melissa Eagleton. Waving to her camera crew, signaling them to wait just one minute, she begins instructions. "I'll just start bombarding you with questions. Answer them honestly, and after ten or fifteen minutes, we'll wrap it up. We won't use all of the tape. My edit team will pick out the best bits." Smiling, she says, "I am so excited. I have been waiting to do a piece about this for years. I never could understand why reeducation was always stalling me. Then suddenly last night, out of the blue, Aaron Hillier calls me, saying they have the perfect couple, you two." She leans forward to clasp each man's hands as she expresses her gratitude. "Thank you!" After leaning back in her chair, she swivels to face the cameraman. She gives him the "one more minute" finger and then asks her guests, "Are we ready?" Both men nod. "All right then." Smiling to the cameraman, she nods her assent.

The cameraman begins calling out, "Five, four," gesturing at the same time with the fingers of his right hand. He is silent for "three, two, one," merely mouthing the words while continuing to gesture. Then after mouthing the word "one," he flicks with his index finger to indicate they are now filming.

"Well, good evening, Hadrian. Tonight's show is a very special event. With us today are Geoffrey and Dean Hunter! This couple met at the Northeast Reeducation Camp." She turns now to face the men. Geoffrey is holding Dean's hands in his. This image makes Melissa smile; it couldn't be any more perfect. "Geoffrey, can you tell my viewers about the first time you met Dean."

"I, ah, I got a job helping out at the Northeast Camp...um, trying to make some money to help pay for my tuition. I, ah, well, um, I wanted to do something to help. I thought this might...was...ah, a good thing."

Melissa smiles. "That's really good," she says encouragingly. "But what my viewers really want to know is how the two of you met."

Dean stares at his hands. He remembers exactly how he and Geoffrey met. Weller had decided it was time for Dean to have sex, and this time he wasn't taking no for an answer. Geoffrey walked in on them by accident. If it hadn't been for Geoffrey Hunter, Gideon Weller would have raped Dean.

Geoffrey answers for them both. "The first time I saw Dean, he was standing in line at the camp cafeteria. I watched him fill up his tray; he sure could eat a lot back then! And the way he walked over to his table really captured my attention. Something about Dean reminded me of a Bengali tiger. His brown curly hair had been left unattended, and I hate to say it, but that unruly look really suited him. I was instantly attracted to the man."

"How romantic."

"Dean, when did you discover that you loved Geoffrey?"

Speaking into his hands, Dean says, "When he said he would never— never force me—and—and I—I—knew I could trust him—that he wouldn't—make me."

"Oh, my," Melissa expresses concern. "You're crying."

"It's a very emotional experience for both of us," Geoffrey explains.

"I see." Tilting her head slightly, hoping to make eye contact with Dean, Melissa presses him with another question. "So, Dean, you must be very grateful to the Northeast Reeducation Camp since it brought you and your husband together."

Dean shudders, his shoulders heave. "I can't do this…" His head shakes.

Geoffrey releases Dean's hands and wraps him in an embrace. "It's all right, Dean; everything's all right."

"I can't, Geoffrey…I can't…I can't say I'm grateful to those bastards for anything! Not even for you. I love you…but I can't."

Geoffrey continues to soothe Dean as he sobs. At one point, the two men kiss—a spontaneous act for which Melissa Eagleton is grateful. There is very little of this interview she can use. Pondering the situation, she realizes this will not be a *Salve! Interview Special*. It will have to be a regular *Salve!*, but with a twist. Her mind works quickly to redesign the show meant to air that very evening. *I'll have the wall screen showing excerpts of their interview.* Considering her options, *At least there's the bit where Geoffrey Hunter explains why he got a job there, his first impression of Dean and their kiss. No wait*, she remembers, *Dean does say "I love you."* With a little creative editing, she realizes they can use that, too. The rest she will simply have to invent. Turning to face her camera crew, Melissa Eagleton signals for them to stop filming.

* * * * *

Salve!

Happily Married After Reeducation
HNN—Melissa Eagleton Reporting

Have you ever wondered what happens to our youth after entering reeducation? Well, today's show is going to answer that question for you. I had the good fortune to interview Geoffrey and Dean Hunter earlier today, and what a lovely couple they make! They met at the Northeast Reeducation Camp over twenty years ago. Records show they even married inside the camp's central meeting hall. On the wall screen to my right, I will be showing you short excerpts from my brief but revealing interview with the Hunters. Here, Geoffrey Hunter is explaining why he went to work at the reeducation camp:

"I wanted to do something to help."

And help he did. He changed Dean's life for the better, so much so that Dean not only agreed to marry the man, but he asked to take Geoffrey's last name as his own! Geoffrey Hunter also told us how he felt the very first time he saw Dean. According to Geoffrey, it was love at first sight for these two.

"Dean was standing in line at the camp cafeteria. I watched him fill up his tray. He sure could eat a lot back then! And the way he walked over to his table, there was something about him. His brown curly hair really suited him. I was instantly attracted to the man."

I just love a good romance story. Dean was so taken by his husband's beautiful words that he was drawn to tears and couldn't help but express his love openly for all our viewers.

"I love you."

And, just look at the way Geoffrey responds to those words. These two men are so much in love they can't help but kiss. Dean Hunter's successful cleansing of his heterosexual tendencies, discovery of his latent homosexuality, and his now loving marriage really show us the good work the people at the Northeast Reeducation Camp do to help bring our wayward youth back into the loving fold.

So, there you have it folks, Geoffrey and Dean Hunter. Happily Married After Reeducation!

Vale!

Het-Row

When Todd wakes, he is lying on a hard mattress. A wooden ceiling spins over his head while rafters lurch down at him. Nauseated, he leans over the side of his bed and retches. A pail, adeptly placed, catches the vomit.

"Water's on the bedside table."

The voice, dull sounding, as if struggling to make itself heard from under a deep green sea, barely registers in Todd's ears. "Huh?"

"Here." A hand blurs into view, holding a tall glass filled with clear liquid.

Todd's hand shakes as he reaches for the water. The strange hand guides the glass into Todd's. "Thanks," Todd mumbles. After rinsing and spitting, Todd throws up again, spilling the remainder of his water.

"Shit, man," the voice utters. "You splashed it all over me."

Todd's head is still hanging over the bucket. "Sorry."

"Fuck it!" the voice replies conciliatory. "It happens to everyone. It's those fucking tranquilizer darts. I don't think they've ever brought in a straight man without them." The hand reaches for the glass, dangling now empty in Todd's hand. Suddenly, two hands are in Todd's blurred vision. One is pouring water from a pitcher into the glass. "Here." The glass floats toward Todd. "No doubt you're not finished. Drink some this time; you're going to need something inside to throw up."

Taking the hand's advice, Todd rinses, spits, and then swallows some water. He immediately throws up again.

"More water?" the voice asks.

"Yeah," Todd mutters, holding the glass up toward the origin of the voice.

"Here. Rinse, spit, drink, and vomit again." Todd takes the glass and does as instructed, except this time he doesn't vomit. He hangs his head over the bucket, waiting, but it seems his nausea is at its end. Todd moves to lie back down when the voice stops him. "I wouldn't do that. It'll only make you puke again."

Figuring he's right, having regained more of his senses so he is now able to determine the voice's sex, Todd chooses to stay sitting up. Pouring water on his hand, Todd rubs it over his face. "Where am I?" he asks when finished.

Laughing sardonically, the voice answers, "Welcome to Eet-Row! Where all the future homos go!"

Looking up, Todd sees the cynical smile of a young man his own age. He has long red hair, a square jaw, and (*are those age wrinkles?*) sparkling blue eyes. Todd drops his head and groans, "Reeducation camp."

"That's what the good folk of Gomorrah like to call it, but really, it's just '*strai* town,' 'cunt hammer village,' or the unruly 'sticker in 'er bog.' Call it what you like, it's home now until you come of age and they exile you, you die—good luck with that (exposing a pair of scarred wrists)—or you get married."

Todd looks up questioningly. "Married?" *Hadrian, no! The only man I thought I could marry was Frank—but no more.*

Responding to the despondent look on Todd's face, the boy quips, "That's right, married! No *strai* leaves here unless he's been poked and successfully latched to another man with the ol' ball and chain, so to speak. It's not good enough to claim you're gay; you have to stay that way under the watchful eye of your loving husband, who, by the way, is required by law to make monthly reports on you for the first year, bi-annual reports for the next five years, and then annually until the day you die!"

"You've got to be fucking kidding me, right?"

"Shit, man, I wish I were." Discontentedly studying his wrists, the boy says, "Ah, to die. Death." Closing his eyes, summoning lines up from memory, he quotes:

"To die: to sleep;
No more; and by a sleep to say we end
The heart-ache and the thousand natural shocks
That flesh is heir to, 'tis a consummation
Devoutly to be wish'd."

"Fuck man," says Todd. "That's morbid."

"Actually, it's Shakespeare, and as for being morbid—" his laugh takes on a derisive edge, "you only just got here, man. Just wait," he harrumphs, "a few more minutes."

Reaching between the two beds, he once again presents his hand. "My name's Matthew Molloy, but don't ever call me Matthew in front of them."

"Why not?" This is too much for Todd to take in.

Losing the cynical edge to his smile, Matthew scowls, "My gay name is Mattie." Scrutinizing Todd, he asks, "You're the Middleton kid, right?"

"Yeah, Todd."

"I wonder what they'll call you? Toddie, Todster, Toddel Bear? Toddly Poo."

Dropping his head into his hands, Todd mutters, "Fuck me."

"I heard that happened, too." Looking at Todd wonderingly, Matthew asks, "Is it true?"

Pissed off, Todd snarls, "Is what true?"

Oblivious to Todd's reaction, Matthew moves in closer to allow for a more conspiratorial tone. "Did you really fuck that girl?" Closing his hands and eyes half in wonder, half in delight, he whispers, "Man, I wish I could have—at least once—shit." Leaning back dejectedly on his bed, he confesses, "I only got a kiss and a little tit. Humph, and we both got shipped off—but you, you actually fucked her, they say, and she never got sent away. They say it was rape, but she wouldn't accuse you because rape is punishable by death. How altruistic of her." The sarcastic slurring suggests that Todd would have been better off with a death sentence. "Is that true? Did you rape her, or did she really fuck with you?" He is shaking with excitement.

"Yes—NO—I didn't rape her—but we did have sex."

"Yes!" Matthew's reaction, aptly enough, is an ejaculation. "What was it like? What did it feel like—in there?"

Todd rests his hand on his forehead. "Fuck, man, too much has happened since then."

"Please tell me!" Matthew is desperate.

"Hot, damp, like being wrapped in warm, wet silk."

"Beautiful. I imagined as much."

But Todd is no longer listening to Matthew. His thoughts have drifted back to a few nights ago. *Only a few nights?* Although only Saturday night, during Pride's National win celebration dance, it feels like a whole world ago when Todd's body sparkled like fireflies dancing over a moonlit river. Stifling a cry, he asks, "How long have I been out?"

Matthew shrugs. "I don't know. That drug usually only lasts twenty-some hours. It's late Wednesday afternoon if that helps. And you were here when I went to bed." Pondering the time difference, he reasons, "They must have really doped you up. Did you fight them?"

Once again, Matthew's words fade into the background as Todd's mind fixates on his memory. *Yes*, Todd figures, *it's only been three nights. Or is it four? Hadrian help me, I can't think.* Shaking his head to try and clear it only causes his mind to spin and his stomach to swirl. Once again, he is vomiting into the bucket, this time only dry heaving since there is nothing left for his stomach to throw up.

"Okay," Matthew quips, "don't shake your head." Reaching for the glass and pitcher, he offers Todd some more water.

Todd accepts the gift but does not acknowledge Matthew's kindness since his mind is still focused on recent events. *And then there was*—grimacing—*the night that was supposed to save me.*

As if reading Todd's mind, Matthew carries on inquisitively, "And the guy? Did you fuck the guy, too?" Todd's shoulders heave as he sobs at the memory. "I'll take that as a yes. And they still brought you here? The fucking is usually the last thing that happens before they marry you to the bastard." Shaking his head sadly, Matthew asks, "So, who did you fuck? The girl, I mean." Still shaking his head in wonder, he adds, "Her mothers must be big in the government."

Todd shakes his head. He doesn't want to say what he remembers Mr. Weller having mentioned in the principal's office: Crystal's second mother is Elena Stiles, the Vice President of Hadrian *and* from a founding family! "I never met Crystal's mothers," is the only response Todd is willing to offer. Thoughts of Crystal remind him of the fairer sex. *Girls.* "Are there any girls here? You said your girlfriend got shipped out, too. Where's the girl's camp?" Todd knows Crystal never got sent away, but a part of him wishes he could somehow find her there.

"Nowhere near here; that's for damn sure. The only cunts that ever walk this place are the ones who come to desensitize you to their flesh." Shuddering at the memory, Matthew adds, "The first time you see a chick in this place, you are going to cringe."

"Ugly?"

"I wish." Shaking his head, Matthew explains, "No, they hire the most beautiful women they can possibly find. All carpet munchers, too, every God damn one of 'em—but don't ever let them hear you say anything derogatory about them—or the men—that'll earn you a paddling."

"They beat us here?"

"If that was all they did," Matthew says, "I think this place would almost be bearable."

"Mattie!" A high pitched, far too feminine voice shrills out. "Is my little Mattie complaining again?" Stephie strolls into the boys' cabin. He is wearing tight-fitting, very short shorts and a tie-up tank top. His hair is up in a high ponytail, classic mid-twentieth century, and his makeup and false eyelashes are garish. As soon as Stephie's voice shrills out, Matthew lies down on his bed, covering his eyes with his arm. His body begins to quiver. Stephie sits down on the edge of Matthew's bed. "Sit up, Mattie." A hint of anger lowers his voice an octave, but gaiety returns as soon as he notices Todd. "Oh, Mattie, your little roommate's awake." His voice is now fully masculine, no longer pretending to be jocular. "I said sit up!" He smacks Matthew's thigh. Matthew obeys, pulling his knees in tight to avoid any physical contact with Stephie.

"Todd Middleton, this is Stephie. Stephie, this is Todd Middleton."

"Much better," Stephie says while eyeing Todd. Now looking over to Matthew, he adds, "I'd hate to have to give you five demerits today." Matthew looks up, his face pale with terror. "Don't play coy with me," says Stephie, tickling Matthew under the chin. The act causes the young man to shake as tears begin to fall. Todd watches on in horror. "First demerit. I heard you call the women who come here for training purposes cunts and carpet munchers." As an aside, he adds, "That should really count for two demerits, but since I don't like women anymore—"

Todd bursts out, "You were het'ro?"

"Yes." Stephie poses happily, pushing out a flat chest forming the S curve with his back. "Believe it or not, Stephie is a tamed little boy. Fully homosexual now." Shaking his head in disgust, he says, "I can't believe I ever thought of girls that way." Assertively, proving even then he knew what was right, he adds, "But I told my dads and they signed me up right away. I had never touched or kissed a girl even. I was only twelve. Being here was the best thing ever to happen to little Stephie. They treated me so well. I was like everyone's little pet."

232

"I was wrong," Matthew quips. "There is one they didn't have to bring in with drugs."

Smiling happily, allowing Matthew his little joke, mostly because he is proud of that fact, Stephie carries on with his life story. "Now I'm fifteen and one of the best tamers ever." Sitting straight and proud, he states, "That's what Papa Gideon—Mr. Weller says." He smiles sadly Matthew's way. "I'm still too young to marry any of my wards, though." He pats Matthew's leg. "I'm hoping Mattie'll wait for me." Matthew groans. Stephie, angered by this subtle act of rejection, squeezes Matthew's leg hard. Looking back Todd's way, feigning serenity in his relationship with Matthew, he explains, "My dads won't let me marry until I'm eighteen." Then looking back over to Matthew, he says, "But Mattie will wait for me, won't you Mattie?"

"They won't let two *strais* marry, remember," Matthew mutters almost too helplessly. Matthew's neck has remained bent the entire time, and now his head drops even lower.

Stephie starts to run his fingers through Matthew's hair, gripping it at the crown and yanking his head up. Tears have flooded Matthew's face. "Papa Gideon says I can marry whomever I want!" He kisses Matthew full on the lips. "And I want you!" A little grimly now, he admits, "But Papa Gideon doesn't think you'll wait for me." Stephie sadly inspects Matthew's face. Tears are streaming down Matthew's neck. When Matthew fails to respond, Stephie leans in and licks away the tears at the base of Matthew's neck up to his closed eyelid. There is no pretense left in Stephie's voice. It is as if his voice has suddenly cracked and lowered in the instant. "Won't you, Mattie?" That Stephie's grip on Matthew's hair has tightened is evidenced by the wince Matthew suddenly expresses.

"Yes," Matthew mumbles. "I'll wait."

Stephie lets go of Matthew's hair and watches with amusement as his head drops down dejectedly against his chest. "You know," Stephie decides, "I am going to have to give you five demerits after all."

Matthew's head rises instantly. He is off the bed and on his knees in front of Stephie. "Please, Stephie, please. I'll be good; I promise. I'll do anything. *Anything!*"

Todd shrinks back on his bed. *Hadrian no! Not in front of me.* Horrified by the thought, he quickly turns his back and squeezes his eyes shut. The thought of what might be about to happen causes Todd's stomach to swirl once more.

Matthew gulps back a wail. "Please don't give me another demerit." Openly crying now, his sobs tear a cleft in Todd's heart. Matthew hides his face in Stephie's lap.

With a motherly, loving smile, Stephie begins petting Matthew's hair. "I don't want to see my Mattie hurt. I just want us to love each other. Because I love you, Mattie." Then softly, in a voice full of hope, he requests, "Kiss me if you love me, Mattie." Stephie ceases the petting, closes his eyes, tilts his head, and waits for a kiss.

Realizing nothing untoward is going to happen, Todd looks back just in time to see Matthew shudder silently, look up at Stephie's attending lips, and comply.

Stephie opens his eyes, his smile now genuine. "Will you do something for me," he sings out, "now that I've done something nice for you?" Matthew nods his assent. Stephie stands, lifting Matthew up with him. They clasp hands and Stephie leads Matthew out.

As they walk over the threshold of the cabin door, they pass Jason Warith entering. He smiles, "Hello, Stephie, Mattie." Matthew remains silent; Stephie smiles, "Hello, Jason. Your little boy is waiting for you." Stephie nods in Todd's direction as he pulls Matthew through the cabin door.

* * * * *

Salve!

Spotlight: Jason Warith
HNN—Melissa Eagleton Reporting

"As I am sure you have noticed, viewers, we have been following a theme these past few weeks. With such a rash of exposures occurring this spring—the most shocking being that of Pride's b-ball star, Todd Middleton—we decided to do a thorough exploration into reeducation. Our focus has been on the most successful of the four male reeducation camps, that being the Northeast Reeducation Camp under the tutelage of Mr. Gideon Weller. Well, tonight we have another guest for you to meet. Before I bring him out on stage, I would like to give you a little background into this extraordinary individual. Jason Warith, now nearing thirty, has just completed his doctorate from Antonius Uni. With a Ph.D. in human sexual orientation, Jason Warith is considered the 'golden boy' of reeducation. Having recently finished his internship at the Southwest Reeducation Camp, located on a farm ten miles east of New Augustus City, Adrian Adams, the camp warden, claims Jason Warith is going to change the way we approach reeducation. 'His methods,' Adams says, 'are innovative and humane ' Warith's approach, Adams maintains, completely dismisses corporal punishment and concentrates on accepting the young man for who he is while simultaneously helping him accept homosexuality as a loving alternative. And on that note, I would like to bring out the man said to be the future reformer of reeducation, Mr. Jason Warith.

"Mr. Warith, welcome and thank you for being on *Salve!*"

"Thank you for having me, Ms. Eagleton."

"Please, Melissa. Tell me, Jason, you don't mind my calling you by your first name, I hope?"

"Not at all."

"Tell me, Jason; what inspired you to pursue reeducation as a career?"

"My mama, Helena, spent three of her teenage years inside a reeducation camp for women. It took a long time for me to get her to open up and tell me what reeducation was like, speaking about what had happened to her was akin to her reliving it all over, but one day she opened up and shared her story."

"Would you mind sharing your Mama Helena's story with my viewers?"

"Yes, I would mind. This is her story and not mine. I cannot share it with the world. What I can say, though, is that her story inspired me. I knew if the way Mama Helena was treated is any indication, the reeducation process needs some serious reformation. It was then that I decided to make the study of human sexual orientation and the ways in which we reeducate our youth my life's vocation. I knew I could not work with young women; the reeducation of females is clearly the domain of our women, but I also knew that if the way my mama was treated is any indication, then our young men must also be brutalized."

"Brutalized?"

"Yes, Ms. Eagleton, brutalized. Think about it. Whom do we hate more—the heterosexual male or the heterosexual female?"

"I—I don't think hate is the right word."

"Really, how many people like barbarians? Hordes? Pedophiles? Rapists?"

"Well, when you put it that way, but really, I think you are over-exaggerating a little."

"Am I? How many times have you referred to the heterosexual male as a barbarian? And you cannot deny that the prevailing attitude toward heterosexual men is that they are violent and dangerous."

"You have to admit there has been a lot of evidence against them."

"Perhaps, coming from those men outside, men who are desperate enough to attack our wall. But I do not believe we should be comparing our young men to fraught and starving marauders."

"I see your point."

"Our boys are merely confused. They are experiencing, what for them, are natural sexual feelings toward women. If, as we believe, many of them are twos on the Kinsey scale, then their heterosexual urges are a lot stronger than their latent homosexual desires. There is nothing wrong with that. The only reason our founding families rejected heterosexual behavior—or rather, I should say the main reason they rejected it, and why we the citizens of Hadrian continue to do so, was and still is, due to the need to quell overpopulation. Rather than punish our boys and girls for their natural feelings, we need to educate them to reason beyond their initial sexual instincts. Once they come to understand the need to avoid procreation, we can then work with them to embrace the latent homosexual inside. It is incumbent upon us to help guide them toward the very same choice we have all made: to be homosexual for the protection of our planet. The key difference here is that these youth need to make this choice consciously, whereas the rest of us have subconsciously agreed to this lifestyle by merely accepting our upbringing."

"Well, this is very interesting. I understand that your first position is to be at the Northeast Camp."

"Yes, I was originally offered a position at the Southwest Camp, and I am sorry to pass that opportunity by, but my services have been requested at the Northeast Camp so I agreed to go."

"Yes, you will be amazed at what you find there. Gideon Weller has done incredible things with his wards. He has the highest success rate in all four male reeducation camps."

"Yes, so I've been told."

"You must look forward to working with such a dedicated and successful man."

"I am certain working with Gideon Weller is going to be an eye-opening experience."

"Indeed it will be. Gideon Weller impressed me as a remarkable man. Reeducation is one of the most commendable of professions. I wish you the best of luck in all your endeavors."

"Thank you, Ms. Eagleton."

"Thank you, Mr. Warith, for if what they say about you is true, then you are the future of reeducation."

Vale!

Warith vs. Weller

Todd is stunned. Matthew, someone Todd is certain is highly intelligent and was very likely once a vibrant young man, has clearly been twisted into something morbid and broken. Lost in contemplation, Todd doesn't even notice Jason Warith until he sits down across from him.

A tall man of mixed Arab and Irish descent, Jason's skin is golden brown. His hair is a rich black, his eyes a very dark brown, and his smile kind and gentle. Jason's calming demeanor had helped him to win over the wards under his guardianship at the Southwest Reeducation Camp. Jason's work during his residency earned him a reputation as the most likely of his graduating class to achieve success in the field of reeducation. Some even hailed him as the future of reeducation.

Not wanting to alienate Todd immediately, Jason chooses to sit on Matthew's bed across from him. In this way, Todd can avoid close physical contact, helping him feel more at his ease. Jason has come to accept that these youth are fearful of men who come on too strong. The best way to win a young man over is to give him a lot of personal space and only enter into his zone when invited. Jason holds out his hand for Todd to shake. "Hello," he says with his famous smile. The sight of Jason's hand repulses Todd, as if it were a cobra ready to strike. "I won't hurt you, I promise," Jason adds reassuringly. When Todd pushes back, Jason lowers his hand. His smile dissipates. This is not working out. He knew meeting his first charge wasn't going to be easy. The file on this boy suggests a hostile youth; yet everything about the young man suggests otherwise. Of course, he is just coming off the effects of the tranquilizer drugs, something else Jason hopes to phase out over time, but still, Todd's reaction is more like a scared child than an angry young man.

Jason crosses his legs and studies Todd. *He sure looks young.* While studying his chart to make sure he got the age correct, he asks, "How old are you, son?"

"Seventeen," Todd answers, but he stares away, avoiding Jason's eyes.

That's his age all right, Jason reaffirms as he shakes his head wonderingly. *Fear,* he muses, *has a way of making a man look younger or older.* And, in the case of Todd Middleton, fright has reduced him into the image of a small child. As well as ensuring the boy's age was accurately recorded, Jason was hoping his question would open the door for further conversation. It hasn't worked. Todd remains despondent, staring first at the wall, now the ceiling, and now the floor.

"My name's Jason." Pausing briefly, a little uneasy about what he has been instructed to say, he adds, "I'm told to call you Tabatha."

Finally eye contact, but glaring hate and anger. *I should have expected as much,* Jason sighs inwardly, *but I have to mark that down—no wait; they can't hear a facial expression, only if he—*

"My name is Todd! I won't wear one of your stupid gay names."

Damn, Jason closes his eyes briefly. He knows he has to jot this down, give the boy his first demerit. Mr. Weller is just outside the cabin door, hanging on their every word. "Listen…" he is about to say, "Tabatha" but decides not to call the boy by any name for the moment. *The last thing this kid needs is for me to exacerbate an already dangerous situation.* Jason knows Mr. Weller seriously hates this boy. He has close ties with Elena Stiles, Crystal Albright's second mother. How to word this? he wonders. Jason Warith does not subscribe to the need to change the ward's name. Yet Mr. Weller made it very clear in their first meeting that this is the way things are done at the Northeast Camp, and under no circumstances is Jason to bring any of his high and mighty radical notions inside his camp. Indeed, Jason's first meeting with Gideon Weller was more than just an eye opener. He was read the riot act and informed beyond a shadow of a doubt that he, Gideon Weller, had not hired him. The only reason Jason Warith is a member of his staff is due to the political clout of one Destiny Stuttgart, Dean's grandmother. Aged eighty-four, Destiny Stuttgart is the last surviving original founding member. For the past twenty-three years, Destiny Stuttgart had thought her grandson dead, so when Dean voc'd her, she had almost refused to listen, thinking he was some sick pervert. It wasn't until Dean had called her Mimi, Dean having been the only grandchild ever to call her Mimi, that she turned on her voc camera and looked into the eyes of the gentleman who had once been the child she had deeply loved. When he explained his and Todd's current circumstances, she decided to take action. She had placed a personal voc to Adrian Adams at the Southwest Camp and asked him for the best man for the job. He had reluctantly recommended Jason Warith. When Jason learned the details of the case, he agreed, knowing full well he would be up against a battle. Rumors abound regarding the treatment of wards at Gideon Weller's camp and Dean Hunter's account only proved to Jason that his presence there was essential, not only for Todd Middleton, but it was critical if real steps were to be made in the reformation of reeducation. Cut out the malignant tumor first; then bombard the body with radiation if you truly hope to kill all the cancer. *But the tumor is still deep inside the brain,* Jason reminds himself. *I haven't dug it out yet, and until I am able to, I have to tread carefully for this boy's sake.* At the moment, this is Gideon Weller's camp. He is in charge and his word, for the time being, is law! During their meeting, Gideon Weller made it perfectly clear, almost too zealously, that the Northeast Camp abides by the demerit system, and as soon as five demerits are given, punishment is swift and brutal. When Jason refused to commit any act that would physically harm a ward under his care, Gideon Weller vowed to be the man's shadow. "Punishment," he stated unequivocally, "will be administered whenever I deem necessary—and I will step in to administer it if you lack the courage to act when necessary!" Jason knows Gideon Weller to be a man of his word. He is standing outside the cabin door, waiting patiently for the opportunity to punish the Middleton boy. Focusing now on Todd, Jason continues, closing his eyes briefly to remember Weller's exact words, "The reason Mr. Weller insists we give you boys new names is to help...to help you transition from the perception of being heterosexual back to a normal gay state."

"Why is being gay normal and heterosexual is not?"

It is a fair question, and back at the southwest camp, Jason would have ignored the fact that it was expelled with such venom and force and answered the boy honestly. Unfortunately, Gideon Weller also heard the question and would only hear the aggravated taunt. Jason knows that the tone of Todd's voice means a second demerit. There is no doubt in Jason's mind that Gideon Weller has added that to the count. Grimacing, Jason knows only too well what lies ahead—how Gideon Weller will emerge as soon as Todd hits the deadly number five. "Neither state is unnatural—"

he begins but is cut short by Todd.

"Then why am I forced to be here?"

Three—damn! "Please, stop speaking and just listen!" Jason had hoped to make a connection with his charge before Mr. Weller came in with the discipline. If he doesn't reach the boy first, he won't have any hope of ever getting Todd to trust him.

"Fuck you!" Todd expostulates.

Four! Jason places his face in his hands. He hasn't even had a chance to explain the demerit system and what is about to happen. Frustrated, he begins rubbing his hands down his face as if to ease tension. Suddenly, like a silent explosion, he grabs the back of Todd's head and gags his mouth with his other hand. "Shut up and listen," he whispers. "Mr. Weller is listening to everything you say. He wants to hurt you, and I'm the only thing standing between you and him. You have to let me help you. Will you please just let me explain to you about this institution—" Jason yelps as Todd bites into his hand. Although no blood is drawn, there are some pretty deep teeth marks.

"Fuck you! And fuck this whole fucking institution!" Todd shouts.

"That's five," says Mr. Weller. Before Jason can even think the number, the man is standing inside the door of the cabin grinning.

"Mr. Weller," Jason intercedes, "give me a minute. I haven't even had a chance to explain the rules to him."

"He understands enough to know that his place is to obey, to listen…" Weller pauses, noting Jason cradling his hand, and having heard the yelp, inferring the damage done, adds with a cynical smile, "and be respectful." Now standing at the small table in the room's center, rubbing the table softly with his hand, Mr. Weller demands, "Bring him here."

"You have five demerits, Tabatha," Jason begins. "You get a demerit every time you are unruly, disobedient, you swear—"

"Enough explanation!" Mr. Weller's voice is dry and curt.

"He should at least be told what is about to happen and why." Jason has never ascribed to the demerit system. At the Southeast Camp, he was able to pilot a new, more gentle approach, one that invites the young man back into the homosexual fold, rather than berates and beats him there. Although he knew the Northeast Camp advocated corporal punishment, Jason was disappointed to learn that Gideon Weller actually utilizes it on a daily basis.

Staring straight ahead at the wall, Todd struggles not to shake. He remembers Matthew's face when Stephie threatened him with a fifth demerit. *It doesn't matter*, he thinks. *I'm not giving in!*

"Bring. Him. Here." Each word is punctuated harshly with a soft tap of his index finger against the table.

As Mr. Weller's order is not to be gainsaid, Jason motions for Todd to stand. When Todd refuses to acknowledge him, Jason grips his arm. Todd yanks it away, looking up at the man with sullen hate. Jason can't bring himself to do this. "No," he insists. "It's too soon after his arrival to punish him. All the research shows that a softer, gentler approach works better than——"

Mr. Weller is having none of this. "We do not pamper our wards here, Mr. Warith!" Then turning toward the door, he yells, "Darrell!" A tall muscular man emerges through the cabin door. Watching as his henchman walks over, Mr. Weller tells Jason, "I knew you were too soft for this job, but it appears Dean Stuttgart has some pull after all."

Just as Dean Stuttgart's name begins to register in Todd's brain, it is yanked away instantly when Darrell reaches across the bed and grabs him by the hair. Todd yelps as the large hand pulls him backwards. In one swift motion, Darrell lifts the youth off the bed and tosses him face first over the table.

Smiling sadistically, Mr. Weller adds, "Fortunately, Dean Stuttgart is still an embarrassment to his family so his hand only extends so far." Jason turns toward the door. Arresting Jason with the shot of a finger, Mr. Weller orders, "You stay right where you are, Mr. Wraith! This boy is your charge, and you are expected to be present for all his reeducation treatment." With a judgmental air, he states, "It should be you doing this, but as you are not up to the task, I shall take over." Mr. Weller takes a moment to enjoy watching Todd's hands flail fruitlessly at Darrell's grip before ordering him to undo his pants.

Todd screeches out, "Fuck you!"

Mr. Weller doesn't reply. He merely crosses over to the wall behind the table to retrieve the paddle hanging there, only to return instantly to slam Todd's backside with it. Appreciating the boy's howl, Mr. Weller waits patiently for it to diminish into a whimper. "Nine more with your pants down, Tabatha. Twenty more with them up."

Crossing over to the table, bending down level to the boy's ear, Jason implores, "Please, Todd, I can't stop him." Closing his eyes briefly, he begs, "Let's not make this worse."

Todd's mind is reeling with pain. *Worse? How can this possibly get worse?* Fumbling for his pants button, he fails to release them fast enough for Mr. Weller. Another smash of the paddle hits his backside. Todd's body convulses as he shakes and screams. Then, wailing out in agony and frustration, he pleads, "I can't. I can't. You won't let me."

Jason stops Mr. Weller from delivering a third blow by grabbing his wrist mid-swing. He stares directly into the warden's eyes. Both men threaten the other. "I'll help him," Jason insists. Mr. Weller struggles against Jason's grip. His lackey, however, cannot aid him since he is currently occupied with keeping a tight grip on Todd's hair. Jason only lets go of his grip when Mr. Weller releases the tension in his arm, showing his willingness to lower the paddle. Jason bends down and undoes Todd's pants, lowering them to his ankles.

"His underwear, too." It is not enough simply to beat the boy. Mr. Weller wants him degraded beyond recognition of his former self. Although Jason wishes to protest, he suspects Mr. Weller will only make things harder for Todd. After his briefs are dangling past his knees, Mr. Weller begins administering the punishment. A third smack is called out as "One!"

"Three!" Jason reminds him.

Again, the two men stare. Oddly enough, Mr. Weller concedes. "Three." Before taking his fourth swing, though, he pauses to inspect the paddle. As he had hoped, as is almost always the case (the drug induces such violent vomiting that inevitably something always shoots out the back end), there are traces of feces on the paddle. He shows it to Darrell, whose grin resembles a rabid hyena. As Darrell shoves Todd to the floor, pushing him into Jason in the process, Mr. Weller spits out his disgust, "You dirty *strai* rat!" Shoving the paddle into Todd's face, he demands, "Didn't your fathers teach you how to wipe your ass?" Looking now at Jason, who has just recovered from the shove, he orders, "Get this dirty little charge of yours a basin of water, soap, and a washcloth." When Jason fails to react on the instant, Mr. Weller explodes, "Now!"

Jason leaps at the order, fear chasing him into the washroom. *Hadrian's lover,* he marvels, *if the man has me this frightened, how must the boy feel?* Todd, in his turn, is lying on the floor, shaking in horror and pain. Within moments, Jason is back. He places the basin next to Todd, rubs some soap on a cloth, and is about to begin washing the boy's behind when Mr. Weller stops him. "One does not stoop to wiping one's ward's ass here, Mr. Warith! The boy must do that himself."

Jason, with infinite tenderness, helps Todd into a child's pose on his knees. He hands him the cloth, guiding his hand to where it needs to be. All the time, he whispers soothingly into Todd's ear. "I will get you out of here, Todd; I promise." But Todd can't hear. His mind is swirling inside an abyss of shame and degradation. He is so consumed by anguish and horror that he can't even accomplish the simple task of wiping himself. Jason ignores Mr. Weller's order and assists the boy. He holds Todd's hand and makes all the necessary motions until he is sure the area is clean. "Let me help you back up, Todd."

Jason's whisper, unfortunately, is loud enough for Mr. Weller to hear. "Have you forgotten his name already, Mr. Warith?"

"Come on, Tabatha," Jason concedes. *No point making things worse.* Lifting Todd to standing, he adds, "I'll help you back to your bed."

"You will help him back to the table! His punishment is not over."

Jason, without turning Todd, looks back at Mr. Weller. "I am the boy's charge, and I say he has been punished enough for his first offense."

"Mr. Jason Warith," Mr. Weller orders, "walk your ward back over to that table. He still has seven hits left. Refuse and I will add the additional twenty."

Additional twenty? Jason looks deep into the headmaster's eyes. Fear begins to scalds him as if he were slowly being lowered into a vat of hot oil. Ironically, a cold shiver rushes up his spine. It dawns on Jason just how dangerous Gideon Weller is. *Hadrian help us; the man is insane.* Not knowing what else to do, and fearing even worse for Todd, Jason Warith turns and directs his ward back to the table. When Todd is placed in front, he literally falls face first onto the tabletop. This time, Darrell grabs Todd's hands to hold him steady. The beatings continue to the count of ten. Mr. Weller, handing the paddle to Jason, demands, "Wash it! And then get the boy ready for indoctrination! We welcome him into the fold at seven."

Jason is stunned. The instrument is bloody, the violent blows having burst veins in the boy's anus. Walking in a daze, Jason enters the washroom.

Looking at his loyal aide, Weller nods. Darrell releases Todd's hands and the boy falls to the floor like wax dripping off a candle.

Jason races out of the washroom as soon as he hears the thud of Todd's body hitting the floor. Through his peripheral vision, Jason catches the sight of Weller and Darrell walking out the cabin door. Directing all his attention to the youth on the floor, he says, "Todd, Todd, my boy." He receives no answer.

* * * * *

Salve!

The Error of Their Ways
HNN—Melissa Eagleton Reporting

Every so often our government reminds HNN of our responsibility to keep Hadrian's citizens informed of the conditions of the outside world. Although we are all aware of the ghastly conditions that exist in other parts of the planet, it never hurts to refresh our consciousness so that our vigilance to maintain and create both a stable human population as well as preserve and resurrect earth's natural resources never abates. It is hoped that a look at the misery wrought by humanity in the outside world will help quell our youth's foolish behaviors; many of our youth persist in experimenting with heterosexual behavior, reminding them yet again of the world's desperate need to stem the tide of world population.

Last year's world report concentrated on the East Asian countries with a strong emphasis on India, perhaps the world's hardest hit, having exceeded 2.5 billion according to the most recent World Pop Clock. Although much of our emphasis has been placed on this country due to its high degree of disparity, Hadrian's government has asked we look at the dwindling state of our closest neighbors; in particular, the splintered anarchy that was once the United States of America.

There is no doubt that many of Hadrian's citizens feel those who used to be American citizens have received their just deserts, but it is hard to hold onto resentment when one views from our satellite cameras the horror of their current existence. Yes, believe it or not, these people once reigned as the world's most dominant power. To think of all the good they could have done to help protect our planet had they but only listened to their own prophets.

One such prophet was a man by the name of Chris Hedges. He wrote back in the early twenty-first century. I dug up one of his articles from Hadrian's editorial archives. This piece is titled, "We Are Breeding Ourselves to Extinction," March 9, 2009. Although it is questionable whether or not humanity still had time to stop its onslaught of destruction, this man at least had the wherewithal to warn humanity of its unfortunate direction. His words also inspired pre-founding family members who established the process of purchasing and creating our own country. Listen to how he opened his article: "All measures to thwart the degradation and destruction of our ecosystem will be useless if we do not cut population growth." Why did humanity ignore this man's voice and the voices of others like him! As we all know and can attest to by virtue of the images of the swarming hordes only two borders below us, that warning was not heeded. More damning evidence against what used to be the United States of America, what used to be the "dominant world power," are echoed in Hedges' words: "The United States alone gobbles up about 25 percent of the oil produced in the world each year." Another key point Hedges reminds us of is that, even though countries like old Canada and the old US of A were not among those countries overpopulating the planet (at this time), their populations continued to grow due to the ever-growing need for immigration. It was these old countries' desperate attempts to stem the excessive waves of the human tide crashing against their shores that wrought many of the bloody conflicts of the mid to late twenty-first century.

Hedges warned us then, "The overpopulated regions of the globe will ravage their local environments, cutting down rainforests and the few remaining wilderness areas, in a desperate bid to grow food." Hedges also pointed out that which every "developed" country but Hadrian now lives with: "the depletion and destruction of resources will eventually create an overpopulation problem in industrialized nations as well." And indeed it did!

Too few listened to Chris Hedges and other learned men and women like him. But Hadrian's pre-founding members heard! And, Hadrian still listens. It was "Earth First!" when Hadrian's borders were created, and it is "Earth First!" to this very day. The human species and the earth will survive, but in order for this to happen, we must all sacrifice. We must all sacrifice for Hadrian. We must all sacrifice to reclaim our beloved Mother Earth.

Vale!

Indoctrination

Jason does not leave Todd's side. Even though the boy is non-responsive, Jason is determined to help him up and onto his bed. He begins by lifting Todd up by his armpits and instructing the lad to step out of his pants and shorts. Todd obeys but says nothing. Helping him over to the bed, Jason ensures Todd is lying face down with his red, swollen buttocks exposed to the air. "There's some salve in the bathroom," Jason says soothingly. "I'm going to get it and put some on your backside." Todd isn't even listening. His mind has entered a dark state—a place void of thought and emotion. Cold and black, it is a place into which Todd can escape—or embrace—insanity. As soon as Jason returns with the ointment, he warns Todd, "It will sting at first, but it will soon become soothing." After applying the ointment, Jason pulls a chair next to Todd's bed where he holds vigil. Humming softly a song his mama used to sing to him when he was sick and couldn't sleep, he gently runs his fingers through Todd's sweaty and matted hair. The boy's eyes are open, but at what they stare, Jason remains oblivious.

Neither Todd nor Jason are aware of time lapsing. Jason is startled back into the present when a small icon appears in the far right corner of his vision. Focusing on it, Jason blinks. "Yes—I know—He's in no condition— It will simply have to wait—No!—I said, NO!—No, you listen to me; this boy is my ward. I am his charge; he is in no shape—Be reasonable—What is wrong with you?—Fine!—Yes!—We're coming!" Annoyed, Jason blinks to sever the connection. Looking down at the boy splayed unconscious before him, he gives him a gentle shake. "Todd, I'm sorry, son, but—" He stops as Todd moans. Closing his eyes, he takes a deep breath. Shaking his head, he wants very much to defy Mr. Weller. *But that will only get me fired*, he reasons, *and then Todd will have no one to help him survive this*. "I am so sorry, son." It is a joke of an apology and Jason knows it. Todd does not acknowledge any of what Jason says. He has fallen back into the black void of his unconsciousness. "You have to get up." Jason closes his eyes, swallowing self-loathing. "I have to get you dressed." Re-opening his eyes, Jason looks around for Todd's pants. Picking them up, he notices how tight they really are. He shakes his head, *stovepipe jeans*. There is no way he will put these back on Todd in his condition. Tossing them aside, he rummages through Matthew's drawers, hoping to find a pair of soft loose-fitting cotton pants. He settles on a pair of fleece pajama bottoms. *These will have to do*, he reasons. He doesn't even bother to make Todd stand. He slips the soft pants under Todd's feet, drawing them up over his legs, taking extra precaution when he lifts them over his buttocks. Even so, Todd groans in agony. As he picks the boy up off the bed, Jason tries to help him stand. Whether it is due to physical agony or simply a lack of will, it is evident Todd will not be walking. Jason lifts him up into his arms and carries him over to the central cabin. Todd rests his head on Jason's shoulder, causing the older man to wonder whether he still has a chance of winning the boy over.

* * * * *

The main cabin is in the center of the complex. All other cabins, those designated to the various wards, encircle it. This much larger log building houses administrative offices, the kitchen galley, cafeteria, small "social rooms" for a charge and ward to conduct private sessions, as well as a large meeting area for indoctrination, dances, parties, sometimes even weddings. It is to this room Jason Warith was instructed to bring Todd for his indoctrination.

Indoctrination consists of the current wards welcoming the newest ward to their commune and reciting, by rote, the rules and rationale for reeducation. For this purpose, the room is set up much like an auditorium in which the new ward's chair is placed front and center while the other wards are seated semi-circle audience-style, facing him. Behind each ward's chair stands his guardian. Currently, seventeen wards are in attendance at the Northeast Camp. Todd Middleton brings that number up to eighteen. Behind Todd's chair is a small riser upon which sits the camp warden, Mr. Weller, his administrative team, and two psychiatric counselors.

Mr. Weller glares at Jason. "Put your ward on his feet and bring him to the front." Jason ignores the man's pointed request and carries Todd forward. Such blatant disregard for his authority bristles down Weller's spine. "Set him down, Mr. Warith!" Jason—suspecting he has already pushed too many buttons for his own—and his ward's good—helps Todd to standing, turning him to face his audience.

"Sit him in his chair," Weller orders.

Jason stares straight ahead, seeing a mixture of animosity, concern, and respect in the other guardians' eyes. He also notes the look of shock and awe from the small collection of wards. Instead of seating Todd, Jason cradles the youth in his arms.

Sensing Warith's refusal to comply, Weller contemplates disciplining his newest employee (a man he never hired but had thrust upon him, no doubt by some vestigial influence Dean Stuttgart still has) right now in front of everyone, but he reconsiders. Warith is being hailed as the "golden boy" and leader of the reformation of reeducation, but Weller thinks, *Reform is not what is needed to quell the heterosexual male. Discipline and a strong hand are all that have ever worked, will ever work, with the male who envisions himself the aggressor.* Still, now is not the moment to fight Warith. He will settle with Jason Warith later. "We shall begin." Mr. Weller's voice booms and echoes throughout the room with over-exaggerated strength and confidence. He is determined that no one charge or ward will take advantage of Warith's show of defiance to treat him similarly. "Wards, let us welcome Tabatha Middleton to our family." There are murmurs of awe. Although he is introduced as Tabatha, Todd Middleton is recognized by everyone because his face and name have been splashed all over *Salve!* for the past month due to his team winning Quadrants and the Nationals and his walking away with the Most Valuable Player award. Their moment of solemn respect is shattered when Mr. Weller orders, "Mattie Malloy, as you are Tabatha's roommate, stand and begin."

Stephie beams. This is a great opportunity to show Papa Gideon how far he's come with Mattie. Tapping Matthew's shoulder, he whispers excitedly, "Stand up, Mattie; stand up."

Obeying, Matthew begins, "Please remember your guardian is here to help you." Stephie smiles. Matthew remembers everything so well. "He will guide you through this transition, remind you of the cornerstones of Hadrian's society, and explain how the loss of one foundation means the loss of our society's strength."

Stephie is thrilled. "Oh, Mattie," he coos, "that is so good." Stephie's beam is seraphic. Mr. Weller rewards him with a smile of reassurance. "What next, Mattie? What next?"

Although focused on Todd, Matthew knows every word he says is falling on deaf ears. It is obvious Todd is already beaten. As Matthew's mind is no longer needed to recite the rules by rote, his thoughts reel back to his first day. His once defiant will earned him five demerits before he even knew what demerits were; these were followed swiftly by the paddle. He shudders at the thought. Everything he does these days is to avoid further encounters with the paddle. He drones on, "Your guardian will guide you through the dangers of heterosexual behavior. How heterosexual men are violent in nature. Always abusive and cruel, it is not uncommon to find rapists and pedophiles among them."

"Oh, Mattie," Stephie sings, "I am so proud of you!"

"Your guardian will help you purge these negative tendencies; guide you toward embracing the more passive loving qualities of our nation."

"Oh, Mattie," Stephie is beside himself. "You did so good." As Matthew resumes his seat, Stephie pats him proudly on the back, kissing the top of his head. Matthew looks straight ahead, acknowledging nothing.

"Jamie," Mr. Weller commands. His guardian yanks the young man to standing. "Inform Tabatha of our daily routine."

When he fails to respond instantly, his guardian slaps the back of his head. "Rise at six," he stammers out. "Breakfast at six-thirty—exercise at seven—classes at eight—lunch at eleven-thirty—exercise again at twelve—rejecting women at one—private session at three—supper at five—visual of the outside world at six—private session at seven—bed by nine."

"Very good, Jamie. Sit down." Glaring at the back of Jason Warith's head, Mr. Weller growls, "Mr. Warith, turn your ward, and his chair, around. Tabatha has missed supper, but he is in time for tonight's visual of the outside world."

After Jason encourages Todd to turn and face Mr. Weller, the warden bores down on the youth. "Tabatha, as you have just heard, we run a very tight ship here at the Northeast Camp. There is no tolerance for rebellion. If you listen to your guardian and obey the rules, your transition back into Hadrian society will be swift and smooth. If not, know this; disciplinary measures will be used to quell all acts of defiance and heterosexual behaviors. We are not going to threaten you with hell and damnation in some foolish afterlife. No, Tabatha. Hell and damnation is out there, on the other side of those walls. It is Hadrian government's strict policy never to send our children out there to fend for themselves. We will either aid in your transition, or retain you here since the only other choice left to you would be to live outside our walls. Today's visuals will remind you why that alternative is not a viable option." Now directing stern attention to Jason, he commands, "And now, Mr. Warith, your ward must sit down!" Each word is spoken emphatically, leaving no room for resistance.

* * * * *

Salve!

The Twenty-Fifth Anniversary of the Terror Attack
HNN—Melissa Eagleton Reporting

It was twenty-five years ago today that a group of well-organized Christian extremists broke through Hadrian's southwest wall. Although well-fortified, those fanatics somehow managed to gain entrance. It is believed one of our soldiers was in collusion with the enemy. Although Corporal Victor Williams was also killed during the attack, it was from his watchtower that the invaders should have been detected. Williams' family, though, ardently defends him, claiming the young man was a patriot and not, as many suspect, a heterosexual sympathizer. Even so, a number of Williams' peers were concerned about his sexual preference. Williams did not date, and a few female soldiers claimed he was creepy. "His eyes follow you everywhere," one female soldier had said in a complaint registered to a senior officer. No formal action was ever taken against Private Williams, though, as no tangible evidence regarding heterosexual tendencies was ever produced.

If Williams were a traitor, he allowed over fifty heterosexual barbarians inside our wall to murder all the soldiers of his compound. Of the fifteen men and eighteen women stationed at the southwest gate that day, all but one died. All the male soldiers were shot, and those women who survived the initial attack were brutally raped and murdered. Footage of the event was found on the body of a dead enemy renegade. These evil brutal animals filmed most of their atrocities, leaving behind a tape that was spine-chilling to say the very least. The torture and raping of the eight surviving female soldiers was cruelty beyond belief.

One soldier survived this brutal attack: Captain Tanya Weller. Before being killed, Corporal Regan Hillier managed to get a message over the wave asking for reinforcements. By the time two heavily armed battalions arrived, though, everyone but Sergeant Weller had been murdered. The heterosexual barbarians were in the process of brutally raping the poor woman while others stood by filming the event. What kind of sick people would film such atrocities? What sort of sick pleasure were they hoping to gain from watching themselves murder, torture, and rape others? Did they actually believe such a film was for posterity?

Even though Sergeant Weller's life was saved, her mind was completely destroyed by the attack. She had to be institutionalized and placed under twenty-four hour watch. She still managed to commit numerous acts of self-mutilation, and eventually, she was successful at taking her own life. Her suicide, as well as the attack against her compatriots, is a bitter reminder of how the outside world views Hadrian's citizens. We must never forget that the ultimate intention of the heterosexual world is to destroy us.

Evidence of the world's hatred is clearly shown in the attack scenes filmed by the attackers. The images seen on this tape are so graphic it was decided not to publicize them; rather, we leave the viewing of them to the discretion of the individual and parents. Anyone needing to be reminded of the violent and brutal nature of heterosexual hordes can access this video, simply titled *Terrorists at the Wall*, over the wave. One viewing of this horrific event is evidence enough to explain why so many citizens of Hadrian shrink with fear at the thought of the outside world breaking through our walls. Extreme religion rules the outside world, and we have been branded as sinners due to our sexual orientation. There is also extreme jealousy that we alone are able to control population and live within a self-sustainable community. The outside world is battering against our walls, desperate to get in, anxious to destroy us and take what we have worked long and hard to create and to preserve.

Hadrian's military will not allow that to happen. The men and women in our service are dedicated to preserving our freedom and saving what little livable earth there is left. We will not allow the heterosexual barbarians, their unnatural hordes, ever to destroy the last vestige of life left on this planet!

Vale!

Gideon's Obsession

Every night after supper, since Todd Middleton's arrival at his camp, Gideon Weller retreats to his office to be alone. He falls into this routine every time a rapist enters his compound. While the wards are kept busy watching images of the outside world, Gideon Weller sits behind his desk, dims the lights, and with the blink of an eye, turns on the small, nearly invisible screen that pops up in front of his vision. Once again, he relives the horror of his mother's rape. He never uses the wall screen for this in case anyone should walk in.

Leaning back now in his large cushioned, swivel office chair, his hand fumbles for his pants zipper. His mind balks, fights against his bodily urges, but they always prove too much for him. Tears stream as he watches four men grab his mother's limbs, pulling her in four opposite directions. The film is grainy as a result of the government having to convert the stream from outside technology to make it compatible with Hadrian's voc wave. After so many viewings, though, Gideon's eyes have adjusted so he doesn't notice the distortions anymore. A fifth man enters the screen. He uses a bowie knife to tear open Gideon's mother's uniform. The man doesn't even bother to strip her fully, only cutting away enough of the fabric to expose her breasts and pubic area. The fifth man steps back and swirls his index finger. The cameraman cackles as the four men holding onto Gideon's mother take their cues. It is grotesque to watch as they pull her in four directions and then spin her, even bounce her up and down, as if this were some children's game. The camera bounces and jerks along with its handler's laughter. Gideon begins to feel nauseous. Ironically, this feeling only adds to the sensations he is creating, sickening both his sense of self and his hatred for all heterosexual men. The men torturing his mother laugh as she screams in terror. Suddenly, the spinning stops and the fifth man, retrieving his penis, begins rubbing it hard. Gideon, too, rubs harder. When ready, the fifth man grabs Gideon's mother's buttocks in preparation for the thrust. His first attempt fails, to the delight of the cameraman, who once again jars the image as he laughs uproariously. The rapist yells at his companions to hold her tighter. Forcing his eyes wide open, Gideon watches as the four men each take a step back and then lean to hold her body taut. Gideon swears he can hear his mother's tendons rip. The rapist's pelvis begins its thrust motion. Gideon's pelvis moves in tandem. A sixth man enters. He yanks his mother's head back and down, forcing her mouth open, and begins to fuck her face. Her body convulses as she chokes clearly, giving the fifth man shivering sensations. Gideon, too, chokes. *Oh, mother, forgive me!* The image is too much for him. He blinks it off. *I am not one of them*, he chants to himself. Softening, alone in the dark, he blinks to retrieve the image. He needs the provocation. The four men holding Gideon's mother shout obscenities along with the cameraman. After both men come, they drop her on the ground and a cascade of urine waterfalls on her face while one man chooses instead to defecate. For this final act of degradation, her mouth is forced open to receive his "special" gift. Gideon's body is shaking, his head thrown back, his chest arched, his eyes raked with tears.

It is not his mother's rape to which he is masturbating. It is the image he has created in his own mind, his raping the men who brutalized her. The impossibility of this act is lost on Gideon at times like this. Even though all those men are long dead, it is not their faces he sees, but the face of the current rapist living inside his compound. It is Todd Middleton's face he envisions. It is Todd Middleton he watches raping and torturing his mother. It is Todd Middleton he aggressively beats and rapes in his own mind. The more violently they torture his mother, the more violently he tortures Middleton until finally, when the first bullet from the reinforcements blows off the head of the man defecating into his mother's mouth (the head of Todd Middleton), Gideon Weller collapses, moaning piteously. Slowly, his eyes close and the horrific image vanishes. Always, without thought, he uses his wet, sticky hand to wipe away the tears. After covering himself with his disgrace, he screams inside his head, *Those Fucking Heterosexual Bastards! I am not one of them! I am not one of them!*

What few people know is that Gideon Weller had once, like Todd Middleton, been caught masturbating to straight porn. His mothers had, after a long discussion with him, decided the best course of action for him was to be reeducated at home. Gideon agreed. Being admitted to a government reeducation camp would have closed off too many doors for his future. As Gideon was scholarship material and destined for uni, he could not afford having a heterosexual stain on his record. From that time forth, he has dedicated himself to finding the latent homosexual within, but the need to eradicate everything heterosexual only came after his mother's brutal rape. The one, and only, time he had visited her in the institution, she had recognized him, but she only saw before her the heterosexual masturbator. She beat him, berated him, cursed him, and called him every ugly name she could muster. She even spat in his face. His whole life since has been dedicated to proving to himself that he is not straight. And, even though he has never formed this need for validation as a conscious thought, he is determined to make all straight men pay for what those murderous marauders did to his mother.

* * * * *

Salve!

The Reeducated
HNN—Melissa Eagleton Reporting

Are we prejudiced against the reeducated? Few people would ever admit to holding animosity toward those of us who have required government assistance when dealing with sexual confusion. Our youth, who have been found acting on heterosexual tendencies and have experienced reeducation, reenter our society fully rehabilitated. One would assume that these individuals can return to life as normal, but there are a few occupations for which these individuals no longer qualify. To begin with, no woman after reeducation has ever been allowed to become a surrogate goddess. Our government's rationale is to avoid further contamination of heterosexual genes into Hadrian's gene pool. This makes perfect sense. If those individuals in reeducation have stronger heterosexual tendencies than the rest of us, it is only reasonable not to contaminate our future children's genes. The surrogate goddess not only provides the womb for our men's fetuses to grow in, but they also provide the eggs. Although sensible not to allow a reeducated woman to become a surrogate goddess, one does have to question why no reeducated man or woman is allowed to enter Hadrian's military, especially at a time when citizens are being asked to reenlist after their four-year tour of duty is over. Why then are the reeducated banned from active military duty?

Angelo Martin, age nineteen, recently applied for and was refused active duty in Hadrian's military on the basis that he had spent eight months in reeducation at the Southwest Reeducation Camp. "I really think it's unfair that even after reeducation, we should be discriminated against. I made a mistake. I know that now. I've been reeducated, and in two years, I will swear an oath of fidelity to Hadrian and our chosen way of life. I love my country, my family, my friends, and my planet as much as any other Hadrian citizen! I want a share in being responsible for our people's protection. It's ironic really. Those of us who have been reeducated are no longer a threat. We've come to accept Hadrian's lifestyle and fully understand its merits. We want to defend our country, too. I know I would be a good soldier if only my country would let me."

Lieutenant-General Birtwistle justifies the army's refusal to allow the reeducated to serve. "We simply cannot risk having anyone who is likely to harbor sympathy for the enemy defending our wall. Just the idea that one of our own could betray us is enough to keep the reeducated off our recruitment list." When asked for evidence of someone with strong heterosexual tendencies actually aiding and abetting the enemy, reference was made to the brutal terror attack on the Southwest Gate over twenty-five years ago. Although Lieutenant-General Birtwistle admits no hard evidence was ever found against Corporal Victor Williams, many in the military still believe he was the one who helped the heterosexual barbarians to break through our wall. As always, it is important to note that the young corporal was exonerated posthumously of all charges. Yet, even just the suspicion that one of our own might well have been swayed to help outsiders based on similar sympathies is enough to bar the door of military service to those citizens who have been reeducated.

Many professions in the areas of medicine, research, and education are also out of reach to the reeducated. I recently learned that our unis deny entrance to anyone who has a reeducation record. This situation is most unfortunate because some of these youth had great careers ahead of them. We most recently lost Todd Middleton to reeducation. You may remember him as the young b-ball star of Pride High's Panthers. He had been offered an early entrance scholarship to Antinous Uni, but that offer was revoked as soon as he was exposed and sent to the Northeast Camp for reeducation. He had even mentioned in an interview with me not too long ago about his wanting to become a bioengineer like his father. His dream had been to alter rice genetically so it would grow in our northern climate. Unfortunately, we will now never know if he could have been successful.

Even with these avenues closed, there are many jobs still open to the reeducated. Many of these men and women, having fallen in love with and married their wards, choose to become stay-at-home spouses. Others go on to work in the trades. As well, the service industry is always hiring, and one does not have to disclose a history of reeducation in any of these jobs. Every job in Hadrian is important, from bioengineering right down to waste disposal. Those, in fact, who work in waste disposal are among the most important citizens in this day and age. It may not be a pretty job, but it is critical if we are to avoid future pollutants damaging our environment.

So don't despair. There is a world of work opportunities awaiting the reeducated. Hadrian loves you. And Hadrian still needs you. You have been welcomed back into the fold. Embrace your new life with joy and energy.

Vale!

Quelling Dissension

"Enough of this," Gideon mutters as he reaches across his desk for a handful of tissue. After wiping his hand and face, Gideon Weller resumes his authoritative bearing. Sitting upright, he zips up his pants before flicking on his reading lamp. Blinking his left eye, he begins peering over the file he keeps open at all times. What he reads brings a sneer to his lips. Todd Middleton has proven to be just as unruly as Gideon Weller had hoped. He is fully aware of the unspoken charge against *Tabatha*. No man should ever be allowed to get away with rape. It never ceases to amaze him that some women haven't the heart to accuse the man, as is their right. Knowing firsthand how rape can tear a woman apart, Mr. Weller sees it as his personal mission never to allow a rapist ever to reenter Hadrian society, for once a man has raped a woman, he will commit the act again and again until he has damned all of Hadrian to a living hell. Every time a rapist comes into his camp, he finds himself compelled to watch his mother's horror over and over, witnessing again and again her bloody and bruised body, her heart-wrenching screams of agony. And then come the memories of her institutionalized life with the rending of hair, the self-mutilations that eventually led to the end of her life.

Gideon Weller has never forgotten the horror of his one visit to his mother after she was institutionalized. Not having seen her since the attack, Gideon was unprepared for how the violence had demented her. The nurse on duty the day of Gideon's visit had tried to warn him. "Your mother is very unstable, Mr. Weller. I do not recommend you visit her. If you wish, I can turn her window on so we can see inside her room." Instinctively, he blinked the window light on, revealing a woman with unkempt hair, muttering and pacing.

Gideon, repulsed by the idea of staring at his mother like an animal in the zoo, demanded, "Turn that off! My mother is not a gorilla!"

Having forgotten whom he was addressing at the moment, the young man protested, "No, she is more like a Tasmanian Devil." Noting the look of horror on Gideon Weller's face, the young nurse apologized, "I am sorry to speak so cruelly about your mother but that is the way it is. She is dangerous." Although Captain Tanya Weller was a short, slightly plump, unassuming woman, her face had that rounded, pointed look of the small devil, not to mention the sharp incisors. "She will lunge at you as soon as you walk through that door. She will dig her teeth into you, and more often than not, she aims for the throat." As a reflex, the young man rubs the side of his neck, caressing the scar. "Thank Hadrian she never bit into the vein," the young nurse muttered to himself.

"I insist you shut off that window and let me in to see my mother," Gideon demanded.

The young man merely shook his head. "That would be unwise. Right now, she appears unresponsive, but the very moment you walk through that door, she will lash out at you, certain you are one of the rapists."

"But she'll know me," Gideon insisted. "I'm her son."

Still doubtful, the young man held off unlocking Tanya Weller's door. "We usually only allow women in there. The last male nurse who went in there, well," he said, again rubbing at the scar on his neck, "she left some mighty nasty scars on his face." He shuddered as he spoke. "Nearly tore out one of his eyeballs. Left him blind on the left side."

"She's my mother," Gideon persisted. "She would never hurt me."

"You are a man!" The nurse's eyes opened wide in emphasis. "She always hurts men."

"I am her son!" Although Gideon's confidence had been shaken, he was determined to see his mother. "I'm family!"

"Oh, sweetie," the young man lamented. "You have no idea what your mother's been through, do you?"

"I know she was brutally beaten and raped." Gideon had been close to shouting by that point. He had been kept away from his mother for too long. His Mama Rena had repeatedly dissuaded him from making the trip and successfully kept him away for over a month. "Honey," Mama Rena had tried to reason softly, "your mother is not responding well to men." Gideon refused to believe his own mother would reject him. "But, baby," Mama

Rena had pleaded, "she's not the same woman she was before the attack." But nothing Mama Rena said had deterred Gideon from visiting his mother.

After a month of battling with Mama Rena, Gideon had been beyond frustration at being forestalled by this nurse. Tired of being kept in the dark, Gideon had started to yell, "Let me into my mother's room now!"

The young nurse sighed, "All right, but you shouldn't go in there alone. Let me voc security first."

"I do not need security to visit my own mother. Let me in her room NOW!" Gideon had been adamant.

The nurse's lips pursed, his head shook, but he had turned and done as Gideon Weller instructed. As soon as Gideon had entered the room, the nurse had locked the door behind him. Under no circumstances was Captain Tanya Weller's room ever to be left open. Her escape, it was feared, would lead to the mass murder of men. As soon as the door was sealed, the nurse had blinked and put in a call to security. "Get up here fast; there's going to be trouble—that's right, the Weller woman—her son—I had no choice—he was adamant! For the love of Hadrian, get up here now!—I can't—I won't go in there! She'll kill us both!" Before he had even had a chance to blink the connection off, four female security guards, accompanied by a female nurse with syringe in hand, had entered Tanya Weller's room. Tanya Weller was sedated and her son, Gideon Weller, was laid out on a stretcher and raced off to emergency.

The attack against her son had been brutal. Captain Tanya Weller was career military. Though short and stocky, she had excelled at hand-to-hand combat. The instant her son had entered the room, she had smiled. "Gideon, is that you?" But before he could even say, "Yes," she had slammed her knuckles into his larynx, shattering his Adam's apple. The damage to his vocal chords provided him with the deep raspy voice that haunts many a ward.

Tanya Weller had watched as her son sunk to his knees. Gasping for air, he had looked up at her in confusion and fear. Captain Tanya Weller was on high alert, every muscle taut, ready to attack, but first, she had wanted to taunt her prey. "You dirty *strai* rat!" And then she had sneered. "You think I don't know? A mother always knows!" Then she had smashed her fist into his face, breaking his nose. Gideon had collapsed to the floor, bleeding profusely from both nostrils. Tanya Weller had successfully managed a kick into his groin just as the door was opened. She had then been tackled, pinned, and injected with a very strong sedative, knocking her out, but not before she had spewed out damaging insults toward her son.

Gideon shudders at the memory. As always, he tells himself, *I am not one of them! These men, these heterosexual rapists*, he repeats over and over, *are the very cancer eating at the heart of Hadrian society, and they must be extricated!*

The worst part about having a known rapist in his camp is knowing that boy is currently being sheltered by that *love and hug and nurture boys back to homosexual health maniac!* Jason Warith is far too easy on the boy, allowing for far too many demerits to slip past without punishment. The boy has already been here for three days, and only once has the paddle been administered. *If I only had the time to follow them everywhere!* His administrative duties, unfortunately, are endless and demanding. It is very bothersome, though, knowing Tabatha is the only ward not to suffer punishment for obvious misdeeds. Warith's leniency toward his ward is starting to nurture seeds of discontent among the other wards whose guardians still adhere to camp rules. And word has gotten back to him that Warith refuses to call Tabatha by his new name, again, spreading dissension among the other wards. Mattie Malloy had to be beaten twice yesterday for refusing to answer to his proper name. Poor Stephie was shaken. Gideon Weller had had to step in and finish the first job for him. When Stephie came to him in tears, informing him of Mattie's tenth demerit of the day, Gideon Weller had ordered his second punishment to be public; a punishment he determined to deliver. Everyone in the camp was ordered to the central meeting room. This public display of humiliation was designed specifically to shut Mattie Molloy down and stem the tide of insurrection Warith had instigated against his rule. And it proved to be very effective. Not a single word of dissent has been heard from Molloy or anyone else since.

Gideon Weller smiles, remembering just how effective this act was. He had ensured Jason Warith and Tabatha were given front row standing (no one was seated for this ritual). With paddle in hand, Weller had wielded it with all his might against Mattie Molloy's already raw and swollen buttock. Having completed the task, he had turned, pointing the paddle (blood dripping from it onto the floor) at his appalled audience, and shouted, "There will be no more dissension in my camp!" His voice had boomed and echoed ominously off the walls. Looking to the top right corner of his eye screen, he had ended the session with an order, "Private sessions, NOW!"

Jason Warith and Todd had been the first to move. Jason had roused his horror-struck ward into action with three simple words, spoken loud enough for everyone in the room to hear, "Let's go, Tabatha." Jason had been quelled and was determined to toe the line from now on—in public at any rate.

* * * * *

Salve!

Debate over Corporal Punishment
HNN—Melissa Eagleton Reporting

A heated debated has risen over the use of corporal punishment inside reeducation camps. As we all know, corporal punishment within our educational institutions is illegal. No teacher would ever think of raising a hand against his or her students today. And, yet, the use of corporal punishment is legal in reeducation camps. It has recently come to the attention of HNN that Jason Warith has requested an investigation be held at the Northeast Reeducation Camp regarding the excessive use of corporal punishment. This request came in the form of a letter complaint written by Jason Warith against Gideon Weller. Jason Warith claims to have witnessed Gideon Weller beating students' backsides with a paddle on more than one occasion, and the beatings were so harsh the man actually drew blood. Warith also states in his letter of complaint that the guardians under Gideon's employ have no qualms following the man's lead. "Young boys are beaten daily at the Northeast Reeducation Camp," Warith wrote in his letter to the reeducation board.

Witnesses are being called forward to speak of these events. Many speak in Gideon Weller's favor. Darrell Jeffreys supports his employer, stating, "These are no ordinary youth we are asked to care for. You can't coddle them. They are violent and abusive when they arrive and only a hard hand teaches them how to obey." Other guardians add support, even Stephie Chatters, the young man I interviewed when I toured that facility. "I hate using the paddle," Stephie admits, "but there are times when it is the only way to deal with noncompliance. Sometimes these boys can be really naughty." When asked if it was true that Mr. Weller had instructed his employees to beat their wards at least once a day, Stephie Chatters denied the charge emphatically. "Oh, no, we are only to use the paddle if a boy earns five demits, not before! Usually you only have to use the paddle once or twice and then they stop misbehaving."

The question of five demerits earning a boy a paddling such as described at the Northeast Reeducation Camp is also being questioned. What exactly earns a boy a demerit? Does the punishment meet the crime? Is such physical force necessary to help reeducate our youth back into Hadrian's loving arms? Jason Warith says no. Gideon Weller insists the answer is yes. No one at HNN is prepared, at this moment, to judge the good folk of the Northeast Reeducation Camp. As none of us has ever had to deal with a young man who believes himself to be heterosexual, we cannot possibly know what it is like having to reeducate these recalcitrant and potentially violent youth. So, we turn to you, Hadrian, and ask for your views. Voc us @HNN#CP-RE/MH and tell us what you think about corporal punishment. Is it a necessary component of the reeducation of our male youth or should its practice be abandoned? We look forward to hearing from you.

Vale!

Private Session

Although memories of having squashed Mattie Molloy and seeing the entire camp shaken please Gideon Weller, he still feels disturbed. An edge of uncertainly has entered into his world. Shaking his head, Gideon Weller resolves that there will be no more niceties, no more leniencies with this Tabatha Middleton! *This one*, he determines, *will suffer*. With a harrumph, he determines, *Vigilante justice must occur since the system has chosen to coddle this one*. Rapists, as far as Gideon Weller is concerned, need the harshest treatment of all. They need to learn what it feels like to be violated by another human being the way they violated his mother!

Blinking open the day's schedule, Gideon Weller notes that Jason Warith and Tabitha Middleton have Room 3 booked for their evening private session. Gideon Weller knows Warith *hasn't the balls* to do what is necessary, so he determines to step in and take charge. Whispering, "Darrell," he waits until a connection is made. "Darrell, meet me outside Room 3." Blinking quickly, he severs the connection and makes his way out of his office and down the hall. Standing outside Room 3, Gideon Weller waits until Darrell Jeffreys arrives before taking any action. Quietly, he opens the door to Room 3 a crack, just enough to hear what is being said inside. Sickened, Gideon Weller realizes that Warith is listening to the youth talk about his attraction to Crystal Albright—the very girl he had raped! With a simple nod of the head, Weller directs Jeffreys to begin the attack. Darrell reacts instantly. He knows his instructions by rote—rip open the door, grab the guardian (in this case Warith), thrust him from the room, slam the door shut, and lock it. His next order of business is to hold the youth in a headlock while Gideon Weller administers medicinal intercourse. Jeffreys always closes his eyes, so he doesn't have to watch.

Jason's first reaction, like many a guardian before him, is to try to re-open the door, but it is locked. Hearing Todd screaming, Jason frantically pulls at the door to no avail. He bangs on it, slams his shoulder against it, shouts down the corridor for help, all to no purpose. He does everything he can think of to get back inside. When the screaming finally stops, Darrell opens his eyes and waits for Gideon Weller to nod before releasing the boy and then unlocking the door. As soon as the door gives, Jason pushes his way into the room, shoving past Darrell, just in time to see Mr. Weller beginning to stuff his penis back inside his pants. Todd, he discovers, is lying senseless on the floor, his pants and shorts a tangled mess around his ankles. He kneels at Todd's side. The boy's anus, Jason notices, is bleeding. No doubt, the internal damage is severe. Weller has clearly bludgeoned the boy. Looking up at Weller, Jason notices blood on the man's hand. His eyes widen in horror. *Hadrian's lover*, he marvels, *did he use his fist?* Raging on the warden, Jason punches Mr. Weller in the head. Stunned, the man flies backwards, with his still hard cock sticking up in the air as he crashes to the floor.

"You will pay for this," Mr. Weller growls after regaining his senses. Returning to his feet, he snarls, "You are fired."

Jason's voice is a low rumble. "You were raping this child!"

"That child," Mr. Weller yells out, pointing down to the floor, "is the rapist! He raped Crystal Albright! He managed to avoid the death penalty, but I'll be damned if he doesn't learn what it feels like to be violated the way he violated that poor girl." Soft now, Mr. Weller tucks his penis back inside his pants and zips them back up.

Jason turns, bends down, and begins gently to lift the boy's briefs and pants up. "Leave him be," Mr. Weller orders.

Jason's voice spits out wrath. "I will not." He lifts Todd into his arms. Defiantly, he stares at Mr. Weller. "I am taking *Todd* to the city central hospital." There is no way Jason is willing to trust anyone at this camp right now! "And then," he states pointedly, "I am calling Quadrant Officials. I intend to see you arrested."

"Really," Weller slurs sarcastically. "And what are you going to tell them?"

"I intend to tell them how you raped this boy, the evidence being the severe damage you caused and no doubt your sperm!"

Mr. Weller laughs, looking to Darrell; reassured by the man's smirk, he turns back to laugh in Jason's face. "Be my guest." He motions for Jason to leave and signals for Darrell to stand aside. As Jason walks out the room, Weller adds, "Good luck making your charge stick." Then, adding acerbically, "My aide here can attest to the fact that Tabatha begged me to help him. He said you weren't willing to do what was necessary so I had to take the initiative." Looking over to his aide, he states, "Isn't that right, Darrell?"

"That's what I heard, sir." Darrell stands next to his boss like an unmovable brick wall.

Stunned and sickened, Jason slowly turns, Todd hanging limp in his arms, to stare horror-struck at the man. "Have you no moral conscience?"

"Do not speak to me about morals." Weller's voice turns into a skewer aimed right at Jason's heart. "You, who shelter and aid a known rapist!" Spitting on the floor at Jason's feet, he yells, "You sicken me!" And then turning his back, he orders Jason Warith, "Get out of my sight!"

* * * * *

When Todd wakes, he is lying on his stomach in a sterile hospital room. Shuddering seizures ravage his body as he relives, during his first conscious moment, the stabbing pain inflicted upon him by Gideon Weller. As the spasms slowly cease, a terrified Todd realizes things can always get worse.

* * * * *

Salve!

Heterosexuals and Suicidal Behavior
HNN—Melissa Eagleton Reporting

Parents, it is critical that you speak openly and honestly with your children about any potential heterosexual feelings they might have. As we are aware, many of us have latent heterosexual tendencies. Only a small percentage of Hadrian's population can claim to be a six on the Kinsey scale. The rest of us exist somewhere between a two and a five. As a result, the period of sexual awakening for our youth can be very confusing. As we grow and mature intellectually, it is much easier for us to reconcile with the first cornerstone of Hadrian's society: that of homosexuality as our preference. As adults, we can understand the logic behind our chosen lifestyle— see how it, combined with strict procreation laws, is essential for creating and maintaining a stable human population. Hadrian's four cornerstones of existence were based on reason and logic, motivated by the very real need to preserve the human species and regain balance with planet earth. As each of us comes of age, with all our cognitive skills developed, we can reaffirm our founding families' oath and swear ourselves, as they did, fealty to the four cornerstones of Hadrian society: Hadrian's chosen lifestyle is homosexual; Hadrian is a safe haven for homosexuals; Hadrian's goal is to create and maintain a stable human population; Hadrian will create an ecologically sound balance between humanity and nature. At twenty-one years of age, after three years of service with our military, Hadrian's citizens are ready to accept the responsibility of fulfilling Hadrian's promise to themselves, the human race and the earth.

Because our children are not yet capable of making that oath, it is incumbent upon parents and teachers to educate, gently guide, and nurture their spirits along Hadrian's chosen path. When we neglect our duty to our youth, we leave them vulnerable to sexual desires that are unwanted here in Hadrian, sexual desires that are in fact dangerous to our society. Allowing heterosexuality to blossom in your youth's bosom is akin to allowing choke weed to grow and destroy our gardens. When a child's sexual education is ignored and he (or she) is left to discover feelings on his (or her) own, havoc can occur. What parents and teachers need to realize is that when a child experiments with heterosexual behaviors, he (or she) is risking more than just unwanted pregnancies. He (or she) is also risking his (or her) life!

Yes, it is true. And, though I do not condone this, the fact remains that individuals pegged as heterosexuals suffer from a great deal of emotional, and sometimes physical, abuse. Children, as we are all aware, are a bundle of paradoxes. Though they may appear to be the most tolerant among us, they also have proven to be the least tolerant, especially with that which they know to be unacceptable by society's standards. Empathy, an intellectual approach toward emotion, is learned behavior. Such lessons often take time—many years in fact—and seldom sink into the cognitive mind until the late teens or early twenties. As a result, youth viewed as straight receive a substantial amount of peer abuse. This abuse, coupled with the growing awareness that their desires are inappropriate, often leads these youth to contemplate suicide. Many, in fact, attempt, and some, unfortunately, succeed. Thus, it is our duty to watch for any signs of heterosexual behavior in our children, to teach them how to counter these feelings, as well as to encourage them to trust our judgment until they are of age and can see the logic and reason behind Hadrian's chosen lifestyle. Hadrian's society is based on choices that require higher level thinking skills, and until our children have acquired this ability, we must protect them from themselves and guide them in the right direction.

Remember, all our children are, at the very least, a two on the Kinsey scale, so given time and the proper education, our youth can be guided gently toward accepting Hadrian's chosen sexual lifestyle: homosexuality. Help your children make the right choice! This lifestyle, coupled with strict procreation laws, is humanity's last hope.

Vale!

"to die, to sleep no more"

Having just woken and experienced the spasms of pain caused by the rape, Todd determines death is his only solution—his only viable escape from hell. What was it Matthew said? No one gets out of here, except through marriage, exile, or death—and regarding death, he wished Todd luck, showing upon his wrists numerous failed attempts. He quoted those lines, the only ones Todd can remember: "to die, to sleep no more." What a pleasure that would be—no more sleep—no more dreams—no more waking up to reality. Simply to cease to be, to disappear into oblivion, is intoxicating. No more thought, no more pain, no more memories, no more betrayal. Eyeing his hospital room, Todd searches for the means necessary to execute his own demise. The IV tubing might work as a noose, but from where would he hang himself? The only hooks in the room are for a pot-holder in the ceiling and one for coats on the door. Neither hook is likely to hold his weight. Inspecting the ceiling offers no hope, either. It is a solid ceiling, no tiles to push aside to wrap the tubing around corner joints. It's as if they thought of everything here. No doubt a hospital is full of poisons, but when mixed properly, they become lifesaving medicines. Still, even if Todd knew which mixtures were deadly, *where in Hadrian's name*, he wonders, *would I find them?* Closing his eyes in despair, he pleads with the unknown, *How am I to die?* Reopening them after letting his head drop dejectedly to the side, Todd finds his answer. *Oh, sweet Mischief*, he almost utters, but stops himself lest anyone in the halls might hear him. There, sitting on the table next to his hospital bed, is a scalpel. Todd does not question how it got there, who "accidently left it behind," or even why there would be a scalpel in his room at all, having no purpose whatsoever in his healing process; he simply rejoices in his breast at having found an instrument ready for action. His first impulse after picking up the sharp implement is to slit his wrists, but the memory of Matthew's scars reminds him that such a death is too slow. No doubt he would be found and revived, which is not part of Todd's plan. This is no cry for help. This is finality! *Dig it into the neck and rip it across the throat*: the thought prompting action simultaneously. Blood begins to stream, and Todd, offering up no resistance, begins to ride the waves of ebb and flow between life and death. Closing his eyes during the final throes, he escapes into his mind, reliving the memory of the last moment on earth when he was truly happy.

* * * * *

Crystal is in her green dress—the tight-fitting one she wore that Sunday when Todd, Frank, and she got together to study. The very same dress that, when left unguarded, would rise up too high. Crystal, Frank, and Todd had been dancing together at the big celebration. The school had thrown a huge party for the b-ball team for having won the Nationals. Wearing high heels, Crystal feigned tripping into Todd so she could whisper in his ear "check your phone" as he had helped her stand back up. After their dance, when Crystal begs leave to go to the bathroom, Todd wanders outside for a bit of fresh air and to cool off, but really, so he can be alone in order to read her clandestine message: "Meet me behind the girls' stairwell." Todd is thrilled. *Behind the girls' stairwell!* What can Crystal want? The girls' back stairwell camera is broken. No one will know they are there. No one will see whatever it is that is going to be done. And Todd wants things done. Stealing his way back into the school, he finds he is shaking more from nerves than the crisp spring night air. Now behind the stairwell, silent in the dark shadows, Todd anxiously awaits Crystal's arrival. His eyes dart up into darkness as he begins to hear her descending the stairs. *She really must have gone to the bathroom*, he surmises. Although her footfalls are light since she is wearing heels, her shoes still manage to click against the stair's tiles. She is wearing some kind of perfume. It smells like cinnamon. Crystal always smells like cinnamon. And then she appears. "Hello, Todd." Is her voice husky? Her walk over to him is like a trance, a dance in slow motion, with her hands sliding along her thighs. Leaning against the wall, Todd steps forward to meet her. Crystal places a hand on his chest. He feels her electric touch. Todd's breath quickens. Crystal leans in and kisses him. Somehow, they have switched positions. Crystal's back is now against the wall. Acting on instinct, unaware of how the first time should feel, Todd is thrilled by how Crystal effectively orchestrates their movements. He tells her he loves her. She kisses him. And then, when it's over, she walks away, with his life in her hands, into darkness.

* * * * *

Salve!

Profile of a Vice President
HNN—Melissa Eagleton Reporting

Vice President Elena Stiles is the third member of the Stiles family to hold a prestigious office in our government. Ester Stiles was Hadrian's first president while Denise Stiles was Hadrian's fifth. Having served under President Nasser for eight years, Vice President Stiles is determined to run in the next campaign. President Nasser has given Elena Stiles her full support. "Having worked with Stiles for both terms of my presidency has convinced me that this is the woman destined to lead our country into the future." President Nasser's endorsement certainly will be a great boost come fall elections. "Elena Stiles is energetic, forthright, forceful, and always looking toward the future. She stands for all that makes Hadrian strong and is determined to ensure the continued power of our military." No one can deny the importance of keeping our military strong. According to Vice President Stiles, "Our military is the main reason we are able to keep Hadrian's values alive. If it were not for our brave young men and women defending our lifestyle and lives, Hadrian's wall would have fallen long ago and the human virus that surrounds us would have overrun and destroyed this last vestige of earth's natural beauty." One key campaign promise Elena Stiles intends to keep after her inauguration is to increase funding to the military.

If voted in as our next president, Vice President Stiles also promises to increase funding toward education. The intellectual growth of our youth must be one of our country's top priorities. "Our children are the future of Hadrian. They are the ones who must continue preserving the natural balance of our country's habitat. They are the ones who must continuously develop new ways to reuse man's pollutants as well as discover ways to counter the poisonous effects already tainting earth's water, soil, and air. The task our foremothers and forefathers burdened us with comes with no simple solutions. Only the strongest and most creative of minds can overcome humanity's past mistakes." She is so right! This woman has Hadrian's priorities as her own: a strong military to protect us from the threat of the outside world and the education of our youth.

When asked how she stands on reeducation camps, Vice President Stiles was circumspect. Although she stressed the importance of reeducating wayward youth, she also seemed to suggest that the way in which our camps are run may not be up to her personal standards. When asked how she felt these institutions should be run, she was unable to offer up any viable suggestions. She did, however, suggest that a thorough inquiry into reeducation camps was essential, and after becoming president ("should I be so lucky as to win the country's confidence"), such an investigation would be held. With respect to the outcome of such an examination, Vice President Stiles hinted at the potential restructuring of these camps. This may very well be the result of a meeting held with the eight camp wardens at the central cabinet. Apparently, some dissension exists between the wardens because disparaging methods are being used at some of the camps. It seems Jason Warith's complaints against the Northeast Reeducation Camp have opened the door for others to express their dissatisfaction at reeducation methods. Vice President Stiles is taking these concerns seriously and is looking at ways of standardizing how we approach reeducation.

Vale!

Extracting a Confession

Five days have passed since Crystal denounced Todd. Every day, she has thought about texting him, though fearful of what she might learn since Frank voc'd and told her he was sentenced to the Northeast Reeducation Camp. Sentenced! Crystal grimaces at the harsh word Frank used. Frank hates her now, but she doesn't care. Her only concern is for Todd. Before Frank had hung up on her, Crystal asked him whether Todd still had his cell phone at the reeducation camp. Frank said no one had mentioned finding it so it was still a secret. But then he said he had tried texting Todd and got no response. Todd might not even have it with him, Crystal reasons, in a feeble attempt to justify not having tried to contact him. It isn't so much cowardice that keeps her from texting Todd; rather, her mother, Gail Albright, having discovered her phone and with whom it was used to converse, confiscated it. Crystal had to find and steal it back before she could try contacting her lover. Her mother is keeping a vigilant eye on her every move. Gail Albright, having taken time off from work, is staying home indefinitely in order to help facilitate Crystal's unofficial reeducation. Although one really doesn't need to reeducate a girl who has been raped, since Crystal refuses to accuse Todd, her mothers are determined to ensure she has not gone astray. As far as Crystal knows, neither of her mothers has seen the digital recording her aunt, Ms. Annabelle Sterne, had forced her to watch early that dreadful morning. Annabelle Sterne insisted Crystal denounce Todd, threatening to tell the girl's mothers what really happened if she didn't. Aunt Annabelle was right. Her exposure was sure to ruin Mama Elena's political career. Mama Elena had worked long and hard to get where she is; Crystal couldn't bear the thought of taking all that away from her, especially now that she has chosen to run for President of Hadrian. Nor could she cope with the threat of her mothers' disappointment in her. She loved both women too much to risk losing their love and respect.

When Crystal adamantly refused to accuse Todd of rape, though, Elena Stiles became suspicious. Elena and Gail held a private conference and decided it would be in Crystal's best interest to reestablish her association with her ex-girlfriend: Lolita Huber (daughter to the secretary of defense). Crystal agreed. Their relationship was easily reestablished since Ms. Huber owed her position in the government to Elena Stiles. Crystal had broken up with Lolita because the two girls have nothing in common. Lolita is an intellect, a big reader, yet dry as desert dust, and deficient in humor whereas Crystal loves to laugh, have fun, roughhouse, and play sports. If given her druthers, Crystal would spend all her time hanging out with Todd and Frank. Very few opportunities exist for a girl to associate with guys, other than on sports teams, so Crystal chose, at a very young age, to become very adept in basketball, baseball, hockey, and wrestling. Her mothers have always approved of her gaming since, on the surface, it appeared as if Crystal were merely trying to prove herself the physical equal of any young man her age. Although she knew both Frank and Todd were miles ahead of her in both speed and strength, Crystal found ways to compensate through skill. In fact, it is fair to say that the only young men Crystal's age who can best her in the sports arena are Todd Middleton and Frank Hunter. Although, at times, she had managed to get the better of Todd, but only in wrestling. *I wonder why that was?* she questions. *I think he liked me on top of him.* A brief smile crosses her lips before once again turning grim. *He'll never love me again*, she reasons. *Not after what I did! Oh, Todd,* tears burgeon once more, *what did I do to you?*

Crystal sighs as she lies on her bed, staring at a blank slate screen. She is supposed to be working on a treatise that validates Hadrian's sexual preference and method of procreation. She is to present her findings at school tomorrow in an oral presentation. Her aunt, Ms. Sterne, assigned it to her in the aftermath of Todd's exposure. She hasn't done any research or written a single word. The only movement on the electronic slate's screen is a blinking curser. Crystal's mind is far too preoccupied with the fate of her lover to worry about homework, especially *extra* homework! Right now the only thing Crystal can think about is what might be happening to Todd—*because of me!* Silencing the hum of the school slate by tapping the power button, Crystal tosses her personal slate aside. Silently, she slips off the bed, tiptoes over to the door, places her ear against the wood, and listens intently for sound in the hallway. When satisfied no one is immediately outside her door, she carefully turns the knob and pushes it open an inch. Peering through the slight crack, she determines no one is in sight. From the basement, she hears the sounds of pool balls clacking. Mom must be practicing. Mama Elena is seldom home, even when she is in town. Crystal knows she is away on business, as usual. Believing it to be safe, Crystal slowly opens her bedroom door, slithers out of her room, and stealthily slips inside her mother's room. Mom is a creature of habit. She would have locked Crystal's phone in her "special drawer" in the master bathroom.

After successfully picking the lock, something Crystal had learned to do years ago (unknown to her mother and simply because she hated the idea of her mother keeping secrets from her—never to steal anything) she slowly pulls open the drawer. Today, this clandestine art serves her need, not her curiosity, as she retrieves her phone. Quickly, Crystal relocks the drawer and returns to her room before anyone knows she was out.

"Todd? Are you out there?" Crystal texts quickly, not daring to try to phone Todd because her mother may hear her speaking out loud. Silence is the better approach. After waiting an intolerably long second, she types again: "Answer me, please."

There is a sudden beep in response. It's from Todd. Crystal sighs her relief and then reads: "What do you want?"

"I'm so sorry."

"Really?"

"Todd, please. Auntie—Ms. Sterne made me denounce you."

"So?"

Crystal drops the phone and begins crying. *Todd hates me! Can I blame him?* Desperate, she reaches out electronically again: "I love you."

"You said it was rape!"

"I never said that!"

"Did you deny it?"

"I can't. You know I can't."

"Why not?"

"Please don't ask me, Todd."

"Was it?"

"What?"

"Rape?"

"How can you ask that?"

"Everyone says it was rape."

"That's not my fault!"

"Isn't it?"

Crystal stares dumbfounded at her phone. *He's right. I know he's right. This is my fault, all my fault. But there's nothing I can do. Auntie Bella's right. If I come out, say anything in Todd's defense, it will ruin Mama Elena's political career.* "Todd, please forgive me."

"How's reeducation at home?"

"It's horrible."

"Try being in camp."

"Is it really bad for you there?"

"What do you think?"

"Todd, you're killing me."

"Reeducation camp is killing me!"

Crystal wants to throw the phone against the wall, but she isn't able to. It is her only link to Todd, and now that she has established contact, she can't let go. *He blames me for everything. And he's right. This is my fault!* Clutching the phone to her breast, Crystal wonders, *Is there anything I can say to explain myself to him?* "Mama Elena wants me to accuse you of rape. But I refuse to!"

"Why don't you? It'd be kinder."

This response terrifies Crystal: "Oh, Todd, what are they doing to you?"

"What are they doing to you?"

"They made me get back together with Lolita."

"Poor you."

"Don't mock me. I'm sorry. I feel horrible. I love you!"

"You didn't answer my question?"

"What question?"

"Was it rape?"

"You know it wasn't!"

"Do I?"

His persistence in such clarification angers Crystal: "No, Todd, it wasn't rape."

"How did it happen, then?"

Why is he asking this? she wonders: "You know how it happened."

"Tell me anyway."

Fine, she grimaces, *I'll answer all his questions. I guess he has a right.* "I texted you a note at the Championship dance."

"Go on."

"We met in the back stairwell."

"The one with the broken camera?"

"Yes."

"Then what happened?"

"I kissed you."

"And then?"

"We made love."

"So, you initiated everything?"

"You know I did. Why are you asking all these questions?"

"Because I'm not Todd!"

Gasping, Crystal drops the phone. It bounces off the bed and clatters to the floor. Crystal leaps up and grabs it, waiting in silence, hoping the sound does not alert any suspicion in her mother. Nothing happens while Crystal holds her breath. Still kneeling on the floor, she looks in horror at the last line of text on her phone: "Because I'm not Todd."

"Who are you?"

"One of the few friends your lover has left."

"What's your name?"

"Do you know what they do to a boy suspected of rape in reeducation?"

This question stops Crystal's heart. Her breath is suspended as she types in her reply: "No" and waits for the answer.

"They bludgeon him!"

"They what?"

"Rape, you stupid girl! They RAPE him!"

Tears are flowing, Crystal is sobbing; had she been speaking, very little of what she types would be comprehensible. As it is, it is barely legible: "ow do u no?"

"I was in reeducation. That year, two boys committed suicide. Both boys suspected of rape. Both boys raped!"

"How do u no? Did u sea?"

"No, but everyone knew. There's more."

Crystal groans; masochistically, she needs to know: "mor?"

"It is impossible to commit suicide in a reeducation camp."

"But u sad—" Realization dawns; Crystal continues her text: "ho did 2 boys die?"

"Suicide."

"I don't understand."

"Curious, isn't it? Two boys suspected of rape were the only two boys able to commit suicide. Think about that for a minute."

"Is Todd—did he—" Crystal is unable to finish.

"He tried. He failed."

"Thank Hadrian for that!"

"You can thank me—or rather, Jason Warith."

"Who?"

"Todd's facilitator."

"Oh."

"I arranged for him to work with Todd—to protect him."

"?"

"Because I knew!"

"Please tell me who you are."

"Will you help Todd?"

"How?"

"Tell the truth."

"I can't."

"We have nothing left to say."

"No, please—"

Crystal pauses, recognition of her character dawning: "Mama Elena— she's VP Stiles."

"We mustn't do anything to hurt one of our founding families."

"Please, you don't understand."

"No. You don't understand! I will not sacrifice Todd on the altar of your stupidity!"

Frightened, knowing herself to be the personification of all that is selfish, Crystal asks: "Will you denounce me?" There is no answer to her plea. She types again, "I'm scared."

"Imagine how Todd feels."

"I can't help him." Her fingers shake before she types in the next phrase. "I can only help myself."

"I DO understand."

Crystal's immediate response to that line is to shut off her phone. Without thought or precaution, she races back into her mothers' personal wash-room. She returns her cell to the locked drawer and swears never to touch it again. Back in her bedroom, Crystal hides herself under the covers, shiv-ering uncontrollably. Frightened and alone, she realizes she forgot to erase all evidence of their conversation. And although she knows with absolute certainty the mystery man at the other end hasn't deleted his version, she still goes through the motion of retrieving her cell and deleting all contact made with Todd's mobile.

* * * * *

Salve!

The World Outside our Walls
HNN—Melissa Eagleton Reporting

To every child, it is revealed what life is like for the unfortunate living outside Hadrian's walls: Images of emaciated bodies lying on desert floors. Children starving. Mothers' breasts bereft of milk. It is truly unfathomable how humanity is still thriving. It is amazing how the words of Dr. Oscar Baumann, written in the late nineteenth century, depict what is happening all over the planet today. "There were women wasted to skeletons from whose eyes the madness of starvation glared…warriors scarcely able to crawl on all fours, and apathetic, languishing elders. Swarms of vultures followed them from high, awaiting their certain victims." The image was frightening enough back then when the calamity of famine only hit one area in Africa, but knowing that this painting of horror is found daily, and in every country but ours, is demoralizing.

Sometimes, I believe it is better not to witness the slow agonizing death throes of humanity's suicide. For, as much as we dearly wish we could do something, anything, to help these wretched creatures, the reality is that providing food, shelter, water, and warmth for the billions dying outside our walls is impossible. We cannot cure the illnesses mankind has festered upon itself. We cannot hope to save those other twenty billion or more individuals. All we can do is cling to the knowledge that we, in Hadrian, are rebuilding humanity's future, that Hadrian is maintaining the necessary balance to help humanity survive.

Vale!

Todd Awakes

When Todd awakes, Frank is clutching his right hand. Having fallen asleep, Frank has his head lying in Todd's lap. Todd sighs when he sees his friend. *Finally*, he mutters.

This is not the first time Todd has risen since his failed suicide attempt. When he first discovered that he was still alive, Todd screamed as best he could through his damaged throat while simultaneously ripping at the bandages around his neck. His intent was to dig his nails deep into his wound, effectively ending his life once and for all! Fortunately for Todd, or perhaps not so fortunately from his perspective, he is under twenty-four hour supervision. The mirror on the right wall is a one-way window for the nurse assigned on observation duty, which explains why his first attempt to kill himself failed. Mia Ocampo, the nurse in attendance his first night at the hospital, managed to call the doctor and effectively stem the flow of blood, saving Todd Middleton's life. It was Gordon McAlister, the second nurse in attendance, who circumvented Todd's second attempt. Although Todd managed to remove most of his bandage, he never got his fingers into the wound. Since then, Todd has been strapped to his bed, has a catheter fitted, and since he refuses to eat, drink, or take any medication, is attached to an IV unit.

When Jason Warith came to visit Todd, he had tried unsuccessfully to reestablish the tenuous bond he had begun forging with the boy. Not that he had any hopes that ties could be rebuilt after what Mr. Weller had done. Since the rape, Todd had completely shut himself off from the rest of the world. Before leaving Todd the last time, Jason had asked the young man whether there was anything at all he could do for him. When Todd asked to see Frank Hunter, Jason smiled. "I can do that for you, son." He had heard that Todd and the Hunter boy were close friends, that prior to

Mr. Weller's interference, they had even begun forming a boyfriend relationship. *Why*, he questioned irritably, *did Weller not leave him with the Hunter family? No*, he reminded himself, *I can't waste thoughts on "what ifs." I only have "what is" to work with.* So, as soon as Todd returned to an induced sleep—an unfortunate necessity as his continued struggles, even with the restraints, caused life-threatening damage to his wounds—Jason Warith contacted the Hunter household.

Frank, having waited at Todd's bedside for over two hours, is now sleeping. Todd would shake his own head, but he can't because it is belted down. All he can do is roll his eyes as his friend snores. *Friend*, he wonders, *can I still call him that?* Studying Frank's profile, Todd considers Frank's motivation. *Would I have done the same if our situations were reversed?* Todd is unable to provide an answer. *I guess I'd only know if I were in his place. At least*, he figures, *he did it because he loves me.* "Frank," he whispers. His voice still hasn't recovered from his suicidal knife attack. When Frank fails to respond, Todd wakes him by shaking his right hand. As soon as Frank stirs, Todd rasps again, "Frank."

Sitting up, rubbing his eyes and face before running his fingers through his hair, Frank mutters, "Todd." Frank leans forward to kiss Todd on the lips; Todd, with closed eyes, remains unresponsive. Frank pretends not to notice. *Keep things cheery, upbeat*, he reminds himself. "Hey, babe. Welcome back."

Todd doesn't waste any time, "Help me."

"You know I will," Frank promises. "I'll do anything for you." Although he remains silent, Frank can see the promise he made to Todd that morning so long ago when they sat hidden (or so they had thought) behind the girl's locker room stairwell. It is like a giant neon sign flashing out of Todd's eyes.

Enunciating each word carefully, lest his voice, hindered by his attempt at self-slaughter, should slur his words, Todd slowly demands, "Help me die." Frank pales. His mind refuses to register what Todd has spoken. Sensing Frank's refusal, Todd insists, "I'd do it for you, *Bob*." Todd says no more. He simply waits for Frank to reach an understanding.

At the beginning of their grade ten school year in their language arts class, Frank and Todd had held a heated debate as to the meaning of Earle Birney's poem "David." Frank had insisted the boys were lovers, making Bob's act of euthanasia a much more powerful moment. Todd took the stance that the boys were just good friends, no sexual innuendoes existed, and Frank was just reading into the poem what he wanted it to say. Frank proved his point, though, by quoting line fourteen, "Then the two of us rolled in the blanket," using the fact that it comes just prior to the pines thrusting up into the sky to emphasize his point. The teacher agreed with Frank and pursued this interpretation.

Now, though, as he lies strapped to his bed, Todd is not thinking of David or Bob's sexual preference. Rather, his thoughts focus on David's request and Bob's agreeing to do it. David, having fallen and broken his back, had begged Bob to push him over so he could die. Bob did not want to comply. He had hoped to find a way to save his friend, but as the poem says, Bob knew that more than a day and a night would pass before he could make his way back down to the camp and bring men "unknowing/ The way of mountains" back to rescue David. "And then, how long? And he knew…and the hell of hours/After that, if he lived till we came, roping him out." Todd thought now of his after hours, the hell of living, if Frank were somehow successfully to "rope him out." He could never go back to thinking that he could be gay now. He could never hope to find that spark somewhere inside now. Looking at Frank, Todd reminds him again, "For Christ's sake push me over!/If I could move…or die…" Another of David's lines. Another desperate plea to die with dignity.

Frank shakes his head sporadically. It is all coming back to him now. Todd wants him to help him commit suicide. "No." His head shake quickens with his heart rate. "No, Todd. No!"

"You promised!" Todd reminds him.

"Never promised this!"

"To do anything!" Todd's brown eyes harden like frozen earth.

"Never. Never this." Frank, unable to bear the accusation in Todd's eyes, turns to leave.

Todd punches him in the back of the head with his words. "You owe me." Frank stumbles. He knows exactly what Todd means. Bitterness strikes like a whip against Frank's heart when Todd spits out, "You're no better than Weller!" Aghast, Frank quickly opens the door and rushes out of Todd's room.

* * * * *

Salve!

Shocking Allegations!
HNN—Melissa Eagleton Reporting

Jason Warith is demanding a thorough investigation be held at the North-east Reeducation Camp, insisting that the administration there be held accountable for abusive treatment of its wards. "The lax approach to the investigation thus far is unacceptable," an enraged Warith stated yester-day at the Reeducation Camp Wardens' Review Board Meeting. It is the responsibility of this board to determine whether or not to press official charges against the Northeast Camp Warden. Jason Warith has laid two very specific charges against Gideon Weller: 1) the over, and unnecessary, use of corporal punishment, and 2) rape. I find these charges extremely hard to believe, having met with Gideon Weller and toured his camp.

These shocking accusations surprise many, considering the numerous accolades hailed upon Gideon Weller over the years. Statistically, the Northeast Camp reeducates more wayward youth than any other. Although Gideon Weller admits corporal punishment is administered at his camp, it is also administered at every other reeducation camp. He believes it is unavoidable when dealing with angry, aggressive youth, particularly young heterosexual males. According to Jason Warith, the success rate of the Northeast Camp does not indicate real success, but rather, young men desperate to escape in any way they can. Jason Warith also pointed out that the Northeast Reeducation Camp has the highest rate of attempted and completed suicides.

Gideon Weller claims that is because his files are accurate; he does not attempt to dissemble. "Every act of self-mutilation discovered in my camp is identified as a suicidal act. Thus," he reminded us, "it only appears as if there are more suicide attempts at my camp. Other camps," Gideon Weller explained recently in response to these charges, "dismiss self-muti-lation as suicidal. We, at the Northeast Camp do not."

I, for one, do not believe these accusations. Having met with Gideon Weller and having toured his facility, I am convinced that these charges are unfounded. We even witnessed a sample of his great success when we aired "Happily Married After Reeducation." It was at the Northeast Camp under Gideon Weller's tutelage that Geoffrey and Dean Hunter met. These two men have been happily married for over twenty years! It is unthinkable that a man of such honor and nobility as Gideon Weller would ever stoop to such abusive strategies to rein in unruly youth. It is my sincere hope that the accusations laid against Gideon Weller are unfounded and that the impending investigation unearths the truth.

Vale!

Heart to Heart

"Todd." Papa Dean's voice is soft, soothing, enticing enough for Todd to surrender to it.

"Papa Dean?"

"Yes, son, it's me." Todd's eyes open. It takes a moment for the image of the man looking down on him to come into focus. Todd is heavily sedated to keep him from thrashing around, even bound the way he is. "Hey, you," Papa Dean says quietly.

"Hi, Papa," Todd mutters. Closing his eyes again, he mumbles, "I'm tired."

"I'm not surprised," Papa Dean replies, "considering all the drugs they've pumped into you."

Todd tries to shake his head. He can't. The leather strap holds him securely. Reopening his eyes, he glances over to the man sitting next to his bed, the man holding and caressing his hand. Papa Dean. Not Papa Mike. "No, Papa Dean, tired of life."

"Please, Todd, no," he whispers softly. "Don't talk like that, son. You're only seventeen years old."

I could just as easily be sixty. Todd sighs fretfully. There is no room for equivocation with the boy. "Do you want me to lie to you?"

"No," Papa Dean answers resolutely. "No, Todd, I don't. Only the truth between us." Sighing deeply, Dean braces himself for the worst. "Only the truth."

"The truth is," Todd says matter-of-factly, "I want to die."

"I know."

"Do you?" Todd is skeptical. How can anyone know? Anyone who hasn't—but, he remembers, *Papa Dean has*. Frank said Papa Dean was straight. "You were in reeducation camp, too, weren't you?"

"Yes, Todd. A very long time ago."

"Tell me the truth, Papa Dean. Why did this happen to me?"

"Because the world is scared."

"Scared of *strais*."

"Hadrian is. The rest of the world—out there—they're scared too."

"Scared of me?"

"No, son. Not you. Scared of living. Scared of dying. Scared of abject poverty, starvation, disease. Twenty billion people battling for life on a planet incapable of sustaining even ten billion. Earth is overburdened, son, overwhelmed with the human virus. They are scared of themselves and of us."

"Us?"

"Hadrian is a haven—we have land—we have clean water—we have space in which to breathe—we have love of our fellow man—"

"Do we?"

"I'm sorry?"

"Love our fellow man?" There is a moment of silence. Papa Dean knows there is no answer he can give to a boy who has had his entire life ripped out from under him—who has been brutally raped. *How*, Dean asks himself, *can Todd possibly believe Hadrian capable of loving man? He can't.* Waking Dean from his reflection, Todd asks, "Don't they?"

"Who son?"

"The outsiders. Don't they love their fellow man?"

Dean ponders this for a moment. All of Hadrian National News' propaganda would have him say no. All he has ever seen of the outside world are the harrowing images of skeleton bodies rushing up against Hadrian's wall, and the images of the starving, dying babies captured from above by Hadrian's satellite camera. Even so, he can't believe them all to be barbarians. "I suppose some of them must. It's just—they have so little food, so little water left that, well, we have to protect ourselves from—" He stops himself from using the now clichéd expressions—*the barbarian heterosexuals; the crazed, insane, and dangerous outsiders.* "Well, from the threat that they'll break through Hadrian's walls, take and destroy all we've managed to preserve." Looking down at the child, he says, "Not just for us, Todd—for the future of humanity. Hadrian is man's last hope for posterity."

"Why can't we share?"

"There just isn't enough."

"Not enough land? Not enough food?"

"No, Todd. Not for twenty billion."

"Is that why we have to be homosexual, Papa?"

"I don't know Todd. That's what we're taught. I mean there are so many ways to prevent pregnancies. But even with all those available, the world is still overpopulated." Shaking his head in wonder, he states, "I may not like all of Hadrian's laws, son, but I don't condemn them either. I mean, if heterosexuals could control procreation, then why is the world so overburdened now?" Looking down at his hands, he remembers the words Geoffrey used to convince him: "Only Hadrian has a stable population. A fully homosexual state may seem drastic, but we are living in an extreme world—even so..." Dean's voice trails off.

"Even so, Papa?"

Trying not to sob, Dean says, looking down on Todd, "What they did to me... What they did to you." Shaking his head, tears flowing. "It all seems so wrong."

"Did you try to die, too, Papa?"

"Yes."

"What stopped you?"

"Geoffrey Hunter."

"Frank's father."

"Yes. Without him," Dean says, closing his eyes in order to shut in the tears, "I don't think I could live."

"Did he rape you?"

Dean is stunned. "No. Of course not." Knowing what happened to the boy has skewed his perspective. Dean adds reassuringly, "Weller is different, Todd. Most men aren't like him." Dean tightens his grip on Todd's hand. "Geoffrey Hunter was good to me. Kind. Gentle. He waited. Like Frank waits for you."

Todd closes his eyes. *Papa Dean doesn't know then.* Memories swirl Todd's stomach. The pounding of fists, his split brow, bruised cheek, and swollen lip; Frank's black eye replays itself in his mind. And then, the stunning blow to his temple, leaving him senseless long enough for Frank to bind his wrists securely to the front bedpost. Todd squeezes his eyes shut. No matter how hard Todd had begged, Frank wouldn't listen. Frank's only words were, "You need to relax, Todd; relax into it or it will hurt." And it did hurt. It had felt as if his backside were being ripped in half. If he could,

Todd would shake his head, but all he can do is say, "No, Papa Dean, Frank can't save me."

"He loves you Todd."

"I know, but—" *I can't tell him,* Todd suddenly realizes. *Knowing the truth about Frank would shatter Papa Dean.* It is evident to Todd that Papa Dean envisions Frank as a duplicate of his father, and although Frank looks exactly like Geoffrey Hunter, Todd knows the two men are as radically different in personality as they are in height. Changing the subject, Todd asks, "Tell me about Frank's father—how he saved you."

"He never tried to turn me. He just—became my friend. He listened, never judged, understood as best he could. He never even tried to kiss me." Smiling, he shrugs, shaking his head wonderingly. "He married me, knowing we might never—"

"Did you? Ever?"

"Yes," he confesses. "Eventually. But he never pressed. I mean, there were times when he thought I might, but he always let go when I said no. But one time, I guess, I no longer had the heart to stop him. I don't know whether I wanted to or not, or whether I felt like I owed him, but when he leaned in, I let him kiss me. For weeks, we just kissed." Dean shakes his head in wonder. "We'd been married two years then. Where he found his patience, I'll never know. And then finally, I went to him, told him I was ready. I knew I wasn't, not really, but something inside me said I need to do this—that Geoffrey loves me and I love him. He was good to me; so gentle with his touch. Even so, I cried. He apologized, but I said, 'No, we needed to do this—I needed to do it—I—'" Dean, now looking at Todd, explains, "I needed to let go. It was cathartic."

"Is it—I mean—do you enjoy it?"

"Sometimes." Sighing a little humph, Dean admits, "Sometimes, I even initiate now." Considering his life with Geoffrey Hunter, Dean adds, "It took me a long time, but now I really do want to be with him." Speaking more hopefully than assuredly, he adds, "I know if you take your time with Frank, you'll feel that way about him someday, too."

He really doesn't know, Todd muses. *I wonder what Frank really told him.*

Sensing the doubt in Todd's eyes, Dean persists, "It's not so bad when the man you're with loves you. When you honestly love him back. Besides," he sighed, "I'd never really been with a girl. We had only just kissed."

"Tell me what happened with the girl, Papa."

"High school," he begins, "grade twelve. Jessica and me—she was one of my best friends. I guess like you and Crystal. We did everything together; always holding hands; always laughing. Then one day at lunch, it just happened. It wasn't planned or nothing—it just happened. We were laughing so hard, and our faces got—well, we just sort of came together. Our lips touched. I burst into flame and started kissing her. Next thing I knew, she was standing up, screaming and pointing my way. Two teachers grabbed me and hauled me into the office. They locked me inside the Vice Principal's office and left me there for over an hour. I didn't know what they'd do or were planning. Then my father came. He was outraged. I had shamed the family name. Me, the genetic offspring of a founding family! They never fiddled with founding family genes in those days." Shaking off sad memories, Dean concludes, "Anyway, he signed me over to the state and disowned me."

Just like Papa Mike. "I'm so sorry, Papa Dean."

"Don't worry about me, Todd; I'm all right. My life's been good, thanks to Geoffrey." Hoping this is the right moment, he adds, "Let Frank help you—I know he can—" But Todd only closes his eyes again.

"What was reeducation camp like for you, Papa?"

"Torture." A sad smile blossoms; Dean knows Todd will understand. "I was Weller's first ward." Todd opens his eyes and gasps. "Yes," Dean admits, "it was horrible."

"Did he…" Todd doesn't finish—he can't finish. "You, too?"

"He tried—he might have succeeded if it hadn't been for Geoffrey."

"Frank's father."

"He walked in just as it was happening. I mean, I tried to fight, but Weller was the stronger man."

"I know." Todd truly does understand.

"Geoffrey was enraged when he saw what Weller was trying to do to me. He pulled him off before Weller could—"

"Weller," Todd interjects, "he had his man grab Jason—throw him out of the room—he locked him out." Papa Dean's story resonates so for him. "Jason would have saved me if he could…" *But it's too late now,* Todd reminds himself. *It's too late for me now.* Shifting his eyes so he can look into Papa Dean's crystal blue orbs, he says, smiling weakly, "Thank you for sharing with me."

"I'd like to tell you more, Todd." Dean takes a moment to brush his fingers through Todd's hair. "About your father, if you'll let me."

"Dad?" It suddenly dawns on Todd. "Was my father…" He whispers now so no one outside the room can hear. "Was my father like me?"

"Yes."

"Tell me." Todd's voice is near pleading. "Tell me, please."

Dean recalls, "I met your father two months after we began high school."

"Grade ten," Todd mutters.

"Yes," Dean's mind begins to drift back into the memory. "Two months into grade ten. I was sitting alone in the cafeteria…" Feeling the need to explain, Dean adds, "I often sat alone in those days."

"Why?" Todd asks.

"I knew—I knew I was different—and was afraid of interaction—afraid of anyone getting to know the real me." Todd's head nods slightly in understanding. "I never had a childhood friend like you. Anyway, Will had been watching me for some time. I often caught him staring at me. I avoided him, thinking he was attracted to me." Dean smiles a little. "Then one day, he just up and joined me at my lunch table. Gave me quite a start." Dean gets lost inside his memory and the words tumble off his lips as if in the moment.

* * * * *

"Dean Stuttgart, right?"

A startled young Dean looks up from his studies. With an egg sandwich poised in his left hand and his computer slate at the ready in his right, Dean freezes at the sight of Will Middleton, the most popular boy in school, smiling down at him, hand extended in greeting. Dean pointedly ignores the offer of friendship and looks back down at his slate. Always studious, Dean throws himself into his studies with fervor because it helps him to avoid interacting with others. Mostly, it is to keep him from staring at girls. If not careful, Dean would be the recipient of many an angry glare. *Study*, he often reminds himself, *study and forget about the others. Study and become a doctor like Dad wants!*

"That's not going to help you this time," Will rejoins.

Dean looks up amazed. He is resorting to talking out loud to himself now. He is going to have to watch out for that. "What?"

"Let's start again, shall we?" Will says with a smile. "Dean Stuttgart, right?"

"Yeah, so?" Dean responds briskly. This man is nothing if not persistent. Extending his hand again, Will says, "Will Middleton."

"Everyone knows who you are," Dean mutters disapprovingly.

"And," Will adds, "everyone knows who you are." Dean rolls his eyes and returns his attention to his slate, though he cannot focus. Laughing now as he retrieves his unwanted hand, Will remains undaunted and persistent. "Mind if I join you?" he asks as he sits across the table from Dean.

Speaking to his slate now, Dean says, "I'd rather be alone, thank you!"

"That's your problem," Will remarks.

Dean's eyes dart up, first in fright, then sparking into anger. "What?" When he gets no response from Will Middleton, he retreats back into the safety of his slate. "I'm studying!" When Will still refuses to take the hint, Dean adds, "Sit there all you want. That doesn't mean I've got to talk to you."

"You're talking to me now," Will adds with a laugh. Then, taking on a serious note, he says, "Yes, you do—we do." Dean sighs, staring intently at the blurred words of his biology text. His left hand is squeezed tightly around his sandwich, having turned it into mulch while his right hand threatens to snap the pencil it is holding. "You see," Will sighs, "I think I know you."

Dean looks up startled, angry. "You don't know me. No one here knows me."

"True, enough," Will replies. "And yet," now waving to the students surrounding them inside the cafeteria, "they all know who you are. You are a Stuttgart." Smiling grimly, "That makes you the most popular unpopular boy in school."

"What do you care?" Dean snaps back.

"I'm like you," Will replies. Dean snorts. "A lot like you," Will insists.

Speaking to his slate, Dean says, "You're the school jock. Everyone looks up to you—"

"And," Will adds pointedly, "expects a lot from me, too. And," he adds grimly, "from you, too, being who you are, who your father is. *Who*," he adds with extra emphasis, "your grandmother is—one of our founding mothers. Everybody watches you."

Dean sinks deeper into his seat, trying to hide his face in his book. "Leave me alone, I'm studying."

Pausing to let the gravity of his words sink in, Will says, "People expect a lot from guys like you and me."

Begrudgingly, Dean asks, "Like what?"

Will's answer is matter-of-fact, "Like dating."

"I'm not dating you!"

Ignoring Dean's adamant rejection, Will continues, "You see, like you, I don't date, and like with you, people want to know why. Like you, some even question if I'm…" in a low whisper, "a *strai*."

Flustered, Dean opens both hands, dropping sandwich crumbs and slate onto the table.

"That's right, Dean." Will stares intently into his soon to be new boyfriend's eyes. "People think you and I just might be…" Now just mouthing the word "straight." After allowing for the reality of their situation to sink in, Will continues, "For the moment, the only thing saving you is your family name, and the only thing saving me are my skills on the b-ball court." Squinting his eyes, planning now to play hard ball, Will says. "If you ever touch one of those girls you ogle—don't try to pretend. I've seen you." Shrugging, he admits, "I've been watching you watch them. I watch them, too, just not so obviously as you." Paling slightly with introspection, Will adds, "At least, I hope not."

Dean is aghast. "How obvious have I been?"

"Very." Will's crisp reply is a cutting reminder that even being a Stuttgart might not be enough to save him if he should ever falter. Finally, having consistent eye contact, Will persists, "The fact is, Dean, you need me, and…" almost a little begrudgingly, "I need you." Holding Dean's crystal blue eyes with his own stone gray orbs, he says, "Here is what I propose." Standing now, Will crosses to Dean's side of the table. "Shove over," he commands. Will has frightened Dean into submission. Thigh snug to thigh, Will begins slowly, very gently to rub Dean's arm with his fingers. So light is his touch that he only manages to caress his arm hair. "We date. You and I become a unit—a tight unit—the serious high school couple. The ones everyone expects to register." Dean swallows hard. "If we can become inseparable, then we can escape the mistrusting, questioning stares, the behind the back whispers we both hear so often, and most importantly," he adds, "we can escape something we both desperately want to escape."

"What?" Dean mutters.

"Actually having to date." Pausing briefly, Will stops his fingers from fluttering. "So," he says coyly, now having his fingers walk up Dean's arm,

297

over his shoulder, and under his chin where he feigns tickling him, "laugh for me." Dean chokes a giggle. Will grimaces and shakes his head slightly. "We'll have to work on your playacting." Will's playacting is obviously exemplary. Using his finger now to turn Dean's face in his direction, Will asks again, "So? Are you in?"

Dean ponders the implications. Thinking back, he has never seen Will with a guy. Never heard of any boy dating him, just a lot of wishes and wants and desires expressed by every other boy in school but him. Even though Will is playing up the player right now, Dean does not mind. There are definite advantages to dating someone who doesn't want to date. "No kissing or any—other stuff?" Dean asks, feeling awkward.

"Definitely no other stuff. As for kissing," Will pauses, "I don't think we can avoid that, but it really only has to be a modest peck between classes."

Dean's mind is highly active at this moment. "Can I—may I introduce you to my dad?"

Will smiles that his plan is actually working. Approaching Dean Stuttgart was a gamble, a huge, extremely dangerous risk, but one he had been right about. Watching Dean ogle Rylie Wineman had made Will decide to act because it looked as if the girl were ready to expose Dean. "I'd be honored to meet the direct descendant of our founding mother."

Dean laughed—not a forced, choked giggle this time, but an honest laugh that piqued the interest of those around them. As Will had known all along, they were under the discreet but vigilant observation of their peers. "Mimi's nice. I'll introduce you to her, too."

"Mimi? I thought her name was Destiny."

"It is," Dean blushes slightly. "Mimi's a pet name for grandmother."

"Cool," Will replies, considering his next move. "Let's seal it with a kiss—just a peck." After a quick meeting of lips, the two boys separate. Will, once he is halfway through the cafeteria, spins back gaily to call out, "See you tonight, then!" Dean blushes for the crowd and nods his head. They hadn't actually made a date, but it was good for the rest of the students to think they had.

* * * * *

"Wow!" Todd's eyes sparkle. "That was quite a story Papa Dean." He had listened so intently to Papa Dean's voice that Todd had almost felt as if he had been there with his father and Dean over twenty-five years ago. Turning his eyes back to Papa Dean, he asks, "Did he—did my father ever get caught? Did he go to reeducation camp, too?"

"No."

"And he married?"

"Yes, your Papa Mike."

"Did he love him?"

"Your Papa Mike loved your father. That I know for sure. But whether your father loved Mike—I think so—but honestly, Todd, I don't know." Dean recalls, "Mike was a cheerleader. He doted on your father. He would do anything for him, and sometimes, your father took advantage of that. I guess that's why he chose to marry Mike. There's safety in marriage." Trying to reassure Todd, he adds, "I'm sure he liked him, appreciated his devotion. Your Papa Mike was thoroughly committed to Will."

"But why would Dad marry if he didn't love the man? Or want sex with him. I mean, marriage means sex."

"Marriage isn't all about sex, Todd."

"I know that, but it is expected, isn't it? That's why you eventually gave in, right? Right?"

"Yes, Todd, you're right."

"Then why would he?"

"Because I warned him—about reeducation." Closing his eyes, Dean remembers the day Will Middleton came to visit him at camp. "You can have visitations after you've come out as gay. When your dad came to see me, I told him how happy I was to find my true self. I even tried to act festive. But it was evident by his eyes that he didn't believe me," Dean harrumphs. "And I didn't blame him because at that point it was all a lie. Anyway, visitors had to sit behind chicken wire stretched up from the countertop to the ceiling. But there were a few inches available for our hands to reach underneath so when I put my hand through, he held onto it. That's when I slipped him the note—a little old school perhaps, but a note is silent and can easily disappear. Anything put on the wave is easily reconstructed."

"What did the note say?" Todd asks in earnest.

"'Never get caught. Find a man you like. Marry him. Trust me. It's better.' He picked Mike Fulton. Your Papa Mike loved your father to distraction. I don't think he could have picked a better man."

"Except he changed," Todd begins.

"Yes, after your father died," Dean agrees. "It was as if something inside Mike died when your father passed."

"He was never the same."

"No, you're right," Dean agrees. "He wasn't."

"Papa Dean?"

"Yes, Todd."

"Please ask Frank to visit me. He hasn't been back since…" *Since I asked him.*

Dean smiles, hopeful. "Sure, I will—of course, I will. And he can help you, Todd—I know he can. Like his father helped me."

No, he can't Papa Dean. Todd closes his eyes so Dean can't read his expression. *Not the way you want him to. Frank's not like his father. But he will help*, Todd determines, *with what I've asked of him. He owes me that much.* "Papa Dean?"

"Yes, Todd."

"I love you."

Dean, smiling through his tears, bends down to kiss Todd. "I love you too, son."

* * * * *

Salve!

Continuing Investigation
HNN—Melissa Eagleton Reporting

The continuing investigation into the alleged abuses reported at the North-east Reeducation Camp is capturing the attention of Hadrian. Parents fear for the health and sanity of their children should they be found acting on their heterosexual tendencies. One mother noted that every one of our children has the potential to experience heterosexual desires. "Sexual education is a parental matter, not a state matter," said one father, expressing his dissatisfaction in the current reeducation system. "Children should remain at home with their parents and a government counselor should attend to them on an as needed basis." This sounds reasonable enough, but when put into the light of economics, only wealthier families could afford such luxuries. We are still left with the necessary means of reeducating the children of our poorer citizens. Such a dichotomic split between the treatment of the wealthy and the poor will only lead to resentment among our citizens. An increase in taxes is not likely to occur, not with another election so close at hand. Hadrian's citizens and businesses already pay the highest taxes in the world to maintain the one remaining zoo as well as our four (and the earth's only remaining) national parks.

Heated debate surrounds the issue of corporal punishment. Some parents are demanding that the paddle be banned as a means of punishment while others concur with Gideon Weller that in order to restrain the passions and aggressions of heterosexual men, one needs to do battle with a hard hand. We have all witnessed firsthand the brutal ways of heterosexual men every time our walls are attacked. These men are truly lunatics and very dangerous. All our exposure to heterosexual men shows that they are not capable of reason and act far too quickly on their emotions. The first instinct of the heterosexual male is to fight. According to Gideon Weller, "When one is responsible for restraining angry young men, one has to use physical force or all of Hadrian will suffer the consequences!" And, as our polls show, many in Hadrian concur.

As for the accusation that Gideon Weller has raped some of the wards at his camp, no evidence has been found, and not a single ward in the past twenty-five years that Gideon Weller has been stationed at the Northeast Camp has come forward with an accusation. It is merely the word of one man who claims to have heard a rape in action. Of that specific incident, Gideon Weller has a witness assuring us that no rape occurred. The young man, the alleged victim in question, remains silent on the issue.

I remain firm in my belief that Gideon Weller is innocent of all charges. His work at the Northeast Reeducation Camp excels all others in the field of reeducation. *Salve!* and HNN stand behind Gideon Weller.

Vale!

A Controversial Lesson

In grade ten, Frank and Todd were in all required courses together. Both boys' favorite class was literature. Much of the material studied was gay literature and the standard interpretation, though often left unexpressed, was that every character read and discussed in class was gay. Todd decided to challenge this rule on the day Mr. Reiner introduced a classic Canadian literature unit with an emphasis on gay literature written when homosexuality was deemed unacceptable.

On that day, unconvinced that either the poet or his characters were gay, Todd raises his hand. After the receptive nod, he asks, "Mr. Reiner, how do you know Earle Birney was gay?"

"Good question, Todd." Mr. Reiner enjoys students with the courage and intelligence to challenge his suppositions. "I don't. I didn't even bother to read the man's bio. All I'm really interested in is the content of his poetry—actually, with the one poem I've chosen for our study, *David*."

"I don't see it. How can you base a man's sexuality on one poem about two friends mountain hiking—especially when there is nothing in the poem to suggest either boy is gay—or the poet for that matter."

Frank instantly raises his hand. Mr. Reiner smiles. Nodding knowingly Frank's way, he waves his hand down. "We'll get to that soon enough, Todd," Mr. Reiner replies, almost condescendingly. "First, I would like to explain the necessity of studying the works of homosexuals from the past—"

Todd refuses to allow the subject to change. "I read a bio of the poet over the wave last night. It said he married a woman, an Edith or Ester Bull, and that they had a son. I think that means the man was a heterosexual."

A slight grimace exposes Mr. Reiner's annoyance. "There were a number of men, and women," he adds for the girls, "who married and lived false heterosexual lives. But," cutting off any further attempt by Todd to recommence his argument, "that is not the topic for today's discussion." Todd had intended to mention how Earle Birney also had a relationship with a female graduate student, but Mr. Reiner is successful in assuaging his attempt. Lifting a finger in front of the boy's face, "Ah, ah, ah," he pronounces sternly, insisting they revert back to his chosen topic. "Those men and women," he continues, "who lived in an oppressed era, had to be subtle about offering the world their expression. It behooves us," Mr. Reiner drones on now, looking directly at his immediate opposition (Todd), "to study the work of those men and women who did not live in a secure and free environment like ourselves. This," he emphasizes, "is an important part of our heritage as homosexuals. And," he reminds his class, "part of the rationale behind why our founding families chose to create a country of our own. Todd—" Although Mr. Reiner is not picking on Todd, he tends to direct most of his questions the young man's way since he is almost always sure to get an intelligent answer from Todd. "Remind the class of the cornerstone I am referring to."

Hadrian's society is founded on four cornerstones of existence, and these cornerstones are drilled into all Hadrian's children from the first days of schooling, so anyone in the room could have answered without thinking. Todd is definitely not thinking at the moment as he answers in far too concise and crisp a manner. He believes he is being picked on for harboring a disparaging interpretation. "Safety for homosexuals."

"Yes," Mr. Reiner's sigh expresses his disappointment. Usually Todd's answers are more in-depth. "Devon," another boy Mr. Reiner can always depend on for bright responses, "elaborate, please."

Devon doesn't even have to turn on the cognitive components of his brain to reply. He simply recites verbatim the words straight out of Hadrian's founding constitution: "First and foremost, it has been decided that Hadrian will provide a safe haven for homosexuals, who have, throughout the history of mankind, suffered discrimination and abuse. Never again shall a homosexual walk in fear or feel the need to hide his identity for the appearance of normalcy in society."

"Very good." Turning on the student who is his favorite most other days, Mr. Reiner scolds, "Now, that, Todd, was a thorough, in-depth response." Todd's nod is acknowledgment enough for Mr. Reiner to move on.

"Now, obviously, Todd read the poem as assigned. Who else in the class read the poem *David* by Earle Birney last night?" Only a few hands rise: Devon, Frank, Millicent, and T'Neal. All other students lower their heads in shame. Mr. Reiner is quite disappointed. Hadrian boasts the brightest minds and the best education system on the planet, yet here, sitting before him, is the deluge of society. His glare is scathing and the class is sufficiently intimidated. Mr. Reiner, notorious for using the voc to contact parents instantly—in class, *and* loud enough for everyone in the room to hear—begins a rapid succession of blinking. Having already set up contact groups with all of his students' parents, it is just a matter of blinking in the right contacts and uttering the appropriate words. "English ten—class two—delete Middleton, Hunter, Rankin, Brown, and Cantos—" The rapid succession of blinks required of Mr. Reiner to organize this message was only comical to those five students not affected. "Parents," the teacher begins his tirade against the wayward members of his class, "I regret to inform you that your child has refrained from completing yesterday's homework. Please note the attached file." Reiner is also notorious for backup plans designed as extra work for students who fail to complete assigned tasks. "I expect all irresponsible students to complete this task tonight in lieu of yesterday's assignment. Please ensure your child completes it and either vocs or waves the assignment to me before tomorrow's lesson." Numerous groans fill the room. Hadrian takes the education of its children seriously, and everyone who failed to read the poem last night knows his or her parents are answering that voc message right now! And Hadrian only knows what horrendous assignment Mr. Reiner has designed for them

"Now," Mr. Reiner continues, "take out your slates and open the Birney poem we downloaded yesterday. T'Neal," (Mr. Reiner always asks T'Neal to read because the young man has a natural actor's voice—and T'Neal always agrees—and knowing he will be asked to read, he always practices the night before) "please read the poem aloud for us."

T'Neal obliges, and when he is done, he offers up the first interpretation. "It's about mountain climbers, isn't it, sir?"

Mr. Reiner quickly aborts the instinctual headshake and scorn he feels whenever a student claims an interpretation already presented by another member of the class. "Yes, T'Neal, it is. That is exactly what Todd pointed out earlier." Hoping for further insight, Mr. Reiner's eyes scan over the other four students who claimed to have read the poem in advance.

Todd immediately pipes up. He likes the poem and read it over four times last night. "Only the one guy was a real climber. The other kid didn't really know what he was doing."

"Good!" Todd is now back in Mr. Reiner's good graces. "How do you know that, Todd?"

"Well, it says here," Todd is pointing to the lines on his slate even though the act is not necessary, "that David taught him how to: 'David showed me/ How to use the give of shale for giant incredible/Strides.'" Scrunching his eyes tight, looking deep inside his brain for the answer, Todd adds, "I think that means David taught him how to jump from one rock to another."

"Not bad, Todd." Mr. Reiner is smiling so hard his cheeks are causing his eyes to squint.

"And here it says," Todd adds, encouraged by his instructor's enthusiasm, "'David taught me/How time on a knife-edge can pass with the guessing of fragments.' I think that means David was the expert here and not his friend."

"Excellent, my boy, but we haven't heard from any of the girls. Millicent, what other evidence can you find in the poem to support the idea that David was an expert climber?"

"Nothing. The poem doesn't make any sense at all." Clearly exasperated, she glares up at Mr. Reiner. "Why does all the stuff we read have to be about boys? Why can't we ever read anything about lesbians?"

Mr. Reiner groans, as do most of the boys. Mr. Reiner so desperately wants to point out that they just finished reading *Fried Green Tomatoes at the Whistle Stop Cafe* by Fannie Flagg. But he doesn't. Millicent Brown would just cry about it to her mothers and make his life a living hell. Instead, he searches for the safest means of escape. "I challenge you to find some for us," Mr. Reiner suggests.

"Sylvia Plath," Millicent responds instantly.

"Fine," Mr. Reiner grumbles. He hates Sylvia Plath's suicidal everybody hates me poetic rants—but all the lesbians love her. "We can download some of her work tomorrow. In the meantime," his eyebrows rise as he speaks briskly, "attempt to understand Birney's poem."

"Yes, sir." Millicent is slightly mollified since she has been assured some study of her favorite poet. "Can we start with *Admonition*?"

Pushing his glasses up to his forehead, and then rubbing the bridge of his nose, Mr. Reiner sighs. "How about you pick the poems?"

"I will," Millicent declares victoriously.

"All right then." Having successfully escaped a scathing remark from the girl's mothers about favoritism to boys, Mr. Reiner directs the class back to today's lesson. "Let's go deeper into the poem, shall we?"

"Oh, oh, oh!" Millicent is practically giggling in delight as she waves her arm about.

"Yes, Millicent." Mr. Reiner is dearly hoping she will talk about *David*.

No such luck. "Can we also study Anne Sexton? She was Sylvia Plath's best friend." She turns and smiles to her best friend, Crystal Albright.

"Were they lovers, too?" Crystal asks Millicent. Before answering, Millicent kisses her girlfriend.

Mr. Reiner puts a stop to this display of affection and any potential response from Millicent. "My classroom is not a bedroom. Please refrain from kissing in here."

Millicent raises her eyes, "You let the boys kiss."

"No, I do not." Mr. Reiner is unimpressed with the accusation. "This is an academic institution, not a social outlet for dating." To mollify the girl some, knowing full well she is going to go home and complain to her mothers, Mr. Reiner offers her a prize. "Here's what you do, Millicent. You choose all the poems and poets for tomorrow's lesson. Voc them to me and I'll approve them. Sound good?"

Victorious, Millicent shakes her fists in front of her and turns for one more kiss from Crystal. Mr. Reiner chooses to let this little act pass since Millicent's mothers are very active in the girl's education. As far as these women are concerned, Millicent is never wrong. Teachers always have to tread lightly with parents of strong influence, regardless of who's right or wrong.

Frank pulls Mr. Reiner out of potential hot water by raising his hand. "I think what Bobbie did for David at the end was incredibly romantic and beautiful."

Romance, Mr. Reiner smiles. *Thank you, Frank. Girls love romance:* "And what was that, Frank?" Better yet, this is the very direction he wants the class discussion to take.

"To help his lover die when his life was clearly over."

"What?" Todd can't believe his ears.

Oh, good! Mr. Reiner grins. *When these two disagree, the class discussion doesn't get any better.*

Frank's shoulders shrug involuntarily as his head shakes and his eyes blink in confusion. "Didn't you hear me?"

"Of course I heard you," Todd retaliates. "I just think you're wrong."

Thank Hadrian for Todd, Mr. Reiner muses. No one else in class has the gumption to disagree with Frank Hunter. That Mr. Reiner silently agrees with Frank is irrelevant. He simply appreciates Todd's ability to spark a debate and get Frank Hunter riled up at the same time.

"So you think assisted suicide is wrong?" Frank is fervent in his position.

"In this case," Todd replies quite matter-of-factly (a tone he knows drives Frank insane), "yes."

"Why?" Frank is almost angry now.

"Because his life isn't over." Then, in deference to Frank's near outburst, Todd raises his hand to calm down his friend. "Okay, I admit he is probably paralyzed for life, but—"

"Probably?" Frank interjects. "Ah, Mr. Reiner, am I right or am I right? I mean, it says David can't even move and he only shifts his eyes…"

"He can move his head," Todd points out.

Frank ignores Todd's input. "On top of all that, *Todd*, he can't feel any pain."

"Where exactly does it say that, Frank?" Mr. Reiner always insists his students provide empirical evidence.

Ignoring his teacher, carrying right on with his harangue, Frank continues, "I mean, he fell a good fifty feet, landed on his back atop a very sharp rock—'a cruel fang' he can't even feel!"

"Good, Frank," Mr. Reiner stops him. "You provided us one quote from the poem, 'a cruel fang,' but that doesn't prove your supposition that David is paralyzed. Find us the evidence, direct evidence from the poem."

"Right here," Frank, too, points to his personal slate, though it does nothing to help the others in the class.

"Which lines?" Mr. Reiner asks since Frank has not provided any direct quotes.

"Um…" Frank really hadn't pointed to the right lines so he begins his search. Tapping his slate triumphantly when he finds it, he exclaims, "Here! Where David says, 'I can't move…If only I felt/Some pain.' See," he says, smiling Todd's way, nodding his head and raising his eyebrows. "He even uses the word 'pain.'"

"Okay," Todd acquiesces. "He's paralyzed for life, but come on; that doesn't mean his life has to end."

"It does for David."

Tilting his head, closing his eyes only to open and roll them Frank's way, Todd asks, "Why?" Mr. Reiner has to stifle a laugh; Todd is so comical with his expressions.

"Listen," Franks says. (Mr. Reiner loves it when the students take over and teach each other.) "It's at the beginning of the poem, 'mountains for David were made to see over,' and then at the end, he rejects the idea of having to live helpless and confined to a wheelchair." Seeing Mr. Reiner's eyebrow cock, Frank looks at the poem and finds the lines he needs for evidence. "Here, when he says, 'For what? A wheelchair,/Bob?'"

"Just because someone wants to die doesn't mean it's right to help him," Todd insists. "He could learn to accept his new life. Learn ways to cope."

Using one of the symbols Birney placed inside his poem, Frank ejaculates, "He was a mountain goat, Todd! He could never live in a wheelchair. He needs to climb mountains. And then," Frank adds, latching onto the other symbol Earle Birney used to foreshadow David's death, "there's the bird with the broken wing. David took it from Bob and killed it, saying, 'Could you teach it to fly?'"

"That was a bird, Frank." Exasperated, Todd practically shouts, "Not a guy." Then turning grim, he says, "I just don't understand how Bobbie could do it." To take a friend's life is incomprehensible to the youth.

"Devon," Mr. Reiner asks, trying to include other class members in the discussion, "do you know the answer to Todd's question?"

Devon is quick to respond. He may not jump into class discussions, but he will always answer a question when asked. "He blames himself for David's fall."

"Good," Mr. Reiner praises the lad, "and where is that found in the poem?" Turning now to the girls, choosing Millicent since she is the only one to have read the poem in advance, he says, "Come, Millicent; show the boys up by finding the evidence."

Millicent scowls but gives in to the challenge. "Here, when David says, 'No, Bobbie! Don't ever blame yourself./I didn't test my foothold.'"

"Not bad," Mr. Reiner acknowledges, "but," he emphasizes, "those lines only show that David doesn't want Bobbie to feel guilty. What lines show that Bobbie *does* feel guilty?" Because Frank's hand is waving like a flag in the wind, Mr. Reiner tosses the reins back to him, "Frank."

"And I knew/He had tested his holds. It was I who had not... I looked/

At the blood on the ledge, and the far valley. I looked/At last in his eyes. He breathed, 'I'd do it for you, Bob.'"

"Very nice, Frank." Although pleased with Frank's in-depth unearthing of the poem exactly as he had hoped, Mr. Reiner still feels obliged to give Todd the last word. The boy looks so dejected and discombobulated by the entire interpretation. "Okay, Todd, what's wrong?"

Todd fumes in frustration because he is unable to break Frank's logic. He truly believes he is right and Frank is wrong. All he wants is for Frank to admit that it's not always right to help another person commit suicide. They have been fighting over this issue ever since one of Hadrian's senators recently tried, and failed, to have the bill legalizing euthanasia revoked. Although referendums are normally only held once a decade, with assisted suicide being such a hot topic, another vote was held mid-decade. Although still a victory in the eyes of the government, 46 percent of the populace voted against the old law. Mr. Reiner purposely chose this poem to match the political mood of the time. He simply had to introduce it as gay literature so he could get the class to this crucial point. "Well," Todd responds, as one who is defeated but determined not to lose, "I just know I could never do what Bobbie did. I could never throw my best friend over the edge of a cliff to his death."

Frank smiles. Of course, everyone in the room knows of his and Todd's friendship so it is evident Todd means he could never kill Frank, but Frank takes the meaning to an even deeper level. Still smiling, he winks at his best friend, clearly enjoying what he is about to say, "But, Todd, Bobbie wasn't just killing his best friend. He was helping his lover to die with dignity."

Todd's blush causes excessive laughter among the students. Even Mr. Reiner is enjoying the show.

With the poem blurring before his eyes, Todd actually begins to stammer. "They weren't lovers. There's nothing in the poem that says they're lovers."

"I disagree," Mr. Reiner pipes up. Now is the time to prove his point. "Frank?" If his suspicion is correct, Frank will know exactly where the line is.

Smiling triumphantly at Todd, Frank quotes the one and only line in the entire poem that is suggestive of a sexual relationship (the one line that enabled Mr. Reiner to claim this poem was homosexual literature) between David and Bobbie: "Then the two of us rolled in the blanket while round us the cold/Pines thrust at the stars." Mr. Reiner beams.

Todd's response is feeble, and he knows it. "That doesn't mean they had sex."

"Oh, yes it does!" Frank retorts. He has won this debate, and there is no doubt about it. Todd has lost face while he has risen victorious.

"Well," says Todd, though defeated, refusing to give in. "I still wouldn't do it."

"Do what?" Frank asks.

Mr. Reiner raises a brow over this line of questioning. It no longer seems as if the boys are discussing David and Bobbie.

"Push you over—" Todd suddenly shuts down; if stripped, his entire body would be plasma purple at having just admitted affection for Frank in front of the whole class.

"Well…" Frank is as happy as if he were in Antinous' bed. "I'd do it for you, *Todd*!"

The line had come straight out of the poem! The class had applauded. Rumor had spread for weeks on end that Frank and Todd were lovers (even if Todd didn't wear the ridiculous purple dog collar denoting Frank's ownership). Frank wished it could have been more than a rumor, but he had enjoyed the accolades while they lasted.

* * * * *

Salve!

A Controversial Law
HNN—Melissa Eagleton Reporting

Euthanasia. Assisted suicide. Call it what you like, helping another person to die has always been a topic of heated debate in Hadrian. This controversial law, in place since the founding families introduced the first constitution, never ceases to spark argument among our citizens. There is a small contingency of religious citizens in Hadrian—mostly Jewish, Islamic, and Christian (historically at odds in the outside world but, ironically, in agreement on this topic)—who have united to fund a campaign against euthanasia. And they are hard at it! There is no doubt about that! Every ten years, Hadrian's citizens gather at the polls to reaffirm our country's policies and beliefs. One such referendum, of course, is to determine whether or not to retain the controversial euthanasia law on our books. So volatile has this debate become that proponents against assisted suicide were able to push for a mid-decade vote, something unheard of previously in Hadrian's short history. Fortunately, as with every other past vote, the majority of Hadrian's citizens determine the "death with dignity" law to be both moral and essential. Even so, radical opposition claims the last referendum to have been a victory since only 54 percent of the populace voted to keep the law in place. As a result, these people are convinced that this decade will be the one when Hadrian votes out the law that permits an individual to commit suicide with the help of loved ones or a medical practitioner if said person feels he or she can no longer live with dignity.

Here at HNN, we are split in our beliefs. I stand for the human right to die with dignity while many others feel that assisted suicide is essentially murder. One cameraman states that death is not a human choice, but the dominion of God. I assure you, he is alone in that opinion. But, at the very least, our production manager would like to see stringent rules in place that will effectively determine what constitutes a life no longer worth living.

Curious to know what our viewers think, we ask that you voc in to our poll at @HNN#E-AS/MDR and let Hadrian know your opinion. Why wait for the next referendum? Let's tell our government how we feel right now! With a presidential election coming up, I can assure you that Hadrian's senate will listen closely to the *Salve!* viewers' opinion.

Vale!

Making Amends

When Frank returns, he is ready. Having visited the darkness of his soul, he has come to realize he is to blame for the pain Todd is suffering. He has been selfish. *Papa Dean was right. When Todd said it would be him and me one day, I should have broken off with T.Neal, but I wanted to get laid!* Scorn and self-recrimination burn deep. *If only I had stayed by Todd's side. Professed myself his boyfriend. Never trusted him alone with that woman! Todd only turned to Crystal because I had abandoned him. Had we been dating, she never would have come on to him.* But even that isn't the reason he decides to help Todd. Anguish is in the truth. *I raped Todd.* Shuddering, he remembers Todd's words, "You're no better than Weller." Those words forced Frank to admit that Todd and he had never made love. *I raped him*, he reminds himself, *and then I shamed him.* With this awareness came understanding. What little spirit and strength Todd had left in him were destroyed inside reeducation camp. All that remains now of his friend is a battered body and a shattered soul desperately seeking rest. Terrified by this reality, Frank realizes there is only one way to make amends, to end Todd's suffering. *I helped put him here*, Frank realizes. *I must help him escape.*

Before walking into Todd's room, Frank charms the nurse on duty. "Why don't you take a five minute break? I'll be in the room with Todd. Everything is going to be okay."

Grateful, the nurse smiles at Frank. He could use a little down time, having been chained to his desk for the past five hours. "I sure could use a break." Wincing slightly and using his eyes to nod toward the washroom, he admits, "I really have to go. I've been farting up a storm."

Frank laughs, then nods, "Go."

As soon as the nurse exits, Frank enters Todd's room. Todd's eyes are closed. "Frank?" he asks without opening them.

"Yes."

There is silence as the boys wait: Frank for Todd to ask; Todd for Frank to say he is ready. Finally, Todd initiates. "Will you do it?"

"Yes."

Todd sighs, "Thank you."

Frank walks over to the bed. His first order of business is to remove from Todd's chest the attached electrodes that keep track of his heartbeat. The sudden elongated beep and straight line on the machine fixes the boys' attention; both are aghast and in awe of the image. Frank jerks back into action, opening his shirt, placing the electrodes on his chest, causing the machine to resume its steady beat, complementing the rise and fall of the heart line. Deciding now is the time, Frank reaches behind Todd's head and pulls at the pillow. He has to yank harder than he had intended to release the pillow since Todd's head is strapped down and the pillow is wedged beneath it. Prior to smothering his friend, Frank bends over and kisses Todd on the lips; then he whispers into his ear, "I love you."

The silence is overpowering, the repeating beeps of Frank's heartbeat failing to register in Frank's stunned mind. Suddenly, the sound explodes in his head like a rapid succession of bombs, an eerie reminder of the corpse lying on the bed—its face still covered by the pillow—Frank's hands still holding it down. Pale, shivering, Frank doesn't move. He knows Todd is dead, but he cannot will himself to let go. He is afraid to release his grip from fear of seeing "It." "It"—the very word Bobbie used to describe David's corpse.

Outside, at the nurse's station, seeing nothing untoward, a young man smiles at the sight of a visiting lover leaning over to comfort his friend. Suddenly, the nurse is shocked into action when he watches Frank slowly straighten and then rip something away from his chest.

* * * * *

Salve!

Murder or Assisted Suicide?
HNN—Melissa Eagleton reporting

The death of Todd Middleton, son of Will Middleton, the bioengineer who brought the soya bean to Hadrian, comes as a shock to everyone who knew and loved the boy. Todd was only seventeen years old and beloved by many. Like his father before him, Todd Middleton was known to Hadrian as a superstar on the b-ball court and had even been offered a full early entrance scholarship to Antinous Uni prior to his having been exposed as a heterosexual male.

What is most shocking about Todd Middleton's death is how he was brutally murdered by his lover. Their peers knew Todd Middleton and Frank Hunter as the best of friends who, shortly after Todd had been exposed as a heterosexual, were said to have coupled. Because Todd had already had sexual intercourse with a young woman, this sudden change in their relationship was insufficient to stem Todd's removal from society and his being placed in a reeducation camp. Todd Middleton was housed at the Northeast Camp under the care of Gideon Weller with Jason Warith as the boy's guardian. Although Frank Hunter has confessed to his crime, Jason Warith insists that the real murderer in this case is Gideon Weller.

Frank Hunter's defense lawyer is Ms. Faial Raboud, renowned for obtaining an acquittal for Andrea Hodgson, who had been exposed as a heterosexual by Darya Danson.

Raboud's strategy of defense for Frank Hunter is to focus on Todd Middleton's death as having been assisted suicide and not an act of murder. As we know, euthanasia is legal in Hadrian if the individual requesting aid is of sound mind and clearly suffering from a debilitating illness. To die with dignity is every Hadrian citizen's right. The question being raised by National Prosecutor Graham Sabine is whether or not Todd Middleton was actually suffering from any weakening and incurable disease. Also, as

Sabine succinctly puts it, "When the euthanasia law was put into place, it is highly unlikely Congress considered depression as life-threatening. Depression," the national prosecutor points out, "cannot be deemed unbearable as it is seldom lifelong and there are always ways to help cure the victim." Medical professionals agree Todd Middleton was in a state of depression at the time of his death, but they are in disagreement whether the quality of his life had been drastically diminished. What validates euthanasia is when the victim can no longer live a quality existence and it would be kinder to allow him to die with dignity. All of this hinges on the individual in question being of sound mind when making the decision to die. As Sabine points out, "Severe depression disables the individual from having a 'sound mind.' Thus," Sabine argues, "Todd Middleton's request to die should have been denied." Defense attorney Faial Raboud must prove to the court that hopelessness is not akin to mental instability and that one can make sound choices while suffering from depression. Raboud has set up quite a challenge for herself if she is going to prove that Todd Middleton had lost all self-respect with no hope of ever restoring his self-esteem.

Vale!

A Private Meeting

Defense attorney Faial Raboud had reluctantly agreed to a private meeting with National Prosecutor Graham Sabine, to be accompanied by Crystal Albright and her mothers. Faial judiciously chose to keep Frank Hunter and his fathers ignorant about this conference. She will reveal all to them after the fact, but emotions are running too high right now for the family—anger, hurt, and disillusionment have built voraciously into a desperate need to scapegoat Crystal Albright. The girl certainly holds her share of responsibility in this tragedy, Faial acknowledges, but she is not deserving of Dean Hunter's severe reaction—his extreme hate for her. The man's anger and pain have taken him beyond the realm of reason.

Scanning the meeting room while she waits, Faial notes that it is the standard issue of the conference meet and greet. Situated on the third floor of the national government's central office building (Hadrian's tallest building), the room has north windows that open onto the building's roof garden. The room is filled with natural light, offering no light fixtures for after daylight hours. No sunrays ever penetrate the room, though, as the sun is always too far southeast or west for any of it to enter the building. Outside this wall-length gemstone is one of the most beautiful roof gardens Faial had ever seen. Being early July, every flower is in bloom, including the tiger lilies and the ever present wild rose. "Ahh," Faial sighs involuntarily, there is a Brown-Eyed Susan. And another! She loves the Brown-Eyed Susan! That had been her genetic father's nickname for her. She also notes a spray of daisies, carnations, and gladiolas.

Blinking and looking to the time display in the upper left of her eye screen, Faial sighs, this time disconcertedly. Graham Sabine is late. Sabine *is always late*, she reminds herself. Graham Sabine is not known for his punctuality. Faial believes he is tardy on purpose in an attempt to unbalance the opposition. By leaving her to sit alone, waiting, worrying, Faial reasons, Sabine means to create tension, bringing on a state of mind he hopes will discombobulate her. This tactic never worked the last two times he tried it, so it amuses Faial that he continues to use it on her. *Who was it that said insanity is to do the same thing over and expect different results?* Even though she can't remember the original author, the thought still makes her giggle.

Bringing her thoughts back to Frank Hunter, Faial's jovial mood diminishes. Though unaffected by Sabine's repetitive tactics, Faial is fully aware of the case's complexities. Getting Frank Hunter off will not be easy. Her partner told her she was crazy to take the case, but there is more to this than a killing. Instinct compels her. The statements of Dean Hunter and Jason Warith have exposed an ugly truth about Hadrian, a truth she has tasted, felt, but prior to this case, has never been able to expose. Andrea Hodgson's case taught her all about the ills of imposing stringent sexual preference laws on individuals. Like her client Andrea, Faial had come to believe Darya Danson dressed in drag to lure women. Though she could never prove this supposition, it had opened her eyes to the realities of imposed sexual preference. Men and women must be free to choose with whom they wish to share their bodies. If society needs law to avoid excessive procreation, so be it, but no one, Faial has come to believe, has the right to decide whom a man or a woman should love. The whole notion that incidents of rape and pedophilia will increase astronomically if heterosexuality becomes legal is sheer nonsense. Rapists and pedophiles are a class all their own. It is unfair to use their despicable behavior against normal sexual drives. Whether Hadrian's citizens are ready to accept it or not, Faial reasons, heterosexual desires are as normal as homosexual ones.

Although she currently lacks proof to support her beliefs, the Frank Hunter case, Faial truly believes, if played right, will reveal the evidence required for much needed reforms. The fact that her client has confessed to murder doesn't make her task any easier. Somehow, she has to get through to the boy that there is more to this case than the act of suffocation. That act, as Faial and the boy's fathers believe, was assisted suicide, but Frank is not helping matters. Using this time alone while waiting for Sabine and the Albrights, Faial turns her mind to the seriousness of this case.

Frank Hunter's confession is damaging. As soon as the nurse entered Todd Middleton's room, Frank confessed. He repeated the same story to government law officials, even to National Prosecutor Graham Sabine prior to speaking with her! When Faial finally had an opportunity to meet with her client, he uttered the exact same words again. It was like listening to a soldier spout off rank, name, and serial number: "Todd is dead. I killed him. I suffocated him with his pillow." Even so, Faial is sure she can work around Frank Hunter's self-damning act. Although her client is taciturn, making it hard for her to uncover motivation, she did get a lot of background information from his fathers and Jason Warith. *Jason Warith*, Faial smiles. *Now there is someone I look forward to working with.* They are like-minded with respect to Hadrian's reeducation system, yet he is not so open-minded regarding the radical change for which she is hoping—making the heterosexual lifestyle legal. Even so, Faial feels almost akin to Jason Warith, as if she has finally encountered a kindred spirit. They may not agree on every point, but together, they can pave the way for some necessary changes to occur in Hadrian. It would help to have some founding family backing, but Faial knows that is asking too much.

Focusing her mind back on today's meeting, Faial considers its potential ramifications; if Graham wants to meet about Crystal Albright, no doubt he knows her testimony will be damaging. *I wonder if he knows about the phone messaging? Not likely*, Faial reasons, *as that would have required the girl to expose herself.* Reaching her hand inside her coat pocket, Faial smiles as her fingers caress the thin metal. Today's meeting will be revealing, especially if what Dean Hunter says is true—*Of course what he says is true; I have all the evidence I need right here.* She taps the phone as she considers this. The text message he judiciously saved says it all, but the evidence will be all the more effective if Faial can get the girl to admit to the truth in court. *I want to hear her say it*, Faial ruminates. *I want the court to hear the words come right out of her mouth.*

As the door opens, Faial turns to see Sabine enter followed by three women, one of whom is Vice President Stiles. Sabine purposely kept Stiles' presence from Faial, hoping to add shock value to the start of this meeting. *So*, she realizes, *he has founding family support.* Fortunately, Faial learned long ago to school her expressions. Although Faial feels the surprise Sabine intended, he is not fortunate enough to witness her distress. Faial's face remains, as it always does when she encounters opposition, impassive. A forced smile blossoms on his pudgy face as Sabine leads his entourage around the oval conference table.

"Graham," Faial nods in greeting.

"Faial." Graham leans forward, casually resting his forearms on the glossy jack pine table, his hands clasped together, unsuccessfully feigning a relaxed countenance.

Graham is not in control, Faial immediately surmises. The three women are all sitting with their backs against their chairs. The youngest, Crystal Albright, no doubt, has dropped her head. Gail Albright, the genetic mother, has all her attention focused on the girl while Vice President Stiles, Crystal's mama most likely, sits with arms folded under her breasts. Stone gray eyes, like a frozen pond, bore down on Faial. She could easily see how this woman won her way into office. Even without her founding family status, she would have accomplished much, maybe even got to where she is today. Smiling now, she returns her gaze back to the prosecution. "It's been a while." Their mutual greeting, though polite, is strained. These two have faced off in court before. Both times, Faial won. Sabine's smile suggests to her that he believes he is on the winning team this time. Faial has no illusions; this is going to be an impossible case to win, but through it, she is going to break a little ice, crack open something she believes needs revealing. *With luck,* she muses, *I may just create an old fashioned river break-up!* Disgusted by Sabine's puffed up confidence, Faial adds, "The Andrea Hodgson case I believe."

Sabine's smile turns quickly to a scowl. He lurches forward, unclasping his right hand and directing his index finger her way. Elena Stiles, sitting next to the man, rests her hand on his shoulder. Sabine resumes his posture of ease, hands re-clasping, and his smile, though strained, once again blossoms on his face. "I see you are alone—no client?"

"I saw no need to bring them." Faial's smile solidifies into confidence. Having successfully exposed Sabine's weakness, that of being a poor loser, she also exposed the true nature of the hierarchy in this room. Elena Stiles, as she had rightly assumed, is the woman in charge. Even so, Faial knows the balance of the meeting has tilted in her favor—for the moment.

"Is it too emotional for them?" Sabine asks sincerely.

"That, and their presence is unnecessary. As, I suspect," she adds assuredly, "is this meeting." In response to Gail Albright's quizzical look, the menacing glare given by Elena Stiles, and Sabine's chagrin, Faial adds, "I have all the evidence I need right here," reaching now into her pocket and retrieving Todd Middleton's cell phone and presenting it, "to subpoena the girl." Faial hones in on Crystal Albright as the girl looks up and stares at the object as if it were a viper ready to strike. Her wide eyes and pale clammy face are all too telling. Sabine glares at the girl, then her mothers. Gail Albright grips her daughter's hand under the table and Crystal's head drops. Sobbing commences and Mama Elena grips Crystal's other hand, silencing her whimpers; even so, her upper body continues to convulse.

"I see." Sabine resumes his smile for Faial, a very tight smile. "And do you really believe that evidence is usable?"

Faial nearly laughs, "Absolutely." *What game is he playing at?* Faial wonders. Elena Stiles gives no clues; she remains stolid and angry, but, for the moment, silent.

"You realize there is no way you can prove Crystal Albright is the author of said text."

Faial's smile widens imperceptibly. "I haven't mentioned a text yet."

Sabine remains in control. "What else could it be?"

"Good guess." She decides to throw Sabine a bone. "And, yes, as I have the original text."

"May I see the text message?" Sabine reaches across the table for the device.

Faial pockets the phone and replies quite congenially, "Of course." She blinks to open her voc line. "Is your voc id the same?"

Sabine sits back, disappointed by the way things are progressing. He had really hoped Faial would have been sufficiently intimidated by the VP's presence simply to hand over the phone and all documentation. "Yes."

With a blink and a quick whisper, "Graham," Faial sends off the link. Sabine's eyes slit as he receives the data.

"Send it to me," Elena Stiles demands, "esHgov33vp—uppercase the 'h.'" Faial obliges. As soon as Elena receives the data, she passes it on to Gail and Crystal. Gail immediately begins blinking and reading. Crystal ignores her voc—she already knows what the document contains.

After finishing his read, Sabine pronounces, "You still can't prove Crystal Albright is the text author." Sabine is reaching here and Faial knows it, but he has serious political clout behind him. "Anyone could have written this."

"Really?" Faial isn't falling for it. She knows better, and one quick look at Crystal proves how easy it is going to be to get the girl to babble once she is on the stand. She is obviously drowning in the deep end of her own fear and guilt. Looking now at the girl's mothers, Faial is held by the arresting stare of Elena Stiles. It feels as if Elena can read her mind. Vice

President Stiles just sits there, impassive, and then suddenly, she cocks her left eye and Faial knows. *This woman will not allow Crystal Albright on the stand.* Looking back to Sabine, grim with determination, "I will subpoena her."

"No, you will not." Elena speaks so softly each word becomes an explosion.

It is hard to stand up against a founding family member, even when one is as formidable as Faial Raboud, but stand up to her she does. "I am merely following the rules of legal engagement established by your forefamily and the other founding forefamilies." Determined not to allow Frank Hunter to be sacrificed on the altar of politics, Faial persists, "My client has the right to a fair trial and he is innocent until proven guilty."

"Your client has already confessed—he is guilty!" Elena Stiles, now in control of the meeting, treats Graham Sabine like a piece of furniture. His head is bowed. *No doubt he is fuming,* Faial reasons. Had it not been her client's life at stake, Faial would have enjoyed watching Sabine so successfully subdued.

Not being one to cave under the bully, Faial announces, "My client is still entitled to a trial. That is the law according to the founding forefamilies' constitution. This case is going to court."

"The national prosecutor can arrange for his sentencing based solely on his confession," Stiles insisted.

Faial instantly lowers her head. Placing her hands atop her head and resting her elbows on the table suggest defeat, adding a long drawn out sigh for emphasis. All the while, she is rapidly blinking out a voc message to her aide—"with Frank?"—"good"—"stick like glue"—"tell you later"—"no visitors"—"no voc contact"—"keep out of his eye"—"no pen, no paper"—"trust me, he'll ask." All the time she is voc'ing, Faial is desperately hoping she is not too late. They must have someone near him right now, and knowing the state her client is in, Frank Hunter would willingly sign his life away.

Sabine, responding to a tap on the shoulder by Elena Stiles, looks up to observe Faial Raboud's physical position. Believing her to have been subdued, he takes full advantage to stick the knife into the jugular. "There is precedent. The Nation vs. Almer." Gerald Almer had murdered Henry Wilfer. It was a crime of passion. Gerald Almer had walked in on Henry and another man. He reacted badly to the sight. Having brooded over his lover's betrayal for months, Gerald eventually took action. Having staked out Wilfer's new home, he waited for a night when his ex was alone. He then snuck into their housing complex and slit his throat. Like Frank, he turned himself in, confessed, and then asked that a trial be waived. He did not want to be exiled, asking instead that the state assist in his suicide. Having given Faial time to register this new information, Sabine now twists the knife. "We plan to do the same with your cli—"

Faial, having finished her silent communication, cuts Graham off. "That action was at the accused's request. My client has made no such declaration!" She adds fervently, "And, any such request must come through me."

"Or your aide," Sabine adds gleefully. Faial's instant anger is unusual, suggesting her back is against the wall—the exact position she hopes he and Elena Stiles believe she is in.

Faial ponders Sabine's comment briefly. It is unlikely Gil would betray her. The two have worked closely for over twenty years. They are very close, Faial being Gil's spouse's son's auntie. When Gil's boy was diagnosed with leukemia, Faial had financed the boy's treatment. Gil may have them convinced he is working for them, but the odds of his betrayal are very unlikely. *But why didn't he say anything when I voc'd? Either they haven't contacted him and are bluffing or I never gave him the opportunity.* Her messaging was sent like a Gatling gun. She had learned years ago how to text with a blink of the eye so she wouldn't have to speak. Most people don't use this feature because it is very hard to master, but master it she did for when she needed to let others know something important quickly; quietly pulling up the keyboard is the only way. *No*, she reasons, *Gil is trustworthy*—yet, Sabine and Stiles seem so sure. She finds herself asking, "Have you received Frank Hunter's consent?"

Both Stiles and Sabine smile, suggesting the answer is yes. Yet Sabine's eyes shift ever so slightly, betraying his confidence. They are waiting on it. Stiles, on the other hand, has the perfect poker face. Faial considers the vice president her real opponent. This woman has substantial power and is now running for president. This court case may very well destroy her chances of winning. Considering just how dangerous Elena Stiles could be, Faial decides to bargain. "Well, I'm not giving you an out of court option. What would you like instead?"

"Keep my daughter out of it!" Elena Stiles answers instead of Sabine. Faial has gauged his role correctly. He is merely Stiles' tool.

Losing Crystal Albright's testimony is huge. It is a key point in Faial's argument. Without the girl's confession, Sabine might very well convince the court that the text message is fraudulent. Faial is only worried slightly over that; at best, Sabine might be able to cast some doubt as to Crystal's authoring it, but there is enough damning information in the text for Faial to open up the idea that Todd Middleton was not a rapist but a young man in love. A young man who had been betrayed by his lover, the woman he loved; a young man who had then been raped while at reeducation camp. Her plan is to show how Todd's mental state deteriorated to such an extent that he could never have accepted life as a homosexual—not after everything that had happened to him. Thus Frank Hunter is no longer a murderer but one who committed the lawful act of euthanasia. Would the text alone be enough? Probably. Even if Sabine does manage to cast some doubt over its authorship, the damage will be done. Graham Sabine is an opponent Faial feels confident in overcoming, but Elena Stiles—Vice President Stiles, soon to be President Stiles—founding family member Stiles—this woman is a hurdle Faial is unsure she can leap. "I'll keep Crystal off the stand, but the text is being used as evidence." Before Elena Stiles can explode, Faial adds, "It is already documented evidence." Stiles' glare is daunting, but Faial is not backing down on this point. She wants her client to live. Elena Stiles' reaction is more subdued than Faial expected. She nods once, and though her face remains grim, her scowl fades ever so slightly. Faial has the sinking feeling that she has just given the woman exactly what she wanted all along. Everything prior to this moment has been a bluff. Faial comes to realize that as much power as a founding family may have, not even its members can circumvent their own laws. Elena Stiles had known all along that she couldn't keep Faial from putting her daughter on the stand until she wrenched the offer out of her. *Thank Hadrian it's Graham I will be up against in the courtroom and not this woman!* Faial takes a brief moment to remind herself never to play poker with Elena Stiles. *She'd clean me right out, down to the very last credit.*

* * * * *

Transcripts: Hadrian vs. Hunter

Defense Questioning of Geneticist Avery Gillis

Defense: Mr. Gillis, you are a geneticist for Hadrian's Procreation Arm of the Government, are you not?

Gillis: Yes.

Defense: How long have you worked in this capacity?

Gillis: Twenty years.

Defense: So, for the last twenty years, you have been working to identify and create the genetically perfect homosexual human gene. Is that not so?

Gillis: We do not consider our work as an attempt to create genetic perfection. We are simply working toward identifying, isolating, and ensuring the DNA most likely to produce homosexuals.

Defense: Why is it so important that every human born in Hadrian be homosexual?

Gillis: Everyone knows the answer to that.

Defense: Of course we do, but humor me and provide us with your reasoning for the record.

Gillis: Obviously, here in Hadrian our goal is to create a stable human population that will live in harmony with the earth.

Defense: And being homosexual is crucial for living in harmony with the earth?

Gillis: No, of course not. But it is critical for controlling human population.

Defense: And why is that?

Gillis: The evidence is all around us in the outside world.

Defense: Once again, humor me, for the record.

Gillis: Over twenty billion people populate the outside world of our earth. Hadrian, on the other hand, has for over fifty years created and maintained a stable population of approximately ten million. This stability has only been accomplished through radical measures with a homosexual population and licensed births.

Defense: Very good. I am sure everyone here agrees with you. Let us go back to your work with genetics. How successful have Hadrian's researchers, such as yourself, been at identifying the homosexual gene within an embryo?

Gillis: Very successful.

Defense: Define *very successful* for me.

Gillis: What's to define? Very successful is very successful.

Defense: Excuse my ignorance, but I am not a geneticist, so I need you to be very specific. For example, can you guarantee that 100 percent of all genetic tracing in embryos will in fact identify if a child will have no homosexual tendencies at all?

Gillis: Yes.

Defense: Really? One hundred percent? No homosexual tendencies at all? Guaranteed? Absolutely? Beyond any shadow of a doubt?

Gillis: Yes.

Defense: And what happens to these embryos?

Gillis: They are destroyed.

Defense: So, is this why you believe you have eradicated all zeros and ones from the Kinsey scale?

Gillis: Yes.

Defense: Does this mean you are able to distinguish the exact ratio of homosexual tendencies that are blended in with hetero-sexual tendencies—in each embryo, of course, prior to it being approved for maturation?

Gillis: No, of course not. But we are so close we honestly believe we have eradicated the majority of zeros and ones from the Kinsey scale.

Defense: The majority of?

Gillis: Yes.

Defense: I'm sorry, Mr. Gillis, but you just stated unequivocally, beyond any shadow of a doubt, that any embryo lacking the gene for homosexuality—every single one—is destroyed, ensuring absolutely no zeros—no pure heterosexuals—exist today in Hadrian. Yet, now you use the phrase "The majority of." When one says the majority, one suggests a minority exists.

Gillis: Yes, but—

Defense:	Wait for the question, Mr. Gillis. Please, correct me if I am wrong, but isn't the Kinsey scale based on behavior patterns? His research, if I recall correctly, was not founded on any genetic studies.
Gillis:	You are correct.
Defense:	So how can you claim to have eliminated *only* "the majority of" the zeros and ones on this scale if it is not a genetic scale?
Prosecution:	M'Lady, I fail to see the purpose behind this line of questioning.
Judge:	Nor I. I would ask the Defense to please explain herself.
Defense:	I am looking to establish the deceased's sexual orientation and the motivation behind my client's act of euthanasia.
Prosecution:	Correction, M'Lady. The defendant is on trial for murder.
Defense:	I am aware of the charges against my client, but it is my intent, M'Lady, to prove his act was, in fact, euthanasia and not murder.
Judge:	And you intend to accomplish this through a study of genetics?
Defense:	Yes, M'Lady.
Judge:	Proceed.
Defense:	Once again, Mr. Gillis, how is it geneticists are able to use a behavioral scale in their genetic research?
Gillis:	We are simply using terminology laypersons can understand.

Defense: So, the Kinsey scale is not, in fact, an accurate representation of what you are capable of with genetics?

Gillis: Well, yes and no.

Defense: Explain.

Gillis: Yes, in the sense that we are very close to identifying the homosexual gene. No, because no work in genetic research will ever be 100 percent.

Defense: Thank you, Mr. Gillis. That brings me to my next point. Let us refer back to your wording "the majority of." Prior to just admitting that any work in genetic research will ever be 100 percent, did you not claim to guarantee—100 percent guarantee—that every fetus could in fact be genetically altered, ensuring all Hadrian's children be born homosexual?

Gillis: Yes.

Defense: Really? A 100 percent guarantee?

Gillis: All right, no, but really, yes.

Defense: No, but really yes? Please explain.

Gillis: We do what is called genetic screening of the fetus. Tests will then reveal if the child to be born has the genetic makeup of someone who is homosexual.

Defense: That sounds straightforward enough, so why did you preface your response with no?

Gillis: Because, as much as we now know about human DNA, it is such a condense microscopic heliograph, it is impossible to ever say fully, 100 percent, exactly what an individual's sexual orientation will be.

Defense: Interesting.

Gillis: That being said—

Defense: That being said, it is possible, is it not, that some of Hadrian's children may in fact be born heterosexual? That perhaps a one or even a zero on the Kinsey scale could be born.

Gillis: It is very unlikely.

Defense: Unlikely does not mean impossible. If it is "unlikely," then you have to admit it is possible; even the most remote possibility still exists, does it not?

Gillis: Not likely.

Defense: Does it not?

Gillis: All right, yes. But we are very careful in our screening process.

Defense: Regardless of how careful you are, did you not just say it is not possible ever to be 100 percent certain of anything when it comes to human DNA?

Gillis: You are correct.

Defense: So it is possible then that one, two, or maybe even more of Hadrian's children may in fact be born not only with heterosexual tendencies but be a zero on the Kinsey scale, to use your own terminology.

Gillis: Although very unlikely, it is possible.

Defense: Thank you, Mr. Gillis. No more questions.

Judge:	Does the prosecution wish to ask any questions of the witness at this time?
Prosecution:	No, M'Lady, but I would like to ask that we approach the bench.
Judge:	Would the prosecution and defense please approach the bench?
Prosecution:	What was the point of all that?
Defense:	My point, M'Lady, is that Todd Middleton was a heterosexual living closeted in a homosexual world. Fearful of reeducation camp, fearful of losing family and friends, fearful of losing the opportunity presented to him by Antinous Uni, Todd Middleton was a young man diminished in morale and esteem. The final toll destroying his will to live was being brutally raped by Mr. Weller—
Prosecution:	Objection, M'Lady. Mr. Weller is not on trial for rape. Nor is there any evidence he committed such an act.
Judge:	Objection noted. The Defense will please rephrase.
Defense:	After his sexual experience with Mr. Weller, the young man turned to thoughts of suicide, evidence of which has already been shown. My client, therefore, chose not to murder Todd Middleton, but rather to assist the young man in an act of suicide.
Judge:	Euthanasia is only legal if the patient is living in pain and wishes to die with dignity. This case still boils down to an act of murder.
Defense:	On the contrary, M'Lady, if Todd Middleton were indeed heterosexual with no hope of reeducation, fearing, no doubt, as all the citizens of Hadrian fear, the "heterosexual

barbarian," his self-loathing, coupled with what I intend to prove was a brutal rape, left the young man living in a state of hopelessness akin to physical pain. Ergo, Frank Hunter's act is no longer that of murder but euthanasia.

Judge: All right, Ms. Raboud. I will allow you to continue—for now.

* * * * *

Salve!

A Captivating Court Case
HNN—Melissa Eagleton reporting

The court case involving Hadrian versus Hunter is all anyone in Hadrian can talk about. Heated debates are being held in every office, classroom, even on the street. Everyone in the HNN newsroom also comments on how the evening dinner table is focused on discussions regarding the innocence or guilt of young Frank Hunter. Seventeen years old and a confessed murderer, yet his lawyer, Ms. Faial Raboud, refuses to enter his guilty plea. Being her client is under age, Ms. Raboud is only entering the plea the boy's fathers agree to: not guilty. The two fathers and Ms. Raboud stand by the plea that Frank Hunter did not murder his friend; rather, he participated in an act of assisted suicide. Today's testimonies by Jason Warith, the boy's guardian at the Northeast Reeducation Camp, and the boy's papa, Mr. Mike Fulton, lend credence to Raboud and the Hunters' assertion.

Mr. Fulton admitted to having abandoned his son to the system when he learned the boy had been exposed as straight. Just knowing one's loving parent no longer desires any contact with you is enough to cause any young man or woman to lose his or her senses. As we know from a previous *Salve!* with Gideon Weller, many of our young men and women who have been exposed find themselves suddenly cast aside by their families. As numerous youth survive the reeducation system and go on to lead productive lives, this evidence alone is not enough to prove that Todd Middleton's depression was extreme enough to allow for euthanasia. It was Mr. Jason Warith's testimony that proved the most damning.

When on the stand, Jason Warith spoke of brutal beatings occurring on a daily basis at the Northeast Camp. The paddle, shown to the right on our wall screen, is said to have been wielded against Todd and nearly every other young man's bare backside while in the custody of our nation. As well as beating the young men, public displays of this abusive treatment also occurred as a warning to others. According to Mr. Warith, Mr. Weller beat one boy to the point where blood dripped off the paddle. Jason Warith goes on to say, "Mr. Weller then pointed the bloody instrument at us, yelling out, 'There will be no dissension in my camp!'" This incident, according to Mr. Warith, wasn't the worst of it. "The man brutally raped my ward." Although Mr. Warith admits he did not witness the actual attack, he claims to have heard the young man crying out for help. "Being locked out of the room," Mr. Warith claims, "made it impossible for me to intervene."

Mr. Weller has yet to take the stand. Tomorrow, prosecuting attorney Graham Sabine intends to examine him and prove beyond a doubt that although Todd Middleton came to the Northeast Camp recalcitrant, he was beginning to soften under Gideon Weller's tutelage and was readying himself for reentry into Hadrian society.

Vale!

Transcripts: Hadrian vs. Hunter

Prosecution questioning of Gideon Weller

Prosecution: Mr. Weller, according to the Defense, Todd Middleton was heterosexual and no amount of reeducation would work for him. Do you agree with his assessment?

Weller: No sir. Todd Middleton knew he had heterosexual leanings, but like everyone in Hadrian, there was inside him a latent homosexual. He asked me to help bring those latent tendencies to the surface.

Prosecution: Which you did by agreeing to make love to him at his request?

Weller: Yes. As the legal age of consent is sixteen and Todd Middleton's Charge was unwilling to assist his ward in this manner, I agreed to help the young man out.

Prosecution: How can you explain Todd Middleton's suicide attempts after your sexual interaction with him?

Weller: Todd Middleton is not the first, nor will he be the last, young man who becomes suicidal after his first sexual experience. These boys are still struggling with their sexual identity, which is why so much care is taken to prevent their attempts from being successful. Inevitably, they learn not only to accept themselves as homosexual, but also eventually to become active, healthy members of society.

Prosecution:	Thank you, Mr. Weller.
Judge:	Defense, you may cross-examine.
Defense:	Mr. Weller, do the men you make love to often scream—
Weller:	Indeed, madam, they do.
Defense:	Allow me to finish the question, sir. "Do the men you make love to often cry—
Weller:	Tears of joy!
Judge:	Mr. Weller, one more outburst and I will hold you in contempt of court.
Weller:	Sorry, M'Lady.
Defense:	Do the men you make love to often cry out in agony, begging Hadrian for help?
Prosecution:	Objection, M'Lady. How Mr. Weller's sexual partners react during their intimate act is of no business to the Defense.
Judge:	Objection noted.
Defense:	Allow me to rephrase. Why is it, if you and Todd Middleton were making love, that the young man was heard to cry out in agony, "For the love of Hadrian, someone help me"?
Weller:	Todd's words were, to the best of my memory, "Please, Mr. Weller, for the love of Hadrian, help me."
Defense:	And never once did he cry out the words, "Please, no, stop, please, stop"?
Weller:	I recall his saying, "Help me stop; please, help me stop."

Defense: How do you explain the difference between what Mr. Warith heard Todd yelling and what you claim him to have said?

Weller: Quite simply, Mr. Warith could only hear the young man's voice muffled through a closed door.

Defense: And your personal assistant, Mr. Darrell Jeffreys, can attest to that.

Weller: Yes, he can.

Defense: One more question, Mr. Weller. Do you often have your personal assistant in the room with you when you make love to a man?

Prosecution: Objection, M'Lady. Mr. Weller's sexual habits are not on trial.

Judge: Objection noted.

Defense: The Defense retracts its question. That will be all; thank you, Mr. Weller.

Judge: Prosecution, you may cross-examine.

Prosecution: Mr. Weller, did you rape Todd Middleton?

Weller: No.

Prosecution: Mr. Weller, did you ever rape any of the charges under your or another guardian's care?

Weller: No.

Prosecution: Mr. Weller, do wards often request sexual intercourse from their guardians?

Weller: Yes.

Prosecution: Mr. Weller, is such sexual activity frowned upon?

Weller: Only if the ward is under the age of consent, that being sixteen.

Prosecution: Thank you, Mr. Weller. That will be all.

* * * * *

Salve!

A Turn for the Worse
HNN—Melissa Eagleton Reporting

Today's testimony by Mr. Gideon Weller has stunned many of Hadrian's citizens. Although Mr. Weller cannot be accused of rape, what he admitted as being a common practice at the Northeast Camp is most shocking. Mr. Weller admitted under oath having had sexual intercourse with Todd Middleton. And, although Todd Middleton, at age seventeen, was of the age of consent, the age difference between the Warden and the young man is far too extreme for comfort. That the act was not rape was confirmed by one of *Salve!*'s investigating reporters, Michael Swahazey. Michael interviewed Mr. Weller's personal assistant who assured us that intercourse occurred between the two men at young Middleton's request. Mr. Weller referred to the act as "medicinal intercourse" and acknowledged it to be a common act between ward and guardian.

HNN has responded to this method of rehabilitating our youth with outrage. We do not believe that any educational institution should have its adult mentors engaging in any form of sexual contact with our youth. The guardian of a ward at a reeducation camp is akin to a teacher in a school. This is a relationship based on trust and, though the focus of these educators is to help our children find their latent homosexuality, it should not be their place to participate in any sexual activity with youth sent to reeducation.

Investigating reporter Michael Swahazey has delved deep into this story and contacted all other reeducation camps throughout Hadrian. Only at the Northeast Reeducation Camp is "medicinal intercourse" used. When a ward tries to seduce a guardian, according to Adrian Adams, camp Warden for the Southwest Reeducation Camp, the guardian is instructed to refuse but speak to the ward positively about such a request. The fact that a ward expresses sexual interest in someone of the same sex is a sign that he (or she as in the case of our female youth) is coming to accept Hadrian's chosen lifestyle as his (or her) own. "Never," Adrian Adams states emphatically, "should a guardian cross the line and participate with his ward in sexual activity."

We, at HNN, agreed with Adrian Adams. I, for one, am not so anxious now to throw all of my support behind Mr. Gideon Weller. He may not have raped Todd Middleton, but he definitely crossed the line when he engaged in sexual activity with the boy. What is your opinion Hadrian? Voc us your views @HNN#GW-RE/MI.

Vale!

Transcripts: Hadrian vs. Hunter

Prosecution Questioning of Dean Stuttgart

Prosecution: Mr. Hunter, when did you first discover the deceased was heterosexual?

Dean: The day Frank voc'd that Todd had been exposed at school.

Prosecution: Surely that wasn't the first time. You must have suspected. When did you first suspect the deceased might be hetero-sexual?

Dean: When the boys were thirteen.

Prosecution: Thirteen. Four years ago.

Dean: Three and a half.

Prosecution: Three and a half then. So, you knew the boy was straight for three and a half years?

Dean: No.

Defense: Objection, M'Lady. The witness never claimed to have known about the deceased's sexual preference, only to have suspected.

Prosecution: Sorry, suspected. So, then, you suspected straight tenden-cies for three and a half years, correct?

Dean: Yes.

Prosecution: In all that time, Mr. Hunter, did you ever sit the boy down to talk to him about the dangers of *strai* behavior?

Defense: M'Lady, that's a sexual slur.

Prosecution: My apologies. Straight behavior—or would the defense prefer I use the word heterosexual—did you ever sit the boy down and discuss the dangers of heterosexual behavior?

Dean: No.

Prosecution: No? That's odd. Tell us, Mr. Hunter, you were reeducated, were you not?

Defense: Objection.

Prosecution: It is important, M'Lady. Since the defense is determined to throw blame on external forces, I am uncovering other external forces from the boy's family and those closely associated with him.

Judge: Proceed.

Defense: M'Lady—

Judge: As I allowed you levity, I will extend the same to the prosecution. Proceed with your questioning.

Prosecution: You were reeducated, were you not?

Dean: Yes.

Prosecution: And in the three whole years you suspected the boy to be straight, you never once spoke to him about being straight or cautioned him about the consequences?

Dean: Of course I did.

Prosecution: How? Did you ever tell him about your being straight?

Defense: Objection, M'Lady. My client was reeducated.

Prosecution: My apologies. Having once been straight, did you ever
               speak to him about that, sir? Did you ever ask him if
               he thought about straight acts? Kissing girls? Touching
               breasts? That sort of thing? Did you ever once think to ask
               him what he liked most about his own sex? Did you ever
               once try to guide him toward a gay lifestyle? Did you ever
               tell him about reeducation camp?

Defense: Objection! M'Lady, the prosecution is bombarding the wit-
               ness, refusing him opportunity to answer.

Judge: Objection noted. Prosecution will restrain himself to one
               question at a time.

Prosecution: Of course, M'Lady. Mr. Hunter, why didn't you share your
               experiences with the boy?

Dean: I...don't talk about it.

Prosecution: Why not?

Defense: M'Lady!

Judge: Answer the question, Mr. Hunter.

Dean: It...

Prosecution: It was what, Mr. Hunter?

Defense: M'Lady, the prosecution is badgering the witness.

Prosecution: M'Lady, please, all I did was request the witness to answer the question.

Judge: Answer the question, Mr. Hunter.

Geoffrey: Dean, it's all right.

Judge: Sit down, Mr. Geoffrey Hunter. Answer the question, Mr. Hunter. If you do not, I will have to charge you for with-holding testimony.

Dean: It was hell! Demeaning! Horrifying! Brutal. I was beaten and tortured.

Prosecution: That smacks of exaggeration, Mr. Hunter.

Dean: You weren't there! They used a paddle on me damn near every day, electric shock therapy, and they overtly encour-aged sexual activity between wards and guardians.

Prosecution: The two methods of discipline and deterrents are legal and an accepted means of maintaining order in reeducation camps, particularly with violent and recalcitrant youth. As for wards choosing to have sex with their guardians, well, there is no law against having sex. No more questions.

Dean: You assume wards have a choice.

Prosecution: You may return to your seat, Mr. Hunter.

Dean: They raped us!

Prosecution: Were you ever raped, Mr. Hunter?

Dean: Weller tri—

Prosecution: Yes or no, Mr. Hunter.

Dean: Weller had me down. He—

Judge: Yes or no, Mr. Hunter.

Dean: But he—

Judge: Yes or no.

Dean: No.

Prosecution: Thank you. No more questions.

Judge: Defense, do you wish to cross-examine?

Defense: Yes. Mr. Hunter, take a moment. I know this is hard for you. Did Gideon Weller ever try to rape you?

Prosecution: Objection!

Defense: M'Lady, if Mr. Weller had attempted to rape another ward, he may well have raped Todd Middleton, too.

Judge: Objection overruled. Proceed.

Defense: Mr. Hunter, did Gideon Weller ever try to rape you?

Dean: Y-yes.

Defense: Please tell us what happened.

Prosecution: Objection!

Defense: M'Lady, I am trying to establish what the conditions at the Northeast Camp are really like in order to prove that Todd's Middleton's state of mind at the time he requested assisted suicide from the accused was in fact beyond repair.

Judge: Objection overruled! Defense may continue with her line of questioning.

Defense: Go ahead, Dean; take your time.

* * * * *

Salve!

A Stunning Revelation
HNN—Melissa Eagleton Reporting

Yesterday's testimony by Dean Hunter was most revealing. One is left to seriously ponder the need for reformation in Hadrian's reeducation system. It appears that Jason Warith's cry for change needs to be met. In fact, Vice-President Elena Stiles has promised, if elected as Hadrian's next president, to establish a committee dedicated to running a thorough investigation into our reeducation camps. It was hinted that she might even choose Mr. Jason Warith as an advisor to the committee.

As equally stunning as Dean Hunter's horror stories about life during reeducation is the text testimony presented by defense lawyer Faial Raboud. Apparently, Mr. Dean Hunter had a text conversation with the young woman Todd Middleton was to have allegedly raped. The young woman, whose name has not been revealed, had refused to accuse the young man of rape. The text message Mr. Hunter allegedly had with this young woman suggests that the sexual act committed by Todd Middleton was not rape, but rather an act instigated by the young woman. This, along with the damning accusation that Mr. Weller may well have raped Todd Middleton lends credence to Faial Raboud's argument that Todd Middleton was suffering from extreme depression. It will be interesting to see the outcome of this case. Will Frank Hunter be found guilty of murder or will the court recognize Todd Middleton's death as an act of kindness? Hadrian, remember to voc us your views. Please note; we have amalgamated all our viewer sites for this case into one: @HNN#RE-GW/MI-FH/AS.

Vale!

Transcripts: Hadrian vs. Hunter

Defense Questioning of Ms. Destiny Stuttgart

Defense: Ms. Stuttgart, please remind the court of the values you and the four other original founding family members established for our country.

Ms. Stuttgart: In order to do that, I must be allowed to start from the beginning.

Prosecution: No objections, M'Lady.

Ms. Stuttgart: When world population topped ten billion, religious extremists with their apoplectic theories and revelations began to war against one another—and us. By us, I mean homosexuals. Regardless of the education and incredible strides made to ensure acceptance in inclusion during the twenty-first century, the abuses against homosexuals grew and persecution became extreme. Anti-gay mobs rose everywhere and even straight men and women were persecuted if they appeared gay or vocally supported us. Sensing the future direction of humanity, finding the need for strength in numbers, a collective was formed. We were, in essence, a secret society. We called ourselves Hadrian's warriors. So, Hadrian was formed as a means of self-preservation and protection. I find it ironic that the very reason we sit in this courtroom today is due to the same type of fear mongering that brought us together as a community.

Prosecution: Objection, M'Lady. With due respect to our founding mother, we are here today to try Frank Hunter with murder.

Judge: Objection stands. Clerk, please strike our founding mother's last statement.

Defense: Please continue, Mother.

Ms. Stuttgart: As I was saying, one reason for gathering our forces together was preservation—however, the word preservation means many things to us. Our efforts were not merely for the self-preservation of the homosexual community but for the preservation of all of humanity and the preservation of a life-sustaining planet. Our planet, as we know it, or rather, as we knew it to be, must be preserved and repaired if humanity is to survive. This preservation became the crux of our constitution.

Prosecution: M'Lady, again, with due respect to our founding mother, I fail to see the purpose behind this line of questioning.

Ms. Stuttgart: That is because you have become as blind as the rest of our society.

Judge: Mother, please.

Ms. Stuttgart: Don't silence me like a wayward child. If any privilege comes of being a founding mother, it is the privilege to speak openly before all as to why our country was founded! Silence, all of you! Fear, hate, distress makes up the basis of humanity—

Prosecution: Yes, outside our walls but—

Ms. Stuttgart: No buts! It is the makeup of all humanity! Not just them but us, too! We are here today because of our fear, our hate, and our distress! They hate us. Now we hate them! They kill us. Now we kill them! They are jealous, fearful, dying We lock them out. Why? Because we have to! But how many of them are exactly like us? We like to quote the Kinsey scale zero to six—and maybe our geneticists have eliminated the zero and the one, and maybe they haven't—and maybe they shouldn't be allowed to. What right do we have to say heterosexual sex is wrong? No more than they have the right to say homosexual sex is wrong. When we founded Hadrian, we were not looking for justifications or the creation of the perfect homosexual human race. We founded our nation on choice. The choice Hadrian citizens made was to reduce the human population now—not tomorrow—not in twenty years—not in the next two hundred years—but now as the critical need is now—is still now! *Stability Now!* became our cry and to do that, we knew we needed a homosexual nation and IVF laws. We asked everyone who joined us, gay or straight, to pledge themselves, to choose with us what we honestly believe to be humanity's last chance at survival. It is why we sacrifice access to higher levels of technology working only with wind, hydro, and thermal power, keeping a store of energy for those days when access to natural energy is lost to us. We were willing to endure those days when we can't drive or run hot water or watch the wall screen. We made these sacrifices because we knew we have more than a claim to this planet; we are responsible to it. But times have changed. We no longer sacrifice for humanity, survival, and our planet. Instead, we demand luxury and—

Prosecution: M'Lady, please. This is getting us nowhere.

Ms. Stuttgart: You sit down, be quiet, and listen. I am here today because my great-grandson is being charged with murder. That's right! Frank Hunter is a Stuttgart by marriage. The poor boy doesn't even know it. I have never even met him! Today is the first time I have ever seen him in my entire life. How wrong is that? How, you ask? Frank's Papa Dean is my grandson. And today is the first day I have seen Dean in over twenty years. I was told he was dead! I only learned otherwise when he voc'd and asked me to help his young friend. Forgive me...

Judge: It's all right, Mother. Take your time.

Ms. Stuttgart: It's hard. I've been denied access to my own grandson and two great-grandsons because of the prejudices of a society I helped to create. I am tired of hiding that reality. There are heterosexuals among us and I don't care. These men and women I hold in the highest esteem as they make the greatest sacrifice for humanity. They choose celibacy or, as in the case of my grandson, some even choose to embrace our lifestyle. This morning, before I agreed to take the stand, I had a chance to meet with my boy because I didn't want to say anything here today that would hurt him any more than he has already suffered. When I asked him if his marriage was a sham, he assured me the answer was no. He loves his partner, Geoffrey Hunter, and I dearly want to get to know the man who won my boy's heart. I want to learn from my grandson and his lover how they managed to find balance in a world where among humanity, balance is damn near unattainable. Yes, balance! Humanity's greatest flaw is in our lack of balance. We swing from one extreme to another, and today, I say Hadrian has taken the pendulum of man's folly from one form of abuse into another. When swung hard enough, the blade meets itself right back up at the top! My great-grandson killed Todd Middleton, but for reasons many of us cannot fathom. He killed his lover out of love. Out of an awareness that our society would never accept him for who he was. Todd Middleton suffered grievously at the hands of Gideon Weller. The man is a rapist—

Prosecution: Objection!

Ms. Stuttgart: Objection be damned! And don't you try to shush me, M'Lady, or strike any of my comments! I am a founding Mother and I say these proceedings go against the very fabric of the values of the country I helped create! You listen to me, and you listen well. I say Gideon Weller is a rapist—not a confessed rapist, one yet to be proven in this court of law—but a rapist nonetheless. I saw the medical report describing Todd Middleton's condition. That alone should be enough to condemn the man! If anyone should be exiled or given henbane to swallow, it should be Gideon Weller and not my great-grandson! That's all I have to say. I'm tired. Let me down.

Defense: Of course, Mother. Thank you.

Judge: Mother Stuttgart, please, the prosecution has the right to cross-examine you.

Prosecution: No questions for now, M'Lady. Mother Stuttgart looks quite drawn; perhaps she will allow for cross-examination tomorrow—if I still feel the need to question her.

Judge: Good. Then, Mother, you may step down from the bench.

* * * * *

Salve!

HNN—Viewer Wave Link
@HNN#RE-GW/MI-FH/AS

April Bolger
Medicinal Sex? What in Hadrian's Name is that all about? How can he get
away with that?

Angel Higgins
Who cares about medicinal sex? The rat was a *strai*. Hadrian is better off
now that he's dead!

Aaron Whyle
*Strai*s make me sick! I say kill 'em and be done with it. Why should our
good money go to reeducating heterosexual pigs? Kick 'em all out.

T'Neal Cantos
I know Frank Hunter. He is a good man. He would never murder anyone.

Angel Higgins
Frank Hunter's my hero! He killed a *strai*!

Duncan Fraser
If our founding mother is not opposed to heterosexuals, then why are we?

Angel Higgins
@ Duncan Fraser—*Strai* lover! Probably a *strai* yourself.

Aaron Whyle
@ Duncan Fraser—Ditto!

Andreas Contreras
All *strai*s should be castrated!

Angel Higgins
@ Andreas Contreas—AGREED!

Toni Freeman
I honestly can't imagine how hard it must be having to tame *strai* males. We all know how violent they are. Of course they have to use corporal punishment. No doubt it's in self-defense! And, I mean, medicinal sex, well maybe *strai* guys need it.

Sebastian Remilard
Didn't anyone listen to our founding mother's testimony today?

Devon Rankin
When I first learned Todd Middleton was a *strai*, I thought castration was in order, but after hearing our founding mother, I don't think that way anymore. I used to date Todd before anyone knew he was that way and he was an amazing guy. The best damn b-ball player I ever had the honor to play with. He spent a whole summer teaching me the game. He may have been straight, but I no longer think that means he was a bad guy. I feel for Frank. I really think he believes he did the right thing by Todd and after reading all these posts—who knows—he might well have. Either way, I hope they don't exile him.

Trina Scaponi
Well said, Devon! I admit, I'm an anti-*strai*. I hate heterosexuals! But after listening to our founding mother today, I'm not so sure anymore. And medicinal sex just doesn't seem right to me.

Shakira Osagi
Hadrian vs. Hunter is an interesting case, and maybe it is okay to be straight just as long as they never act on it.

Bronek Sobanski
Say no to *Strai*s!

Adolfo Gaafar
Exile is too good for *strai*s. Don't give 'em a choice. Just give 'em the death penalty!

Fernando Pereira
It's not illegal to be straight. It's only illegal to have heterosexual sex. I agree with Shakira Osagi, just as long as they don't act on it.

Bromek Sobranski
Strai men are sluts! They have to have sex. No woman is safe around a *strai* man.

Sissy Hildebrand
You people are sick! You have no idea what you are talking about.

Aaron Whyle
@ Bromek Sobranski—The slogan is, "Go away, Mr. Strai!"

Duncan Fraser
People, please, these are our mothers and fathers, our sisters and brothers you're talking about. Listen to Mother Stuttgart and learn a little tolerance and acceptance. Love, not hate, should be the order of the day.

* * * * *

Transcripts: Hadrian vs. Hunter

Defense Questioning of Darrell Jeffreys, Warden's Personal Assistant

Defense: M'Lady, the Defense would like to call Darrell Jeffreys, Mr. Weller's personal assistant, to the stand.

Clerk: Mr. Darrell Jeffreys to the stand.

Defense: Mr. Jeffreys, how long have you been Mr. Weller's personal assistant?

Jeffreys: Over twenty years.

Defense: And during that time, how many times were you on hand when Mr. Weller was helping young men discover their latent homosexual?

Jeffreys: I don't understand the question, madam.

Defense: How many times were you in the same room as Mr. Weller while he was having sex with a young ward under his charge?

Jeffreys: I don't remember, madam.

Defense: Really? From the way Mr. Weller was describing his prowess, one would assume witnessing such intensity would be hard to forget.

Jeffreys: I really don't remember.

Defense:	Let me help jog your memory. Was it once, twice, three times, five maybe?
Jeffreys:	I don't remember.
Prosecution:	Objection! The defense is badgering the witness.
Defense:	M'Lady, determining how many times Mr. Jeffreys was privy to Mr. Weller's special moments with his wards is crucial to my client's defense.
Judge:	Proceed, but tread carefully.
Defense:	Yes, M'Lady. Mr. Jeffreys, according to the records of the North-East Reeducation Camp, you were in attendance five times while Mr. Weller was administering medicinal intercourse, not including Todd Middleton. Can you confirm these numbers?
Jeffreys:	That sounds about right.
Defense:	Can you tell me how these young men are doing today?
Jeffreys:	I do not keep track of the whereabouts of wards once they leave the compound. My job is simply to assist Mr. Weller whenever required.
Defense:	So you really don't know where any of these men are today?
Jeffreys:	No, ma'am, I do not.
Defense:	Would it shock you to learn that, like Todd Middleton, all five of these men are dead? That all five of these men committed suicide shortly after Mr. Weller administered the medicinal intercourse you were so fortunate to have been in the presence of?

Jeffreys:	I—ah—had no idea.
Defense:	Was Mr. Weller actually administering medicinal intercourse, or was he, in fact, raping these men?
Prosecution:	Objection!
Judge:	Objection denied. Answer the question, Mr. Jeffreys.
Jeffreys:	I—I honestly thought it was for medicinal purposes—that he was helping them. I swear on Hadrian's lover I had no idea any of them died.
Defense:	Did any of these men, did Todd Middleton, agree to medicinal intercourse with Mr. Weller?
Jeffreys:	No. No, ma'am, they didn't.
Defense:	Did Jason Warith accidently lock himself out of the room?
Jeffreys:	No, ma'am, he did not.
Defense:	How was it he was unable to reenter?
Jeffreys:	I was instructed to remove him from the room and then lock the door behind him so Mr. Weller could administer— while he—
Defense:	While he raped Todd Middleton.
Prosecution:	Objection. The Defense is putting words in the witness's mouth.
Judge:	Objection noted.
Defense:	Mr. Jeffreys, in your opinion, did Mr. Weller rape Todd Middleton?

Jeffreys: Yes, ma'am, he did.

Defense: No more questions.

Judge: Prosecution. Do you wish to cross-examine?

Prosecution: No, M'Lady.

Judge: This session is adjourned. We will reconvene tomorrow morning at 8:00 a.m. when I will execute judgment.

* * * * *

Transcripts: Hadrian vs. Hunter

An Unprecedented Sentence

Clerk: Frank Hunter, please rise for your verdict.

Judge: I must say this has been a most disturbing and unique
                case. Todd Middleton's death was murder, and not, as
                the defense lawyer eloquently suggests, an act of assisted
                suicide. Although Hadrian law allows for euthanasia in
                cases of the terminally ill, these laws do not extend to the
                emotionally distressed. One can overcome a mental illness
                brought on by circumstance. Todd Middleton's depres-
                sion was not the result of an incurable chemical disorder
                of the brain. Thus, it is the decision of this court that,
                you, Frank Hunter, are guilty of murder. Under normal
                circumstances, the penalty for said crime is death and I
                would hang you. However, there are extenuating circum-
                stances that require leniency. Nor will you be exiled to the
                outside world. I am fully aware that I will be setting prece-
                dent here today, but as your lawyer uncovered for us, Todd
                Middleton's situation, his sexual preference compounded
                by his having been raped, did make life for the young man
                unbearable in Hadrian. I believe that you, and Todd Mid-
                dleton, saw his death, your aiding him in his suicide, as
                an act of mercy. I recognize the need for reform within
                our reeducation system as well as a complete rethinking
                of our nation's attitudes toward our heterosexual citizens.
                As a result, I have chosen to sentence you to a life of ser-
                vice within Hadrian's military. Your rank upon entrance,
                until the day you die, will be that of ensign. There will be

no opportunity for promotion. No opportunity for parole. You will spend the rest of your days serving your country by protecting Hadrian from the outside world. This court is now adjourned.

* * * * *

Salve!

An End to an Era
HNN—Melissa Eagleton Reporting

As all my viewers are aware, *Salve!* is the voice of Hadrian—that of the government and of the people. When the tune of those voices changes, so must its mouthpiece. I am not retiring as the host of *Salve!* but I have been forced to face some very ugly truths about much of what I have been saying to you over the years. I still believe, as I am sure do many of you, that Hadrian is the future hope for humanity, but that future cannot be forged by the blood of our youth. I do not refer to those who die defending our wall. The threat of the outside world remains as prevalent as ever. I refer, rather, to those who have suffered and died at the hands of Gideon Weller—six young men over the past twenty years. Are those numbers too small for Hadrian to take notice? No. Every single boy's death is a slap in the face of our good country Hadrian. The charges laid against Gideon Weller based on the evidence that surfaced in the wake of Frank Hunter's murder trial and the reeducation camp's ex-warden's subsequent sentence of exile has shattered citizens' faith in Hadrian's reeducation system. As Judge Julia Reznikoff said in her final address at Weller's trial: "Gideon Weller is a man who became judge, jury, and executioner of these young men. He determined them to be pure heterosexuals with no hope of reformation and acted believing their end justified. Unfortunately," Judge Reznikoff added, "as we condemn this man, we must also condemn ourselves, for his warped attitude was born of our country's prevailing prejudice." As Mother Stuttgart succinctly reminded us when she spoke at her great-grandson's trial: "Humanity's greatest flaw is in our lack of balance." We swing from one extreme to another, and today, I say Hadrian has taken the pendulum of man's folly from one form of abuse into another. Gideon Weller acted based on our country's lack of balance—our country's prevailing prejudice against heterosexuals. The six youth Gideon Weller raped all committed suicide. That these young men all chose death as their only escape proves beyond a shadow of a doubt that we have allowed our hopes for the future to act as a steamroller over the fringes of our youth. These six young men were our children. Our fear of the outside world, our warped perception of heterosexuals—especially viewing heterosexual men as aggressive, violent, and abusive—has twisted the way we view some of our youth.

Todd Middleton proved how we do not truly understand our heterosexual youth. His potential, his gifts, much like those of his father, whom we learned during Frank Hunter's trial was also a *strai*—I'm sorry, heterosexual, are lost to our society. As we know, Will Middleton is revered in Hadrian for his genetically altering the soya bean, an ingenious genetic alteration which helped Hadrian enter into the self-sustaining age we now appreciate. An act brought into existence by a straight man—a het'ro. Had we known of his sexual preference when he was still in high school, our country would have been denied all of his talents. Just as we are now denied all the potential talents his son, Todd Middleton, had. Todd Middleton had hoped to follow in his father's footsteps. His dream was to alter the DNA of rice so we could grow that life-saving crop in our northern climate. Because rice is the last remaining crop Hadrian imports, Todd's dream would have offered us complete anonymity and self-reliance. We will never know if he, like his father, could have been successful.

Why is it we only ever stop to think about our actions when the one who dies, or the person who speaks out, is deemed a member of our elite? Stop and think, we have, finally. Recently elected President Stiles vows to look into the state of reeducation camps and has appointed Jason Warith to work in conjunction with the Minister of Education. As you know, Jason Warith was the man who helped expose Gideon Weller's abusive methods of reeducation. Mr. Warith states that his first act as assistant to the Minister of Education is to ban the use of corporal punishment. Only one paddle will remain—Gideon Weller's—a paddle stained with the blood of his victims. This instrument of torture used against our children for far too many years will now hang in the Government Hall as a bloody reminder of his ruthless rule forged by our fear of the outside world and unreasonable prejudice against heterosexuals.

And although positive changes are being made, needless to say, many are out there who actually approve of Gideon Weller's methods. Hadrian's transition back to a state of tolerance and understanding will not be easy, but suffice to say, the spark that lights the way for that transition is burning brightly, and women and men like Faial Raboud and Jason Warith are more than willing to carry that torch in the hopes of creating a better future for our children.

Vale!

Love Recovers

Four years have passed since Frank's trial. Dramatic changes have occurred in the Hunter family as a result. Dean moved out, taking up residence in his grandmother Destiny Stuttgart's abode. She purchased a home in the New Augustus City, rebuilt closer to the Canadian border and growing after that dirty nuclear assault. When he left, Dean had insisted on a separation. Time was needed, he said, for him to come to grips with what had happened: Todd's death, Frank's confession, the legalization of heterosexuality, and now, the lengthy court battles he and countless other victims of the Northeast Reeducation Camp have filed. Most important for Dean is the reemergence of Destiny Stuttgart, his Mimi, in his life. As both an elder and family member, Mimi does not cause Dean to suffer the negative effects of the shock treatment that successfully conditioned his body against feminine influence. Mimi, knowing this brutal effect on her grandson, determined the last important goal of her life would be to help Dean overcome this psychological prison.

The separation is hardest on Geoffrey and Roger. The pain of losing his lover spirals Geoffrey into a state of depression that twists him into a severe workaholic. He is now indispensable to Hadrian National Fisheries (HNF) and is the top CEO of the entire corporation. Roger is torn between two fathers. As much as he longs for the loving arms of his papa, Roger is too afraid to leave Geoffrey alone even for a day. Thus, his only visits with Dean are through visual voc. Whenever Dean suggests he come to live with him, or even just enjoy a short visit, Roger refuses. Roger knows he is his father's only link to life outside the work world. Roger is the only reason Geoffrey leaves the office to come home for dinner. More times than not, though, Geoffrey's mind stays at the office, and then after eating, he either disappears into his study or returns to work. Roger is more often alone than not. And he misses Frank dearly.

Frank feels none of this. His sentence to life in the military has him living at the southwest wall. He has cut off all communication with family and friends, greeting them cordially when they insist on making a visit, which he is allowed once a month with a maximum of three people. Only two ever show up: Geoffrey and Roger. This monthly vigil is a daytrip on which Geoffrey brings his work. Roger brings homework and reading material since his father is uncommunicative. Roger makes this visit regardless of Frank's now formal aloofness. He refuses to believe his brother no longer feels any love. He knows that deep inside, locked away by fear and self-loathing, is the fun-loving tenderhearted brother he grew up with. And even if the old Frank never again emerges, Roger continues his monthly visits and determines to do so until the day he dies.

With the legalization of heterosexuality, and the uni of New Augustus suffering economically due to fear resulting from the name association (Augustus now being synonymous with nuclear strike and cancer), Dean gained reluctant acceptance into the campus. Of course, Mimi's influence was critical. Very few people are willing to refuse a founding mother. Thus, Dean is now working toward building a life in the field of medicine. He has chosen nursing for his vocation because he will be able to graduate and begin work in the field before the age of fifty. Mimi and Geoffrey share the cost of his tuition and living expenses. At first, Dean felt it wrong to have Geoffrey help pay for his education since he was the one who filed for separation and had left, but both grandmother and partner had insisted Geoffrey be allowed to help. Dean, having reclaimed his last name at Mimi's insistence, registered as Dean Stuttgart. Once precedence was set, Dean advocated for other heterosexuals to be allowed uni entrance, and coupled with Mimi's powerful influence and the university's crippled financial status, the New Augustus Campus became a beacon of hope for heterosexuals throughout Hadrian. By the end of his second year of schooling, Dean had established the first straight/gay alliance on campus, the first of its kind in the history of Hadrian. Dean, of course, is its president and his vice-president is Cantara Raboud, Faial Raboud's daughter. Thanks to her mother's efforts, Cantara is now free to come out and express her sexuality. Dean and she are not lovers. Dean is restrained in three ways: 1) age appropriate heterosexual attraction—Cantara is only twenty-three to Dean's forty-four years, 2) electric shock conditioning—although he has managed to overcome most of it, Dean still has a long way to go before he can ever hope to hold a woman in his arms, and 3) Geoffrey—Dean loves Geoffrey and every time he thinks of trying to be with a woman, the thought of hurting his former lover acts as more of an abatement than his previous conditioning. During their separation, Dean often found himself not only thinking about his partner, but longing for him. In many ways, Dean has come to conclude, one's sexual preference has as much to do with love as it has with physical yearnings—perhaps even more so. Having confessed this revelation to Mimi, Dean is continuously encouraged by her to invite Geoffrey down for a visit. Now that the school year is nearing its end, Dean agrees and vocs his old lover.

Geoffrey is overwhelmed with conflicting emotions: relief, love, and desire, muddy when mixed with anger, resentment, and pain. It takes time to win Geoffrey's trust back, but soon the two men are voc'ing on a daily basis. Within six months, Geoffrey makes his first visit to New Augustus.

Mimi's home consists of two levels, a ground floor and a level below ground. The car park is also below ground. One drives down a small hill inside the compound. Mimi, being a founding mother, is wealthy and her home consists of four bedrooms and a family room on the ground level, with the living room, kitchen, and a fifth (guest) bedroom below ground. When Mimi opens the door to her underground vehicle park, she greets Geoffrey, inviting him in. Turning to face the stairs, she calls up to Dean, who is working in one of the rooms he has converted into his study. "Your room," she instructs Geoffrey as they await Dean's arrival, "is the first door on the right." She points to the room just past the stairs. To their left is the living room, and down the hall, past the guest room on the right, is the kitchen.

Within seconds, Dean has leaped down the stairs like a young mountain goat. As soon as his eyes meet Geoffrey's, he lunges forward, pulling him into his arms. Mimi discreetly backs away into the living room to give the two men their privacy. While kissing and awkwardly banging against walls, Dean and Geoffrey make their way into the guest bedroom where they remain for three days with Dean periodically emerging to prepare a meal in the kitchen.

By the end of Dean's final year, Geoffrey and he are planning their re-registration ceremony. The decision came quite suddenly and at Dean's suggestion. After a bout of unabashed lovemaking, while Geoffrey is lying with his head cradled into Dean's shoulder, he shudders a soft sigh. "I thought I had lost you forever."

Dean closes his eyes. "Do you remember the first time we made love?"

"It was at The Cattle Ranch." The memory provokes a smile.

"Did you know that I had the chance to be with a woman while we were there?"

Sitting up in surprise, Geoffrey battles with his emotions. He is appalled that the ranch was a front for heterosexual behavior while at the same time trying to remind himself he has no right to judge. "Did you?" Fear imbues his being as he worries that Dean may well have been with another partner.

"No." Pausing briefly, knowing his next words will be painful, Dean confesses, "I wanted to, but I couldn't. The conditioning was too strong." With a slight harrumph, he admits, "I still have trouble being in the same room with a woman for too long." Smiling, he concludes, "Mimi's helping me with that, though."

"So," Geoffrey gulps back the truth, "if you could have, you would have then?"

"Yes." Dean is not purposely trying to hurt Geoffrey. He is simply trying to share with him the complete truth. "Back then, but not today." He looks his lover in the eye and emphasizes, "The only person I ever want to be with now is you." Geoffrey begins to sob and Dean envelops him in his arms. "I am so sorry I hurt you. Please understand. I needed this time to decide who I wanted to be." Wiping the tears from Geoffrey's eyes, he adds, "This time, Geoffrey, I can honestly say I choose to be with you. No one else is deciding for me. Not fear, not Weller, not society…" With a little smirk, he concludes, "not even you." Now, with the eyes and smile of honesty, he says, "I love you, Geoffrey Hunter, and I want to spend the rest of my life with you."

After the two men decide to reestablish their bond, Geoffrey steps down as the conglomerate head, resuming his former position as President of Hunter Fisheries. Roger is thrilled, not just to have his family back, but to have his father restored to his former, more jovial self. Geoffrey asks Roger to stand up for him at the ceremony and Dean also makes a request. He needs Geoffrey and Roger to speak to Frank on his behalf. It is time to heal the rift between papa and son. It is time to make their family whole again.

* * * * *

Hadrian's Wall

At the wall, Frank Hunter stands at the ready, watchful of any movement on the outside. Before him lies a wasteland scarred by bombings,
blackened shards of rock, shrapnel, and the decimated skeletal remains
of enemy vehicles. Beyond Hadrian's firing range are the scattered and
stunted beginnings of black pine, the heartiest of all northern trees, no
doubt attempting to resurrect the Lazarus of old Canada's once abundant
boreal forest. Frank watches the horizon of the wastelands for any sign of
heterosexual barbarians. He doesn't call them that. He doesn't even think
of them as the enemy. But it is the military term for the enemy; anyone
outside the wall, in fact, is a heterosexual barbarian; it is the term he uses
when addressing a senior officer about a kill, and he always writes, "Shot
and killed one (or more) heterosexual barbarian" in every report. Frank
has a sharp eye and exceptional aim. He kills, on average, five heterosexuals a month. Frank doesn't think of this act as shooting the enemy. He
doesn't see it as necessary for his nation's security. There is not a single
patriotic bone left in Frank Hunter's body. He doesn't even consider himself a citizen of Hadrian anymore. Frank Hunter is a mercy killer. Every
kill is, for Frank, and very likely for his every victim, an act of euthanasia.
After every kill, he whispers, "I did it for you, Todd."

Frank's post is atop the central watchtower. He takes no days off unless sick
or ordered to. He breaks for meals and the odd trip to the bathroom. He won't
watch news streams or vids, he plays no wave games, and takes no lover. Most
of all, he tries not to think. He mans his station, kills every human straight that
wanders into his site, and suffers restless, nightmarish sleep. Frank cannot stop
his mind from remembering when he succumbs to weariness.

When forced to rest by a senior officer, usually one new to his platoon,
Frank runs. He runs the three-mile length of the wall his tactile tattoo

restraint allows him. He then runs back. Back and forth and up and down. When Frank runs the three mile stretch, he runs up and down every set of stairs leading up the three stories of the wall as well as up and down the fourth set of stairs, leading up to each of the watchtowers within his limits. For Frank, running is the most effective method of emptying his mind. It does not please the MPs assigned to guard him day and night. Whenever Private Frank Hunter runs, the MP is obliged to run alongside him. More often than not, though, the MP trails behind, unable to keep pace with the lithe, powerful man. One MP actually shot Frank in the leg when he was unable to keep up. He claimed he had ordered Frank to halt, and very likely did, but the gap formed between them made it impossible for Frank to hear him. Nor could he have simply voc'd Frank. Being that military service is a life sentence for Frank, he is not allowed any luxuries such as the voc or access to Hadrian's wave network. Nor does he wish for any. Being granted access to the historic library on his one enforced day off is all he cares for. When he is not running, Frank will retreat to the historic library and read one of the archaic books. The feel of the book in his hand, its weight combined with the scent of the paper as he flips the pages, is oddly relaxing.

Contact with family is also limited to one downloaded letter a week, which one of the senior officers projects from his voc onto the wall screen for Frank to read. Once a month, Frank is entitled to a vid conference or personal visit with family. Frank is forever being ordered to attend these and must be escorted to the meeting room by his MP. Always, his father and Roger come. Dean, initially by his own design and also at Frank's request, has never attended or participated in any family conference or visit. On this day, however, unknown to Frank, Dean Stuttgart arrives. He does not come into the room immediately. Geoffrey and Roger intend to prepare Frank. They begin with the usual trite conversation about how healthy Frank looks—so tanned, so fit—and then move on to how little activity there has been at the wall of late while Frank tallies off his kills for the month. Neither Geoffrey nor Roger care to hear about that aspect of Frank's life, but Frank always lists them off anyway. It is grizzly how detailed Frank is when he describes each man or woman's death. It is as if he has engrained the image of each heterosexual he kills into his mind's eye. Finally, nearing the end of their visit, Frank asks, as always, "And how is your schooling, Roger? Are you excelling?"

"Uni is great!" Roger ejaculates.

"Do you know he plans to attend for at least six years?" Geoffrey is proud of Roger's decision to study agricultural engineering and his determination to obtain, at the very least, a Master's degree.

"Eight," Roger adds excitedly. "I'm definitely going for my Ph.D. Professor Joel Lipman, the same man who taught Will Middleton and Quintin Laugharne, says I show real promise for an undergrad."

"Well, get your Bachelor's degree first," Geoffrey adds judiciously. "Then you can work on your Master's. You can talk Ph.D. six years from now!"

On this particular visit, Roger made sure to take a few days off from uni to be with Frank, his father, and Papa Dean for this most important reunion.

"Good work, Roger." Frank remains civil, containing all show of affection, sitting upright and at attention, as if he were addressing senior officers.

"Roger's average," a proud father interjects, "is eighty-eight percent!"

Although there is no sign of emotion, Frank replies, "I am pleased, Roger. Todd would be proud." The only sign of emotion that threatens to crack the veneer of Frank's self-imposed emotional exile is the closing of his eyes and an intake of breath held momentarily before slowly exhaling.

"Thanks, Frank. That means a lot to me," says Roger. Reaching into his pocket, he retrieves a small burlap bag. "I brought you a present." Handing the package to Frank, he says, "Smell it."

Working to keep his voice flat, Frank replies, "It smells really good. What is it?"

"Ground cocoa."

Frank's eyes moisten. Once more, he must breathe slowly to contain the threat of an outpouring of emotion. "Todd had promised to grow these for Papa Dean."

"I know. Professor Lipman lets me grow these in one of the Antinous Uni hot houses. He was reluctant at first, hot houses being critical for growing plants for life saving medicines, and the beans having to come from Hadrian's Global Seed Vault, but when I explained about how Todd...well... how he...well, how I want to...you know, genetically alter them...like he wanted to...anyway, I get to grow a little crop. I roasted and ground these figuring they'd make a great gift for..." Looking now to his father, Roger asks, "May I tell him?" Geoffrey nods; he does not contain his emotions;

tears begin to stream, creating an odd image on a face suddenly shining with delight. "And, I figured they'd make a great wedding present for Papa Dean."

Frank starts. "Pa—Pa—Papa Dean is—but, Dad—he—you—never divorced—did you?"

"No son," Geoffrey smiles through the tears. "We are getting remarried. Papa Dean wants you—he wants you to stand up for him. He came with us today and is waiting outside until you ask him to enter. May I please go get him, Frank? He misses you dearly. He loves you and wants you back in his life." Frank is speechless. Afraid to talk, afraid to move from fear of breaking down, he just sits in his chair, waiting. Geoffrey stands, "I'll—I'll go get him." As soon as he opens the door, he calls out and Dean steps into the room. Franks stands, the two men facing one another.

Dean opens his arms, "Frank—"

Frank crumples to his knees, wailing in a sudden burst of emotion expelled from him like an explosion. Sobs and tears rack his body like a tempest-tossed bark. Papa Dean bends down and cradles him. "I'm so sorry, son. I'm so sorry I abandoned you for all these years."

Through his sobs, Frank manages a plea. "Forgive me."

* * * * *

Bibliography

Although fictional, a substantial amount of research went into the production of *Hadrian's Lover*. Resources used while writing this novel include:

About.com Geography. Current World Population. http://geography.about.com/od/obtainpopulationdata/a/worldpopulation.htm

About.com Geography. How fast is the world's population growing? http://geography.about.com/library/faq/blqzworldgrowth.htm

About.com Geography. Most Populous Countries Today. The 24 Most Populous Countries on Earth Today. By Matt Rosenburg. About.com Guide. http://geography.about.com/cs/worldpopulation/a/mostpopulous.htm

About.com Geography. Population Statistics. http://geography.about.com/od/obtainpopulationdata/Population_Statistics.htm

About.com Geography. Trash Islands. Trash Islands of the Pacific and Atlantic Oceans. From Amanda Briney, Contributing Writer. Updated March 24, 2009. http://geography.about.com/od/globalproblemsandissues/a/trashislands.htm

About.com Geography. Seven Billion People. Will seven billion people be overpopulation? http://geography.about.com/od/obtainpopulationdata/a/seven-7-billion-people.htm

American Institute of Biological Sciences. Articles. Forecasting the Effects of Global Warming on Biodiversity. Daniel B. Bodkin. Henrik Saxe. Miguel B. Araujo. Richard Betts. Richard H. W. Bradshaw. Thomas Cedhagen. Peter Chesson. Terry P. Dawson. Julie R. Etterson. Daniel P. Faith. Simon Ferrier. Antoine Guisan. Anja Skjoldborg Hansen. David W. Hilbert. Craig Loehle. Chris Margules. Mark New. Matthew J. Sobel. David R. B. Stockwell. http://ibcperu.org/doc/isis/7086.pdf

Annenberg Learner. The Habitable Planet: A Systems Approach to Environmental Science. http://www.learner.org/resources/series209.html

Arctic Institute of North America. Arctic, Vol. 54, No. 2 (June 2001) P. 142-148. Climate Change Scenarios for Hudson Bay Canada, from General Circulation Models. William A. Gough and Edmund Wolfe. (Received May 16, 2000: accepted in revised form September 19, 2000). http://arctic.synergiesprairies.ca/arctic/index.php/arctic/article/view/773/799

Arctic. Vol. 57, No. 3 (September 2004) P. 299-305. Trends in Seasonal sea Ice Duration in Southwestern Hudson Bay. William A. Gough, Adam R. Cornwell and Leonard J. S. Tsuji. (Received 22 August 2003; accepted in revised form April 1, 2004). http://pubs.aina.ucalgary.ca/arctic/Arctic57-3-299.pdf

blog.modernature.ca. MODERN LIFE vs. HUMAN NATURE. Garbage Island: Floating Plastic Ocean. Posted on June 6, 2008. http://blog.modernature.ca/?p=90

Blythe, David, Director. "Circadian Rhthyms". 1976. http://www.youtube.com/watch?v=3Xyy9OgCOZE. Published on Oct. 9, 2012. Note: the You Tube account associated with this video has been closed.

BMJ Helping doctors make better decisions. Falling grain stocks and rising population spell disaster and demand debate. A. J. McMichael. http://www.bmj.com/content/311/7021/1651

Calendar 2210. http://www.hf.rim.or.jp/~kaji/cal/cal.cgi?2210

Daily News. Scientists uncover possible source of homosexuality. By Christine Roberts. New York Daily News. Tuesday, December 11, 2012. 6:11 PM. www.nydailynews.com/news/national/scientists-uncover-source-homosexuality-article-1.1218017

Genesis of Eden. The World Population "Bomb." http://dhushara.com/book/diversit/bomb.htm

Government. no. Ministry of Agriculture and Food. Svalbard Global Seed Vault. http://www.regjeringen.no/en/dep/lmd/campain/svalbard-global-seed-vault.html?id=462220

Hinton Parklander.com. News Local. Breeding a forest to survive climate change. By Craig Palmer. Hinton Parklander. Wednesday, July 4, 2012 10:58:28 MDT AM. http://www.hintonparklander.com/2012/07/04/breeding-a-forest-to-thrive-during-climate-change

Hus, Tim. *Alberta Crude.* "The Bull Rider". Track 2. Saved by Radio Records. 2004. Festival Distribution

Hus, Tim. *Alberta Crude.* "Silver in the Buckle". Track 6. Saved by Radio Records. 2004. Festival Distribution.

Jones, Lisa. "Why Bad Sex is Shortening Your Life". Cosmopolitan. Love/Sex. http://www.cosmopolitan.com/sex-love/tips-moves/orgasm-news.

Live Science. Stephanie Pappas. Why Gay Parents May Be the Best Parents. By Stephanie Pappas. http://www.livescience.com/17913-advantages-gay-parents.html

National Geographic. The Ocean. Photo Gallery: Polluted Oceans. http://ocean.nationalgeographic.com/ocean/photos/ocean-pollution/#/alaska-dump_46_600x450.jpg

New Statesman. The Staggers. The New Statesman's rolling politics blog. "Top Ten: the world's most populated countries." By Samira Shackle.

Published 08 July 2:10 9:44. http://www.newstatesman.com/blogs/
the-staggers/2010/07/population-index-overpopulated

One More Generation. Is ocean garbage killing whales? By Jim Ries.
Published July 11, 2011. http://onemoregeneration.org/2011/07/11/
is-ocean-garbage-killing-whales/

Overpopulation – America's Greatest Calamity. By Frosty Wooldridge.
March 12, 2009. http://rense.com/general85/over.htm

Overpopulation in Africa. Effects of overpopulation. By Derek and Ryan.
http://geojoedr.tripod.com/id3.html

Overpopulation. The Population Explosion. By Paul and Anne Ehrlich.
http://dieoff.org/page27.htm

Parviz, Babak. Electrical Engineer at the University of Washington. As
told to Flora Lichtman. Popular Science. "Terminator Vision." P. 33.
March 2012.

POPSCI: The Future Now. How We're Creating "Terminator Vision"
in Your Future Contact Lenses. By Babak Parviz, as told to Flora Lichtman. Posted February 21, 2012 at 10:13 AM. http://www.popsci.com/
science/article/2012-02/terminator-vision

Softpedia. The Effects of Global Warming in Africa. http://news.softpe-
dia.com/news/The-Effects-of-Global-Warming-in-Africa-41077.shtml

Suite101. Ancient History. The Scandal of Hadrian and Antinous. By
Brenda Ralph Lewis. http://suite101.com/article/the-scandal-of-hadri-
an-and-antinous-a186176

Sustainable Development in the Hudson Bay. James Bay Bioregion.
Canadian Arctic Resources Committee. Environmental Committee of
Sanikiluaq. Rawson Academy of Aquatic Science. http://www.carc.org/
pubs/v19no3/2.htm

The Daily. Report points to radical Arctic warming. November 9, 2004 at 12:00 AM. Usha Lee McFarling \ Los Angeles Times. http://dailyuw.com/archive/2004/11/09/imported/report-points-radical-arctic-warming#.UPxwlY7C5Wg

The Daily. Studies show warming in Antarctic regions. September 28, 2006 at 12:00 AM. Staci Miner. http://dailyuw.com/archive/2006/09/28/imported/studies-show-warming-antarctic-regions#.UPxwHI7C5Wg

The Sustainability Report. Canada's Population. http://www.sustreport.org/signals/canpop_ttl.html

treehugger. World Population to Hit 7 Billion by 2011, New Stats Show. Mat McDermott Business / Corporate Responsibility August 14, 2009. http://www.treehugger.com/corporate-responsibility/world-population-to-hit-7-billion-by-2011-new-stats-show.html

Truthdig drilling beneath the headlines. We Are Breeding Ourselves to Extinction. By Chris Hedges. Posted March 8, 2009. http://www.truthdig.com/report/item/20090309_we_are_breeding_ourselves_to_extinction//

UNRV. History. Hadrian. http://www.unrv.com/five-good-emperors/hadrian.php

University of Toronto Libraries. Canadian Poetry Online. Earle Birney: Biography. Source: Wailan Low. http://www.library.utoronto.ca/canpoetry/birney/

University of Toronto Libraries: RPO (Representative Poetry Online). David. Birney, Earle (1904-1995). http://rpo.library.utoronto.ca/poems/david

U.S. Department of Commerce. United States Census Bureau. World POPClock Projection. http://www.census.gov/population/popclock-world.html

WebMD. Health & Sex. Is There a Gay Gene? New Genetic Regions Associated With Male Sexual Orientation Found. WebMD Health News. January 28, 2005. http://www.webmd.com/sex-relationships/news/20050128/is-there-gay-gene

Wikipedia: The Free Encyclopedia. Human population control. http://en.wikipedia.org/wiki/Human_population_control

Wikipedia: The Free Encyclopedia. Hudson Bay. http://en.wikipedia.org/wiki/Hudson_Bay#Climate

WWF Global. Marine problems: Climate change. http://wwf.panda.org/about_our_earth/blue_planet/problems/climate_change/

WWF Global. Marine problems: Pollution. http://wwf.panda.org/about_our_earth/blue_planet/problems/pollution/

Yahoo! News. Business. The world of 2030: U.S. declines; food water may be scarce. By Olivier Knox, Yahoo! News. The Ticket – Mon. December 10, 2012. http://ca.news.yahoo.com/blogs/ticket/world-2030-u-declines-food-water-may-scarce-162757458--politics.html

Yahoo! News. Canada. Next Great Depression? MIT study predicting 'global economic collapse' by 2030 still on track. By Eric Pfeiffer, Yahoo! News. The Sideshow – Wed. April 4, 2012. http://ca.news.yahoo.com/blogs/sideshow/next-great-depression-mit-researchers-predict-global-economic-190352944.html

YouTube CA. 7 Billion, National Geographic Magazine. 3,915 videos. http://www.youtube.com/watch?v=sc4HxPxNrZ0

2208 Hanke-Henry Permanent Calendar. http://henry.pha.jhu.edu/calendardir/ccctdir/ccctHTML/2208.0.html

Disclaimer: The author of this text cannot be held responsible for any links that have been disengaged since the publication of this novel.